Trigger Warning

By Neil Gaiman and published by Headline

American Gods
Stardust
Neverwhere
Smoke and Mirrors
Anansi Boys
Fragile Things
The Ocean at the End of the Lane

The Truth is a Cave in the Black Mountains
(illustrated by Eddie Campbell)

NEIL GAIMAN

Trigger Warning

SHORT FICTIONS & DISTURBANCES

headline

First published in Great Britain in 2015 by
HEADLINE PUBLISHING GROUP

3

Cataloguing in Publication Data is
available from the British Library

ISBN 978 1 4722 1768 4 (Hardback)
ISBN 978 1 4722 1769 1 (Trade paperback)

Typeset in Zapf Elliptical by Palimpsest Book Production Limited,
Falkirk, Stirlingshire

Printed and bound in Great Britain by Clays Ltd, St Ives plc

Headline's policy is to use papers that are natural, renewable and recyclable
products and made from wood grown in well-managed forests and other controlled
sources. The logging and manufacturing processes are expected to conform to the
environmental regulations of the country of origin.

HEADLINE PUBLISHING GROUP
An Hachette UK Company
338 Euston Road
London NW1 3BH

www.headline.co.uk
www.hachette.co.uk

I'm not sure how I wound up with an honourable Hollywood agent who reads books for pleasure but I did, eighteen years ago. He's still my agent, still honourable, and he still likes short stories best of all. This book of tales is for Jon Levin.

Contents

Introduction

I. LITTLE TRIGGERS

There are things that upset us. That's not quite what we're talking about here, though. I'm thinking rather about those images or words or ideas that drop like trapdoors beneath us, throwing us out of our safe, sane world into a place much more dark and less welcoming. Our hearts skip a ratatat drumbeat in our chests, and we fight for breath. Blood retreats from our faces and our fingers, leaving us pale and gasping and shocked.

And what we learn about ourselves in those moments, where the trigger has been squeezed, is this: the past is not dead. There are things that wait for us, patiently, in the dark corridors of our lives. We think we have moved on, put them out of mind, left them to desiccate and shrivel and blow away; but we are wrong. They have been waiting there in the darkness, working out, practising their most vicious blows, their sharp hard thoughtless punches into the gut, killing time until we came back that way.

The monsters in our cupboards and our minds are always there in the darkness, like mould beneath the floorboards and behind the wallpaper, and there is so much darkness, an inexhaustible supply of darkness. The universe is amply supplied with night.

What do we need to be warned about? We each have our little triggers.

I first encountered the phrase *Trigger Warning* on the Internet, where it existed primarily to warn people of links to images or ideas that could upset them and trigger flashbacks or anxiety or terror, in order that the images or ideas could be filtered out of a feed, or that the person reading could be mentally prepared before encountering them.

I was fascinated when I learned that trigger warnings had crossed the divide from the Internet to the world of things you could touch. Several colleges, it was announced, were considering putting trigger warnings on works of literature, art or film, to warn students of what was waiting for them, an idea that I found myself simultaneously warming to (of course you want to let people who may be distressed know that this might distress them) while at the same time being deeply troubled by it: when I wrote *Sandman* and it was being published as a monthly comic, it had a warning on each issue, telling the world it was Suggested for Mature Readers, which I thought was wise. It told potential readers that this was not a children's comic and it might contain images or ideas that could be troubling, and also suggests that if you are mature (whatever that happens to mean) you are on your own. As for what they would find that might disturb them, or shake them, or make them think something they had never thought before, I felt that that was their own lookout. We are mature, we decide what we read or do not read.

What we read as adults should be read, I think, with no warnings or alerts beyond, perhaps: enter at your own risk. We need to find out what fiction is, what it means, to us, an experience that is going to be unlike anyone else's experience of the story.

We build the stories in our heads. We take words, and we give them power, and we look out through other eyes, and we see, and experience, what others see. I wonder, *Are fictions safe places?* And then I ask myself, *Should they be safe places?* There are stories I read as a child I wished, once I had read them, that I had never encountered, because I was not ready for them and they upset me: stories which contained helplessness, in which people were embarrassed, or mutilated, in which adults were made vulnerable and parents could be of no assistance. They troubled me and haunted my nightmares and my daydreams, worried and upset me on profound levels, but they also taught me that, if I was going to read fiction, sometimes I would only know what my comfort zone was by leaving it; and now, as an adult, I would not erase the experience of having read them if I could.

There are still things that profoundly upset me when I encounter them, whether it's on the Web or the word or in the world. They never get easier, never stop my heart from trip-trapping, never let me escape, this time, unscathed. But they teach me things, and they open my eyes, and if they hurt, they hurt in ways that make me think and grow and change.

I wondered, reading about the college discussions, whether, one day, people would put a trigger warning on my fiction. I wondered whether or not they would be justified in doing it. And then I decided to do it first.

There are things in this book, as in life, that might upset you. There is death and pain in here, tears and discomfort, violence of all kinds, cruelty, even abuse. There is kindness, too, I hope, sometimes. Even a handful of happy endings. (Few stories end unhappily for all participants, after all.) And there's more than that: I know a lady called Rocky who is triggered by tentacles, and who genuinely needs warnings for things that have tentacles in them, especially tentacles with suckers, and who, confronted with an unexpected slice of squid or octopus, will dive, shaking, behind the nearest sofa. There is an enormous tentacle somewhere in these pages.

Many of these stories end badly for at least one of the people in them. Consider yourself warned.

II. PRE-FLIGHT SAFETY DEMONSTRATION

Sometimes huge truths are uttered in unusual contexts. I fly too much, a concept and a sentence that would have been impossible for me to understand as a young man, when every plane journey was exciting and miraculous, when I would stare out of the window at the clouds below and imagine that they were a city, or a world, somewhere I could walk safely. Still, I find myself, at the start of each flight, meditating and pondering the wisdom offered by the flight attendants as if it were a koan or a tiny parable, or the high point of all wisdom.

This is what they say:

Secure your own mask before helping others.

And I think of us, all the people, and the masks we wear, the masks we hide behind and the masks that reveal. I imagine people pretending to be what they truly are, and discovering that other people are so much more and so much less than they imagined themselves to be or present themselves as. And then, I think about the need to help others, and how we mask ourselves to do it, and how unmasking makes us vulnerable . . .

We are all wearing masks. That is what makes us interesting.

These are stories about those masks, and the people we are underneath them.

We authors, who trade in fictions for a living, are a continuum of all that we have seen and heard, and most importantly, all that we have read.

I have friends who fulminate and bark and explode in frustration because people do not know the references, do not know what is being pointed at, have forgotten authors and stories and worlds. I tend to look at these things from another direction: I was once a blank piece of parchment too, waiting to be inscribed. I learned about things and people from stories, and I learned about other authors from stories.

Many, perhaps most, of the stories in this book are part of
that same continuum. They exist because other authors, other
voices, other minds, have existed. I hope you will not mind if,
in this introduction, I take the opportunity to point you at some
of the writers and places without whom these tales might not
have ever seen the light.

III. THE LUCK OF THE DRAW

This is my third collection of short fiction, and I know just how
lucky I am.

I grew up loving and respecting short stories. They seemed
to me to be the purest and most perfect things people could
make: not a word wasted, in the best of them. An author would
wave her hand and suddenly there was a world, and people in
it, and ideas. A beginning and a middle and an end that would
take you across the universe and bring you back. I loved all
kinds of short-story collections, from the anthologies of ghost
and horror stories I'd pick up as a boy, to the single-author
collections that would reshape the inside of my head.

My favourite collections would not just give me short stories
but they would also tell me things I didn't know, about the
stories in the book and the craft of writing. I would respect
authors who did not write an introduction, but I could not truly
love them as I loved the authors who made me realise that each
of the stories in the anthology was written, actually made up
word by word and written down, by someone human, who
thought and breathed and walked and probably even sang in
the shower, like me.

The wisdom in publishing is that short-story collections don't
sell. All too often short-story collections are viewed as vanity

projects or are published by small presses, are not seen as real
in the way that novels are real. Still, for me, the short stories
are the places where I get to fly, to experiment, to play. I get to
make mistakes and to go on small adventures, and there is
something about the process of putting together a collection like
this that is both scary and eye-opening: when I put stories together
themes reoccur, reshape and become clear. I learn what I've been
writing about for the previous decade.

IV. GENERAL APOLOGY

I firmly believe that short-story collections should be the same
sort of thing all the way through. They should not, hodgepodge
and willy-nilly, assemble stories that were obviously not intended
to sit between the same covers. They should not, in short, contain
horror and ghost stories, science fiction and fairy tales, fabulism
and poetry, all in the same place. They should be respectable.

This collection fails this test.

For this failure, as for so much, I request your indulgence and
forgiveness, and hope only that somewhere in these pages you
may encounter a story you might otherwise never have read.
Look. Here is a very small one, waiting for you now:

Shadder

Some creatures hunt. Some creatures forage. The Shadder lurk.
Sometimes, admittedly, they skulk. But mostly, they just lurk.

The Shadder do not make webs. The world is their web. The
Shadder do not dig pits. If you are here you have already fallen.

There are animals that chase you down, run fast as the wind, tirelessly, to sink their fangs into you, to drag you down. The Shadder do not chase. They simply go to the place where you will be, when the chase is over, and they wait for you there, somewhere dark and indeterminate. They find the last place you would look, and abide there, as long as they need to abide, until it becomes the last place that you look and you see them.

You cannot hide from the Shadder. They were there first. You cannot outrun the Shadder. They are waiting at your journey's end. You cannot fight the Shadder, because they are patient, and they will tarry until the last day of all, the day that the fight has gone out of you, the day that you are done with fighting, the day the last punch has been thrown, the last knife-blow struck, the last cruel word spoken. Then, and only then, will the Shadder come out.

They eat nothing that is not ready to be eaten. Look behind you.

V. ABOUT THE CONTENT OF THIS BOOK

Welcome to these pages. You can read about the stories you will encounter here, or you can skip this and come back and see what I have to say after you've read the stories. I'm easy.

Making a Chair

Some days the words won't come. On those days, I normally try to revise something that already exists. On that day, I made a chair.

A Lunar Labyrinth

I met Gene Wolfe over thirty years ago, when I was a twenty-two-year-old journalist, and I interviewed him about his four-part novel, *The Book of the New Sun*. Over the next five years we became friends, and we have been friends ever since. He is a good man and a fine, deep writer, always tricky, always wise. His third novel, *Peace,* written when I was almost a boy, is one of my favourite books. His most recent novel, *The Land Across,* was the book I read with the most enjoyment this year, and is as deceptive and dangerous as any book he has written.

One of Gene's finest short stories is called 'A Solar Labyrinth'. It's about a labyrinth made of shadows and is a darker story than it seems on the surface.

I wrote this story for Gene. If there are solar labyrinths, there should be lunar ones too, after all, and a Wolfe to bay at the moon.

The Thing About Cassandra

When I was about fourteen, it seemed much easier to imagine a girlfriend than to have one – that would involve actually talking to a girl, after all. So I would, I decided, write a girl's name on the cover of my exercise books and deny all knowledge of her when asked, thus, I fondly imagined, causing everyone to think that I actually had a girlfriend. I do not believe it worked. I never actually got around to imagining anything about her but the name.

I wrote this story in August of 2009, on the Isle of Skye, while my then-girlfriend Amanda had flu and tried to sleep it off. When she woke I would bring her soup and honeyed drinks, then read her what I had written of the story. I am not certain how much of it she remembers.

I gave the story to Gardner Dozois and George R. R. Martin for their anthology *Songs of Love and Death,* and was inordinately relieved when they liked it.

Down to a Sunless Sea

The *Guardian* newspaper was celebrating World Water Day with a week of stories about water. I was in Austin, Texas, during the South by Southwest Festival, where I was recording the audiobooks of *The Ocean at the End of the Lane* and my first short-story collection, *Smoke and Mirrors.*

I was thinking of Grand Guignol, of heartbreaking monologues whispered by lonely performers to a captive audience, and remembering some of the more painful tales from *The Newgate Calendar.* And London, in the rain, a long long way from Texas.

'The Truth Is a Cave in the Black Mountains . . .'

There are stories you build, and there are stories you construct, then there are stories that you hack out of rock, removing all the things that are not the story.

I wanted to edit an anthology of stories which were cracking good reads with, perhaps, a fantasy or SF edge, but mostly that simply kept people turning the pages. Al Sarrantonio became my coeditor on the project. We called the book *Stories,* which might have been a good title for it, before Google. It was not enough to edit the book. I had to write a story for it.

I have visited many peculiar places in the world, places that can hold your mind and your soul tightly and will not let them go. Some of those places are exotic and unusual, some are mundane. The strangest of all of them, at least for me, is the Isle of Skye, off the west coast of Scotland. I know I am not alone in this. There are people who discover Skye and will not leave, and even for those of us who do leave, the misty island haunts us and holds us in its own way. It is where I am happiest and where I am most alone.

Otta F. Swire wrote books about the Hebrides and about Skye in particular, and she filled her books with strange and arcane knowledge. (Did you know May the third was the day that the devil was cast out of heaven, and thus the day on which it is unpardonable to commit a crime? I learned that in her book on the myths of the Hebrides.) And in one of her books, she mentioned the cave in the Black Cuillins where you could go, if you were brave, and get gold, with no cost, but each visit you paid to the cave would make you more evil, would eat your soul.

And that cave, and its promise, began to haunt me.

I took several true stories (or stories that are said to be true, which is almost the same thing) and gave them to two men, set them in a world that was almost, but not quite, ours, and told a story of revenge and of travel, of desire for gold and of secrets. It won the Shirley Jackson Award for Best Novelette (*Stories* won for Best Anthology) and the Locus Award for Best Novelette, and I was very proud of it, my story.

Before it was published, I was set to appear on the stage of the Sydney Opera House and was asked if I could do something with Australian string quartet FourPlay (they are the rock band of string quartets, an amazing, versatile bunch with a cult following): perhaps something with art that could be projected onto the stage.

I thought about 'The Truth Is a Cave in the Black Mountains . . .': it would take about seventy minutes to read. I wondered what would happen if a string quartet created a moody and glorious soundtrack while I told the story, as if it were a movie. And what if Scottish artist Eddie Campbell, he who drew Alan Moore's *From Hell*, writer and artist of *Alec*, my favourite comic, created illustrations for this most Scottish of my stories and projected them above me while I read?

I was scared, going out onto the stage of the Sydney Opera House, but the experience was amazing: the story was received with a standing ovation, and we followed it with an interview (artist Eddie Campbell was the interviewer) and a poem, also with FourPlay.

Six months later, we performed it again, with more paintings by Eddie, in Hobart, Tasmania, in front of three thousand people, in a huge shed at a festival, and again, they loved it.

Now we had a problem. The only people who had ever seen the show were in Australia. It seemed unfair, somehow. We needed an excuse to travel, to bring the FourPlay string quartet across the world (pop-culture-literate and brilliant musicians, they are: I fell in love with their version of the *Doctor Who* theme before I ever knew them). Fortunately, Eddie Campbell had taken his paintings, and done many more, and then laid out the text into something halfway between an illustrated story and a graphic novel, and HarperCollins were publishing it in the U.S. and Headline publishing it in the UK.

We went on tour, FourPlay and Eddie and me, to San Francisco, to New York, to London and to Edinburgh. We got a standing ovation at Carnegie Hall, and it doesn't get much better than that.

And still I wonder how much of the story I wrote, and how much was simply waiting there for me, like the grey rocks that sit like bones on the low hills of Skye.

My Last Landlady

This was written for a publication of the World Horror Convention. That year, it was in Brighton. Brighton these days is a bustling, arty, go-ahead, exciting seaside metropolis. When I was a boy, though, we would go to Brighton out of season, and it was dreary and cold and murderous.

Obviously, this story is set in that long-gone Brighton and not the current one. You have nothing to be scared of if you stay in a bed-and-breakfast there now.

Adventure Story

I was asked to write this story by Ira Glass for his *This American Life* radio show. He liked it, but his producers didn't, so I wrote them an op-ed instead, about how 'adventures are all very well in their place, but there is a lot to be said for regular meals and freedom from pain', and this story went on to be published in *McSweeney's Quarterly*.

I had been thinking a lot about death, and the way that when people die they take their stories with them. It's a sort of companion piece to my novel *The Ocean at the End of the Lane*, I think, at least in that respect.

Orange

Jonathan Strahan is a nice man and a good editor. He lives in Perth, Western Australia. I have a bad habit of breaking his heart by writing something for an anthology he is editing and then taking it away. I always try and mend his broken heart by writing something else, though. This is one of those something elses.

The way a story is told is as important as the story being told, although the way that the story is told is usually a little less obvious than it is here. I had a story in my head, but it wasn't until I thought of the questionnaire format that it all fell into place. I wrote the story in airports and on the plane to Australia, where I was going to be attending the Sydney Writers' Festival, and read it a day or so after I had landed to an audience of many people and to my pale and scary goddaughter, Hayley Campbell, whose grumblings about orange tan smears on the fridge might have inspired the story in the first place.

A Calendar of Tales

This was one of the oddest and most pleasant things I've done in the last few years.

When I was young, I would read Harlan Ellison's short-story collections with delight. I loved the stories, and I loved his accounts of how the stories had come to be written just as much. I learned many things from Harlan, but the thing that I took away from his introductions that made the most impact was just the idea that the way that you wrote the stories was, you did the work. You showed up, and you did it.

And that never seemed more clear or obvious than when Harlan would explain that he had written such and such a short story in a bookshop window, or live on air on the radio, or in a similar situation. That people had suggested titles or words. He was demonstrating to the world that writing was a craft, that it was not an act of magic. Somewhere, a writer was sitting down and writing. I loved the idea of trying to write in a shop window.

But, I thought, the world had changed. You could now have a shop window that allowed hundreds of thousands of people to press their faces to the glass and watch.

BlackBerry came to me and asked if I would be willing to do a social media project, anything I wanted, and seemed perfectly happy when I suggested that I'd like to write 'A Calendar of Tales', each story spinning off a reply to a tweet about the months of the year – questions like 'Why is January dangerous?' 'What's the strangest thing you've ever seen in July?' (Someone named @mendozacarla replied, 'An Igloo made of books,' and I knew what my story would be.) 'Who would you like to see again in December?'

I asked the questions, got tens of thousands of replies, and chose twelve.

I wrote the twelve stories (March was the first, December the last), then invited people to make their own art based on the stories. Five short films were made about the process, and the whole thing was blogged, tweeted, and put out into the world, for free, on the Web. It was a joy to make stories in public. Harlan Ellison isn't a big fan of things like Twitter, but I phoned him when the project was over, and I told him it was his fault and that I hoped it would inspire someone who had been following it, as much as his bookshop window tales had inspired me.

(My most grateful thanks to @zyblonius, @TheAstralGypsy, @MorgueHumor, @_NikkiLS_, @StarlingV, @DKSakar, @mendozacarla, @gabiottasnest, @TheGhostRegion, @elainelowe, @MeiLinMiranda, and @Geminitm for their inspirational tweets.)

The Case of Death and Honey

I encountered the Sherlock Holmes stories as a boy, and fell in love, and never forgot Holmes or the redoubtable Dr Watson who chronicled his detective work; Mycroft Holmes, Sherlock's brother; or Arthur Conan Doyle, the mind behind it all. I loved the rationalism, the idea that an intelligent, observant person could take a handful of clues and build them up into a world. I loved learning who these people were, a story at a time.

Holmes coloured things. When I began to keep bees, I was always aware that I was merely following in Holmes's footsteps. But then I would wonder why Holmes had taken up beekeeping. After all, it's not the most labour intensive of retirement hobbies. And Sherlock Holmes was never happy unless he was working on a case: indolence and inactivity were death to him.

I met Les Klinger at the first meeting of the Baker Street Irregulars I attended, in 2002. I liked him very much. (I liked all the people there: grown-up women and men who, when not being eminent jurists, journalists, surgeons and wastrels, had elected to believe that somewhere it was always 1889 in 221b Baker Street, and Mrs Hudson would soon be bringing up both the tea and an eminent client.)

This story was written for Les and for Laurie King for their collection *A Study in Sherlock*. It was inspired by a jar of snow-white honey I was offered on the side of a mountain in China.

I wrote this story over a week in a hotel room, while my wife and my youngest daughter and her friend were at the beach.

'The Case of Death and Honey' was nominated for an Anthony Award, an Edgar Award, and a Crime Writers' Association Silver Dagger Award. That it didn't win any of them made me no less happy: I'd never been nominated for a crime-writing award before, probably never would again.

The Man Who Forgot Ray Bradbury

I forgot my friend. Or rather, I remembered everything about him except his name. He had died over a decade before. I remembered our phone conversations, our time together, the way he talked and gestured, the books he had written. I resolved that I would not go to the Internet and look. I would simply remember his name. I would walk around trying to remember his name, and began to be haunted by the idea that if I could not remember his name he would never have existed. Foolishness, I knew, but still . . .

I wrote 'The Man Who Forgot Ray Bradbury' as a ninetieth-birthday present for Ray Bradbury, and as a way of talking about the impact that Ray Bradbury had on me as a boy, and as an adult, and, as far as I could, about what he had done to the world. I wrote it as a love letter and as a thank-you and as a birthday present for an author who made me dream, taught me about words and what they could accomplish, and who never let me down as a reader or as a person as I grew up.

My editor at William Morrow, Jennifer Brehl went to his bedside and read the story to him. The thank-you message he sent me by video meant the world to me.

My friend Mark Evanier told me that he met Ray Bradbury when he was a boy of eleven or twelve. When Bradbury found out that Mark wanted to be a writer, he invited him to his office and spent half a day telling him the important stuff: if you want to be a writer, you have to write. Every day. Whether you feel like it or not. That you can't just write one book and stop. That it's work, but the best kind of work. Mark grew up to be a writer, the kind who writes and supports himself through writing.

Ray Bradbury was the kind of person who would give half a day to a kid who wanted to be a writer when he grew up.

I encountered Ray Bradbury's stories as a boy. The first one I read was 'Homecoming', about a human child in a world of *Addams Family*-style monsters, who wanted to fit in. It was the first time anyone had ever written a story that spoke to me personally. There was a copy of *The Silver Locusts* (the UK title of *The Martian Chronicles*) knocking about my house. I read it, loved it, and bought all the Bradbury books I could from the travelling bookshop that set up once a term in my school. I learned about Poe from Bradbury. There was poetry in the short stories, and it didn't matter that I was missing so much: what I took from the stories was enough.

Some authors I read and loved as a boy disappointed me as I aged. Bradbury never did. His horror stories remained as chilling, his dark fantasies as darkly fantastic, his science fiction (he never cared about the science, only about the people, which was why the stories worked so well) as much of an exploration of the sense of wonder as they had been when I was a child.

He was a good writer, and he wrote well in many disciplines. He was one of the first science fiction writers to escape the 'pulp' magazines and to be published in the 'slicks'. He wrote scripts for Hollywood films. Good films were made from his novels and stories. Long before I was a writer Bradbury was one of the writers that other writers aspired to become.

A Ray Bradbury story meant something on its own – it told you nothing of what the story would be about, but it told you about atmosphere, about language, about some sort of magic escaping into the world. *Death Is a Lonely Business*, his detective novel, is as much a Bradbury story as *Something Wicked This Way Comes* or *Fahrenheit 451* or any of the horror, or science fiction, or magical realism, or realism you'll find in the short-story collections. He was a genre on his own, and on his own terms. A young man from Waukegan, Illinois, who went to Los Angeles, educated himself in libraries, and wrote until he got good, then transcended genre and became a genre of one, often emulated, absolutely inimitable.

I met him first when I was a young writer and he was in the UK for his seventieth-birthday celebrations, held at the Natural History Museum. We became friends in an odd, upside-down way, sitting beside each other at book signings, at events. I would be there when Ray spoke in public over the years. Sometimes I'd introduce him to the audience. I was the master of ceremonies when Ray was given his Grand Master Award by the Science Fiction and Fantasy Writers of America: he told them about a child he had watched, teased by his friends for wanting to enter a toy shop because they said it was too young for him, and how much Ray had wanted to persuade the child to ignore his friends and play with the toys.

He'd speak about the practicalities of a writer's life ('You have to write!' he would tell people. 'You have to write every day! I still write every day!') and about being a child inside (he said he had a photographic memory, going back to babyhood, and perhaps he did), about joy, about love.

He was kind, and gentle, with that midwestern niceness that's a positive thing rather than an absence of character. He was enthusiastic, and it seemed that that enthusiasm would keep him going forever. He genuinely liked people. He left the world a better place, and left better places in it: the red sands and canals of Mars, the midwestern Hallowe'ens and small towns and dark carnivals. And he kept writing.

'Looking back over a lifetime, you see that love was the answer to everything,' Ray said once, in an interview.

He gave people so many reasons to love him. We did. And, so far, we have not forgotten.

Jerusalem

This story was commissioned by the BBC for its William Blake Week. They asked if I could write a story to be read on Radio Four, inspired by a Blake poem.

I had recently visited Jerusalem, and wondered what it would actually take to build Jerusalem in England's green and pleasant land. And what kind of person would want to.

I make many things up, but Jerusalem syndrome is a real thing.

Click-Clack the Rattlebag

I wrote this in the house of my friends Peter Nicholls and Clare Coney, in Surrey Hills, Melbourne, Australia. It was Christmas. Oddly enough, despite the sweltering temperatures, it was a white Christmas: thick, marble-sized hail fell during our Christmas dinner and blanketed the Coney–Nicholls lawn. I wrote it for a book of new monsters, edited by Kasey Lansdale, but it was first published as an audiobook by Audible in the U.S. and the UK. They gave it away for free, for Hallowe'en, and gave money to good causes for each person who downloaded it. So everyone was happy, except the people who had downloaded the story, and listened to it late at night, and then had to go around turning all the lights on.

The house in the story is based on my friend Tori's house in Kinsale, Ireland, which is obviously not actually haunted, and the sound of people upstairs moving wardrobes around when you are downstairs there and alone is probably just something that old houses do when they think they are unobserved.

An Invocation of Incuriosity

Children are driven by a sense of injustice, and it sticks around as we age, bury it however we try. It still rankles that, almost forty years ago, when I was fifteen, I wrote a short story for my mock English O level that was graded down from an A to a C with an explanatory comment from the teacher that it 'was too original. Must obviously have copied it from somewhere.' Many years later, I took my favourite idea from that tale and put it into this. I'm pretty sure that the idea was original, but it gave me pleasure to put it into a story dedicated to Jack Vance and set in the world of *The Dying Earth*.

Writers live in houses other people built.

They were giants, the men and the women who made the houses we inhabit. They started with a barren place and they built Speculative Fiction, always leaving the building unfinished so the people who came by after they were gone could put on another room, or another story. Clark Ashton Smith dug the foundations of the *Dying Earth* stories, and Jack Vance came along and built them high and glorious, as he made so much high and glorious, and built a world in which all science is now magic, at the very end of the world, when the sun is dim and preparing to go out.

I discovered *The Dying Earth* when I was thirteen, in an anthology called *Flashing Swords*. The story was called 'Morreion', and it started me dreaming. I found a British paperback copy of *The Dying Earth*, filled with strange misprints, but the stories were there and they were as magical as 'Morreion' had been. In a dark secondhand bookshop where men in overcoats bought used pornography I found a copy of *The Eyes of the Overworld* and then tiny dusty books of short stories – 'The Moon Moth' is, I felt then and feel now, the most perfectly built SF short story that anyone has ever written – and around that point Jack Vance books began to be published in the UK and suddenly all I had to do to read Jack Vance books was buy them. And I did: *The Demon Princes*, the *Alastor* trilogy, and the rest. I loved the way he would digress, I loved the way he would imagine, and most of all I loved the way he wrote it all down: wryly, gently, amused, like a god would be amused, but never in a way that made less of what he wrote, like James Branch Cabell but with a heart as well as a brain.

Every now and again I've noticed myself crafting a Vance sentence, and it always makes me happy when I do – but he's not a writer I'd ever dare to imitate. I don't think he's imitable. There are few enough of the writers I loved when I was thirteen I can see myself going back to twenty years from now. Jack Vance I will reread forever.

'An Invocation of Incuriosity' won the Locus Award for Best Short Story, which delighted me, although I considered it as much an award for Jack Vance as for my tale, and it thrilled and vindicated my inner mock-O-level-taking teenager.

'And Weep, Like Alexander'

It has long been a source of puzzlement to me that none of the inventions we were promised when I was a boy, the ones that were due to make our lives much more fun and interesting in the world to come, ever arrived. We got computers, and phones which do everything that computers used to do, but no flying cars, no glorious spaceships, no easy travel to other planets (as Ted Mooney put it).

This story was written as part of a fund-raising book for the Arthur C. Clarke Awards. The book, *Fables from the Fountain*, edited by Ian Whates, was based on Arthur C. Clarke's *Tales from the White Hart,* itself modelled on the club stories of the early twentieth century. (Lord Dunsany's stories of Mr Joseph Jorkens are my favourite club stories.) I took the name Obediah Polkinghorn from one of Arthur C. Clarke's stories, as a tribute to Clarke himself. (I met and interviewed him, back in 1985. I remember being surprised by the West Country burr in his voice.)

It is a very silly story, so I gave it a slightly pompous title.

Nothing O'Clock

I have wholeheartedly and unashamedly loved the television series *Doctor Who* since I was a three-year-old boy at Mrs Pepper's School in Portsmouth, and William Hartnell was the Doctor. Writing actual episodes of the show, almost fifty years later, was one of the most fun things I've done. (One of them even won a Hugo Award.) By this time Matt Smith played the eleventh Doctor. Puffin Books asked if I would write a story for their book *Doctor Who: 11 Doctors, 11 Stories*. I chose to set the story during the first season of Matt's run.

You might think you need to know a lot about *Doctor Who*, given that it is a fifty-year-old show, to enjoy this story, but you don't need to know much. The Doctor is an alien, a Time Lord, the last of his race, who travels through time and space in a blue box that is bigger on the inside than it is on the outside. It sometimes lands where he wanted to go. If there's something wrong, he may well sort it out. He's very clever.

There is a game in England, or there was when I was growing up, called What's the Time, Mister Wolf? It's a fun game. Sometimes Mister Wolf tells you the time. Sometimes he tells you something much more disquieting.

Diamonds and Pearls: A Fairy Tale

I first spent time with the woman who would become my wife because she wanted to make a book of photographs of herself dead, to accompany her album *Who Killed Amanda Palmer?* She had been taking photographs of herself dead since she was eighteen. She wrote to me and pointed out that nobody was going to buy a book of photos of a dead woman who wasn't even actually dead, but perhaps if I wrote some captions they might.

Photographer Kyle Cassidy and Amanda and I gathered in Boston for a few days of making art. The photographs Kyle took were like stills from lost films, and I would write stories to accompany them. Unfortunately, most of the stories don't work when separated from their photographs. (My favourite was a murder mystery, involving a woman killed by a typewriter.)

I like this one, though, and you do not need the photograph (of young Amanda with her mouth open and a floor covered with costume jewellery) to understand it.

The Return of the Thin White Duke

The title is a quote from a David Bowie song, and the story began, some years ago, with a fashion magazine asking the remarkable Japanese artist Yoshitaka Amano to do some fashion drawings of Bowie and his wife, Iman. Mr Amano asked if I would like to write a story to accompany them. I wrote the first half of a story, with plans to conclude it in the next issue of the magazine. But the magazine lost interest before they had published the first part, and the story was forgotten. For this anthology I thought it would be an adventure to finish it, and find out what was going to happen, and where it was all heading. If I had known once (I *must* have known once), I still found myself reading the story like a stranger, and walking alone into the mist to learn where it was going.

Feminine Endings

Life imitates art, but clumsily, copying its movements when it thinks it isn't looking.

There are stories it feels almost impious to put on paper, for fear of allowing the things in the story to begin to influence the real world.

I was asked to write a love letter, for a book of love letters. I remembered a human statue I had seen in the square in Kraków, a city with a smoke dragon beneath it.

When I met the woman I would one day marry, we traded stories of our lives. She had once, she told me, been a human statue. I sent her this story, and it did not frighten her away.

For my birthday, shortly after we met, she surprised me in a park in her human-statue incarnation. As a human statue she wore a wedding dress that she had bought for $20, and stood on a box. They called her the Eight-Foot Bride. She wore the wedding dress she had been a statue in on the day we were married. Nobody has seen the dress since that day.

Observing the Formalities

I am not scared of bad people, of wicked evildoers, of monsters and creatures of the night.

The people who scare me are the ones who are certain of their own rightness. The ones who know how to behave, and what their neighbours need to do to be on the side of the good.

We are all the heroes of our own stories.

In this case, *Sleeping Beauty*. Which, seen from another direction, is also the subject of . . .

The Sleeper and the Spindle

Written for Melissa Marr and Tim Pratt's anthology *Rags and Bones*, subtitled *New Twists on Timeless Tales*. They asked a few writers to create stories based on stories that had influenced us. I chose two fairy tales.

I love fairy tales. I remember the first one I encountered, 'Snow White and the Seven Dwarfs', in a beautiful illustrated book my mother would read to me when I was two. I loved everything about that story and those pictures. She read it to me, and soon enough I was reading it to myself. It wasn't until I was older that I started pondering the stranger parts of the story, and I wrote 'Snow, Glass, Apples' (in *Smoke and Mirrors*).

I loved Sleeping Beauty too, in all her incarnations. When I was a young journalist I read a dozen thick bestsellers, and realised I could retell the story of Sleeping Beauty as a huge, sex-and-shopping blockbuster, complete with an evil multinational corporation, a noble young scientist, and a young girl in a mysterious coma. I decided not to write it: it seemed too calculated, and the sort of thing that might actually put me off the writing career I was hoping for.

When Melissa and Tim asked me for a story, I had been pondering what would happen if two stories were happening at the same time. And what if the women who were already the subjects of the stories had a little more to do, and were active and not passive . . . ?

I love this story more than, perhaps, I should. (It is now available as an illustrated storybook in its own right, pictures by the redoubtable Chris Riddell.)

Witch Work

When I was a child and read books of poems I would wonder more than was healthy about the person telling the story. I still do, even with my own poems. In this case there is a witch, and there is a watcher. This was also written as an apologetic gift for Jonathan Strahan, after I realised that *The Ocean at the End of the Lane* was turning into a novel.

In Relig Odhráin

This is a true story. Well, as true as any story about a sixth-century Irish saint can be. The churchyard is there, on Iona. You can even visit it.

I didn't mean to write this as a poem, but the metre turned up in my head and after that I simply had no say in the matter.

They used to bury people alive in the walls or the foundations, to ensure that buildings remained standing. Even saints.

Black Dog

We first met Baldur 'Shadow' Moon in *American Gods,* in which he gets caught up in a war between gods in America. In 'The Monarch of the Glen', a story in the *Fragile Things* collection, Shadow found himself a bouncer at a party in northern Scotland.

He is on his way back to America, but in this story has only made it as far as Derbyshire's Peak District. (This was the very last of the stories in this book to be written and is, as they say on the book jackets, original to this collection.)

I want to thank my friends Colin Greenland and Susanna Clarke for taking me to the Three Stags Heads pub in Wardlow, which, cat, lurchers and all, inspired the opening, and to Colin for telling me that Black Shuck walked Trot Lane, when I asked him about black dogs.

There is one last story to be told, about what happens to Shadow when he reaches London. And then, if he survives that, it will be time to send him back to America. So much has changed, after all, since he went away.

VI. FINAL WARNING

There are monsters in these pages, but as Ogden Nash pointed out in my first short-story collection, *Smoke and Mirrors,* where there's a monster, there's also a miracle.

There are some long stories and some short ones. There are a handful of poems, which perhaps might need their own warning for the people who are frightened, disturbed, or terminally puzzled by poetry. (In my second short-story collection, *Fragile Things,* I tried to explain that the poems come free. They are bonuses for the kind of people who do not need to worry about sneaky and occasional poems lurking inside their short-story collections.)

There. Consider yourself warned. There are so many little triggers out there, being squeezed in the darkness even as I write this. This book is correctly labelled. Now all we have to worry about is all the other books, and, of course, life, which is huge and complicated and will not warn you before it hurts you.

Thank you for coming. Enjoy the things that never happened. Secure your own mask again after you read these stories, but do not forget to help others.

NEIL GAIMAN

In a cabin in the dark woods, 2014

Trigger Warning

Making a Chair

Today I intended to begin to write.
Stories are waiting like distant thunderstorms
grumbling and flickering on the grey horizon
and there are emails and introductions
and a book, a whole damn book
about a country and a journey and belief
I'm here to write.

I made a chair.
I opened a cardboard box with a blade
(I assembled the blade)
removed the parts, carried them, carefully, up the stairs.

'Functional seating for today's workplace'
I pressed five casters into the base,
learned that they press in with a most satisfying pop.
Attached the armrests with the screws,
puzzling over the left and the right of it,
the screws not being what they should be
as described in the instructions. And then the base
beneath the seat,
which attached with six 40 mm screws (that were
puzzlingly six 45 mm screws).

Then the headpiece to the chairback,
the chairback to the seat, which is where the problems start
as the middle screw on either side declines
to penetrate and thread.

This all takes time. Orson Welles is Harry Lime
on the old radio as I assemble my chair. Orson meets a dame
and a crooked fortune-teller, and a fat man,
and a New York gang boss in exile,
and has slept with the dame, solved the mystery,
read the script
and pocketed the money
before I have assembled my chair.

Making a book is a little like making a chair.
Perhaps it ought to come with warnings,
like the chair instructions.
A folded piece of paper slipped into each copy,
warning us:
'Only for one person at a time.'
'Do not use as a stool or a stepladder.'
'Failure to follow these warnings can result in serious
    injury.'

One day I will write another book, and when I'm done
I will climb it,
like a stool or a stepladder,
or a high old wooden ladder propped against the side of
    a plum tree,
in the autumn,
and I will be gone.
But for now I shall follow these warnings,
and finish making the chair.

A Lunar Labyrinth

We were walking up a gentle hill on a summer's evening. It was gone eight thirty, but it still felt like midafternoon. The sky was blue. The sun was low on the horizon, and it splashed the clouds with gold and salmon and purple-grey.

'So how did it end?' I asked my guide.

'It never ends,' he said.

'But you said it's gone,' I said. 'The maze.'

I had found the lunar labyrinth mentioned online, a small footnote on a website that told you what was interesting and noteworthy wherever you were in the world. Unusual local attractions: the tackier and more man-made the better. I do not know why I am drawn to them: stoneless henges made of cars or of yellow school buses, polystyrene models of enormous blocks of cheese, unconvincing dinosaurs made of flaking powdery concrete and all the rest.

I need them, and they give me an excuse to stop driving, wherever I am, and actually to talk to people. I have been invited into people's houses and into their lives because I wholeheartedly appreciated the zoos they made from engine parts, the houses they had built from tin cans, stone blocks and then covered with aluminium foil, the historical pageants made from shop-window dummies, the paint on their faces flaking off. And those people, the ones who made the roadside attractions, they would accept me for what I am.

* * *

'We burned it down,' said my guide. He was elderly, and he walked with a stick. I had met him sitting on a bench in front of the town's hardware store, and he had agreed to show me the site that the lunar labyrinth had once been built upon. Our progress across the meadow was not fast. 'The end of the lunar labyrinth. It was easy. The rosemary hedges caught fire and they crackled and flared. The smoke was thick and drifted down the hill and made us all think of roast lamb.'

'Why was it called a lunar labyrinth?' I asked. 'Was it just the alliteration?'

He thought about this. 'I wouldn't rightly know,' he said. 'Not one way or the other. We called it a labyrinth, but I guess it's just a maze . . .'

'Just amazed,' I repeated.

'There were traditions,' he said. 'We would start to walk it the day *after* the full moon. Begin at the entrance. Make your way to the centre, then turn around and trace your way back. Like I say, we'd only start walking the day the moon began to wane. It would still be bright enough to walk. We'd walk it any night the moon was bright enough to see by. Come out here. Walk. Mostly in couples. We'd walk until the dark of the moon.'

'Nobody walked it in the dark?'

'Oh, some of them did. But they weren't like us. They were kids, and they brought flashlights, when the moon went dark. They walked it, the bad kids, the bad seeds, the ones who wanted to scare each other. For those kids it was Hallowe'en every month. They loved to be scared. Some of them said they saw a torturer.'

'What kind of a torturer?' The word had surprised me. You did not hear it often, not in conversation.

'Just someone who tortured people, I guess. I never saw him.'

A breeze came down towards us from the hilltop. I sniffed the air but smelled no burning herbs, no ash, nothing that seemed unusual on a summer evening. Somewhere there were gardenias.

'It was only kids when the moon was dark. When the crescent moon appeared, then the children got younger, and parents would come up to the hill and walk with them. Parents and children. They'd walk the maze together to its centre and the adults would point up to the new moon, how it looks like a smile in the sky, a huge yellow smile, and little Romulus and Remus, or whatever the kids were called, they'd smile and laugh, and wave their hands as if they were trying to pull the moon out of the sky and put it on their little faces.

'Then, as the moon waxed, the couples would come. Young couples would come up here, courting, and elderly couples, comfortable in each other's company, the ones whose courting days were long forgotten.' He leaned heavily on his stick. 'Not forgotten,' he said. 'You never forget. It must be somewhere inside you. Even if the brain has forgotten, perhaps the teeth remember. Or the fingers.'

'Did they have flashlights?'

'Some nights they did. Some nights they didn't. The popular nights were always the nights where no clouds covered the moon, and you could just walk the labyrinth. And sooner or later, everybody did. As the moonlight increased, day by day – night by night, I should say. That world was so beautiful.

'They parked their cars down there, back where you parked yours, at the edge of the property, and they'd come up the hill on foot. Always on foot, except for the ones in wheelchairs, or the ones whose parents carried them. Then, at the top of the hill some of them'd stop to canoodle. They'd walk the labyrinth too. There were benches, places to stop as you walked it. And they'd stop and canoodle some more. You'd think it was just the young ones, canoodling, but the older folk did it, too. Flesh to flesh. You would hear them sometimes, on the other side of the hedge, making noises like animals, and that always was your cue to slow down, or maybe explore another branch of the path for a while. Doesn't come by too often, but when it does I think I appreciate it more now than I did then. Lips touching skin. Under the moonlight.'

'How many years exactly was the lunar labyrinth here before it was burned down? Did it come before or after the house was built?'

My guide made a dismissive noise. 'After, before . . . these things all go back. They talk about the labyrinth of Minos, but that was nothing by comparison to this. Just some tunnels with a horn-headed fellow wandering lonely and scared and hungry. He wasn't really a bull-head. You know that?'

'How do you know?'

'Teeth. Bulls and cows are ruminants. They don't eat flesh. The minotaur did.'

'I hadn't thought of that.'

'People don't.' The hill was getting steeper now.

I thought, *There are no torturers, not any longer.* And I was no torturer. But all I said was, 'How high were the bushes that made up the maze? Were they real hedges?'

'They were real. They were high as they needed to be.'

'I don't know how high rosemary grows in these parts.' I didn't. I was far from home.

'We have gentle winters. Rosemary flourishes here.'

'So why exactly did the people burn it all down?'

He paused. 'You'll get a better idea of how things lie when we get to the top of the hill.'

'How do they lie?'

'At the top of the hill.'

The hill was getting steeper and steeper. My left knee had been injured the previous winter, in a fall on the ice, which meant I could no longer run fast, and these days I found hills and steps extremely taxing. With each step my knee would twinge, reminding me, angrily, of its existence.

Many people, on learning that the local oddity they wished to visit had burned down some years before, would simply have gotten back into their cars and driven on towards their final destination. I am not so easily deterred. The finest things I have seen are dead places: a shuttered amusement park I entered by bribing a night watchman with the price of a drink; an abandoned barn in which, the farmer said, half a dozen bigfoots had been living the summer before. He said they howled at night, and that they stank, but that they had moved on almost a year ago. There was a rank animal smell that lingered in that place, but it might have been coyotes.

'When the moon waned, they walked the lunar labyrinth with love,' said my guide. 'As it waxed, they walked with desire, not with love. Do I have to explain the difference to you? The sheep and the goats?'

'I don't think so.'

'The sick came, too, sometimes. The damaged and the disabled came, and some of them needed to be wheeled through the labyrinth, or carried. But even they had to choose the path they travelled, not the people carrying them or wheeling them. Nobody chose their paths but them. When I was a boy people called them cripples. I'm glad we don't call them cripples any longer. The lovelorn came, too. The alone. The lunatics – they were brought here, sometimes. Got their name from the moon, it was only fair the moon had a chance to fix things.'

We were approaching the top of the hill. It was dusk. The sky

was the colour of wine, now, and the clouds in the west glowed
with the light of the setting sun, although from where we were
standing it had already dropped below the horizon.

'You'll see, when we get up there. It's perfectly flat, the top
of the hill.'

I wanted to contribute something, so I said, 'Where I come
from, five hundred years ago the local lord was visiting the king.
And the king showed off his enormous table, his candles, his
beautiful painted ceiling, and as each one was displayed, instead
of praising it, the lord simply said, "I have a finer, and bigger,
and better one." The king wanted to call his bluff, so he told
him that the following month he would come and eat at this
table, bigger and finer than the king's, lit by candles in candle-
holders bigger and finer than the king's, under a ceiling painting
bigger and better than the king's.'

My guide said, 'Did he lay out a tablecloth on the flatness of
the hill, and have twenty brave men holding candles, and did
they dine beneath God's own stars? They tell a story like that
in these parts, too.'

'That's the story,' I admitted, slightly miffed that my contribu-
tion had been so casually dismissed. 'And the king acknowledged
that the lord was right.'

'Didn't the boss have him imprisoned, and tortured?' asked
my guide. 'That's what happened in the version of the story
they tell hereabouts. They say that the man never even made it
as far as the Cordon-bleu dessert his chef had whipped up. They
found him on the following day with his hands cut off, his
severed tongue placed neatly in his breast pocket and a final
bullet-hole in his forehead.'

'Here? In the house back there?'

'Good lord, no. They left his body in his nightclub. Over in
the city.'

I was surprised how quickly dusk had ended. There was still

a glow in the west, but the rest of the sky had become night, plum-purple in its majesty.

'The days before the full of the moon, in the labyrinth,' he said. 'They were set aside for the infirm, and those in need. My sister had a women's condition. They told her it would be fatal if she didn't have her insides all scraped out, and then it might be fatal anyway. Her stomach had swollen up as if she was carrying a baby, not a tumour, although she must have been pushing fifty. She came up here when the moon was a day from full and she walked the labyrinth. Walked it from the outside in, in the moon's light, and she walked it from the centre back to the outside, with no false steps or mistakes.'

'What happened to her?'

'She lived,' he said, shortly.

We crested the hill, but I could not see what I was looking at. It was too dark.

'They delivered her of the thing inside her. It lived as well, for a while.' He paused. Then he tapped my arm. 'Look over there.'

I turned and looked. The size of the moon astonished me. I know it's an optical illusion, that the moon grows no smaller as it rises, but this moon seemed to take up so much of the horizon as it rose that I found myself thinking of the old Frank Frazetta paperback covers, where men with their swords raised would be silhouetted in front of huge moons, and I remembered paintings of wolves howling on hilltops, black cutouts against the circle of snow-white moon that framed them. The enormous moon that was rising was the creamy yellow of freshly churned butter.

'Is the moon full?' I asked.

'That's a full moon, all right.' He sounded satisfied. 'And there's the labyrinth.'

We walked towards it. I had expected to see ash on the ground, or nothing. Instead, in the buttery moonlight, I saw a maze, complex and elegant, made of circles and whorls inside a huge square. I could not judge distances properly in that light, but I thought that each side of the square must be two hundred feet or more.

The plants that outlined the maze were low to the ground, though. None of them was more than a foot tall. I bent down, picked a needle-like leaf, black in the moonlight, and crushed it between finger and thumb. I inhaled, and thought of raw lamb, carefully dismembered and prepared, and placed in an oven on a bed of branches and needles that smelled just like this.

'I thought you people burned all this to the ground,' I said.

'We did. They aren't hedges, not any longer. But things grow again, in their season. There's no killing some things. Rosemary's tough.'

'Where's the entrance?'

'You're standing in it,' he said. He was an old man, who walked with a stick and talked to strangers. Nobody would ever miss him.

'So what happened up here when the moon was full?'

'Locals didn't walk the labyrinth then. That was the one night that paid for all.'

I took a step into the maze. There was nothing difficult about it, not with the bushes that marked it no higher than my shins, no higher than a kitchen garden. If I got lost, I could simply step over the bushes, walk back out. But for now I followed the path into the labyrinth. It was easy to make out in the light of the full moon. I could hear my guide, as he continued to talk.

'Some folk thought even that price was too high. That was why we came up here, why we burned the lunar labyrinth. We came up that hill when the moon was dark, and we carried burning torches, like in the old black-and-white movies. We all did. Even me. But you can't kill everything. It don't work like that.'

'Why rosemary?' I asked.

'Rosemary's for remembering,' he told me.

The butter-yellow moon was rising faster than I imagined or expected. Now it was a pale ghost-face in the sky, calm and compassionate, and its colour was white, bone-white.

The man said, 'There's always a chance that you could get out safely. Even on the night of the full moon. First you have to get to the centre of the labyrinth. There's a fountain there. You'll see. You can't mistake it. Then you have to make it back from the centre. No missteps, no dead ends, no mistakes on the way in or on the way out. It's probably easier now than it was when the bushes were high. It's a chance. Otherwise, the labyrinth gets to cure you of all that ails you. Of course, you'll have to run.'

I looked back. I could not see my guide. Not any longer. There was something in front of me, beyond the bush-path pattern, a black shadow padding silently along the perimeter of the square. It was the size of a large dog, but it did not move like a dog.

It threw back its head and howled to the moon with amusement and with merriment. The huge flat table at the top of the hill echoed with joyous howls, and, my left knee aching from the long hill-climb, I stumbled forward.

The maze had a pattern; I could trace it. Above me the moon shone, bright as day. She had always accepted my gifts in the past. She would not play me false at the end.

'Run,' said a voice that was almost a growl.

I ran like a lamb to his laughter.

The Thing About Cassandra

So there's Scallie and me wearing Starsky-and-Hutch wigs, complete with sideburns, at five o'clock in the morning by the side of a canal in Amsterdam. There had been ten of us that night, including Rob, the groom, last seen handcuffed to a bed in the red-light district with shaving foam covering his nether regions and his future brother-in-law giggling and patting the hooker holding the straight razor on the arse, which was the point I looked at Scallie and he looked at me, and he said, 'Maximum deniability?' and I nodded, because there are some questions you don't want to be able to answer when a bride starts asking pointed questions about the stag weekend, so we slipped off for a drink, leaving eight men in Starsky-and-Hutch wigs (one of whom was mostly naked, attached to a bed by fluffy pink handcuffs, and seemed to be starting to think that this adventure wasn't such a good idea after all) behind us, in a room that smelled of disinfectant and cheap incense, and we went and sat by a canal and drank cans of Danish lager and talked about the old days.

Scallie – whose real name is Jeremy Porter, and these days people call him Jeremy, but he had been Scallie when we were eleven – and the groom-to-be, Rob Cunningham, had been at school with me. We had drifted out of touch, more or less, had found each other the lazy way you do these days, through Friends Reunited and Facebook and such, and now Scallie and I were together for the first time since we were nineteen. The Starsky-and-Hutch wigs, which had been Scallie's idea, made us look like we were playing brothers in some made-for-TV movie – Scallie the short, stocky brother with the thick moustache, me, the tall one. Given that I've made a significant part of my income since leaving school modelling, I'd add the tall good-looking one, but nobody looks good in a Starsky-and-Hutch wig complete with sideburns.

Also, the wig itched.

We sat by the canal, and when the lager had all gone we kept talking and we watched the sun come up.

Last time I saw Scallie he was nineteen and filled with big plans. He had just joined the RAF as a cadet. He was going to fly planes, and do double duty using the flights to smuggle drugs, and so get incredibly rich while helping his country. It was the kind of mad idea he used to have all the way through school. Usually the whole thing would fall apart. Sometimes he'd get the rest of us into trouble on the way.

Now, twelve years later, his six months in the RAF ended early because of an unspecified problem with his ankle, he was a senior executive in a firm that manufactured double-glazed windows, he told me, with, since the divorce, a smaller house than he felt that he deserved and only a golden retriever for company.

He was sleeping with a woman in the double-glazing firm, but had no expectations of her leaving her boyfriend for him, seemed to find it easier that way. 'Of course, I wake up crying sometimes, since the divorce. Well, you do,' he said at one point. I could not imagine him crying, and anyway he said it with a huge, Scallie grin.

I told him about me: still modelling, helping out in a friend's antique shop to keep busy, more and more painting. I was lucky; people bought my paintings. Every year I would have a small gallery show at the Little Gallery in Chelsea, and while initially the only people to buy anything had been people I knew – photographers, old girlfriends and the like – these days I have actual collectors. We talked about the days that only Scallie seemed to remember, when he and Rob and I had been a team of three, inviolable, unbreakable. We talked about teenage heart-break, about Caroline Minton (who was now Caroline Keen, and married to a vicar), about the first time we brazened our way into an 18 film, although neither of us could remember what the film actually was.

Then Scallie said, 'I heard from Cassandra the other day.'

'Cassandra?'

'Your old girlfriend. Cassandra. Remember?'

'. . . No.'

'The one from Reigate. You had her name written on all your books.' I must have looked particularly dense or drunk or sleepy, because he said, 'You met her on a skiing holiday. Oh, for heaven's sake. *Your first shag.* Cassandra.'

'Oh,' I said, remembering, remembering everything. 'Cassandra.'

And I did remember.

'Yeah,' said Scallie. 'She dropped me a line on Facebook. She's running a community theatre in East London. You should talk to her.'

'Really?'

'I think, well, I mean, reading between the lines of her message, she may still have a thing for you. She asked after you.'

I wondered how drunk he was, how drunk I was, staring at the canal in the early light. I said something, I forget what, then I asked whether Scallie remembered where our hotel was, because I had forgotten, and he said he had forgotten too, and that Rob had all the hotel details and really we should go and find him and rescue him from the clutches of the nice hooker with the handcuffs and the shaving kit, which, we realised, would be easier if we knew how to get back to where we'd left him, and looking for some clue to where we had left Rob I found a card with the hotel's address on it in my back pocket, so we headed back there and the last thing I did before I walked away from the canal and that whole strange evening was to pull the itchy Starsky-and-Hutch wig off my head and throw it into the canal.

It floated.

Scallie said, 'There was a deposit on that, you know. If you didn't want to wear it, I'd've carried it.' Then he said, 'You should drop Cassandra a line.'

I shook my head. I wondered who he had been talking to online, who he had confused for her, knowing it definitely wasn't Cassandra.

The thing about Cassandra is this: I'd made her up.

* * *

I was fifteen, almost sixteen. I was awkward. I had just experienced my teenage growth spurt and was suddenly taller than most of my friends, self-conscious about my height. My mother owned and ran a small riding stables, and I helped out there, but the girls – competent, horsey, sensible types – intimidated me. At home I wrote bad poetry and painted watercolours, mostly of ponies in fields; at school – there were only boys at my school – I played cricket competently, acted a little, hung around with my friends playing records (the CD was newly around, but CD players were expensive and rare, and we had all inherited record players and hi-fis from parents or older siblings). When we didn't talk about music, or sports, we talked about girls.

Scallie was older than me. So was Rob. They liked having me as part of their gang, but they liked teasing me, too. They acted like I was a kid, and I wasn't. They had both done it with girls. Actually, that's not entirely true; they had both done it with the same girl, Caroline Minton, famously free with her favours and always up for it once, as long as the person she was with had a moped.

I did not have a moped. I was not old enough to get one, my mother could not afford one (my father had died when I was small, of an accidental overdose of anaesthetic, when he was in hospital to have a minor operation on an infected toe. To this day, I avoid hospitals). I had seen Caroline Minton at parties, but she terrified me and even had I owned a moped, I would not have wanted my first sexual experience to be with her.

Scallie and Rob also had girlfriends. Scallie's girlfriend was taller than he was, had huge breasts and was interested in football, which meant Scallie had to feign an interest in football, mostly Crystal Palace, while Rob's girlfriend thought that Rob and she should have things in common, which meant that Rob stopped listening to the mideighties electropop the rest of us liked and started listening to hippy bands from before we were born, which was bad, and that Rob got to raid her dad's amazing collection of old TV on video, which was good.

I had no girlfriend.

Even my mother began to comment on it.

There must have been a place where it came from, the name, the idea: I don't remember though. I just remember writing 'Cassandra' on my exercise books. Then, carefully, not saying anything.

'Who's Cassandra?' asked Scallie, on the bus to school.

'Nobody,' I said.

'She must be somebody. You wrote her name on your maths exercise book.'

'She's just a girl I met on the skiing holiday.' My mother and I had gone skiing, with my aunt and cousins, the month before, in Austria.

'Are we going to meet her?'

'She's from Reigate. I expect so. Eventually.'

'Well, I hope so. And you *like* her?'

I paused, for what I hoped was the right amount of time, and said, 'She's a really good kisser,' then Scallie laughed and Rob wanted to know if this was French kissing, with tongues and everything, and I said, 'What do *you* think,' and by the end of the day, they both believed in her.

My mum was pleased to hear I'd met someone. Her questions – what Cassandra's parents did, for example – I simply shrugged away.

I went on three 'dates' with Cassandra. On each of our dates, I took the train up to London, and took myself to the cinema. It was exciting, in its own way.

I returned from the first trip with more stories of kissing, and of breast-feeling.

Our second date (in reality, spent watching *Weird Science* on my own in Leicester Square) was, as told to my mum, merely spent holding hands together at what she still called 'the pictures', but as reluctantly revealed to Rob and Scallie (and, over that week, to several other school friends who had heard rumours from sworn-to-secrecy Rob and Scallie, and now needed to find out if any of it was true) it was actually The Day I Lost My Virginity, in Cassandra's aunt's flat in London: the aunt was away, Cassandra had a key. I had (for proof) a packet of three condoms missing the one I had thrown away and a strip of four black-and-white photographs I had found on my first trip to London, abandoned in the basket of a photo booth in Victoria Station. The photo strip showed a girl about my age with long straight hair (I could not be certain of the colour. Dark blond? Red? Light brown?) and a friendly, freckly, not unpretty, face. I pocketed it. In art class I did a pencil sketch of the third of the pictures, the one I liked the best, her head half-turned as if calling out to an unseen friend beyond the tiny curtain. She looked sweet, and charming. I would have liked her to be my girlfriend.

I put the drawing up on my bedroom wall, where I could see it from my bed.

After our third date (it was to see *Who Framed Roger Rabbit?*) I came back to school with bad news: Cassandra's family was going to Canada (a place that sounded more convincing to my ears than America), something to do with her father's job, and I would not see her for a long time. We hadn't really broken up, but we were being practical: those were the days when transatlantic phone calls were too expensive for teenagers. It was over.

I was sad. Everyone noticed how sad I was. They said they would have loved to have met her, and maybe when she comes back at Christmas? I was confident that by Christmas, she would be forgotten.

She was. By Christmas I was going out with Nikki Blevins and the only evidence that Cassandra had ever been a part of my life was her name, written on a couple of my exercise books, and the pencil drawing of her on my bedroom wall, with 'Cassandra, 19th February, 1985' written underneath it.

When my mother sold the riding stable, the drawing was lost in the move. I was at art college at the time, considered my old pencil drawings as embarrassing as the fact that I had once invented a girlfriend, and did not care.

I do not believe I had thought of Cassandra for twenty years.

***

My mother sold the stables, the attached house and the meadows to a property developer, who built a housing estate where we had once lived, and, as part of the deal, gave her a small, detached house at the end of Seton Close. I visit her at least once a fortnight, arriving on Friday night, leaving Sunday morning, a routine as regular as the grandmother clock in the hall.

Mother is concerned that I am happy in life. She has started to mention that various of her friends have eligible daughters. This trip we had an extremely embarrassing conversation that began with her asking if I would like her to introduce me to the organist at her church, a very nice young man of about my age.

'Mother. I'm not gay.'

'There's nothing wrong with it, dear. All sorts of people do it. They even get married. Well, not proper marriage, but it's the same thing.'

'I'm still not gay.'

'I just thought, still not married, and the painting and the modelling.'

'I've had girlfriends, Mummy. You've even met some of them.'

'Nothing that ever stuck, dear. I just thought there might be something you wanted to tell me.'

'I'm not gay, Mother. I would tell you if I was.' And then I said, 'I snogged Tim Carter at a party when I was at art college but we were drunk and it never went beyond that.'

She pursed her lips. 'That's quite enough of that, young man.' And then, changing the subject, as if to get rid of an unpleasant taste in her mouth, she said, 'You'll never guess who I bumped into in Tesco's last week.'

'No, I won't. Who?'

'Your old girlfriend. Your first girlfriend, I should say.'

'Nikki Blevins? Hang on, she's married, isn't she? Nikki Woodbridge?'

'The one before her, dear. Cassandra. I was behind her, in the line. I would have been ahead of her, but I forgot that I needed cream for the berries today, so I went back to get it, and she was in front of me, and I knew her face was familiar. At first, I thought she was Joanie Simmond's youngest, the one with the speech disorder, what we used to call a stammer but apparently you can't say that any more, but then I thought, *I know where I know that face from,* it was over your bed for five years, of course I said, "It's not Cassandra, is it?" and she said, "It is," and I said, "You'll laugh when I say this, but I'm Stuart Innes's mum." She says, "Stuart Innes?" and her face lit up. Well, she hung around while I was putting my groceries in my shopping bag, and she said she'd already been in touch with your friend Jeremy Porter on Bookface, and they'd been talking about you—'

'You mean Facebook? She was talking to Scallie on Facebook?'

'Yes, dear.'

I drank my tea and wondered who my mother had actually been talking to. I said, 'You're quite sure this was the Cassandra from over my bed?'

'Oh yes, dear. She told me about how you took her to Leicester Square, and how sad she was when they had to move to Canada. They went to Vancouver. I asked her if she ever met my cousin Leslie, he went to Vancouver after the war, but she said she didn't believe so, and it turns out it's actually a big sort of a place. I told her about the pencil drawing you did, and she seemed very up-to-date on your activities. She was thrilled when I told her that you were having a gallery opening this week.'

'You *told* her that?'

'Yes, dear. I thought she'd like to know.' Then my mother said, almost wistfully, 'She's very pretty, dear. I think she's doing something in community theatre.' Then the conversation went over to the retirement of Dr Dunnings, who had been our GP since before I was born, and how he was the only non-Indian doctor left in his practice and how my mother felt about this.

I lay in bed that night in my small bedroom at my mother's house and turned over the conversation in my head. I am no longer on Facebook and thought about rejoining to see who

Scallie's friends were, and if this pseudo-Cassandra was one of them, but there were too many people I was happy not to see again, and I let it be, certain that when there was an explanation, it would prove to be a simple one, and I slept.

* * *

I have been showing in the Little Gallery in Chelsea for over a decade now. In the old days, I had a quarter of a wall and nothing priced at more than three hundred pounds. Now I get my own show every October, for a month, and it would be fair to say that I only have to sell a dozen paintings to know that my needs, rent and life are covered for another year. The unsold paintings remain on the gallery walls until they are gone and they are always gone by Christmas.

The couple who own the gallery, Paul and Barry, still call me 'the beautiful boy' as they did twelve years ago, when I first exhibited with them, when it might actually have been true. Back then, they wore flowery, open-necked shirts and gold chains: now, in middle age, they wear expensive suits and talk too much for my liking about the stock exchange. Still, I enjoy their company. I see them three times a year: in September when they come to my studio to see what I've been working on, and select the paintings for the show; at the gallery, hanging and opening in October; and in February, when we settle up.

Barry runs the gallery. Paul co-owns it, comes out for the parties, but also works in the wardrobe department of the Royal Opera House. The preview party for this year's show was on a Friday evening. I had spent a nervous couple of days hanging the paintings. Now, my part was done, and there was nothing to do but wait, and hope people liked my art, and not to make a fool of myself. I did as I had done for the previous twelve years, on Barry's instructions: 'Nurse the champagne. Fill up on water. There's nothing worse for the collector than encountering a drunken artist, unless he's famous for being drunk, and you are not, dear. Be amiable but enigmatic, and when people ask for the story behind the painting, say, "My lips are sealed." But for god's sake, imply there *is* one. It's the story they're buying.'

I rarely invite people to the preview any longer: some artists do, regarding it as a social event. I do not. While I take my art seriously, as art, and am proud of my work (the latest exhibition was called 'People in Landscapes', which pretty much says it all about my work anyway), I understand that the party exists solely as a commercial event, a come-on for eventual buyers and those who might say the right thing to other eventual buyers. I tell you this so you will not be surprised that Barry and Paul manage the guest list to the preview, not I.

The preview always begins at six thirty p.m. I had spent the afternoon hanging paintings, making sure everything looked as good as it could, as I have done every other year. The only thing that was different about the day of this particular event was how excited Paul looked, like a small boy struggling with the urge to tell you what he had bought you for a birthday present. That, and Barry, who said, while we were hanging, 'I think tonight's show will put you on the map.'

I said, 'I think there's a typo on the Lake District one.' An oversized painting of Windermere at sunset, with two children staring lostly at the viewer from the banks. 'It should say three thousand pounds. It says three hundred thousand.'

'Does it?' said Barry, blandly. 'My, my.' But he did nothing to change it.

It was perplexing, but the first guests had arrived, a little early, and the mystery could wait. A young man invited me to eat a mushroom puff from a silver tray. I took my glass of nurse-this-slowly champagne from the table in the corner, and I prepared to mingle.

All the prices were high, and I doubted that the Little Gallery would be able to sell the paintings at those prices, and I worried about the year ahead.

Barry and Paul always take responsibility for moving me around the room, saying, 'This is the artist, the beautiful boy who makes all these beautiful things, Stuart Innes,' and I shake hands, and smile. By the end of the evening I will have met everyone, and Paul and Barry are very good about saying, 'Stuart, you remember David, he writes about art for the *Telegraph* . . .', and I for my part am good about saying, 'Of course, how are you? So glad you could come.'

The room was at its most crowded when a striking red-haired woman to whom I had not yet been introduced began shouting, 'Representational bullshit!'

I was in conversation with the *Daily Telegraph* art critic and we turned. He said, 'Friend of yours?'

I said, 'I don't think so.'

She was still shouting, although the sounds of the party had now quieted. She shouted, 'Nobody's interested in this shit! Nobody!' Then she reached her hand into her coat pocket and pulled out a bottle of ink, shouted, 'Try selling this now!' and threw ink at *Windermere Sunset*. It was blue-black ink.

Paul was by her side then, pulling the ink bottle away from her, saying, 'That was a three-hundred-thousand-pound painting, young lady.' Barry took her arm, said, 'I think the police will want a word with you,' and walked her back into his office. She shouted at us as she went, 'I'm not afraid! I'm proud! Artists like him, just feeding off you gullible art buyers. You're all sheep! Representational crap!'

And then she was gone, and the party people were buzzing, and inspecting the ink-fouled painting and looking at me, and the *Telegraph* man was asking if I would like to comment and how I felt about seeing a three-hundred-thousand-pound painting destroyed, and I mumbled about how I was proud to be a painter, and said something about the transient nature of art, and he said that he supposed that tonight's event was an artistic happening in its own right, and we agreed that, artistic happening or not, the woman was not quite right in the head.

Barry reappeared, moving from group to group, explaining that Paul was dealing with the young lady, and that her eventual disposition would be up to me. The guests were still buzzing excitedly as he ushered them out of the door. Barry apologised as he did so, agreed that we lived in exciting times, explained that he would be open at the regular time tomorrow.

'That went well,' he said, when we were alone in the gallery.

'*Well?* That was a disaster.'

'Mm. "Stuart Innes, the one who had the three-hundred-thousand-pound painting destroyed." I think you need to be forgiving, don't you? She was a fellow artist, even one with different goals. Sometimes you need a little something to kick you up to the next level.'

We went into the back room.

I said, 'Whose idea was this?'

'Ours,' said Paul. He was drinking white wine in the back room with the red-haired woman. 'Well, Barry's mostly. But it needed a good little actress to pull it off, and I found her.' She grinned, modestly: managed to look both abashed and pleased with herself.

'If this doesn't get you the attention you deserve, beautiful boy,' said Barry, smiling at me, 'nothing will. *Now* you're important enough to be attacked.'

'The Windermere painting's ruined,' I pointed out.

Barry glanced at Paul, and they giggled. 'It's already sold, ink-splatters and all, for seventy-five thousand pounds,' Barry said. 'It's like I always say, people think they are buying the art, but really, they're buying the story.'

Paul filled our glasses: 'And we owe it all to you,' he said to the woman. 'Stuart, Barry, I'd like to propose a toast. *To Cassandra.*'

'Cassandra,' we repeated, and we drank. This time I did not nurse my drink. I needed it.

Then, as the name was still sinking in, Paul said, 'Cassandra, this ridiculously attractive and talented young man is, as I am sure you know, Stuart Innes.'

'I know,' she said. 'Actually, we're very old friends.'

'Do tell,' said Barry.

'Well,' said Cassandra, 'twenty years ago, Stuart wrote my name on his maths exercise notebook.'

She looked like the girl in my drawing, yes. Or like the girl in the photographs, all grown-up. Sharp-faced. Intelligent. Assured.

I had never seen her before in my life.

'Hello, Cassandra,' I said. I couldn't think of anything else to say.

* * *

We were in the wine bar beneath my flat. They serve food there, too. It's more than just a wine bar.

I found myself talking to her as if she was someone I had known since childhood. And, I reminded myself, she wasn't. I had only met her that evening. She still had ink stains on her hands.

We had glanced at the menu, ordered the same thing – the vegetarian meze – and when it had arrived, both started with the dolmades, then moved on to the hummus.

'I made you up,' I told her.

It was not the first thing I had said: first we had talked about her community theatre, how she had become friends with Paul,

his offer to her – a thousand pounds for this evening's show –
and how she had needed the money but mostly said yes to him
because it sounded like a fun adventure. Anyway, she said, she
couldn't say no when she heard my name mentioned. She thought
it was fate.

That was when I said it. I was scared she would think I was
mad, but I said it. 'I made you up.'

'No,' she said. 'You didn't. I mean, obviously you didn't. I'm
really here.' Then she said, 'Would you like to touch me?'

I looked at her. At her face, and her posture, at her eyes. She
was everything I had ever dreamed of in a woman. Everything
I had been missing in other women. 'Yes,' I said. 'Very much.'

'Let's eat our dinner first,' she said. Then she said, 'How long
has it been since you were with a woman?'

'I'm not gay,' I protested. 'I have girlfriends.'

'I know,' she said. 'When was the last one?'

I tried to remember. Was it Brigitte? Or the stylist the ad
agency had sent me to Iceland with? I was not certain. 'Two
years,' I said. 'Perhaps three. I just haven't met the right person
yet.'

'You did once,' she said. She opened her handbag then, a big
floppy purple thing, pulled out a cardboard folder, opened it,
removed a piece of paper, tape-browned at the corners. 'See?'

I remembered it. How could I not? It had hung above my bed
for years. She was looking around, as if talking to someone
beyond the curtain. *Cassandra*, it said, *19th February, 1985*. And
it was signed, *Stuart Innes*. There is something at the same time
both embarrassing and heartwarming about seeing your hand-
writing from when you were fifteen.

'I came back from Canada in '89,' she said. 'My parents'
marriage fell apart out there, and Mum wanted to come home.
I wondered about you, what you were doing, so I went to your
old address. The house was empty. Windows were broken. It

was obvious nobody lived there any more. They'd knocked down the riding stables already – that made me so sad, I'd loved horses as a girl, obviously, but I walked through the house until I found your bedroom. It was obviously your bedroom, although all the furniture was gone. It still smelled like you. And this was still pinned to the wall. I didn't think anyone would miss it.'

She smiled.

'Who *are* you?'

'Cassandra Carlisle. Aged thirty-four. Former actress. Failed playwright. Now running a community theatre in Norwood. Drama therapy. Hall for rent. Four plays a year, plus workshops, and a local panto. Who are *you*, Stuart?'

'You know who I am.' Then, 'You know I've never met you before, don't you?'

She nodded. She said, 'Poor Stuart. You live just above here, don't you?'

'Yes. It's a bit loud sometimes. But it's handy for the tube. And the rent isn't painful.'

'Let's pay the bill, and go upstairs.'

I reached out to touch the back of her hand. 'Not yet,' she said, moving her hand away before I could touch her. 'We should talk first.'

So we went upstairs.

'I like your flat,' she said. 'It looks exactly like the kind of place I imagine you being.'

'It's probably time to start thinking about getting something a bit bigger,' I told her. 'But it does me fine. There's good light out the back for my studio – you can't get the effect now, at night. But it's great for painting.'

It's strange, bringing someone home. It makes you see the place you live as if you've not been there before. There are two oil paintings of me in the lounge, from my short-lived career as an artists' model (I did not have the patience to stand and pose for very long, a failing I know), blown-up advertising photos of me in the little kitchen and the loo, book covers with me on – romance covers, mostly – over the stairs.

I showed her the studio, and then the bedroom. She examined the Edwardian barbers' chair I had rescued from an ancient place that closed down in Shoreditch. She sat down on the chair, pulled off her shoes.

'Who was the first grown-up you liked?' she asked.

'Odd question. My mother, I suspect. Don't know. Why?'

'I was three, perhaps four. He was a postman called Mister Postie. He'd come in his little post van and bring me lovely things. Not every day. Just sometimes. Brown paper packages with my name on, and inside would be toys or sweets or something. He had a funny, friendly face with a knobby nose.'

'And he was real? He sounds like somebody a kid would make up.'

'He drove a post van inside the house. It wasn't very big.'

She began to unbutton her blouse. It was cream-coloured, still flecked with splatters of ink. 'What's the first thing you actually remember? Not something you were told you did. That you really remember.'

'Going to the seaside when I was three, with my mum and my dad.'

'Do you remember it? Or do you remember being told about it?'

'I don't see what the point of this is . . .'

She stood up, wiggled, stepped out of her skirt. She wore a white bra, dark green panties, frayed. Very human: not something you would wear to impress a new lover. I wondered what her breasts would look like, when the bra came off. I wanted to stroke them, to touch them to my lips.

She walked from the chair to the bed, where I was sitting.

'Lie down, now. On that side of the bed. I'll be next to you. Don't touch me.'

I lay down, my hands at my sides. She looked down at me. She said, 'You're so beautiful. I'm not honestly sure whether you're my type. You would have been when I was fifteen, though. Nice and sweet and unthreatening. Artistic. Ponies. A riding stable. And I bet you never make a move on a girl unless you're sure she's ready, do you?'

'No,' I said. 'I don't suppose that I do.'

She lay down beside me.

'You can touch me now,' said Cassandra.

* * *

I had started thinking about Stuart again late last year. Stress, I think. Work was going well, up to a point, but I'd broken up with Pavel, who may or may not have been an actual bad hat although he certainly had his finger in many dodgy East European pies, and I was thinking about Internet dating. I had spent a stupid week joining the kind of websites that link you to old friends, and from there it was no distance to Jeremy 'Scallie' Porter, and to Stuart Innes.

I don't think I could do it any more. I lack the single-mindedness, the attention to detail. Something else you lose when you get older.

Mister Postie used to come in his van when my parents had no time for me. He would smile his big gnomey smile, wink an eye at me, hand me a brown-paper parcel with *Cassandra* written on it in big block letters, and inside would be a chocolate, or a doll, or a book. His final present was a pink plastic microphone, and I would walk around the house singing into it or pretending to be on TV. It was the best present I had ever been given.

My parents did not ask about the gifts. I did not wonder who was actually sending them. They came with Mister Postie, who drove his little van down the hall and up to my bedroom door, and who always knocked three times. I was a demonstrative girl, and the next time I saw him, after the plastic microphone, I ran to him and threw my arms around his legs.

It's hard to describe what happened then. He fell like snow, or like ash. For a moment I had been holding someone, then there was just powdery white stuff, and nothing.

I used to wish that Mister Postie would come back, after that, but he never did. He was over. After a while, he became embarrassing to remember: I had fallen for *that*.

So strange, this room.

I wonder why I could ever have thought that somebody who made me happy when I was fifteen would make me happy now. But Stuart was perfect: the riding stables (with ponies), and the painting (which showed me he was sensitive), and the inexperience with girls (so I could be his first) and how very, very tall, dark and handsome he would be. I liked the name, too: it was vaguely Scottish and (to my mind) sounded like the hero of a novel.

I wrote Stuart's name on my exercise books.

I did not tell my friends the most important thing about Stuart: that I had made him up.

And now I'm getting up off the bed and looking down at the outline of a man, a silhouette in flour or ash or dust on the black satin bedspread, and I am getting into my clothes.

The photographs on the wall are fading, too. I didn't expect that. I wonder what will be left of his world in a few hours, wonder if I should have left well enough alone, a masturbatory fantasy, something reassuring and comforting. He would have gone through his life without ever really touching anyone, just a picture and a painting and a half-memory for a handful of people who barely ever thought of him any more.

I leave the flat. There are still people at the wine bar downstairs. They are sitting at the table, in the corner, where Stuart and I had been sitting earlier. The candle has burned way down but I imagine that it could almost be us. A man and a woman, in conversation. And soon enough, they will get up from their table and walk away, and the candle will be snuffed and the lights turned off and that will be that for another night.

I hail a taxi. Climb in. For a moment – for, I hope, the last time – I find myself missing Stuart Innes.

Then I sit back in the seat of the taxi, and I let him go. I hope I can afford the taxi fare and find myself wondering whether there will be a cheque in my bag in the morning, or just another blank sheet of paper. Then, more satisfied than not, I close my eyes, and I wait to be home.

Down to a Sunless Sea

The Thames is a filthy beast: it winds through London like a blindworm, or a sea serpent. All the rivers flow into it, the Fleet and the Tyburn and the Neckinger, carrying all the filth and scum and waste, the bodies of cats and dogs and the bones of sheep and pigs down into the brown water of the Thames, which carries them east into the estuary and from there into the North Sea and oblivion.

It is raining in London. The rain washes the dirt into the gutters, and it swells streams into rivers, rivers into powerful things. The rain is a noisy thing, splashing and pattering and rattling the rooftops. If it is clean water as it falls from the skies it only needs to touch London to become dirt, to stir dust and make it mud.

Nobody drinks it, neither the rainwater nor the river water. They make jokes about Thames water killing you instantly, and it is not true. There are mudlarks who will dive deep for thrown pennies, then come up again, spout the river water, shiver and hold up their coins. They do not die, of course, or not of that, although there are no mudlarks over fifteen years of age.

The woman does not appear to care about the rain.

She walks the Rotherhithe docks, as she has done for years, for decades: nobody knows how many years, because nobody cares. She walks the docks, or she stares out to sea. She examines the ships, as they bob at anchor. She must do something, to keep body and soul from dissolving their partnership, but none of the folk of the dock have the foggiest idea what this could be.

You take refuge from the deluge beneath a canvas awning put up by a sailmaker. You believe yourself to be alone under there, at first, for she is statue-still and staring out across the water, even though there is nothing to be seen through the curtain of rain. The far side of the Thames has vanished.

And then she sees you. She sees you and she begins to talk, not to you, oh no, but to the grey water that falls from the grey sky into the grey river. She says, 'My son wanted to be a sailor,' and you do not know what to reply, or how to reply. You would have to shout to make yourself heard over the roar of the rain, but she talks, and you listen. You discover yourself craning and straining to catch her words.

'My son wanted to be a sailor.

'I told him not to go to sea. I'm your mother, I said. The sea won't love you like I love you, she's cruel. But he said, Oh Mother, I need to see the world. I need to see the sun rise in the tropics, and watch the Northern Lights dance in the Arctic sky, and most of all I need to make my fortune and then, when it's made I will come back to you, and build you a house, and you will have servants, and we will dance, Mother, oh how we will dance . . .

'And what would I do in a fancy house? I told him. You're a fool with your fine talk. I told him of his father, who never came back from the sea – some said he was dead and lost overboard, while some swore blind they'd seen him running a whorehouse in Amsterdam.

'It's all the same. The sea took him.

'When he was twelve years old, my boy ran away, down to the docks, and he shipped on the first ship he found, to Flores in the Azores, they told me.

'There's ships of ill omen. Bad ships. They give them a lick of paint after each disaster, and a new name, to fool the unwary.

'Sailors are superstitious. The word gets around. This ship was run aground by its captain, on orders of the owners, to defraud the insurers; and then, all mended and as good as new, it gets taken by pirates; and then it takes a shipment of blankets and becomes a plague ship crewed by the dead, and only three men bring it into port in Harwich . . .

'My son had shipped on a stormcrow ship. It was on the homeward leg of the journey, with him bringing me his wages – for he was too young to have spent them on women and on grog, like his father – that the storm hit.

'He was the smallest one in the lifeboat.

'They said they drew lots fairly, but I do not believe it. He was smaller than them. After eight days adrift in the boat, they were so hungry. And if they did draw lots, they cheated.

'They gnawed his bones clean, one by one, and they gave them to his new mother, the sea. She shed no tears and took them without a word. She's cruel.

'Some nights I wish he had not told me the truth. He could have lied.

'They gave my boy's bones to the sea, but the ship's mate – who had known my husband, and known me too, better than my husband thought he did, if truth were told – he kept a bone, as a keepsake.

'When they got back to land, all of them swearing my boy was lost in the storm that sank the ship, he came in the night, and he told me the truth of it, and he gave me the bone, for the love there had once been between us.

'I said, you've done a bad thing, Jack. That was your son that you've eaten.

'The sea took him too, that night. He walked into her, with his pockets filled with stones, and he kept walking. He'd never learned to swim.

'And I put the bone on a chain to remember them both by,

late at night, when the wind crashes the ocean waves and tumbles them onto the sand, when the wind howls around the houses like a baby crying.'

The rain is easing, and you think she is done, but now, for the first time, she looks at you, and appears to be about to say something. She has pulled something from around her neck, and now she is reaching it out to you.

'Here,' she says. Her eyes, when they meet yours, are as brown as the Thames. 'Would you like to touch it?'

You want to pull it from her neck, to toss it into the river for the mudlarks to find or to lose. But instead you stumble out from under the canvas awning, and the water of the rain runs down your face like someone else's tears.

'The Truth is a Cave in the Black Mountains . . .'

You ask me if I can forgive myself? I can forgive myself for many things. For where I left him. For what I did. But I will not forgive myself for the year that I hated my daughter, when I believed her to have run away, perhaps to the city. During that year I forbade her name to be mentioned, and if her name entered my prayers when I prayed, it was to ask that she would one day learn the meaning of what she had done, of the dishonour that she had brought to our family, of the red that ringed her mother's eyes.

I hate myself for that, and nothing will ease the hatred, not even what happened that final night, on the side of the mountain.

I had searched for nearly ten years, although the trail was cold. I would say that I found him by accident, but I do not believe in accidents. If you walk the path, eventually you must arrive at the cave.

But that was later. First, there was the valley on the mainland, the whitewashed house in the gentle meadow with the burn splashing through it, a house that sat like a square of white sky against the green of the grass and the heather just beginning to purple.

And there was a boy outside the house, picking wool from off a thornbush. He did not see me approaching, and he did not look up until I said, 'I used to do that. Gather the wool from the thornbushes and twigs. My mother would wash it, then she would make me things with it. A ball, and a doll.'

He turned. He looked shocked, as if I had appeared out of nowhere. And I had not. I had walked many a mile, and had many more miles to go. I said, 'I walk quietly. Is this the house of Calum MacInnes?'

The boy nodded, drew himself up to his full height, which was perhaps two fingers bigger than mine, and he said, 'I am Calum MacInnes.'

'Is there another of that name? For the Calum MacInnes that I seek is a grown man.'

The boy said nothing, just unknotted a thick clump of sheep's wool from the clutching fingers of the thornbush. I said, 'Your father, perhaps? Would he be Calum MacInnes as well?'

The boy was peering at me. 'What are you?' he asked.

'I am a small man,' I told him. 'But I am a man, nonetheless, and I am here to see Calum MacInnes.'

'Why?' The boy hesitated. Then, 'And why are you so small?'

I said, 'Because I have something to ask your father. Man's business.' And I saw a smile start at the tips of his lips. 'It's not a bad thing to be small, young Calum. There was a night when the Campbells came knocking on my door, a whole troop of them, twelve men with knives and sticks, and they demanded of my wife, Morag, that she produce me, as they were there to kill me, in revenge for some imagined slight. And she said, "Young Johnnie, run down to the far meadow, and tell your father to come back to the house, that I sent for him." And the Campbells watched as the boy ran out the door. They knew that I was a most dangerous person. But nobody had told them that I was a wee man, or if that had been told them, it had not been believed.'

'Did the boy call you?' said the lad.

'It was no boy,' I told him, 'but me myself, it was. And they'd had me, and still I walked out the door and through their fingers.'

The boy laughed. Then he said, 'Why were the Campbells after you?'

'It was a disagreement about the ownership of cattle. They thought the cows were theirs. I maintained the Campbells' ownership of them had ended the first night the cows had come with me over the hills.'

'Wait here,' said young Calum MacInnes.

I sat by the burn and looked up at the house. It was a good-sized house: I would have taken it for the house of a doctor or a man of law, not of a border reaver. There were pebbles on the ground and I made a pile of them, and I tossed the pebbles, one by one, into the burn. I have a good eye, and I enjoyed rattling the pebbles over the meadow and into the water. I had thrown a hundred stones when the boy returned, accompanied by a tall, loping man. His hair was streaked with grey, his face was long and wolfish. There are no wolves in those hills, not any longer, and the bears have gone too.

'Good day to you,' I said.

He said nothing in return, only stared. I am used to stares. I said, 'I am seeking Calum MacInnes. If you are he, say so, I will greet you. If you are not he, tell me now, and I will be on my way.'

'What business would you have with Calum MacInnes?'

'I wish to hire him, as a guide.'

'And where is it you would wish to be taken?'

I stared at him. 'That is hard to say,' I told him. 'For there are some who say it does not exist. There is a certain cave on the Misty Isle.'

He said nothing. Then he said, 'Calum, go back to the house.'

'But, Da—'

'Tell your mother I said she was to give you some tablet. You like that. Go on.'

Expressions crossed the boy's face – puzzlement, hunger,

happiness – and then he turned and ran back to the white house.

Calum MacInnes said, 'Who sent you here?'

I pointed to the burn as it splashed its way between us on its journey down the hill. 'What's that?' I asked.

'Water,' he replied.

'And they say there is a king across it,' I told him.

I did not know him then at all, and never knew him well, but his eyes became guarded, and his head cocked to one side. 'How do I know you are who you say you are?'

'I have claimed nothing,' I said. 'Just that there are those who have heard there is a cave on the Misty Isle, and that you might know the way.'

He said, 'I will not tell you where the cave is.'

'I am not here asking for directions. I seek a guide. And two travel more safely than one.'

He looked me up and down, and I waited for the joke about my size, but he did not make it, and for that I was grateful. He just said, 'When we reach the cave, I will not go inside. You must bring out the gold yourself.'

I said, 'It is all one to me.'

He said, 'You can only take what you carry. I will not touch it. But yes, I will take you.'

I said, 'You will be paid well for your trouble.' I reached into my jerkin, handed him the pouch I had in there. 'This for taking me. Another, twice the size, when we return.'

He poured the coins from the pouch into his huge hand, and he nodded. 'Silver,' he said. 'Good.' Then, 'I will say goodbye to my wife and son.'

'Is there nothing you need to bring?'

He said, 'I was a reaver in my youth, and reavers travel light. I'll bring a rope, for the mountains.' He patted his dirk, which hung from his belt, and went back into the whitewashed house.

I never saw his wife, not then, nor at any other time. I do not know what colour her hair was.

I threw another fifty stones into the burn as I waited, until he returned, with a coil of rope thrown over one shoulder, and then we walked together away from a house too grand for any reaver, and we headed west.

* * *

The mountains between the rest of the world and the coast are gradual hills, visible from a distance as gentle, purple, hazy things, like clouds. They seem inviting. They are slow mountains, the kind you can walk up easily, like walking up a hill, but they are hills that take a full day and more to climb. We walked up the hill, and by the end of the first day we were cold.

I saw snow on the peaks above us, although it was high summer.

We said nothing to each other that first day. There was nothing to be said. We knew where we were going.

We made a fire, from dried sheep dung and a dead thornbush: we boiled water and made our porridge, each of us throwing a handful of oats and a fingerpinch of salt into the little pan I carried. His handful was huge, and my handful was small, like my hands, which made him smile and say, 'I hope you will not be eating half of the porridge.'

I said I would not and indeed, I did not, for my appetite is smaller than that of a full-grown man. But this is a good thing, I believe, for I can keep going in the wild on nuts and berries that would not keep a bigger person from starving.

A path of sorts ran across the high hills, and we followed it and encountered almost nobody: a tinker and his donkey, piled high with old pots, and a girl leading the donkey, who smiled at me when she thought me to be a child, and then scowled when she perceived me to be what I am, and would have thrown a stone at me had the tinker not slapped her hand with the switch he had been using to encourage the donkey; and, later, we overtook an old woman and a man she said was her grandson, on their way back across the hills. We ate with her, and she told us that she had attended the birth of her first great-grandchild, that it was a good birth. She said she would tell our fortunes from the lines in our palms, if we had coins to cross her palm. I gave the old biddy a clipped lowland groat, and she looked at the palm of my right hand.

She said, 'I see death in your past and death in your future.'

'Death waits in all our futures,' I said.

She paused, there in the highest of the highlands, where the summer winds have winter on their breath, where they howl and whip and slash the air like knives. She said, 'There was a woman in a tree. There will be a man in a tree.'

I said, 'Will this mean anything to me?'

'One day. Perhaps.' She said, 'Beware of gold. Silver is your friend.' And then she was done with me.

To Calum MacInnes she said, 'Your palm has been burned.' He said that was true. She said, 'Give me your other hand, your left hand.' He did so. She gazed at it, intently. Then, 'You return to where you began. You will be higher than most other men. And there is no grave waiting for you, where you are going.'

He said, 'You tell me that I will not die?'

'It is a left-handed fortune. I know what I have told you, and no more.'

She knew more. I saw it in her face.

That was the only thing of any importance that occurred to us on the second day.

We slept in the open that night. The night was clear and cold, and the sky was hung with stars that seemed so bright and close I felt as if I could have reached out my arm and gathered them, like berries.

We lay side by side beneath the stars, and Calum MacInnes said, 'Death awaits you, she said. But death does not wait for me. I think mine was the better fortune.'

'Perhaps.'

'Ah,' he said. 'It is all a nonsense. Old-woman talk. It is not truth.'

I woke in the dawn mist to see a stag, watching us, curiously.

The third day we crested those mountains, and we began to walk downhill.

My companion said, 'When I was a boy, my father's dirk fell into the cooking fire. I pulled it out, but the metal hilt was as hot as the flames. I did not expect this, but I would not let the dirk go. I carried it away from the fire, and plunged the sword into the water. It made steam. I remember that. My palm was burned, and my hand curled, as if it was meant to carry a sword until the end of time.'

I said, 'You, with your hand. Me, only a little man. It's fine heroes we are, who seek our fortunes on the Misty Isle.'

He barked a laugh, short and without humour. 'Fine heroes,' was all he said.

The rain began to fall then, and did not stop falling. That night we passed a small croft house. There was a trickle of smoke from its chimney, and we called out for the owner, but there was no response.

I pushed open the door and called again. The place was dark, but I could smell tallow, as if a candle had been burning and had recently been snuffed.

'No one at home,' said Calum, but I shook my head and walked forward, then leaned down into the darkness beneath the bed.

'Would you care to come out?' I asked. 'For we are travellers, seeking warmth and shelter and hospitality. We would share with you our oats and our salt and our whisky. And we will not harm you.'

At first the woman hidden beneath the bed said nothing, and then she said, 'My husband is away in the hills. He told me to hide myself away if the strangers come, for fear of what they might do to me.'

I said, 'I am but a little man, good lady, no bigger than a child, you could send me flying with a blow. My companion is a full-sized man, but I do swear that he shall do nothing to you, save partake of your hospitality, and we would dry ourselves. Please do come out.'

All covered with dust and spiderwebs she was when she emerged, but even with her face all begrimed, she was beautiful, and even with her hair all webbed and greyed with dust it was still long and thick, and golden-red. For a heartbeat she put me in the mind of my daughter, but that my daughter would look a man in the eye, while this one glanced only at the ground fearfully, like something expecting to be beaten.

I gave her some of our oats, and Calum produced strips of dried meat from his pocket, and she went out to the field and returned with a pair of scrawny turnips, and she prepared food for the three of us.

I ate my fill. She had no appetite. I believe that Calum was still hungry when his meal was done. He poured whisky for the three of us: she took but a little, and that with water. The rain rattled on the roof of the house, and dripped in the corner, and, unwelcoming though it was, I was glad that I was inside.

It was then that a man came through the door. He said nothing, only stared at us, untrusting, angry. He pulled off his cape of sheepskin, and his hat, and he dropped them on the earth floor. They dripped and puddled. The silence was oppressive.

Calum MacInnes said, 'Your wife gave us hospitality, when we found her. Hard enough she was in the finding.'

'We asked for hospitality,' I said. 'As we ask it of you.'

The man said nothing, only grunted.

In the high lands, people spend words as if they were golden coins. But the custom is strong there: strangers who ask for hospitality must be granted it, though you have blood-feud against them and their clan or kin.

The woman – little more than a girl she was, while her husband's beard was grey and white, so I wondered if she was his daughter for a moment, but no: there was but one bed, scarcely big enough for two – went outside, into the sheep-pen that adjoined the house, and returned with oatcakes and a dried ham she must have hidden there, which she sliced thin, and placed on a wooden trencher before the man.

Calum poured the man whisky, and said, 'We seek the Misty Isle. Do you know if it is there?'

The man looked at us. The winds are bitter in the high lands, and they would whip the words from a man's lips. He pursed his mouth, then he said, 'Aye. I saw it from the peak this morning. It's there. I cannot say if it will be there tomorrow.'

We slept on the hard-earth floor of that cottage. The fire went out, and there was no warmth from the hearth. The man and his woman slept in their bed, behind the curtain. He had his way with her, beneath the sheepskin that covered that bed, and before he did that, he beat her for feeding us and for letting us in. I heard them, and could not stop hearing them, and sleep was hard in the finding that night.

I have slept in the homes of the poor, and I have slept in palaces, and I have slept beneath the stars, and would have told you before that night that all places were one to me. But I woke before first light, convinced we had to be gone from that place, but not knowing why, and I woke Calum by putting a finger to his lips, and silently we left that croft on the mountainside without saying our farewells, and I have never been more pleased to be gone from anywhere.

We were a mile from that place when I said, 'The island. You asked if it would be there. Surely, an island is there, or it is not there.'

Calum hesitated. He seemed to be weighing his words, and then he said, 'The Misty Isle is not as other places. And the mist that surrounds it is not like other mists.'

We walked down a path worn by hundreds of years of sheep and deer and few enough men.

He said, 'They also call it the Winged Isle. Some say it is because the island, if seen from above, would look like butterfly wings. And I do not know the truth of it.' Then, *'And what is truth? said jesting Pilate.'*

It is harder coming down than it is going up.

I thought about it. 'Sometimes I think that truth is a place. In my mind, it is like a city: there can be a hundred roads, a thousand paths, that will all take you, eventually, to the same place. It does not matter where you come from. If you walk towards the truth, you will reach it, whatever path you take.'

Calum MacInnes looked down at me and said nothing. Then, 'You are wrong. The truth is a cave in the black mountains. There is one way there, and one only, and that way is treacherous and hard, and if you choose the wrong path you will die alone, on the mountainside.'

We crested the ridge, and we looked down to the coast. I could see villages below, beside the water. And I could see high black mountains before me, on the other side of the sea, coming out of the mist.

Calum said, 'There's your cave. In those mountains.'

The bones of the earth, I thought, seeing them. And then I became uncomfortable, thinking of bones, and to distract myself, I said, 'And how many times is it you have been there?'

'Only once.' He hesitated. 'I searched for it all my sixteenth year, for I had heard the legends, and I believed if I sought I should find. I was seventeen when I reached it, and brought back all the gold coins I could carry.'

'And were you not frightened of the curse?'

'When I was young, I was afraid of nothing.'

'What did you do with your gold?'

'A portion I buried and I alone know where. The rest I used as bride-price for the woman I loved, and to build a fine house.'

He stopped as if he had already said too much.

There was no ferryman at the jetty. Only a small boat on the shore, hardly big enough for three full-sized men, tied to a tree trunk all twisted and half-dead, and a bell beside it.

I sounded the bell, and soon enough a fat man came down the shore.

He said to Calum, 'It will cost you a shilling for the ferry, and your boy, three pennies.'

I stood tall. I am not as big as other men are, but I have as much pride as any of them. 'I am also a man,' I said, 'I'll pay your shilling.'

The ferryman looked me up and down, then he scratched his beard. 'I beg your pardon. My eyes are not what they once were. I shall take you to the island.'

I handed him a shilling. He weighed it in his hand, 'That's ninepence you did not cheat me out of. Nine pennies are a lot of money in this dark age.' The water was the colour of slate, although the sky was blue, and whitecaps chased one another across the water's surface. He untied the boat and hauled it, rattling, down the shingle to the water. We waded out into the cold channel, and clambered inside.

The splash of oars on seawater, and the boat was propelled forward in easy movements. I sat closest to the ferryman. I said, 'Ninepence. It is good wages. But I have heard of a cave in the mountains on the Misty Isle, filled with gold coins, the treasure of the ancients.'

He shook his head dismissively.

Calum was staring at me, lips pressed together so hard they were white. I ignored him and asked the man again, 'A cave filled with golden coins, a gift from the Norsemen or the Southerners or from those who they say were here long before any of us: those who fled into the West as the people came.'

'Heard of it,' said the ferryman. 'Heard also of the curse of it. I reckon that the one can take care of the other.' He spat into the sea. Then he said, 'You're an honest man, dwarf. I see it in your face. Do not seek this cave. No good can come of it.'

'I am sure you are right,' I told him, without guile.

'I am certain I am,' he said. 'For not every day it is that I take a reaver and a little dwarfy man to the Misty Isle.' Then he said, 'In this part of the world, it is not considered lucky to talk about those who went to the West.'

We rode the rest of the boat journey in silence, though the sea became choppier, and the waves splashed into the side of the boat, such that I held on with both hands for fear of being swept away.

And after what seemed like half a lifetime the boat was tied to a long jetty of black stones. We walked the jetty, as the waves crashed around us, the salt spray kissing our faces. There was a humpbacked man at the landing selling oatcakes and plums dried until they were almost stones. I gave him a penny and filled my jerkin pockets with them.

We walked on into the Misty Isle.

I am old now, or at least, I am no longer young, and everything I see reminds me of something else I've seen, such that I see nothing for the first time. A bonny girl, her hair fiery red, reminds me only of another hundred such lasses, and their mothers, and what they were as they grew, and what they looked like when they died. It is the curse of age, that all things are reflections of other things.

I say that, but my time on the Misty Isle that is also called, by the wise, the Winged Isle, reminds me of nothing but itself.

It is a day from that jetty until you reach the black mountains.

Calum MacInnes looked at me, half his size or less, and he set off at a loping stride, as if challenging me to keep up. His legs propelled him across the ground, which was wet, and all ferns and heather.

Above us, low clouds were scudding, grey and white and black, hiding each other and revealing and hiding again.

I let him get ahead of me, let him press on into the rain, until he was swallowed by the wet, grey haze. Then, and only then, I ran.

This is one of the secret things of me, the things I have not revealed to any person, save to Morag, my wife, and Johnnie and James, my sons, and Flora, my daughter (may the Shadows rest her poor soul): I can run, and I can run well, and, if I need to, I can run faster and longer and more sure-footedly than any full-sized man; and it was like this that I ran then, through the mist and the rain, taking to the high ground and the black-rock ridges, yet keeping below the skyline.

He was ahead of me, but I spied him soon, and I ran on and I ran past him, on the high ground, with the brow of the hill between us. Below us was a stream. I can run for days without stopping. That is the first of my secrets, but there is one secret I have revealed to no man.

We had discussed already where we would camp that first night on the Misty Isle, and Calum had told me that we would spend the night beneath the rock that is called Man and Dog, for it is said that it looks like an old man with his dog by his side, and I reached it late in the afternoon. There was a shelter beneath the rock, which was protected and dry, and some of those who had been before us had left firewood behind, sticks and twigs and branches. I made a fire and dried myself in front of it and took the chill from my bones. The wood smoke blew out across the heather.

It was dark when Calum loped into the shelter and looked at me as if he had not expected to see me that side of midnight. I said, 'What took you so long, Calum MacInnes?'

He said nothing, only stared at me. I said, 'There is trout, boiled in mountain water, and a fire to warm your bones.'

He nodded. We ate the trout, drank whisky to warm ourselves. There was a mound of heather and of ferns, dried and brown, piled high in the rear of the shelter, and we slept upon that, wrapped tight in our damp cloaks.

I woke in the night. There was cold steel against my throat – the flat of the blade, not the edge. I said, 'And why would you ever kill me in the night, Calum MacInnes? For our way is long, and our journey is not yet over.'

He said, 'I do not trust you, dwarf.'

'It is not me you must trust,' I told him, 'but those that I serve. And if you left with me but return without me, there are those who will know the name of Calum MacInnes, and cause it to be spoken in the shadows.'

The cold blade remained at my throat. He said, 'How did you get ahead of me?'

'And here was I, repaying ill with good, for I made you food and a fire. I am a hard man to lose, Calum MacInnes, and it ill-becomes a guide to do as you did today. Now, take your dirk from my throat and let me sleep.'

He said nothing, but after a few moments, the blade was removed. I forced myself neither to sigh nor to breathe, hoping he could not hear my heart pounding in my chest; and I slept no more that night.

For breakfast, I made porridge, and threw in some dried plums to soften them.

The mountains were black and grey against the white of the

sky. We saw eagles, huge and ragged of wing, circling above us. Calum set a sober pace and I walked beside him, taking two steps for every one of his.

'How long?' I asked him.

'A day. Perhaps two. It depends upon the weather. If the clouds come down then two days, or even three . . .'

The clouds came down at noon and the world was blanketed by a mist that was worse than rain: droplets of water hung in the air, soaked our clothes and our skin; the rocks we walked upon became treacherous and Calum and I slowed in our ascent, stepped carefully. We were walking up the mountain, not climbing, up goat paths and craggy sharp ways. The rocks were black and slippery: we walked, and climbed and clambered and clung, we slipped and slid and stumbled and staggered, yet even in the mist, Calum knew where he was going, and I followed him.

He paused at a waterfall that splashed across our path, thick as the trunk of an oak. He took the thin rope from his shoulders, wrapped it about a rock.

'This waterfall was not here before,' he told me. 'I'll go first.' He tied the other end of the rope about his waist and edged out along the path, into the waterfall, pressing his body against the wet rock-face, edging slowly, intently through the sheet of water.

I was scared for him, scared for both of us: holding my breath as he passed through, only breathing when he was on the other side of the waterfall. He tested the rope, pulled on it, motioned me to follow him, when a stone gave way beneath his foot and he slipped on the wet rock, and fell into the abyss.

The rope held, and the rock beside me held. Calum MacInnes dangled from the end of the rope. He looked up at me, and I sighed, anchored myself by a slab of crag, and I wound and pulled him up and up. I hauled him back onto the path, dripping and cursing.

He said, 'You're stronger than you look,' and I cursed myself for a fool. He must have seen it on my face for, after he shook himself (like a dog, sending droplets flying), he said, 'My boy Calum told me the tale you told him about the Campbells coming for you, and you being sent into the fields by your wife, with them thinking she was your ma, and you a boy.'

'It was just a tale,' I said. 'Something to pass the time.'

'Indeed?' he said. 'For I heard tell of a raiding party of Campbells sent out a few years ago, seeking revenge on someone who had taken their cattle. They went, and they never came back. If a small fellow like you can kill a dozen Campbells . . . well, you must be strong, and you must be fast.'

I must be *stupid*, I thought ruefully, telling that child that tale.

I had picked them off one by one, like rabbits, as they came out to piss or to see what had happened to their friends: I had killed seven of them before my wife killed her first. We buried them in the glen, built a small cairn of stacking stones above them, to weigh them down so their ghosts would not walk, and we were sad: that Campbells had come so far to kill me, that we had been forced to kill them in return.

I take no joy in killing: no man should, and no woman. Sometimes death is necessary, but it is always an evil thing. That is something I am in no doubt of, even after the events I speak of here.

I took the rope from Calum MacInnes, and I clambered up and up, over the rocks, to where the waterfall came out of the side of the hill, and it was narrow enough for me to cross. It was slippery there, but I made it over without incident, tied the rope in place, came down it, threw the end of it to my companion, walked him across.

He did not thank me, neither for rescuing him, nor for getting us across: and I did not expect thanks. I also did not expect what he actually said, though, which was: 'You are not a whole man, and you are ugly. Your wife: is she also small and ugly, like yourself?'

I decided to take no offence, whether offence had been intended or no. I simply said, 'She is not. She is a tall woman, almost as tall as you, and when she was young – when we were both younger – she was reckoned by some to be the most beautiful girl in the lowlands. The bards wrote songs praising her green eyes and her long red-golden hair.'

I thought I saw him flinch at this, but it is possible that I imagined it, or more likely, wished to imagine I had seen it.

'How did you win her, then?'

I spoke the truth: 'I wanted her, and I get what I want. I did not give up. She said I was wise and I was kind, and I would always provide for her. And I have.'

The clouds began to lower, once more, and the world blurred at the edges, became softer.

'She said I would be a good father. And I have done my best to raise my children. Who are also, if you are wondering, normal-sized.'

'I beat sense into young Calum,' said older Calum. 'He is not a bad child.'

'You can only do that as long as they are there with you,' I said. And then I stopped talking, and I remembered that long year, and also I remembered Flora when she was small, sitting on the floor with jam on her face, looking up at me as if I were the wisest man in the world.

'Ran away, eh? I ran away when I was a lad. I was twelve. I went as far as the court of the king over the water. The father of the current king.'

'That's not something you hear spoken aloud.'

'I am not afraid,' he said. 'Not here. Who's to hear us? Eagles? I saw him. He was a fat man, who spoke the language of the foreigners well, and our own tongue only with difficulty. But he was still our king.' He paused. 'And if he is to come to us again, he will need gold, for vessels and weapons and to feed the troops that he raises.'

I said, 'So I believe. That is why we go in search of the cave.'

He said, 'This is bad gold. It does not come free. It has its cost.'

'Everything has its cost.'

I was remembering every landmark: climb at the sheep skull, cross the first three streams, then walk along the fourth until the five heaped stones and find where the rock looks like a seagull and walk on between two sharply jutting walls of black rock, and let the slope bring you with it . . .

I could remember it, I knew. Well enough to find my way down again. But the mists confused me, and I could not be certain.

We reached a small loch, high in the mountains, and drank fresh water, caught huge white creatures that were not shrimps or lobsters or crayfish, and ate them raw like sausages, for we could not find any dry wood to make our fire, that high.

We slept on a wide ledge beside the icy water and woke into clouds before sunrise, when the world was grey and blue.

'You were sobbing in your sleep,' said Calum.

'I had a dream,' I told him.

'I do not have bad dreams,' Calum said.

'It was a good dream,' I said. It was true. I had dreamed that Flora still lived. She was grumbling about the village boys, and telling me of her time in the hills with the cattle, and of things of no consequence, smiling her great smile and tossing her hair the while, red-golden like her mother's, although her mother's hair is now streaked with white.

'Good dreams should not make a man cry out like that,' said Calum. A pause, then, 'I have no dreams, not good, not bad.'

'No?'

'Not since I was a young man.'

We rose. A thought struck me: 'Did you stop dreaming after you came to the cave?'

He said nothing. We walked along the mountainside, into the mist, as the sun came up.

The mist seemed to thicken and fill with light, in the sunshine, but did not fade away and I realised that it must be a cloud. The world glowed. And then it seemed to me that I was staring at a man of my size, a small, humpty man, his face a shadow, standing in the air in front of me, like a ghost or an angel, and it moved as I moved. It was haloed by the light, and shimmered, and I could not have told you how near it was or how far away. I have seen miracles and I have seen evil things, but never have I seen anything like that.

'Is it magic?' I asked, although I smelled no magic on the air. Calum said, 'It is nothing. A property of the light. A shadow. A reflection. No more. I see a man beside me, as well. He moves as I move.' I glanced back, but I saw nobody beside him.

And then the little glowing man in the air faded, and the cloud, and it was day, and we were alone.

We climbed all that morning, ascending. Calum's ankle had twisted the day before, when he had slipped at the waterfall. Now it swelled in front of me, swelled and went red, but his pace did not ever slow, and if he was in discomfort or in pain it did not show upon his face.

I said, 'How long?' as the dusk began to blur the edges of the world.

'An hour, less, perhaps. We will reach the cave, and then we will sleep for the night. In the morning you will go inside. You can bring out as much gold as you can carry, and we will make our way back off the island.'

I looked at him, then: grey-streaked hair, grey eyes, so huge and wolfish a man, and I said, 'You would sleep outside the cave?'

'I would. There are no monsters in the cave. Nothing that will come out and take you in the night. Nothing that will eat us. But you should not go in until daylight.'

And then we rounded a rockfall, all black rocks and grey half-blocking our path, and we saw the cave mouth. I said, 'Is that all?'

'You expected marble pillars? Or a giant's cave from a gossip's fireside tales?'

'Perhaps. It looks like nothing. A hole in the rockface. A shadow. And there are no guards?'

'No guards. Only the place, and what it is.'

'A cave filled with treasure. And you are the only one who can find it?'

Calum laughed then, like a fox's bark. 'The islanders know how to find it. But they are too wise to come here, to take its gold. They say that the cave makes you evil: that each time you visit it, each time you enter to take gold, it eats the good in your soul, so they do not enter.'

'And is that true? Does it make you evil?'

'. . . No. The cave feeds on something else. Not good and evil. Not really. You can take your gold, but afterwards, things are' – he paused – 'things are *flat*. There is less beauty in a rainbow, less meaning in a sermon, less joy in a kiss . . .' He looked at the cave mouth and I thought I saw fear in his eyes. 'Less.'

I said, 'There are many for whom the lure of gold outweighs the beauty of a rainbow.'

'Me, when young, for one. You, now, for another.'

'So we go in at dawn.'

'You will go in. I will wait for you out here. Do not be afraid. No monster guards the cave. No spells to make the gold vanish, if you do not know some cantrip or rhyme.'

We made our camp, then: or rather we sat in the darkness, against the cold rock wall. There would be no sleep there.

I said, 'You took the gold from here, as I will do tomorrow. You bought a house with it, a bride, a good name.'

His voice came from the darkness. 'Aye. And they meant nothing to me, once I had them, or less than nothing. And if your gold pays for the king over the water to come back to us and rule us and bring about a land of joy and prosperity and warmth, it will still mean nothing to you. It will be as something you heard of that happened to a man in a tale.'

'I have lived my life to bring the king back,' I told him.

He said, 'You take the gold back to him. Your king will want more gold, because kings want more. It is what they do. Each time you come back, it will mean less. The rainbow means nothing. Killing a man means nothing.'

Silence then, in the darkness. I heard no birds: only the wind that called and gusted about the peaks like a mother seeking her babe.

I said, 'We have both killed men. Have you ever killed a woman, Calum MacInnes?'

'I have not. I have killed no women, no girls.'

I ran my hands over my dirk in the darkness, seeking the wood and silver of the hilt, the steel of the blade. It was there in my hands. I had not intended ever to tell him, only to strike when we were out of the mountains, strike once, strike deep, but now I felt the words being pulled from me, would I or never-so. 'They say there was a girl,' I told him. 'And a thorn-bush.'

Silence. The whistling of the wind. 'Who told you?' he asked. Then, 'Never mind. I would not kill a woman. No man of honour would kill a woman . . .'

If I said a word, I knew, he would be silent on the subject, and never talk about it again. So I said nothing. Only waited.

Calum MacInnes began to speak, choosing his words with care, talking as if he was remembering a tale he had heard as a child and had almost forgotten. 'They told me the kine of the lowlands were fat and bonny, and that a man could gain honour and glory by adventuring off to the south and returning with the fine red cattle. So I went south, and never a cow was good enough, until on a hillside in the lowlands I saw the finest, reddest, fattest cows that ever a man has seen. So I began to lead them away, back the way I had come.

'She came after me with a stick. The cattle were her father's, she said, and I was a rogue and a knave and all manner of rough things. But she was beautiful, even when angry, and had I not already a young wife I might have dealt more kindly with her. Instead I pulled a knife, and touched it to her throat, and bade her to stop speaking. And she did stop.

'I would not kill her – I would not kill a woman, and that is the truth – so I tied her, by her hair, to a thorn tree, and I took her knife from her waistband, to slow her as she tried to free herself, and pushed the blade of it deep into the sod. I tied her to the thorn tree by her long hair, and I thought no more of her as I made off with her cattle.

'It was another year before I was back that way. I was not after cows that day, but I walked up the side of that bank – it was a lonely spot, and if you had not been looking, you might not have seen it. Perhaps nobody searched for her.'

'I heard they searched,' I told him. 'Although some believed her taken by reavers, and others believed her run away with a tinker, or gone to the city. But still, they searched.'

'Aye. I saw what I did see – perhaps you'd have to have stood where I was standing, to see what I did see. It was an evil thing I did, perhaps.'

'Perhaps?'

He said, 'I have taken gold from the cave of the mists. I cannot tell any longer if there is good or there is evil. I sent a message, by a child, at an inn, telling them where she was, and where they could find her.'

I closed my eyes but the world became no darker.

'There is evil,' I told him.

I saw it in my mind's eye: her skeleton picked clean of clothes, picked clean of flesh, as naked and white as anyone would ever be, hanging like a child's puppet against the thornbush, tied to a branch above it by its red-golden hair.

'At dawn,' said Calum MacInnes, as if we had been talking of provisions or the weather, 'you will leave your dirk behind, for such is the custom, and you will enter the cave, and bring out as much gold as you can carry. And you will bring it back with you, to the mainland. There's not a soul in these parts, knowing what you carry or where it's from, would take it from you. Then send it to the king over the water, and he will pay his men with it, and feed them, and buy their weapons. One day, he will return. Tell me on that day, that there is evil, little man.'

* * *

When the sun was up, I entered the cave. It was damp in there. I could hear water running down one wall, and I felt a wind on my face, which was strange, because there was no wind inside the mountain.

In my mind, the cave would be filled with gold. Bars of gold would be stacked like firewood, and bags of golden coins would sit between them. There would be golden chains and golden rings, and golden plates, heaped high like the china plates in a rich man's house.

I had imagined riches, but there was nothing like that here. Only shadows. Only rock.

Something was here, though. Something that waited.

I have secrets, but there is a secret that lies beneath all my other secrets, and not even my children know it, although I believe my wife suspects, and it is this: my mother was a mortal woman, the daughter of a miller, but my father came to her from out of the West, and to the West he returned, when he had had his sport with her. I cannot be sentimental about my parentage: I am sure he does not think of her, and doubt that he ever knew of me. But he left me a body that is small, and fast, and strong; and perhaps I take after him in other ways – I do not know. I am ugly, and my father was beautiful, or so my mother told me once, but I think that she might have been deceived.

I wondered what I would have seen in that cave if my father had been an innkeeper from the lowlands.

You would be seeing gold, said a whisper that was not a whisper, from deep in the heart of the mountain. It was a lonely voice, and distracted, and bored.

'I would see gold,' I said aloud. 'Would it be real, or would it be an illusion?'

The whisper was amused. *You are thinking like a mortal man, making things always to be one thing or another. It is gold they would see, and touch. Gold they would carry back with them, feeling the weight of it the while, gold they would trade with other mortals for what they needed. What does it matter if it is there or no, if they can see it, touch it, steal it, murder for it? Gold they need and gold I give them.*

'And what do you take, for the gold you give them?'

Little enough, for my needs are few, and I am old; too old to follow my sisters into the West. I taste their pleasure and their joy. I feed, a little, feed on what they do not need and do not value. A taste of heart, a lick and a nibble of their fine consciences, a sliver of soul. And in return a fragment of me leaves this cave with them and gazes out at the world through their eyes, sees what they see until their lives are done and I take back what is mine.

'Will you show yourself to me?'

I could see, in the darkness, better than any man born of man and woman could see. I saw something move in the shadows, and then the shadows congealed and shifted, revealing formless things at the edge of my perception, where it meets imagination. Troubled, I said the thing it is proper to say at times such as this: 'Appear before me in a form that neither harms nor is offensive to me.'

Is that what you wish?

The drip of distant water. 'Yes,' I said.

From out of the shadows it came, and it stared down at me with empty sockets, smiled at me with wind-weathered ivory teeth. It was all bone, save its hair, and its hair was red and gold, and wrapped about the branch of a thornbush.

'That offends my eyes.'

I took it from your mind, said a whisper that surrounded the skeleton. Its jawbone did not move. *I chose something you loved. This was your daughter, Flora, as she was the last time you saw her.*

I closed my eyes, but the figure remained.

It said, *The reaver waits for you at the mouth of the cave. He waits for you to come out, weaponless and weighed down with gold. He will kill you, and take the gold from your dead hands.*

'But I'll not be coming out with gold, will I?'

I thought of Calum MacInnes, the wolf-grey in his hair, the grey of his eyes, the line of his dirk. He was bigger than I am, but all men are bigger than I am. Perhaps I was stronger, and faster, but he was also fast, and he was strong.

He killed my daughter, I thought, then wondered if the thought was mine or if it had crept out of the shadows into my head. Aloud, I said, 'Is there another way out of this cave?'

You leave the way you entered, through the mouth of my home.

I stood there and did not move, but in my mind I was like

an animal in a trap, questing and darting from idea to idea, finding no purchase and no solace and no solution.

I said, 'I am weaponless. He told me that I could not enter this place with a weapon. That it was not the custom.'

It is the custom now, to bring no weapon into my place. It was not always the custom. Follow me, said the skeleton of my daughter.

I followed her, for I could see her, even when it was so dark that I could see nothing else.

In the shadows it said, *It is beneath your hand.*

I crouched and felt it. The haft felt like bone – perhaps an antler. I touched the blade cautiously in the darkness, discovered that I was holding something that felt more like an awl than a knife. It was thin, sharp at the tip. It would be better than nothing.

'Is there a price?'

There is always a price.

'Then I will pay it. And I ask one other thing. You say that you can see the world through his eyes.'

There were no eyes in that hollow skull, but it nodded.

'Then tell me when he sleeps.'

It said nothing. It melded with the darkness, and I felt alone in that place.

Time passed. I followed the sound of the dripping water, found a rockpool, and drank. I soaked the last of the oats and I ate them, chewing them until they dissolved in my mouth. I slept and woke and slept again, and dreamed of my wife, Morag, waiting for me as the seasons changed, waiting for me just as we had waited for our daughter, waiting for me forever.

Something, a finger I thought, touched my hand: it was not bony and hard. It was soft, and human-like, but too cold. *He sleeps.*

I left the cave in the blue light, before dawn. He slept across the cave, cat-like, I knew, such that the slightest touch would have woken him. I held my weapon in front of me, a bone handle and a needle-like blade of blackened silver, and I reached out and took what I was after, without waking him.

Then I stepped closer, and his hand grasped for my ankle and his eyes opened.

'Where is the gold?' asked Calum MacInnes.

'I have none.' The wind blew cold on the mountainside. I had danced back, out of his reach, when he had grabbed at me. He stayed on the ground, pushed himself up onto one elbow.

Then he said, 'Where is my dirk?'

'I took it,' I told him. 'While you slept.'

He looked at me, sleepily. 'And why ever would you do that? If I was going to kill you I would have done it on the way here. I could have killed you a dozen times.'

'But I did not have gold, then, did I?'

He said nothing.

I said, 'If you think you could have got me to bring the gold from the cave, and that not bringing it out yourself would have saved your miserable soul, then you are a fool.'

He no longer looked sleepy. 'A fool, am I?'

He was ready to fight. It is good to make people who are ready to fight angry.

I said, 'Not a fool. No. For I have met fools and idiots, and they are happy in their idiocy, even with straw in their hair. You are too wise for foolishness. You seek only misery and you bring misery with you and you call down misery on all you touch.'

He rose then, holding a rock in his hand like an axe, and he came at me. I am small, and he could not strike me as he would have struck a man of his own size. He leaned over to strike. It was a mistake.

I held the bone haft tightly, and stabbed upward, striking fast with the point of the awl, like a snake. I knew the place I was aiming for, and I knew what it would do.

He dropped his rock, clutched at his right shoulder. 'My arm,' he said. 'I cannot feel my arm.'

He swore then, fouling the air with curses and threats. The dawn-light on the mountaintop made everything so beautiful and blue. In that light, even the blood that had begun to soak his garments was purple. He took a step back, so he was between me and the cave. I felt exposed, the rising sun at my back.

'Why do you not have gold?' he asked me. His arm hung limply at his side.

'There was no gold there for such as I,' I said.

He threw himself forward, then, ran at me and kicked at me. My awl-blade went flying from my hand. I threw my arms around his leg, and I held on to him as together we hurtled off the mountainside.

His head was above me, and I saw triumph in it, and then I saw sky, and then the valley floor was above me and I was rising to meet it and then it was below me and I was falling to my death.

A jar and a bump, and now we were turning over and over on the side of the mountain, the world a dizzying whirligig of rock and pain and sky, and I knew I was a dead man, but still I clung to the leg of Calum MacInnes.

I saw a golden eagle in flight, but below me or above me I could no longer say. It was there, in the dawn sky, in the shattered fragments of time and perception, there in the pain. I was not afraid: there was no time and no space to be afraid in: no space in my mind and no space in my heart. I was falling through the sky, holding tightly to the leg of a man who was trying to kill me; we were crashing into rocks, scraping and bruising and then . . .

. . . we stopped.

Stopped with force enough that I felt myself jarred, and I was almost thrown off Calum MacInnes and to my death beneath. The side of the mountain had crumbled, there, long ago, sheared off, leaving a sheet of blank rock, as smooth and as featureless as glass. But that was below us. Where we were, there was a ledge, and on the ledge there was a miracle: stunted and twisted, high above the tree line, where no trees have any right to grow, was a twisted hawthorn tree, not much larger than a bush, although it was old. Its roots grew into the side of the mountain, and it was this hawthorn that had caught us in its grey arms.

I let go of the leg, clambered off Calum MacInnes's body and onto the side of the mountain. I stood on the narrow ledge and looked down at the sheer drop. There was no way down from here. No way down at all.

I looked up. It might be possible, I thought, climbing slowly, with fortune on my side, to make it up that mountain. If it did not rain. If the wind was not too hungry. And what choice did I have? The only alternative was death.

A voice: 'So. Will you leave me here to die, dwarf?'

I said nothing. I had nothing to say.

His eyes were open. He said, 'I cannot move my right arm, since you stabbed it. I think I broke a leg in the fall. I cannot climb with you.'

I said, 'I may succeed, or I may fail.'

'You'll make it. I've seen you climb. After you rescued me, crossing that waterfall. You went up those rocks like a squirrel going up a tree.'

I did not have his confidence in my climbing abilities.

He said, 'Swear to me by all you hold holy. Swear by your king, who waits over the sea as he has since we drove his subjects from this land. Swear by the things you creatures hold dear – swear by shadows and eagle-feathers and by silence. Swear that you will come back for me.'

'You know what I am?' I said.

'I know nothing,' he said. 'Only that I want to live.'

I thought. 'I swear by these things,' I told him. 'By shadows and by eagle-feathers and by silence. I swear by green hills and standing stones. I will come back.'

'I would have killed you,' said the man in the hawthorn bush, and he said it with humour, as if it was the biggest joke that ever one man had told another. 'I had planned to kill you, and take the gold back as my own.'

'I know.'

His hair framed his face like a wolf-grey halo. There was red blood on his cheek where he had scraped it in the fall. 'You could come back with ropes,' he said. 'My rope is still up there, by the cave mouth. But you'd need more than that.'

'Yes,' I said. 'I will come back with ropes.' I looked up at the rock above us, examined it as best I could. Sometimes good eyes mean the difference between life and death, if you are a climber. I saw where I would need to be as I went, the shape of my journey up the face of the mountain. I thought I could see the ledge outside the cave, from which we had fallen as we fought. I would head for there. Yes.

I blew on my hands, to dry the sweat before I began to climb. 'I will come back for you,' I said. 'With ropes. I have sworn.'

'When?' he asked, and he closed his eyes.

'In a year,' I told him. 'I will come here in a year.'

I began to climb. The man's cries followed me as I stepped and crawled and squeezed and hauled myself up the side of that mountain, mingling with the cries of the great raptors; and they followed me back from the Misty Isle, with nothing to show for my pains and my time, and I will hear him screaming, at the edge of my mind, as I fall asleep or in the moments before I wake, until I die.

It did not rain, and the wind gusted and plucked at me, but did not throw me down. I climbed, and I climbed in safety.

When I reached the ledge the cave entrance seemed like a darker shadow in the noonday sun. I turned from it, turned my back on the mountain, and from the shadows that were already gathering in the cracks and the crevices and deep inside my skull, and I began my slow journey away from the Misty Isle. There were a hundred roads and a thousand paths that would take me back to my home in the lowlands, where my wife would be waiting.

My Last Landlady

My last landlady? She was nothing like you, nothing at
   all alike. Her rooms
were damp. The breakfasts were unpleasant: oily eggs
leathery sausages, a baked orange sludge of beans.
Her face could have curdled beans. She was not kind.
You strike me as a kind person. I hope your world is kind.
By which I mean, I've heard we see the world not as it is
but as we are. A saint sees a world of saints, a killer
sees only murderers and victims. I see the dead.
My landlady told me she would not willingly walk upon
   the beach
for it was littered with weapons: huge, hand-fitting rocks,
each ripe for striking. She only had a little money in her
   tiny purse,
she said, but they would take the notes, oily from her
   fingers,
and leave the purse tucked underneath a stone.
And the water, she would say: hold anyone
under, chill salt-water, grey and brown. Heavy as sin, all
   ready
to drag you away: children went like that so easily, in the
   sea,
when they were surplus to requirements or had learned
awkward facts they might be inclined to pass on

to those who would listen. There were
people on the West Pier the night it burned, she said.

The curtains were dusty lace, and blocked each town-
    grimed window.
Sea View: that was a laugh. The morning she saw me
    twitch
her curtains, to see if it was properly raining, she rapped
    my knuckles.
'Mister Maroney,' she said. 'In this house,
we do not look at the sea through the windows. It brings
bad luck.' She said, 'People come to the beach to forget
    their problems.
It's what we do. It's what the English do. You chop your
    girlfriend up
because she's pregnant and you're worried what the wife
    would say
if she found out. Or you poison the banker you're
    sleeping with,
for the insurance, marry a dozen men in a dozen little
    seaside towns.
Margate. Torquay. Lord love them, but why must they
    stand so still?'
When I asked her who, who stood so still, she told me
it was none of my beeswax, and to be sure to be out
of the house between midday and four, as the char was
    coming,
and I would be underfoot and in the way.

I'd been in that B & B for three weeks now, looking for
    permanent digs.
I paid in cash. The other guests were loveless folk on
    holiday,

and did not care if this was Hove or Hell. We'd eat
our slippery eggs together. I'd watch them promenade
if the day was fine, or huddle under awnings if it rained.
  My landlady
cared only that they were out of the house until teatime.
A retired dentist from Edgbaston, down for a week
of loneliness and drizzle by the sea, would nod at me
  over breakfast,
or if we passed on the seafront. The bathroom was down
  the hall. I was up
in the night. I saw him in his dressing gown. I saw him
  knock upon
her door. I saw it open. He went in. There's nothing
  more to tell.
My landlady was there at breakfast, bright and cheery.
  She said
the dentist had left early, owing to a death in the family.
  She told the truth.

That night the rain rattled the windows. A week passed,
and it was time: I told my landlady I'd found a place
and would be moving on, and paid the rent.
That night she gave me a glass of whisky, and then
  another, and said
I had always been her favourite, and that she was a
  woman of needs,
a flower ripe for plucking, and she smiled, and it was the
  whisky made me nod,
and think she was perhaps a whit less sour of face and
  form. And so
I knocked upon her door that night. She opened it: I
  remember
the whiteness of her skin. The whiteness of her gown. I
  can't forget.

'Mister Maroney,' she whispered. I reached for her, and
　　that was forever
that. The Channel was cold and salt-wet, and she filled
　　my pockets with rocks
to keep me under. So when they find me, if they find me,
I could be anyone, crab-eaten flesh and sea-washed
　　bones and all.

I think I shall like it here in my new digs, here on the
　　seashore. And you
have made me welcome. You have all made me feel so
　　welcome.

How many of us are here? I see us, but I cannot count.
We cluster on the beach and stare at the light in the
　　uppermost room
of her house. We see the curtains twitch, we see a white
　　face
glaring through the grime. She looks afraid, as if one
　　loveless day we might
start up the pebbles towards her, to rebuke her for her
　　lack of hospitality,
to tear her for her bad breakfasts and her sour holidays
　　and our fates.

We stand so still.
Why must we stand so still?

Adventure Story

In my family 'adventure' tends to be used to mean 'any minor disaster we survived' or even 'any break from routine'. Except by my mother, who still uses it to mean *'what she did that morning'*. Going to the wrong part of a supermarket car park and, while looking for her car, getting into a conversation with someone whose sister, it turns out, she knew in the 1970s would qualify, for my mother, as a full-blown adventure.

She is getting older, now. She no longer gets out of the house as she used to. Not since my father died.

My last visit to her, we were clearing out some of his possessions. She gave me a black leather lens-case filled with tarnished cuff links, and invited me to take any of my father's old sweaters and cardigans I wanted, to remember him by. I loved my father, but couldn't imagine wearing one of his sweaters. He was much bigger than me, all my life. Nothing of his would fit me.

And then I said, 'What's that?'

'Oh,' said my mother. 'That's something that your father brought back from Germany when he was in the army.' It was carved out of mottled red stone, the size of my thumb. It was a person, a hero or perhaps a god, with a pained expression on its rough-carved face.

'It doesn't look very German,' I said.

'It wasn't, dear. I think it's from . . . Well, these days, it's Kazakhstan. I'm not sure what it was back then.'

'What was Dad doing in Kazakhstan in the army?' This would have been about 1950. My father ran the officers' club in Germany during his national service, and, in none of his post-war army after-dinner stories, had ever done anything more than borrow a truck without permission, or take delivery of some dodgily sourced whisky.

'Oh.' She looked as if she'd said too much. Then she said, 'Nothing, dear. He didn't like to talk about it.'

I put the statue with the cuff links, and the small pile of curling black-and-white photographs I had decided to take home with me to scan.

I slept in the spare bedroom at the end of the hall, in the narrow spare bed.

The next morning, I went into the room that had been my father's office, to look at it one final time. Then I walked across the hall into the living room, where my mother had already laid breakfast.

'What happened to that little stone carving?'

'I put it away, dear.' My mother's lips were set.

'Why?'

'Well, your father always said he shouldn't have held on to it in the first place.'

'Why not?'

She poured tea from the same china teapot she had poured it from all my life.

'There were people after it. In the end, their ship blew up. In the valley. Because of those flappy things getting into their propellers.'

'Flappy things?'

She thought for a moment. 'Pterodactyls, dear. With a P. That was what your father said they were. Of course, he said the people in the airship deserved all that was coming to them, after what they did to the Aztecs in 1942.'

'Mummy, the Aztecs died out years ago. Long before 1942.'

'Oh yes, dear. The ones in America. Not in that valley. These other people, the ones in the airship, well, your father said they weren't really people. But they looked like people, even though they came from somewhere with such a funny name. Where was it?' She thought for a while. Then, 'You should drink your tea, dear.'

'Yes. No. Hang on. So what were these people? And pterodactyls have been extinct for fifty million years.'

'If you say so, dear. Your father never really talked about it.' She paused. Then, 'There was a girl. This was at least five years before your father and I started going out. He was very good-looking back then. Well, I always thought he was handsome. He met her in Germany. She was hiding from people who were looking for that statue. She was their queen or princess or wise woman or something. They kidnapped her, and he was with her, so they kidnapped him too. They weren't actually aliens. They were more like, those people who turn into wolves on the television . . .'

'Werewolves?'

'I suppose so, dear.' She seemed doubtful. 'The statue was an oracle, and if you owned it, even if you had it, you were the ruler of those people.' She stirred her tea. 'What did your father say? The entrance to the valley was through a tiny footpath, and after the German girl, well, she wasn't German, obviously, but they blew up the pathway with a . . . a ray machine, to cut off the way to the outside world. So your father had to make his own way home. He would have got into such a lot of trouble, but the man who escaped with him, Barry Anscome, he was in Military Intelligence, and—'

'Hang on. Barry Anscome? Used to come and stay for the weekend, when I was a kid. Gave me fifty pence every time. Did bad coin tricks. Snored. Silly moustache.'

'Yes, dear, Barry. He went to South America when he retired. Ecuador, I think. That was how they met. When your father was in the army.' My father had told me once that my mother had never liked Barry Anscome, that he was my dad's friend.

'And?'

She poured me another cup of tea. 'It was such a long time ago, dear. Your father told me all about it once. But he didn't tell the story immediately. He only told me when we were married. He said I ought to know. We were on our honeymoon. We went to a little Spanish fishing village. These days it's a big tourist town, but back then, nobody had ever heard of it. What was it called? Oh yes. Torremolinos.'

'Can I see it again? The statue?'

'No, dear.'

'You put it away?'

'I threw it away,' said my mother, coldly. Then, as if to stop me from rummaging in the rubbish, 'The bin-men already came this morning.'

We said nothing, then.

She sipped her tea.

'You'll never guess who I met last week. Your old schoolteacher. Mrs Brooks? We met in Safeways. She and I went off to have coffee in the Bookshop because I was hoping to talk to her about joining the town carnival committee. But it was closed. We had to go to the Olde Tea Shoppe instead. It was quite an adventure.'

Orange

(Third Subject's Responses to
Investigator's Written Questionnaire.)

EYES ONLY.

1) Jemima Glorfindel Petula Ramsey.

2) Seventeen on June the ninth.

3) The last five years. Before that we lived in Glasgow (Scotland). Before that, Cardiff (Wales).

4) I don't know. I think he's in magazine publishing now. He doesn't talk to us any more. The divorce was pretty bad and Mum wound up paying him a lot of money. Which seems sort of wrong to me. But maybe it was worth it just to get shot of him.

5) An inventor and entrepreneur. She invented the Stuffed Muffin™, and started the Stuffed Muffin chain. I used to like them when I was a kid, but you can get kind of sick of stuffed muffins for every meal, especially because Mum used us as guinea pigs. The Complete Turkey Dinner Christmas Stuffed Muffin was the worst. But she sold out her interest in the Stuffed Muffin chain about five years ago, to start work on My Mum's Coloured Bubbles (not actually ™ yet).

6) Two. My sister, Nerys, who was just fifteen, and my brother, Pryderi, twelve.

7) Several times a day.

8) No.

9) Through the Internet. Probably on eBay.

10) She's been buying colours and dyes from all over the world ever since she decided that the world was crying out for brightly coloured Day-Glo bubbles. The kind you can blow, with bubble mixture.

11) It's not really a laboratory. I mean, she calls it that, but really it's just the garage. Only she took some of the Stuffed Muffins ™ money and converted it, so it has sinks and bathtubs and Bunsen burners and things, and tiles on the walls and the floor to make it easier to clean.

12) I don't know. Nerys used to be pretty normal. When she turned thirteen she started reading these magazines and putting pictures of these strange bimbo women up on her wall like Britney Spears and so on. Sorry if anyone reading this is a Britney fan ;) but I just don't get it. The whole orange thing didn't start until last year.

13) Artificial tanning creams. You couldn't go near her for hours after she put it on. And she'd never give it time to dry after she smeared it on her skin, so it would come off on her sheets and on the fridge door and in the shower leaving smears of orange everywhere. Her friends would wear it too, but they never put it on like she did. I mean, she'd slather on the cream, with no attempt to look even human-coloured, and she thought she looked great. She did the tanning salon thing once, but I don't think she liked it, because she never went back.

14) Tangerine Girl. The Oompa-Loompa. Carrot-top. Go-Mango. Orangina.

15) Not very well. But she didn't seem to care, really. I mean, this is a girl who said that she couldn't see the point of science or maths because she was going to be a pole dancer as soon as she left school. I said, nobody's going to pay to see you in the altogether, and she said how do you know? and I told her that I saw the little QuickTime films she'd made of herself dancing nuddy and left in the camera and she screamed and said give me that, and I told her I'd wiped them. But honestly, I don't think she was ever going to be the next Bettie Page or whoever. She's a sort of squarish shape, for a start.

16) German measles, mumps, and I think Pryderi had chicken-pox when he was staying in Melbourne with the grandparents.

17) In a small pot. It looked a bit like a jam jar, I suppose.

18) I don't think so. Nothing that looked like a warning label anyway. But there was a return address. It came from abroad, and the return address was in some kind of foreign lettering.

19) You have to understand that Mum had been buying colours and dyes from all over the world for five years. The thing with the Day-Glo bubbles is not that someone can blow glowing coloured bubbles, it's that they don't pop and leave splashes of dye all over everything. Mum says that would be a lawsuit waiting to happen. So, no.

20) There was some kind of shouting match between Nerys and Mum to begin with, because Mum had come back from the shops and not bought anything from Nerys's shopping list except the shampoo. Mum said she couldn't find the tanning cream at the supermarket but I think she just forgot. So Nerys stormed off and slammed the door and went into her bedroom and played something that was probably Britney Spears really loudly. I was out the back, feeding the three cats, the chinchilla, and

a guinea pig named Roland who looks like a hairy cushion, and I missed it all.

21) On the kitchen table.

22) When I found the empty jam jar in the back garden the next morning. It was underneath Nerys's window. It didn't take Sherlock Holmes to figure it out.

23) Honestly, I couldn't be bothered. I figured it would just be more yelling, you know? And Mum would work it out soon enough.

24) Yes, it was stupid. But it wasn't uniquely stupid, if you see what I mean. Which is to say, it was par-for-the-course-for-Nerys stupid.

25) That she was glowing.

26) A sort of pulsating orange.

27) When she started telling us that she was going to be worshipped like a god, as she was in the dawn times.

28) Pryderi said she was floating about an inch above the ground. But I didn't actually see this. I thought he was just playing along with her newfound weirdness.

29) She didn't answer to 'Nerys' any more. She described herself mostly as either My Immanence, or the Vehicle. ('It is time to feed the Vehicle.')

30) Dark chocolate. Which was weird because in the old days I was the only one in the house who even sort of liked it. But Pryderi had to go out and buy her bars and bars of it.

31) No. Mum and me just thought it was more Nerys. Just a bit more imaginatively weirdo Nerys than usual.

32) That night, when it started to get dark. You could see the

orange pulsing under the door. Like a glowworm or something. Or a light show. The weirdest thing was that I could still see it with my eyes closed.

33) The next morning. All of us.

34) It was pretty obvious by this point. She didn't really even look like Nerys any longer. She looked sort of *smudged*. Like an afterimage. I thought about it, and it's . . . Okay. Suppose you were staring at something really bright, that was a blue colour. Then you closed your eyes, and you'd see this glowing yellowy-orange afterimage in your eyes? That was what she looked like.

35) They didn't work either.

36) She let Pryderi leave to get her more chocolate. Mum and I weren't allowed to leave the house any more.

37) Mostly I just sat in the back garden and read a book. There wasn't very much else I really could do. I started wearing dark glasses, so did Mum, because the orange light hurt our eyes. Other than that, nothing.

38) Only when we tried to leave or call anybody. There was food in the house, though. And Stuffed Muffins™ in the freezer.

39) 'If you'd just stopped her wearing that stupid tanning cream a year ago we wouldn't be in this mess!' But it was unfair, and I apologised afterwards.

40) When Pryderi came back with the dark chocolate bars. He said he'd gone up to a traffic warden and told him that his sister had turned into a giant orange glow and was controlling our minds. He said the man was extremely rude to him.

41) I don't have a boyfriend. I did, but we broke up after he went to a Rolling Stones concert with the evil bottle-blond former

friend whose name I do not mention. Also, I mean, the Rolling Stones? These little old goat-men hopping around the stage pretending to be all rock-and-roll? Please. So, no.

42) I'd quite like to be a vet. But then I think about having to put animals down, and I don't know. I want to travel for a bit before I make any decisions.

43) The garden hose. We turned it on full, while she was eating her chocolate bars, and distracted, and we sprayed it at her.

44) Just orange steam, really. Mum said that she had solvents and things in the laboratory, if we could get in there, but by now Her Immanence was hissing mad (literally) and she sort of fixed us to the floor. I can't explain it. I mean, I wasn't stuck, but I couldn't leave or move my legs. I was just where she left me.

45) About half a metre above the carpet. She'd sink down a bit to go through doors, so she didn't bump her head. And after the hose incident she didn't go back to her room, just stayed in the main room and floated about grumpily, the colour of a luminous carrot.

46) Complete world domination.

47) I wrote it down on a piece of paper and gave it to Pryderi.

48) He had to carry it back. I don't think Her Immanence really understood money.

49) I don't know. It was Mum's idea more than mine. I think she hoped that the solvent might remove the orange. And at that point, it couldn't hurt. Nothing could have made things worse.

50) It didn't even upset her, like the hose-water did. I'm pretty sure she liked it. I think I saw her dipping her chocolate bars into it, before she ate them, although I had to sort of squint

up my eyes to see anything where she was. It was all a sort of a great orange glow.

51) That we were all going to die. Mum told Pryderi that if the Great Oompa-Loompa let him out to buy chocolate again, he just shouldn't bother coming back. And I was getting really upset about the animals – I hadn't fed the chinchilla or Roland the guinea pig for two days, because I couldn't go into the back garden. I couldn't go anywhere. Except the loo, and then I had to ask.

52) I suppose because they thought the house was on fire. All the orange light. I mean, it was a natural mistake.

53) We were glad she hadn't done that to us. Mum said it proved that Nerys was still in there somewhere, because if she had the power to turn us into goo, like she did the firefighters, she would have done. I said that maybe she just wasn't powerful enough to turn us into goo at the beginning and now she couldn't be bothered.

54) You couldn't even see a person in there any more. It was a bright orange pulsing light, and sometimes it talked straight into your head.

55) When the spaceship landed.

56) I don't know. I mean, it was bigger than the whole block, but it didn't crush anything. It sort of materialised around us, so that our whole house was inside it. And the whole street was inside it too.

57) No. But what else could it have been?

58) A sort of pale blue. They didn't pulse, either. They twinkled.

59) More than six, less than twenty. It's not that easy to tell if

this is the same intelligent blue light you were just speaking to five minutes ago.

60) Three things. First of all, a promise that Nerys wouldn't be hurt or harmed. Second, that if they were ever able to return her to the way she was, they'd let us know, and bring her back. Thirdly, a recipe for fluorescent bubble mixture. (I can only assume they were reading Mum's mind, because she didn't say anything. It's possible that Her Immanence told them, though. She definitely had access to some of 'the Vehicle's' memories.) Also, they gave Pryderi a thing like a glass skateboard.

61) A sort of a liquid sound. Then everything became transparent. I was crying, and so was Mum. And Pryderi said, 'Cool beans,' and I started to giggle while crying, and then it was just our house again.

62) We went out into the back garden and looked up. There was something blinking blue and orange, very high, getting smaller and smaller, and we watched it until it was out of sight.

63) Because I didn't want to.

64) I fed the remaining animals. Roland was in a state. The cats just seemed happy that someone was feeding them again. I don't know how the chinchilla got out.

65) Sometimes. I mean, you have to bear in mind that she was the single most irritating person on the planet, even before the whole Her Immanence thing. But yes, I guess so. If I'm honest.

66) Sitting outside at night, staring up at the sky, wondering what she's doing now.

67) He wants his glass skateboard back. He says that it's his, and the government has no right to keep it. (You are the government,

aren't you?) Mum seems happy to share the patent for the Coloured Bubbles recipe with the government though. The man said that it might be the basis of a whole new branch of molecular something or other. Nobody gave me anything, so I don't have to worry.

68) Once, in the back garden, looking up at the night sky. I think it was only an orangeyish star, actually. It could have been Mars, I know they call it the red planet. Although once in a while I think that maybe she's back to herself again, and dancing, up there, wherever she is, and all the aliens love her pole dancing because they just don't know any better, and they think it's a whole new art form, and they don't even mind that she's sort of square.

69) I don't know. Sitting in the back garden talking to the cats, maybe. Or blowing silly-coloured bubbles.

70) Until the day that I die.

I attest that this is a true statement of events.
Jemima Glorfindel Petula Ramsey

A Calendar of Tales

January Tale

Whap!

'Is it always like this?' The kid seemed disoriented. He was glancing around the room, unfocused. That would get him killed, if he wasn't careful.

Twelve tapped him on the arm. 'Nope. Not always. If there's any trouble, it'll come from up there.'

He pointed to an attic door, in the ceiling above them. The door was askew, and the darkness waited behind it like an eye.

The kid nodded. Then he said, 'How long have we got?'

'Together? Maybe another ten minutes.'

'One thing I kept asking them at Base, they wouldn't answer. They said I'd see for myself. Who *are* they?'

Twelve didn't answer. Something had changed, ever so slightly, in the darkness of the attic above them. He touched his finger to his lips, then raised his weapon, and indicated for the kid to do likewise.

They came tumbling down from the attic-hole: brick-grey and mould-green, sharp-toothed and fast, so fast. The kid was still fumbling at the trigger when Twelve started shooting, and he took them out, all five of them, before the kid could fire a shot.

He glanced to his left. The kid was shaking.

'There you go,' he said.

'I guess I mean, *what* are they?'

'What or who. Same thing. They're the enemy. Slipping in at the edges of time. Right now, at handover, they're going to be coming out in force.'

They walked down the stairs together. They were in a small, suburban house. A woman and a man sat in the kitchen, at a table with a bottle of champagne upon it. They did not appear to notice the two men in uniform who walked through the room. The woman was pouring the champagne.

The kid's uniform was crisp and dark blue and looked unworn. His yearglass hung on his belt, full of pale sand. Twelve's uniform was frayed and faded to a bluish grey, patched up where it had been sliced into, or ripped, or burned. They reached the kitchen door and—

Whap!

They were outside, in a forest, somewhere very cold indeed.

'DOWN!' called Twelve.

The sharp thing went over their heads and crashed into a tree behind them.

The kid said, 'I thought you said it wasn't always like this.'

Twelve shrugged.

'Where are they coming from?'

'Time,' said Twelve. 'They're hiding behind the seconds, trying to get in.'

In the forest close to them something went *whumpf*, and a tall fir tree began to burn with a flickering copper-green flame.

'Where are they?'

'Above us, again. They're normally above you or beneath you.'

They came down like sparks from a sparkler, beautiful and white and possibly slightly dangerous.

The kid was getting the hang of it. This time the two of them fired together.

'Did they brief you?' asked Twelve. As they landed, the sparks looked less beautiful and much more dangerous.

'Not really. They just told me that it was only for a year.'

Twelve barely paused to reload. He was grizzled and scarred. The kid looked barely old enough to pick up a weapon. 'Did they tell you that a year would be a lifetime?'

The kid shook his head. Twelve remembered when he was a kid like this, his uniform clean and unburned. Had he ever been so fresh-faced? So innocent?

He dealt with five of the spark-demons. The kid took care of the remaining three.

'So it's a year of fighting,' said the kid.

'Second by second,' said Twelve.

Whap!

The waves crashed on the beach. It was hot here, a Southern Hemisphere January. It was still night, though. Above them fireworks hung in the sky, unmoving. Twelve checked his yearglass: there were only a couple of grains left. He was almost done.

He scanned the beach, the waves, the rocks.

'I don't see it,' he said.

'I do,' said the kid.

It rose from the sea as he pointed, something huge beyond the mind's holding, all bulk and malevolent vastness, all tentacles and claws, and it roared as it rose.

Twelve had the rocket launcher off his back and over his shoulder. He fired it, and watched as flame blossomed on the creature's body.

'Biggest I've seen yet,' he said. 'Maybe they save the best for last.'

'Hey,' said the kid, 'I'm only at the beginning.'

It came for them then, crab-claws flailing and snapping, tentacles lashing, maw opening and vainly closing. They sprinted up the sandy ridge.

The kid was faster than Twelve: he was young, but sometimes that's an advantage. Twelve's hip ached, and he stumbled. His final grain of sand was falling through the yearglass when something – a tentacle, he figured – wrapped itself around his leg, and he fell.

He looked up.

The kid was standing on the ridge, feet planted like they teach you in boot camp, holding a rocket launcher of unfamiliar design – something after Twelve's time, he assumed. He began mentally to say his goodbyes as he was hauled down the beach, sand scraping his face, and then a dull bang and the tentacle was whipped from his leg as the creature was blown backwards, into the sea.

He was tumbling through the air as the final grain fell and Midnight took him.

Twelve opened his eyes in the place the old years go. Fourteen helped him down from the dais.

'How'd it go?' asked Nineteen Fourteen. She wore a floor-length white skirt and long, white gloves.

'They're getting more dangerous every year,' said Twenty Twelve. 'The seconds, and the things behind them. But I like the new kid. I think he's going to do fine.'

February Tale

Grey February skies, misty white sands, black rocks, and the sea seemed black too, like a monochrome photograph, with only the girl in the yellow raincoat adding any colour to the world.

Twenty years ago the old woman had walked the beach in all weathers, bowed over, staring at the sand, occasionally bending, laboriously, to lift a rock and look beneath it. When she had stopped coming down to the sands, a middle-aged woman, her daughter I assumed, came, and walked the beach with less enthusiasm than her mother. Now that woman had stopped coming, and in her place there was the girl.

She came towards me. I was the only other person on the beach in that mist. I don't look much older than her.

'What are you looking for?' I called.

She made a face. 'What makes you think I'm looking for anything?'

'You come down here every day. Before you it was the lady, before her the very old lady, with the umbrella.'

'That was my grandmother,' said the girl in the yellow raincoat.

'What did she lose?'

'A pendant.'

'It must be very valuable.'

'Not really. It has sentimental value.'

'Must be worth more than that, if your family has been looking for it for umpteen years.'

'Yes.' She hesitated. Then she said, 'Grandma said it would take her home again. She said she only came here to look around. She was curious. And then she got worried about having the pendant on her, so she hid it under a rock, so she'd be able to find it again, when she got back. And then, when she got back, she wasn't sure which rock it was, not any more. That was fifty years ago.'

'Where was her home?'

'She never told us.'

The way the girl was talking made me ask the question that scared me. 'Is she still alive? Your grandmother?'

'Yes. Sort of. But she doesn't talk to us these days. She just stares out at the sea. It must be horrible to be so old.'

I shook my head. It isn't. Then I put my hand into my coat pocket and held it out to her. 'Was it anything like this? I found it on this beach a year ago. Under a rock.'

The pendant was untarnished by sand or by salt water.

The girl looked amazed, then she hugged me, and thanked me, and she took the pendant, and ran up the misty beach, in the direction of the little town.

I watched her go: a splash of gold in a black-and-white world, carrying her grandmother's pendant in her hand. It was a twin to the one I wore around my own neck.

I wondered about her grandmother, my little sister, whether she would ever go home; whether she would forgive me for the joke I had played on her if she did. Perhaps she would elect to stay on the earth, and would send the girl home in her place. That might be fun.

Only when my great-niece was gone and I was alone did I swim upward, letting the pendant pull me home, up into the vastness above us, where we wander with the lonely sky-whales and the skies and seas are one.

March Tale

. . . only this we know, that she was not executed.
– CHARLES JOHNSON, A GENERAL HISTORY OF THE ROBBERIES
AND MURDERS OF THE MOST NOTORIOUS PIRATES

It was too warm in the great house, and so the two of them went out onto the porch. A spring storm was brewing far to the west. Already the flicker of lightning, and the unpredictable chilly gusts blew about them and cooled them. They sat decorously on the porch swing, the mother and the daughter, and

they talked of when the woman's husband would be home, for
he had taken ship with a tobacco crop to faraway England.

Mary, who was thirteen, so pretty, so easily startled, said, 'I
do declare. I am glad that all the pirates have gone to the gallows,
and Father will come back to us safely.'

Her mother's smile was gentle, and it did not fade as she said,
'I do not care to talk about pirates, Mary.'

* * *

She was dressed as a boy when she was a girl, to cover up her
father's scandal. She did not wear a woman's dress until she
was on the ship with her father, and with her mother, his serving-
girl mistress whom he would call wife in the New World, and
they were on their way from Cork to the Carolinas.

She fell in love for the first time, on that journey, enveloped
in unfamiliar cloth, clumsy in her strange skirts. She was eleven,
and it was no sailor who took her heart but the ship itself: Anne
would sit in the bows, watching the grey Atlantic roll beneath
them, listening to the gulls scream, and feeling Ireland recede
with each moment, taking with it all the old lies.

She left her love when they landed, with regret, and even as
her father prospered in the new land she dreamed of the creak
and slap of the sails.

Her father was a good man. He had been pleased when she
had returned, and did not speak of her time away: the young
man whom she had married, how he had taken her to Providence.
She had returned to her family three years after, with a baby at
her breast. Her husband had died, she said, and although tales
and rumours abounded, even the sharpest of the gossiping
tongues did not think to suggest that Annie Riley was the pirate-
girl Anne Bonny, Red Rackham's first mate.

'If you had fought like a man, you would not have died like

a dog.' Those had been Anne Bonny's last words to the man who put the baby in her belly, or so they said.

* * *

Mrs Riley watched the lightning play, and heard the first rumble of distant thunder. Her hair was greying now, and her skin just as fair as that of any local woman of property.

'It sounds like cannon fire,' said Mary (Anne had named her for her own mother, and for her best friend in the years she was away from the great house).

'Why would you say such things?' asked her mother, primly. 'In this house, we do not speak of cannon fire.'

The first of the March rain fell, then, and Mrs Riley surprised her daughter by getting up from the porch swing and leaning into the rain, so it splashed her face like sea spray. It was quite out of character for a woman of such respectability.

As the rain splashed her face she thought herself there: the captain of her own ship, the cannonade around them, the stench of the gunpowder smoke blowing on the salt breeze. Her ship's deck would be painted red, to mask the blood in battle. The wind would fill her billowing canvas with a snap as loud as cannon's roar, as they prepared to board the merchant ship, and take whatever they wished, jewels or coin – and burning kisses with her first mate when the madness was done . . .

'Mother?' said Mary. 'I do believe you must be thinking of a great secret. You have such a strange smile on your face.'

'Silly girl, *acushla*,' said her mother. And then she said, 'I was thinking of your father.' She spoke the truth, and the March winds blew madness about them.

April Tale

You know you've been pushing the ducks too hard when they stop trusting you, and my father had been taking the ducks for everything he could since the previous summer.

He'd walk down to the pond. 'Hey, ducks,' he'd say to the ducks.

By January they'd just swim away. One particularly irate drake – we called him Donald, but only behind his back, ducks are sensitive to that kind of thing – would hang around and berate my father. 'We ain't interested,' he'd say. 'We don't want to buy nothing you're selling: not life insurance, not encyclopedias, not aluminium siding, not safety matches, and especially not damp-proofing.'

'"Double or nothing"!' quacked a particularly indignant mallard. 'Sure, you'll toss us for it. With a double-sided quarter . . . !'

The ducks, who had got to examine the quarter in question when my father had dropped it into the pond, all honked in agreement, and drifted elegantly and grumpily to the other side of the pond.

My father took it personally. 'Those ducks,' he said. 'They were always there. Like a cow you could milk. They were suckers – the best kind. The kind you could go back to again and again. And I queered the pitch.'

'You need to make them trust you again,' I told him. 'Or better still, you could just start being honest. Turn over a new leaf. You have a real job now.'

He worked at the village inn, opposite the duck pond.

My father did not turn over a new leaf. He barely even turned over the old leaf. He stole fresh bread from the inn kitchens, he took unfinished bottles of red wine, and he went down to the duck pond to win the ducks' trust.

All of March he entertained them, he fed them, he told them

jokes, he did whatever he could to soften them up. It was not until April, when the world was all puddles, and the trees were new and green and the world had shaken off winter, that he brought out a pack of cards.

'How about a friendly game?' asked my father. 'Not for money?'

The ducks eyed each other nervously. 'I don't know . . . ,' some of them muttered, warily.

Then one elderly mallard I did not recognise extended a wing graciously. 'After so much fresh bread, after so much good wine, we would be churlish to refuse your offer. Perhaps, gin rummy? Or happy families?'

'How about poker?' said my father, with his poker face on, and the ducks said yes.

My father was so happy. He didn't even have to suggest that they start playing for money, just to make the game more interesting – the elderly mallard did that.

I'd learned a little over the years about dealing off the bottom: I'd watch my father sitting in our room at night, practising, over and over, but that old mallard could have taught my father a thing or two. He dealt from the bottom. He dealt from the middle. He knew where every card in that deck was, and it just took a flick of the wing to put them exactly where he wanted them.

The ducks took my father for everything: his wallet, his watch, his shoes, his snuffbox, and the clothes he stood up in. If the ducks had accepted a boy as a bet, he would have lost me as well, and perhaps, in a lot of ways, he did.

He walked back to the inn in just his underwear and socks. Ducks don't like socks, they said. It's a duck thing.

'At least you kept your socks,' I told him.

That was the April that my father learned not to trust ducks.

May Tale

In May I received an anonymous Mother's Day card. This puzzled me. I would have noticed if I had ever had children, surely?

In June I found a notice saying, 'Normal Service Will Be Resumed as Soon as Possible', taped to my bathroom mirror, along with several small tarnished copper coins of uncertain denomination and origin.

In July I received three postcards, at weekly intervals, all postmarked from the Emerald City of Oz, telling me the person who sent them was having a wonderful time, and asking me to remind Doreen about changing the locks on the back door and to make certain that she had cancelled the milk. I do not know anyone named Doreen.

In August someone left a box of chocolates on my doorstep. It had a sticker attached saying it was evidence in an important legal case, and under no circumstances were the chocolates inside to be eaten before they had been dusted for fingerprints. The chocolates had melted in the August heat into a squidgy brown mass, and I threw the whole box away.

In September I received a package containing *Action Comics* #1, a first folio of Shakespeare's plays, and a privately published copy of a novel by Jane Austen I was unfamiliar with, called *Wit and Wilderness*. I have little interest in comics, Shakespeare, or Jane Austen, and I left the books in the back bedroom. They were gone a week later, when I needed something to read in the bath, and went looking.

In October I found a notice saying, 'Normal Service Will Be Resumed as Soon as Possible. Honest', taped to the side of the goldfish tank. Two of the goldfish appeared to have been taken and replaced by identical substitutes.

In November I received a ransom note telling me exactly what to do if ever I wished to see my uncle Theobald alive again. I do not have an Uncle Theobald, but I wore a pink carnation in my buttonhole and ate nothing but salads for the entire month anyway.

In December I received a Christmas card postmarked THE NORTH POLE, letting me know that, this year, due to a clerical error, I was on neither the Naughty nor the Nice list. It was signed with a name that began with an S. It might have been Santa but it seemed more like Steve.

In January I woke to find someone had painted SECURE YOUR OWN MASK BEFORE HELPING OTHERS on the ceiling of my tiny kitchen, in vermilion paint. Some of the paint had dripped onto the floor.

In February a man came over to me at the bus stop and showed me the black statue of a falcon in his shopping bag. He asked for my help keeping it safe from the Fat Man, and then he saw someone behind me and he ran away.

In March I received three pieces of junk mail, the first telling me I might have already won a million dollars, the second telling me that I might already have been elected to the Académie Française, and the last telling me I might already have been installed as the titular head of the Holy Roman Empire.

In April I found a note on my bedside table apologising for the problems in service, and assuring me that henceforward all faults in the universe had now been remedied forever. WE APOLOGISE OF THE INCONVENIENTS, it concluded.

In May I received another Mother's Day card. Not anonymous, this time. It was signed, but I could not read the signature. It started with an S but it almost definitely wasn't Steve.

June Tale

My parents disagree. It's what they do. They do more than disagree. They argue. About everything. I'm still not sure that I understand how they ever stopped arguing about things long enough to get married, let alone to have me and my sister.

My mum believes in the redistribution of wealth, and thinks that the big problem with Communism is it doesn't go far enough. My dad has a framed photograph of the Queen on his side of the bed, and he votes as Conservative as he can. My mum wanted to name me Susan. My dad wanted to name me Henrietta, after his aunt. Neither of them would budge an inch. I am the only Susietta in my school or, probably, anywhere. My sister's name is Alismima, for similar reasons.

There is nothing that they agree on, not even the temperature. My dad is always too hot, my mum always too cold. They turn the radiators on and off, open and close windows, whenever the other one goes out of the room. My sister and I get colds all year, and we think that's probably why.

They couldn't even agree on what month we'd go on holiday. Dad said definitely August, Mum said unquestionably July. Which meant we wound up having to take our summer holiday in June, inconveniencing everybody.

Then they couldn't decide where to go. Dad was set on pony trekking in Iceland, while Mum was only willing to compromise as far as a camelback caravan across the Sahara, and both of them simply looked at us as if we were being a bit silly when we suggested that we'd quite like to sit on a beach in the South of France or somewhere. They stopped arguing long enough to tell us that that wasn't going to happen, and neither was a trip to Disneyland, and then they went back to disagreeing with each other.

They finished the Where Are We Going for Our Holidays in

June Disagreement by slamming a lot of doors and shouting a lot of things like 'Right then!' at each other through them.

When the inconvenient holiday rolled around, my sister and I were only certain of one thing: we weren't going anywhere. We took a huge pile of books out of the library, as many as we could between us, and prepared to listen to lots of arguing for the next ten days.

Then the men came in vans and brought things into the house and started to install them.

Mum had them put a sauna in the cellar. They poured masses of sand onto the floor. They hung a sunlamp from the ceiling. She put a towel on the sand beneath the sunlamp, and she'd lie down on it. She had pictures of sand dunes and camels taped to the cellar walls until they peeled off in the extreme heat.

Dad had the men put the fridge – the biggest fridge he could find, so big you could walk into it – in the garage. It filled the garage so completely that he had to start parking the car in the driveway. He'd get up in the morning, dress warmly in a thick Icelandic wool sweater, he'd get a book and thermos-flask filled with hot cocoa, and some Marmite and cucumber sandwiches, and he'd head in there in the morning with a huge smile on his face, and not come out until dinner.

I wonder if anybody else has a family as weird as mine. My parents never agree on anything at all.

'Did you know Mum's been putting her coat on and sneaking into the garage in the afternoons?' said my sister suddenly, while we were sitting in the garden, reading our library books.

I didn't, but I'd seen Dad wearing just his bathing trunks and dressing gown heading down into the cellar that morning to be with Mum, with a big, goofy smile on his face.

I don't understand parents. Honestly, I don't think anybody ever does.

July Tale

The day that my wife walked out on me, saying she needed to be alone and to have some time to think things over, on the first of July, when the sun beat down on the lake in the centre of the town, when the corn in the meadows that surrounded my house was knee-high, when the first few rockets and firecrackers were let off by over-enthusiastic children to startle us and to speckle the summer sky, I built an igloo out of books in my backyard.

I used paperbacks to build it, scared of the weight of falling hardbacks or encyclopedias if I didn't build it soundly.

But it held. It was twelve feet high, and had a tunnel, through which I could crawl to enter, to keep out the bitter arctic winds.

I took more books into the igloo I had made out of books, and I read in there. I marvelled at how warm and comfortable I was inside. As I read the books, I would put them down, make a floor out of them, and then I got more books, and I sat on them, eliminating the last of the green July grass from my world.

My friends came by the next day. They crawled on their hands and knees into my igloo. They told me I was acting crazy. I told them that the only thing that stood between me and the winter's cold was my father's collection of 1950s paperbacks, many of them with racy titles and lurid covers and disappointingly staid stories.

My friends left.

I sat in my igloo imagining the arctic night outside, wondering whether the Northern Lights would be filling the sky above me. I looked out, but saw only a night filled with pinprick stars.

I slept in my igloo made of books. I was getting hungry. I made a hole in the floor, lowered a fishing line and waited until something bit. I pulled it up: a fish made of books – green-covered vintage Penguin detective stories. I ate it raw, fearing a fire in my igloo.

When I went outside I observed that someone had covered the whole world with books: pale-covered books, all shades of white and blue and purple. I wandered the ice floes of books.

I saw someone who looked like my wife out there on the ice. She was making a glacier of autobiographies.

'I thought you left me,' I said to her. 'I thought you left me alone.'

She said nothing, and I realised she was only a shadow of a shadow.

It was July, when the sun never sets in the Arctic, but I was getting tired, and I started back towards the igloo.

I saw the shadows of the bears before I saw the bears themselves: huge they were, and pale, made of the pages of fierce books: poems ancient and modern prowled the ice floes in bear-shape, filled with words that could wound with their beauty. I could see the paper, and the words winding across them, and I was frightened that the bears could see me.

I crept back to my igloo, avoiding the bears. I may have slept in the darkness. And then I crawled out, and I lay on my back on the ice and stared up at the unexpected colours of the shimmering Northern Lights, and listened to the cracks and snaps of the distant ice as an iceberg of fairy tales calved from a glacier of books on mythology.

I do not know when I became aware that there was someone else lying on the ground near to me. I could hear her breathing.

'They are very beautiful, aren't they?' she said.

'It is aurora borealis, the Northern Lights,' I told her.

'It's the town's Fourth of July fireworks, baby,' said my wife. She held my hand and we watched the fireworks together.

When the last of the fireworks had vanished in a cloud of golden stars, she said, 'I came home.'

I didn't say anything. But I held her hand very tightly, and I left my igloo made of books, and I went with her back into the house we lived in, basking like a cat in the July heat.

I heard distant thunder, and in the night, while we slept, it began to rain, tumbling my igloo of books, washing away the words from the world.

August Tale

The forest fires started early that August. All the storms that might have dampened the world went south of us, and they took their rain with them. Each day we would see the helicopters going over above us, with their cargoes of lake water ready to drop on the distant flames.

Peter, who is Australian, and owns the house in which I live, cooking for him, and tending the place, said, 'In Australia, the eucalypts use fire to survive. Some eucalyptus seeds won't germinate unless a forest fire has gone through and cleared out all the undergrowth. They need the intense heat.'

'Weird thought,' I said. 'Something hatching out of the flames.'

'Not really,' said Peter. 'Very normal. Probably a lot more normal when the Earth was hotter.'

'Hard to imagine a world any hotter than this.'

He snorted. 'This is nothing,' he said, and then talked about intense heat he had experienced in Australia when he was younger.

The next morning the TV news said that people in our area were advised to evacuate their property: we were in a high-risk area for fire.

'Load of old tosh,' said Peter, crossly. 'It'll never cause a problem for us. We're on high ground, and we've got the creek all around us.'

When the water was high, the creek could be four, even five feet deep. Now it was no more than a foot, or two at the most.

By late afternoon, the smell of woodsmoke was heavy on the air, and the TV and the radio were both telling us to get out, now, if we could. We smiled at each other, and drank our beers, and congratulated each other on our understanding of a difficult situation, on not panicking, on not running away.

'We're complacent, humanity,' I said. 'All of us. People. We see the leaves cooking on the trees on a hot August day, and we still don't believe anything's really going to change. Our empires will go on forever.'

'Nothing lasts forever,' said Peter, and he poured himself another beer and told me about a friend of his back in Australia who had stopped a bushfire burning down the family farm by pouring beer on the little fires whenever they sprang up.

The fire came down the valley towards us like the end of the world, and we realised how little protection the creek would be. The air itself was burning.

We fled then, at last, pushing ourselves, coughing in the choking smoke, ran down the hill until we reached the creek, and we lay down in it, with only our heads above the water.

From the inferno we saw them hatch from the flames, and rise, and fly. They reminded me of birds, pecking at the flaming ruins of the house on the hill. I saw one of them lift its head, and call out triumphantly. I could hear it over the crackling of the burning leaves, over the roar of the flames. I heard the call of the phoenix, and I understood that nothing lasts forever.

A hundred birds of fire ascended into the skies as the creek water began to boil.

September Tale

My mother had a ring in the shape of a lion's head. She used it to do small magics – find parking spaces, make the queue she was in at the supermarket move a bit faster, make the squabbling couple at the next table stop squabbling and fall in love again, that sort of thing. She left it to me when she died.

The first time I lost it I was in a café. I think I had been fiddling with it nervously, pulling it off my finger, putting it on again. Only when I got home did I realise that I was no longer wearing it.

I returned to the café, but there was no sign of it.

Several days later, it was returned to me by a taxi driver, who had found it on the pavement outside the café. He told me my mother had appeared to him in a dream and given him my address and her recipe for old-fashioned cheesecake.

The second time I lost the ring I was leaning over a bridge, idly tossing pinecones into the river below. I didn't think it was loose, but the ring left my hand with a pinecone. I watched its arc as it fell. It landed in the wet dark mud at the edge of the river with a loud *pollup* noise, and was gone.

A week later, I bought a salmon from a man I met in the pub: I collected it from a cooler in the back of his ancient green van. It was for a birthday dinner. When I cut the salmon open, my mother's lion ring tumbled out.

The third time I lost it, I was reading and sunbathing in the back garden. It was August. The ring was on the towel beside me, along with my dark glasses and some suntan lotion, when a large bird (I suspect it was a magpie or a jackdaw, but I may be wrong. It was definitely a corvid of some kind) flew down, and flapped away with my mother's ring in its beak.

The ring was returned the following night by a scarecrow, awkwardly animated. He gave me quite a start as he stood there, unmoving under the back door light, and then he lurched off into the darkness once again as soon as I had taken the ring from his straw-stuffed glove hand.

'Some things aren't meant to be kept,' I told myself.

The next morning, I put the ring into the glove compartment of my old car. I drove the car to a wrecker, and I watched, satisfied, as the car was crushed into a cube of metal the size of an old television set, and then put in a container to be shipped to Romania, where it would be processed into useful things.

In early September I cleared out my bank account. I moved to Brazil, where I took a job as a web designer under an assumed name.

So far there's been no sign of Mother's ring. But sometimes I wake from a deep sleep with my heart pounding, soaked in sweat, wondering how she's going to give it back to me next time.

October Tale

'That feels good,' I said, and I stretched my neck to get out the last of the cramp.

It didn't just feel good, it felt great, actually. I'd been squashed up inside that lamp for so long. You start to think that nobody's ever going to rub it again.

'You're a genie,' said the young lady with the polishing cloth in her hand.

'I am. You're a smart girl, toots. What gave me away?'

'The appearing in a puff of smoke,' she said. 'And you look like a genie. You've got the turban and the pointy shoes.'

I folded my arms and blinked. Now I was wearing blue jeans, grey sneakers, and a faded grey sweater: the male uniform of this time and this place. I raised a hand to my forehead, and I bowed deeply.

'I am the genie of the lamp,' I told her. 'Rejoice, O fortunate one. I have it in my power to grant you three wishes. And don't try the "I wish for more wishes" thing – I won't play and you'll lose a wish. Right. Go for it.'

I folded my arms again.

'No,' she said. 'I mean thanks and all that, but it's fine. I'm good.'

'Honey,' I said. 'Toots. Sweetie. Perhaps you misheard me. I'm a genie. And the three wishes? We're talking anything you want. You ever dreamed of flying? I can give you wings. You want to be wealthy, richer than Croesus? You want power? Just say it. Three wishes. Whatever you want.'

'Like I said,' she said, 'thanks. I'm fine. Would you like something to drink? You must be parched after spending so much time in that lamp. Wine? Water? Tea?'

'Uh . . .' Actually, now she came to mention it, I was thirsty. 'Do you have any mint tea?'

She made me some mint tea in a teapot that was almost a twin to the lamp in which I'd spent the greater part of the last thousand years.

'Thank you for the tea.'

'No problem.'

'But I don't get it. Everyone I've ever met, they start asking for things. A fancy house. A harem of gorgeous women – not that you'd want that, of course . . .'

'I might,' she said. 'You can't just make assumptions about people. Oh, and don't call me toots, or sweetie, or any of those things. My name's Hazel.'

'Ah!' I understood. 'You want a beautiful woman then? My apologies. You have but to wish.' I folded my arms.

'No,' she said. 'I'm good. No wishes. How's the tea?'

I told her that the mint tea was the finest I had ever tasted.

She asked me when I had started feeling a need to grant people's wishes, and whether I felt a desperate need to please. She asked about my mother, and I told her that she could not judge me as she would judge mortals, for I was a djinn, powerful and wise, magical and mysterious.

She asked me if I liked hummus, and when I said that I did, she toasted a pitta bread, and sliced it up, for me to dip into the hummus.

I dipped my bread slices into the hummus, and ate it with delight. The hummus gave me an idea.

'Just make a wish,' I said, helpfully, 'and I could have a meal fit for a sultan brought in to you. Each dish would be finer than the one before, and all served upon golden plates. And you could keep the plates afterwards.'

'It's good,' she said, with a smile. 'Would you like to go for a walk?'

We walked together through the town. It felt good to stretch my legs after so many years in the lamp. We wound up in a public park, sitting on a bench by a lake. It was warm, but gusty, and the autumn leaves fell in flurries each time the wind blew.

I told Hazel about my youth as a djinn, of how we used to eavesdrop on the angels and how they would throw comets at us if they spied us listening. I told her of the bad days of the djinn-wars, and how King Suleiman had imprisoned us inside hollow objects: bottles, lamps, clay pots, that kind of thing.

She told me of her parents, who were both killed in the same plane crash, and who had left her the house. She told me of her job, illustrating children's books, a job she had backed into, accidentally, at the point she realised she would never be a really competent medical illustrator, and of how happy she became whenever she was sent a new book to illustrate. She told me she taught life drawing to adults at the local community college one evening a week.

I saw no obvious flaw in her life, no hole that she could fill by wishing, save one.

'Your life is good,' I told her. 'But you have no one to share it with. Wish, and I will bring you the perfect man. Or woman. A film star. A rich . . . person . . .'

'No need. I'm good,' she said.

We walked back to her house, past houses dressed for Hallowe'en.

'This is not right,' I told her. 'People always want things.'

'Not me. I've got everything I need.'

'Then what do *I* do?'

She thought for a moment. Then she pointed at her front yard. 'Can you rake the leaves?'

'Is that your wish?'

'Nope. Just something you could do while I'm getting our dinner ready.'

I raked the leaves into a heap by the hedge, to stop the wind from blowing it apart. After dinner, I washed up the dishes. I spent the night in Hazel's spare bedroom.

It wasn't that she didn't want help. She let me help. I ran errands for her, picked up art supplies and groceries. On days she had been painting for a long time, she let me rub her neck and shoulders. I have good, firm hands.

Shortly before Thanksgiving I moved out of the spare bedroom, across the hall, into the main bedroom, and Hazel's bed.

I watched her face this morning as she slept. I stared at the shapes her lips make when she sleeps. The creeping sunlight touched her face, and she opened her eyes and stared at me, and she smiled.

'You know what I never asked,' she said, 'is what about you? What would you wish for if I asked what your three wishes were?'

I thought for a moment. I put my arm around her, and she snuggled her head into my shoulder.

'It's okay,' I told her. 'I'm good.'

November Tale

The brazier was small and square and made of an aged and fire-blackened metal that might have been copper or brass. It had caught Eloise's eye at the garage sale because it was twined with animals that might have been dragons and might have been sea-snakes. One of them was missing its head.

It was only a dollar, and Eloise bought it, along with a red hat with a feather on the side. She began to regret buying the hat even before she got home, and thought perhaps she would give it to someone as a gift. But the letter from the hospital had been waiting for her when she got home, and she put the brazier in the back garden and the hat in the closet as you went into the house, and had not thought of either of them again.

The months had passed, and so had the desire to leave the house. Every day made her weaker, and each day took more from her. She moved her bed to the room downstairs, because it hurt to walk, because she was too exhausted to climb the stairs, because it was simpler.

November came, and with it the knowledge that she would never see Christmas.

There are things you cannot throw away, things you cannot leave for your loved ones to find when you are gone. Things you have to burn.

She took a black cardboard folder filled with papers and letters and old photographs out into the garden. She filled the brazier with fallen twigs and brown paper shopping bags, and she lit it with a barbecue lighter. Only when it was burning did she open the folder.

She started with the letters, particularly the ones she would not want other people to see. When she had been at university there had been a professor and a relationship, if you could call it that, which had gone very dark and very wrong very fast. She had all his letters paper-clipped together, and she dropped them, one by one, into the flames. There was a photograph of the two of them together, and she dropped it into the brazier last of all, and watched it curl and blacken.

She was reaching for the next thing in the cardboard folder when she realised that she could not remember the professor's name, or what he taught, or why the relationship had hurt her as it did, left her almost suicidal for the following year.

The next thing was a photograph of her old dog, Lassie, on her back beside the oak tree in the backyard. Lassie was dead these seven years, but the tree was still there, leafless now in the November chill. She tossed the photograph into the brazier. She had loved that dog.

She glanced over to the tree, remembering . . .

There was no tree in the backyard.

There wasn't even a tree stump; only a faded November lawn, strewn with fallen leaves from the trees next door.

Eloise saw it, and she did not worry that she had gone mad. She got up stiffly and walked into the house. Her reflection in the mirror shocked her, as it always did these days. Her hair so thin, so sparse, her face so gaunt.

She picked up the papers from the table beside her makeshift bed: a letter from her oncologist was on the top, beneath it a dozen pages of numbers and words. There were more papers beneath it, all with the hospital logo on the top of the first page. She picked them up and, for good measure, she picked up the hospital bills as well. Insurance covered so much of it, but not all.

She walked back outside, pausing in the kitchen to catch her breath.

The brazier waited, and she threw her medical information into the flames. She watched them brown and blacken and turn to ash on the November wind.

Eloise got up, when the last of the medical records had burned away, and she walked inside. The mirror in the hall showed her an Eloise both familiar and new: she had thick brown hair, and she smiled at herself from the looking glass as if she loved life and trailed comfort in her wake.

Eloise went to the hall closet. There was a red hat on the shelf she could barely remember, but she put it on, worried that the red might make her face look washed out and sallow. She looked in the mirror. She appeared just fine. She tipped the hat at a jauntier angle.

Outside the last of the smoke from the black snake-wound brazier drifted on the chilly November air.

December Tale

Summer on the streets is hard, but you can sleep in a park in the summer without dying from the cold. Winter is different. Winter can be lethal. And even if it isn't, the cold still takes you as its special homeless friend, and it insinuates itself into every part of your life.

Donna had learned from the old hands. The trick, they told her, is to sleep wherever you can during the day – the Circle line is good, buy a ticket and ride all day, snoozing in the carriage, and so are the kinds of cheap cafés where they don't mind an eighteen-year-old girl spending fifty pence on a cup of tea and then dozing off in a corner for an hour or three, as long as she looks more or less respectable – but to keep moving at night, when the temperatures plummet, and the warm places close their doors, and lock them, and turn off the lights.

It was nine at night and Donna was walking. She kept to well-lit areas, and she wasn't ashamed to ask for money. Not any more. People could always say no, and mostly they did.

There was nothing familiar about the woman on the street corner. If there had been, Donna wouldn't have approached her. It was her nightmare, someone from Biddenden seeing her like this: the shame, and the fear that they'd tell her mum (who never said much, who only said 'good riddance' when she heard Gran had died) and then her mum would tell her dad, and he might just come down here and look for her, and try to bring her home. And that would break her. She didn't ever want to see him again.

The woman on the corner had stopped, puzzled, and was looking around as if she was lost. Lost people were sometimes good for change, if you could tell them the way to where they wanted to go.

Donna stepped closer, and said, 'Spare any change?'

The woman looked down at her. And then the expression on her face changed and she looked like . . . Donna understood the cliché then, understood why people would say *She looked like she had seen a ghost.* She did. The woman said, '*You?*'

'Me?' said Donna. If she had recognised the woman she might have backed away, she might even have run off, but she didn't know her. The woman looked a little like Donna's mum, but kinder, softer, plump where Donna's mum was pinched. It was hard to see what she really looked like because she was wearing thick black winter clothes, and a thick woollen bobble hat, but her hair beneath the hat was as orange as Donna's own.

The woman said, 'Donna.' Donna would have run then, but she didn't, she stayed where she was because it was just too crazy, too unlikely, too ridiculous for words.

The woman said, 'Oh god. Donna. You are you, aren't you? I remember.' Then she stopped. She seemed to be blinking back tears.

Donna looked at the woman, as an unlikely, ridiculous idea filled her head, and she said, 'Are you who I think you are?'

The woman nodded. 'I'm you,' she said. 'Or I will be. One day. I was walking this way remembering what it was like back when I . . . when you . . .' Again she stopped. 'Listen. It won't be like this for you forever. Or even for very long. Just don't do anything stupid. And don't do anything permanent. I promise it will be all right. Like the YouTube videos, you know? *It Gets Better.*'

'What's a you tube?' asked Donna.

'Oh, lovey,' said the woman. And she put her arms around Donna and pulled her close and held her tight.

'Will you take me home with you?' asked Donna.

'I can't,' said the woman. 'Home isn't there for you yet. You haven't met any of the people who are going to help you get off the street, or help you get a job. You haven't met the person who's going to turn out to be your partner. And you'll both make a place that's safe, for each other and for your children. Somewhere warm.'

Donna felt the anger rising inside her. 'Why are you telling me this?' she asked.

'So you know it gets better. To give you hope.'

Donna stepped back. 'I don't want hope,' she said. 'I want somewhere warm. I want a home. I want it now. Not in twenty years.'

A hurt expression on the placid face. 'It's sooner than twen—'

'I don't *care*! It's not tonight. I don't have anywhere to go. And I'm *cold*. Have you got any change?'

The woman nodded. 'Here,' she said. She opened her purse and took out a twenty-pound note. Donna took it, but the money didn't look like any currency she was familiar with. She looked back at the woman to ask her something, but she was gone, and when Donna looked back at her hand, so was the money.

She stood there shivering. The money was gone, if it had ever been there. But she had kept one thing: she knew it would all work out someday. In the end. And she knew that she didn't need to do anything stupid. She didn't have to buy one last Underground ticket just to be able to jump down onto the tracks when she saw a train coming, too close to stop.

The winter wind was bitter, and it bit her and it cut her to the bone, but still, she spotted something blown up against a shop doorway, and she reached down and picked it up: a five-pound note. Perhaps tomorrow would be easier. She didn't have to do any of the things she had imagined herself doing.

December could be lethal, when you were out on the streets. But not this year. Not tonight.

The Case of Death and Honey

I t was a mystery in those parts for years what had happened to the old white ghost man, the barbarian with his huge shoulder-bag. There were some who supposed him to have been murdered, and, later, they dug up the floor of Old Gao's little shack high on the hillside, looking for treasure, but they found nothing but ash and fire-blackened tin trays.

This was after Old Gao himself had vanished, you understand, and before his son came back from Lijiang to take over the beehives on the hill.

* * *

This is the problem, *wrote Holmes in 1899*: Ennui. And lack of interest. Or rather, it all becomes too easy. When the joy of solving crimes is the challenge, the possibility that you cannot, why then the crimes have something to hold your attention. But when each crime is soluble, and so easily soluble at that, why then there is no point in solving them.

Look: this man has been murdered. Well then, someone murdered him. He was murdered for one or more of a tiny handful of reasons: he inconvenienced someone, or he had something that someone wanted, or he had angered someone. Where is the challenge in that?

I would read in the dailies an account of a crime that had the police baffled, and I would find that I had solved it, in broad strokes if not in detail, before I had finished the article. Crime is too soluble. It dissolves. Why call the police and tell them the answers to their mysteries? I leave it, over and over again, as a challenge for them, as it is no challenge for me.

I am only alive when I perceive a challenge.

* * *

The bees of the misty hills, hills so high that they were sometimes called a mountain, were humming in the pale summer sun as they moved from spring flower to spring flower on the slope. Old Gao listened to them without pleasure. His cousin, in the village across the valley, had many dozens of hives, all of them already filling with honey, even this early in the year; also, the honey was as white as snow-jade. Old Gao did not believe that the white honey tasted any better than the yellow or light-brown honey that his own bees produced, although his bees produced it in meagre quantities, but his cousin could sell his white honey for twice what Old Gao could get for the best honey he had.

On his cousin's side of the hill, the bees were earnest, hardworking, golden-brown workers, who brought pollen and nectar back to the hives in enormous quantities. Old Gao's bees were ill-tempered and black, shiny as bullets, who produced as much honey as they needed to get through the winter and only a little more: enough for Old Gao to sell from door to door, to his fellow villagers, one small lump of honeycomb at a time. He would charge more for the brood-comb, filled with bee-larvae, sweet-tasting morsels of protein, when he had brood-comb to sell, which was rarely, for the bees were angry and sullen and every-thing they did, they did as little as possible, including make more bees, and Old Gao was always aware that each piece of brood-comb he sold were bees he would not have to make honey for him to sell later in the year.

Old Gao was as sullen and as sharp as his bees. He had had a wife once, but she had died in childbirth. The son who had killed her lived for a week, then died himself. There would be nobody to say the funeral rites for Old Gao, no one to clean his grave for festivals or to put offerings upon it. He would die unremembered, as unremarkable and as unremarked as his bees.

The old white stranger came over the mountains in late spring of that year, as soon as the roads were passable, with a huge brown bag strapped to his shoulders. Old Gao heard about him before he met him.

'There is a barbarian who is looking at bees,' said his cousin.

Old Gao said nothing. He had gone to his cousin to buy a pailful of second-rate comb, damaged or uncapped and liable soon to spoil. He bought it cheaply to feed to his own bees, and if he sold some of it in his own village, no one was any the wiser. The two men were drinking tea in Gao's cousin's hut on the hillside. From late spring, when the first honey started to flow, until first frost, Gao's cousin left his house in the village and went to live in the hut on the hillside, to live and to sleep beside his beehives, for fear of thieves. His wife and his children would take the honeycomb and the bottles of snow-white honey down the hill to sell.

Old Gao was not afraid of thieves. The shiny black bees of Old Gao's hives would have no mercy on anyone who disturbed them. He slept in his village, unless it was time to collect the honey.

'I will send him to you,' said Gao's cousin. 'Answer his questions, show him your bees and he will pay you.'

'He speaks our tongue?'

'His dialect is atrocious. He said he learned to speak from sailors, and they were mostly Cantonese. But he learns fast, although he is old.'

Old Gao grunted, uninterested in sailors. It was late in the morning, and there was still four hours' walking across the valley to his village, in the heat of the day. He finished his tea. His cousin drank finer tea than Old Gao had ever been able to afford.

He reached his hives while it was still light, put the majority of the uncapped honey into his weakest hives. He had eleven hives. His cousin had over a hundred. Old Gao was stung twice doing this, on the back of the hand and the back of the neck. He had been stung over a thousand times in his life. He could not have told you how many times. He barely noticed the stings of other bees, but the stings of his own black bees always hurt, even if they no longer swelled or burned.

The next day a boy came to Old Gao's house in the village, to tell him that there was someone – and that the someone was a giant foreigner – who was asking for him. Old Gao simply grunted. He walked across the village with the boy at his steady pace, while the boy ran ahead, and soon was lost to sight.

Old Gao found the stranger sitting drinking tea on the porch of the Widow Zhang's house. Old Gao had known the Widow Zhang's mother, fifty years ago. She had been a friend of his wife. Now she was long dead. He did not believe anyone who had known his wife still lived. The Widow Zhang fetched Old Gao tea, introduced him to the elderly barbarian, who had removed his bag and sat beside the small table.

They sipped their tea. The barbarian said, 'I wish to see your bees.'

***

Mycroft's death was the end of Empire, and no one knew it but the two of us. He lay in that pale room, his only covering a thin white sheet, as if he were already becoming a ghost from the popular imagination, and needed only eyeholes in the sheet to finish the impression.

I had imagined that his illness might have wasted him away, but he seemed huger than ever, his fingers swollen into white suet sausages.

I said, 'Good evening, Mycroft. Doctor Hopkins tells me you have two weeks to live, and stated that I was under no circumstances to inform you of this.'

'The man's a dunderhead,' said Mycroft, his breath coming in huge wheezes between the words. 'I will not make it to Friday.'

'Saturday at least,' I said.

'You always were an optimist. No, Thursday evening and then I shall be nothing more than an exercise in practical geometry for Hopkins and the funeral directors at Snigsby and Malterson, who will have the challenge, given the narrowness of the doors and corridors, of getting my carcass out of this room and out of the building.'

'I had wondered,' I said. 'Particularly given the staircase. But they will take out the window-frame and lower you to the street like a grand piano.'

Mycroft snorted at that. Then, 'I am fifty-four years old, Sherlock. In my head is the British government. Not the ballot and hustings nonsense, but the business of the thing. There is no one else knows what the troop movements in the hills of Afghanistan have to do with the desolate shores of North Wales, no one else who sees the whole picture. Can you imagine the mess that this lot and their children will make of Indian Independence?'

I had not previously given any thought to the matter. '*Will* it become independent?'

'Inevitably. In thirty years, at the outside. I have written several recent memoranda on the topic. As I have on so many other subjects. There are memoranda on the Russian Revolution – that'll be along within the decade I'll wager – and on the German problem and . . . oh, so many others. Not that I expect them to be read or understood.' Another wheeze. My brother's lungs rattled like the windows in an empty house. 'You know, if I were to live, the British Empire might last another thousand years, bringing peace and improvement to the world.'

In the past, especially when I was a boy, whenever I heard Mycroft make a grandiose pronouncement like that I would say something to bait him. But not now, not on his deathbed. And also I was certain that he was not speaking of the Empire as it was, a flawed and fallible construct of flawed and fallible people, but of a British Empire that existed only in his head, a glorious force for civilisation and universal prosperity.

I do not, and did not, believe in empires. But I believed in Mycroft.

Mycroft Holmes. Four-and-fifty years of age. He had seen in the new century but the Queen would still outlive him by several months. She was more than thirty years older than he was, and in every way a tough old bird. I wondered to myself whether this unfortunate end might have been avoided.

Mycroft said, 'You are right of course, Sherlock. Had I forced myself to exercise. Had I lived on birdseed and cabbages instead of porterhouse steak. Had I taken up country dancing along with a wife and a puppy and in all other ways behaved contrary to my nature, I might have bought myself another dozen or so years. But what is that in the scheme of things? Little enough. And sooner or later, I would enter my dotage. No. I am of the opinion that it would take two hundred years to train a functioning civil service, let alone a secret service . . .'

I had said nothing.

The pale room had no decorations on the wall of any kind. None of Mycroft's citations. No illustrations, photographs or paintings. I compared his austere digs to my own cluttered rooms in Baker Street and I wondered, not for the first time, at Mycroft's mind. He needed nothing on the outside, for it was all on the inside – everything he had seen, everything he had experienced, everything he had read. He could close his eyes and walk through the National Gallery, or browse the British Museum Reading Room – or, more likely, compare intelligence reports from the edge of the Empire with the price of wool in Wigan and the unemployment statistics in Hove, and then, from this and only this, order a man promoted or a traitor's quiet death.

Mycroft wheezed enormously, and then he said, 'It is a crime, Sherlock.'

'I beg your pardon?'

'A crime. It is a crime, my brother, as heinous and as monstrous as any of the penny-dreadful massacres you have investigated. A crime against the world, against nature, against order.'

'I must confess, my dear fellow, that I do not entirely follow you. What is a crime?'

'My death,' said Mycroft, 'in the specific. And Death in general.' He looked into my eyes. 'I mean it,' he said. 'Now isn't *that* a crime worth investigating, Sherlock, old fellow? One that might keep your attention for longer than it will take you to establish that the poor fellow who used to conduct the brass band in Hyde Park was murdered by the third cornet using a preparation of strychnine.'

'Arsenic,' I corrected him, almost automatically.

'I think you will find,' wheezed Mycroft, 'that the arsenic, while present, had in fact fallen in flakes from the green-painted bandstand itself onto his supper. Symptoms of arsenical poison a complete red herring. No, it was strychnine that did for the poor fellow.'

Mycroft said no more to me that day or ever. He breathed his last the following Thursday, late in the afternoon, and on the Friday the worthies of Snigsby and Malterson removed the casing from the window of the pale room, and lowered my brother's remains into the street, like a grand piano.

His funeral service was attended by me, by my friend Watson, by our cousin Harriet and, in accordance with Mycroft's express wishes – by no one else. The Civil Service, the Foreign Office, even the Diogenes Club – these institutions and their representatives were absent. Mycroft had been reclusive in life; he was to be equally as reclusive in death. So it was the three of us, and the parson, who had not known my brother, and had no conception that it was the more omniscient arm of the British government itself that he was consigning to the grave.

Four burly men held fast to the ropes and lowered my brother's remains to their final resting place, and did, I daresay, their utmost not to curse at the weight of the thing. I tipped each of them half a crown.

Mycroft was dead at fifty-four, and, as they lowered him into his grave, in my imagination I could still hear his clipped, grey wheeze as he seemed to be saying, 'Now *there* is a crime worth investigating.'

***

The stranger's accent was not too bad, although his vocabulary was limited, but he seemed to be talking in the local dialect, or something near to it. He was a fast learner. Old Gao hawked and spat into the dust of the street. He said nothing. He did not wish to take the stranger up the hillside; he did not wish to disturb his bees. In Old Gao's experience, the less he bothered his bees, the better they did. And if they stung the barbarian, what then?

The stranger's hair was silver–white, and sparse; his nose, the first barbarian nose that Old Gao had seen, was huge and curved and put Old Gao in mind of the beak of an eagle; his skin was tanned the same colour as Old Gao's own, and was lined deeply. Old Gao was not certain that he could read a barbarian's face as he could read the face of a person, but he thought the man seemed most serious and, perhaps, unhappy.

'Why?'

'I study bees. Your brother tells me you have big black bees here. Unusual bees.'

Old Gao shrugged. He did not correct the man on the relationship with his cousin.

The stranger asked Old Gao if he had eaten, and when Gao said that he had not the stranger asked the Widow Zhang to bring them soup and rice and whatever was good that she had in her kitchen, which turned out to be a stew of black tree-fungus and vegetables and tiny transparent river-fish, little bigger than tadpoles. The two men ate in silence. When they had finished eating, the stranger said, 'I would be honoured if you would show me your bees.'

Old Gao said nothing, but the stranger paid Widow Zhang well and he put his bag on his back. Then he waited, and, when Old Gao began to walk, the stranger followed him. He carried his bag as if it weighed nothing to him. He was strong for an old man, thought Old Gao, and wondered whether all such barbarians were so strong.

'Where are you from?'

'England,' said the stranger.

Old Gao remembered his father telling him about a war with the English, over trade and over opium, but that was long ago.

They walked up the hillside, that was, perhaps, a moun-tainside. It was steep, and the hillside was too rocky to be cut into fields. Old Gao tested the stranger's pace, walking faster than usual, and the stranger kept up with him, with his pack on his back.

The stranger stopped several times, however. He stopped to examine flowers – the small white flowers that bloomed in early spring elsewhere in the valley, but in late spring here on the side of the hill. There was a bee on one of the flowers, and the stranger knelt and observed it. Then he reached into his pocket, produced a large magnifying glass and examined the bee through it, and made notes in a small pocket notebook, in an incomprehensible writing.

Old Gao had never seen a magnifying glass before, and he leaned in to look at the bee, so black and so strong and so very different from the bees elsewhere in that valley.

'One of your bees?'

'Yes,' said Old Gao. 'Or one like it.'

'Then we shall let her find her own way home,' said the stranger, and he did not disturb the bee, and he put away the magnifying glass.

* * *

The Croft
East Dene, Sussex
11th August, 1922

My dear Watson,

I have taken our discussion of this afternoon to heart, considered it carefully, and am prepared to modify my previous opinions.

I am amenable to your publishing your account of the incidents of 1903, specifically of the final case before my retirement, under the following condition.

In addition to the usual changes that you would make to disguise actual people and places, I would suggest that you replace the entire scenario we encountered (I speak of Professor Presbury's garden. I shall not write of it further here) with monkey glands, or some such extract from the testes of an ape or lemur, sent by some foreign mystery-man. Perhaps the monkey-extract could have the effect of making Professor Presbury move like an ape – he could be some kind of 'creeping man', perhaps? – or possibly make him able to clamber up the sides of buildings and up trees. Perhaps he could grow a tail, but this might be too fanciful even for you, Watson, although no more fanciful than many of the rococo additions you have made in your histories to otherwise humdrum events in my life and work.

In addition, I have written the following speech, to be delivered by myself, at the end of your narrative. Please make certain that something much like this is there, in which I inveigh against living too long, and the foolish urges that push foolish people to do foolish things to prolong their foolish lives.

There is a very real danger to humanity. If one could live forever, if youth were simply there for the taking, that the material, the sensual, the worldly would all prolong their worthless lives. The spiritual would not avoid the call to something higher. It would be the survival of the least fit. What sort of cesspool may not our poor world become?

Something along those lines, I fancy, would set my mind at rest.

Let me see the finished article, please, before you submit it to be published.

I remain, old friend, your most obedient servant,

Sherlock Holmes

* * *

They reached Old Gao's bees late in the afternoon. The beehives were grey wooden boxes piled behind a structure so simple it could barely be called a shack. Four posts, a roof, and hangings of oiled cloth that served to keep out the worst of the spring rains and the summer storms. A small charcoal brazier served for warmth, if you placed a blanket over it and yourself, and to cook upon; a wooden pallet in the centre of the structure, with an ancient ceramic pillow, served as a bed on the occasions that Old Gao slept up on the mountainside with the bees, particularly in the autumn, when he harvested most of the honey. There was little enough of it compared to the output of his cousin's hives, but it was enough that he would sometimes spend two or three days waiting for the comb that he had crushed and stirred into a slurry to drain through the cloth into the buckets and pots that he had carried up the mountainside. He would melt the remainder, the sticky wax and bits of pollen and dirt and bee slurry, in a pot, to extract the beeswax, and he would give the sweet water back to the bees. Then he would carry the honey and the wax blocks down the hill to the village to sell.

He showed the barbarian stranger the eleven hives, watched impassively as the stranger put on a veil and opened a hive, examining first the bees, then the contents of a brood box, and finally the queen, through his magnifying glass. He showed no fear, no discomfort: in everything he did the stranger's movements were gentle and slow, and he was not stung, nor did he crush or hurt a single bee. This impressed Old Gao. He had assumed that barbarians were inscrutable, unreadable, mysterious creatures, but this man seemed overjoyed to have encountered Gao's bees. His eyes were shining.

Old Gao fired up the brazier, to boil some water. Long before the charcoal was hot, however, the stranger had removed from his bag a contraption of glass and metal. He had filled the upper half of it with water from the stream, lit a flame, and soon a kettleful of water was steaming and bubbling. Then the stranger took two tin mugs from his bag, and some green tea leaves wrapped in paper, and dropped the leaves into the mug, and poured on the water.

It was the finest tea that Old Gao had ever drunk: better by far than his cousin's tea. They drank it cross-legged on the floor.

'I would like to stay here for the summer, in this house,' said the stranger.

'Here? This is not even a house,' said Old Gao. 'Stay down in the village. Widow Zhang has a room.'

'I will stay here,' said the stranger. 'Also I would like to rent one of your beehives.'

Old Gao had not laughed in years. There were those in the village who would have thought such a thing impossible. But still, he laughed then, a guffaw of surprise and amusement that seemed to have been jerked out of him.

'I am serious,' said the stranger. He placed four silver coins on the ground between them. Old Gao had not seen where he got them from: three silver Mexican pesos, a coin that had become popular in China years before, and a large silver yuan. It was as much money as Old Gao might see in a year of selling honey. 'For this money,' said the stranger, 'I would like someone to bring me food: every three days should suffice.'

Old Gao said nothing. He finished his tea and stood up. He pushed through the oiled cloth to the clearing high on the hillside. He walked over to the eleven hives: each consisted of two brood boxes with one, two, three or, in one case, even four boxes above that. He took the stranger to the hive with four boxes above it, each box filled with frames of comb.

'This hive is yours,' he said.

* * *

They were plant extracts. That was obvious. They worked, in their way, for a limited time, but they were also extremely poisonous. But watching poor Professor Presbury during those final days – his skin, his eyes, his gait – had convinced me that he had not been on entirely the wrong path.

I took his case of seeds, of pods, of roots, and of dried extracts and I thought. I pondered. I cogitated. I reflected. It was an intellectual problem, and could be solved, as my old maths tutor had always sought to demonstrate to me, by intellect.

They were plant extracts, and they were lethal.

Methods I used to render them nonlethal rendered them quite ineffective.

It was not a three-pipe problem. I suspect it was something approaching a three-hundred-pipe problem before I hit upon an initial idea – a notion perhaps – of a way of processing the plants that might allow them to be ingested by human beings.

It was not a line of investigation that could easily be followed in Baker Street. So it was, in the autumn of 1903, that I moved to Sussex, and spent the winter reading every book and pamphlet and monograph so far published, I fancy, upon the care and keeping of bees. And so it was that in early April of 1904, armed only with theoretical knowledge, I took delivery from a local farmer of my first package of bees.

I wonder, sometimes, that Watson did not suspect anything. Then again, Watson's glorious obtuseness has never ceased to surprise me, and sometimes, indeed, I had relied upon it. Still, he knew what I was like when I had no work to occupy my mind, no case to solve. He knew my lassitude, my black moods when I had no case to occupy me.

So how could he believe that I had truly retired? He knew my methods.

Indeed, Watson was there when I took receipt of my first bees. He watched, from a safe distance, as I poured the bees from the package into the empty, waiting hive, like slow, gently humming treacle.

He saw my excitement, and he saw nothing.

And the years passed, and we watched the Empire crumble, we watched the government unable to govern, we watched those poor heroic boys sent to the trenches of Flanders to die, all these things confirmed me in my opinions. I was not doing the right thing. I was doing the only thing.

As my face grew unfamiliar, and my finger joints swelled and ached (not so much as they might have done, though, which I attributed to the many bee stings I had received in my first few years as an investigative apiarist) and as Watson, dear, brave, obtuse Watson, faded with time and paled and shrank, his skin becoming greyer, his moustache becoming the same shade of grey as his skin, my resolve to conclude my researches did not diminish. If anything, it increased.

So: my initial hypotheses were tested upon the South Downs, in an apiary of my own devising, each hive modelled upon Langstroth's. I do believe that I made every mistake that ever a novice beekeeper could or has ever made, and in addition, due to my investigations, an entire hiveful of mistakes that no beekeeper has ever made before, or shall, I trust, ever make again. *The Case of the Poisoned Beehive,* Watson might have called many of them, although *The Mystery of the Transfixed Women's Institute* would have drawn more attention to my researches, had anyone been interested enough to investigate. (As it was, I chided Mrs Telford for simply taking a jar of honey from the shelves here without consulting me, and I ensured that, in the future, she was given several jars for her cooking from the more regular hives, and that honey from the experimental hives was locked away once it had been collected. I do not believe that this ever drew comment.)

I experimented with Dutch bees, with German bees and with Italians, with Carniolans and Caucasians. I regretted the loss of our British bees to blight and, even where they had survived, to interbreeding, although I found and worked with a small hive I purchased and grew up from a frame of brood and a queen cell, from an old abbey in St Albans, which seemed to me to be original British breeding stock.

I experimented for the best part of two decades, before I concluded that the bees that I sought, if they existed, were not to be found in England, and would not survive the distances they would need to travel to reach me by international parcel post. I needed to examine bees in India. I needed to travel perhaps further afield than that.

I have a smattering of languages.

I had my flower-seeds, and my extracts and tinctures in syrup. I needed nothing more.

I packed them up, arranged for the cottage on the Downs to be cleaned and aired once a week, and for Master Wilkins – to whom I am afraid I had developed the habit of referring, to his obvious distress, as 'Young Villikins' – to inspect the beehives, and to harvest and sell surplus honey in Eastbourne market, and to prepare the hives for winter.

I told them I did not know when I should be back.

I am an old man. Perhaps they did not expect me to return.

And, if this was indeed the case, they would, strictly speaking, have been right.

* * *

Old Gao was impressed, despite himself. He had lived his life among bees. Still, watching the stranger shake the bees from the boxes, with a practised flick of his wrist, so cleanly and so sharply that the black bees seemed more surprised than angered, and simply flew or crawled back into their hive, was remarkable. The stranger then stacked the boxes filled with comb on top of one of the weaker hives, so Old Gao would still have the honey from the hive the stranger was renting.

So it was that Old Gao gained a lodger.

Old Gao gave the Widow Zhang's granddaughter a few coins to take the stranger food three times a week – mostly rice and vegetables, along with an earthenware pot filled, when she left at least, with boiling soup.

Every ten days Old Gao would walk up the hill himself. He went initially to check on the hives, but soon discovered that under the stranger's care all eleven hives were thriving as they had never thrived before. And indeed, there was now a twelfth hive, from a captured swarm of the black bees the stranger had encountered while on a walk along the hill.

Old Gao brought wood, the next time he came up to the shack, and he and the stranger spent several afternoons wordlessly working together, making extra boxes to go on the hives, building frames to fill the boxes.

One evening the stranger told Old Gao that the frames they were making had been invented by an American, only seventy years before. This seemed like nonsense to Old Gao, who made frames as his father had, and as they did across the valley, and as, he was certain, his grandfather and his grandfather's grandfather had, but he said nothing.

He enjoyed the stranger's company. They made hives together, and Old Gao wished that the stranger was a younger man. Then he would stay there for a long time, and Old Gao would have someone to leave his beehives to, when he died. But they were two old men, nailing boxes together, with thin frosty hair and old faces, and neither of them would see another dozen winters.

Old Gao noticed that the stranger had planted a small, neat garden beside the hive that he had claimed as his own, which he had moved away from the rest of the hives. He had covered it with a net. He had also created a 'back door' to the hive, so that the only bees that could reach the plants came from the hive that he was renting. Old Gao also observed that, beneath the netting, there were several trays filled with what appeared to be sugar solution of some kind, one coloured bright red, one green, one a startling blue, one yellow. He pointed to them, but all the stranger did was nod and smile.

The bees were lapping up the syrups, though, clustering and crowding on the sides of the tin dishes with their tongues down, eating until they could eat no more, and then returning to the hive.

The stranger had made sketches of Old Gao's bees. He showed the sketches to Old Gao, tried to explain the ways that Old Gao's bees differed from other honeybees, talked of ancient bees preserved in stone for millions of years, but here the stranger's Chinese failed him, and, truthfully, Old Gao was not interested. They were his bees, until he died, and after that, they were the bees of the mountainside. He had brought other bees here, but they had sickened and died, or been killed in raids by the black bees, who took their honey and left them to starve.

The last of these visits was in late summer. Old Gao went down the mountainside. He did not see the stranger again.

* * *

It is done.

It works. Already I feel a strange combination of triumph and of disappointment, as if of defeat, or of distant storm clouds teasing at my senses.

It is strange to look at my hands and to see, not my hands as I know them, but the hands I remember from my younger days: knuckles unswollen, dark hairs, not snow-white, on the backs.

It was a quest that had defeated so many, a problem with no apparent solution. The first emperor of China died and nearly destroyed his empire in pursuit of it, three thousand years ago, and all it took me was, what, twenty years?

I do not know if I did the right thing or not (although any 'retirement' without such an occupation would have been, literally, maddening). I took the commission from Mycroft. I investigated the problem. I arrived, inevitably, at the solution.

Will I tell the world? I will not.

And yet, I have half a pot of dark brown honey remaining in my bag; a half a pot of honey that is worth more than nations. (I was tempted to write, *worth more than all the tea in China*, perhaps because of my current situation, but fear that even Watson would deride it as cliché.)

And speaking of Watson . . .

There is one thing left to do. My only remaining goal, and it is small enough. I shall make my way to Shanghai, and from there I shall take ship to Southampton, a half a world away.

And once I am there, I shall seek out Watson, if he still lives – and I fancy he does. It is irrational, I acknowledge, and yet I am certain that I would know, somehow, had Watson passed beyond the veil.

I shall buy theatrical makeup, disguise myself as an old man, so as not to startle him, and I shall invite my old friend over for tea.

There will be honey on buttered toast served with the tea that afternoon, I fancy.

* * *

There were tales of a barbarian who passed through the village on his way east, but the people who told Old Gao this did not believe that it could have been the same man who had lived in Gao's shack. This one was young and proud, and his hair was dark. It was not the old man who had walked through those parts in the spring, although, one person told Gao, the bag was similar.

Old Gao walked up the mountainside to investigate, although he suspected what he would find before he got there.

The stranger was gone, and the stranger's bag.

There had been much burning, though. That was clear. Papers had been burnt – Old Gao recognised the edge of a drawing the stranger had made of one of his bees, but the rest of the papers were ash, or blackened beyond recognition, even had Old Gao been able to read barbarian writing. The papers were not the only things to have been burnt; parts of the hive that stranger had rented were now only twisted ash; there were blackened, twisted strips of tin that might once have contained brightly coloured syrups.

The colour was added to the syrups, the stranger had told him once, so that he could tell them apart, although for what purpose Old Gao had never inquired.

He examined the shack like a detective, searching for a clue as to the stranger's nature or his whereabouts. On the ceramic pillow four silver coins had been left for him to find – two yuan coins and two silver pesos – and he put them away.

Behind the shack he found a heap of used slurry, with the last bees of the day still crawling upon it, tasting whatever sweetness was still on the surface of the still-sticky wax.

Old Gao thought long and hard before he gathered up the slurry, wrapped it loosely in cloth, and put it in a pot, which he filled with water. He heated the water on the brazier, but did not let it boil. Soon enough the wax floated to the surface, leaving the dead bees and the dirt and the pollen and the propolis inside the cloth.

He let it cool.

Then he walked outside, and he stared up at the moon. It was almost full.

He wondered how many villagers knew that his son had died as a baby. He remembered his wife, but her face was distant, and he had no portraits or photographs of her. He thought that there was nothing he was so suited for on the face of the earth as to keep the black, bullet-like bees on the side of this high, high hill. There was no other man who knew their temperament as he did.

The water had cooled. He lifted the now solid block of beeswax out of the water, placed it on the boards of the bed to finish cooling. Then he took the cloth filled with dirt and impurities out of the pot. And then, because he too was, in his way, a detective, and once you have eliminated the impossible whatever remains, however unlikely, must be the truth, he drank the sweet water in the pot. There is a lot of honey in slurry, after all, even after the majority of it has dripped through a cloth and been purified. The water tasted of honey, but not a honey that Gao had ever tasted before. It tasted of smoke, and metal, and strange flowers, and odd perfumes. It tasted, Gao thought, a little like sex.

He drank it all down, and then he slept, with his head on the ceramic pillow.

When he woke, he thought, he would decide how to deal with his cousin, who would expect to inherit the twelve hives on the hill when Old Gao went missing.

He would be an illegitimate son, perhaps, the young man who would return in the days to come. Or perhaps a son. Young Gao. Who would remember, now? It did not matter.

He would go to the city and then he would return, and he would keep the black bees on the side of the mountain for as long as days and circumstances would allow.

The Man Who Forgot Ray Bradbury

I am forgetting things, which scares me.

I am losing words, although I am not losing concepts. I hope that I am not losing concepts. If I am losing concepts, I am not aware of it. If I am losing concepts, how would I know?

Which is funny, because my memory was always so good. Everything was in there. Sometimes my memory was so good that I even thought that I could remember things I didn't know yet. Remembering forward . . .

I don't think there's a word for that, is there? Remembering things that haven't happened yet. I don't have that feeling I get when I go looking in my head for a word that isn't there, as if someone must have come and taken it in the night.

When I was a young man I lived in a big, shared house. I was a student, then. We had our own shelves in the kitchen, neatly marked with our names, and our own shelves in the fridge, upon which we kept our own eggs, cheese, yogurt, milk. I was always punctilious about using only my own provisions. Others were not so . . . there. I lost a word. One that would mean, 'careful to obey the rules'. The other people in the house were . . . not so. I would go to the fridge, but my eggs would have vanished.

I am thinking of a sky filled with spaceships, so many of them that they seem like a plague of locusts, silver against the luminous mauve of the night.

Things would go missing from my room back then as well. Boots. I remember my boots going. Or 'being gone', I should say, as I did not ever actually catch them in the act of leaving. Boots do not just 'go'. Somebody 'went' them. Just like my big dictionary. Same house, same time period. I went to the small bookshelf beside my bed (everything was by my bed: it was my room, but it was not much larger than a cupboard with a bed in it). I went to the shelf and the dictionary was gone, just a dictionary-sized hole in my shelf to show where my dictionary wasn't.

All the words and the book they came in were gone. Over the next month they also took my radio, a can of shaving foam, a pad of notepaper and a box of pencils. And my yogurt. And, I discovered during a power cut, my candles.

Now I am thinking of a boy with new tennis shoes, who believes he can run forever. No, that is not giving it to me. A dry town in which it rained forever. A road through the desert, on which good people see a mirage. A dinosaur that is a movie producer. The mirage was the pleasure dome of Kublai Khan. No . . .

Sometimes when the words go away I can find them by creeping up on them from another direction. Say I go and look for a word – I am discussing the inhabitants of the planet Mars, say, and I realise that the word for them has gone. I might also realise that the missing word occurs in a sentence or a title. The _____ Chronicles. My Favourite _____. If that does not give it to me I circle the idea. Little green men, I think, or tall, dark-skinned, gentle: dark they were and golden-eyed . . . and suddenly the word *Martians* is waiting for me, like a friend or a lover at the end of a long day.

I left that house when my radio went. It was too wearing, the slow disappearance of the things I had thought so safely mine, item by item, thing by thing, object by object, word by word.

When I was twelve I was told a story by an old man that I have never forgotten.

A poor man found himself in a forest as night fell, and he had no prayer book to say his evening prayers. So he said, 'God who knows all things, I have no prayer book and I do not know any prayers by heart. But you know all the prayers. You are God. So this is what I am going to do. I am going to say the alphabet, and I will let you put the words together.'

There are things missing from my mind, and it scares me.

Icarus! It's not as if I have forgotten all names. I remember Icarus. He flew too close to the sun. In the stories, though, it's worth it. Always worth it to have tried, even if you fail, even if you fall like a meteor forever. Better to have flamed in the darkness, to have inspired others, to have *lived*, than to have sat in the darkness, cursing the people who borrowed, but did not return, your candle.

I have lost people, though.

It's strange when it happens. I don't actually *lose* them. Not in the way one loses one's parents, either as a small child, when you think you are holding your mother's hand in a crowd and then you look up, and it's not your mother . . . or later. When you have to find the words to describe them at a funeral service or a memorial, or when you are scattering ashes on a garden of flowers or into the sea.

I sometimes imagine I would like my ashes to be scattered in a library. But then the librarians would just have to come in early the next morning to sweep them up again, before the people got there.

I would like my ashes scattered in a library or, possibly, a funfair. A 1930s funfair, where you ride the black . . . the black . . . the . . .

I have lost the word. Carousel? Roller coaster? The thing you ride, and you become young again. The Ferris wheel. Yes. There is another carnival that comes to town as well, bringing evil. 'By the pricking of my thumbs . . .'

Shakespeare.

I remember Shakespeare, and I remember his name, and who he was and what he wrote. He's safe for now. Perhaps there are people who forget Shakespeare. They would have to talk about 'the man who wrote to be or not to be' – not the film, starring Jack Benny, whose real name was Benjamin Kubelsky, who was raised in Waukegan, Illinois, an hour or so outside Chicago. Waukegan, Illinois, was later immortalised as Green Town, Illinois, in a series of stories and books by an American author who left Waukegan and went to live in Los Angeles. I mean, of course, the man I am thinking of. I can see him in my head when I close my eyes.

I used to look at his photographs on the back of his books. He looked mild and he looked wise, and he looked kind.

He wrote a story about Poe, to stop Poe being forgotten, about a future where they burn books and they forget them, and in the story we are on Mars although we might as well be in Waukegan or Los Angeles, as critics, as those who would repress or forget books, as those who would take the words, all the words, dictionaries and radios full of words, as those people are walked through a house and murdered, one by one, by orangutan, by pit and pendulum, for the love of God, Montressor . . .

Poe. I know Poe. And Montressor. And Benjamin Kubelsky and his wife, Sadie Marks, who was no relation to the Marx Brothers and who performed as Mary Livingstone. All these names in my head.

I was twelve.

I had read the books, I had seen the film, and the burning point of paper was the moment where I knew that I would have to remember this. Because people would have to remember books, if other people burn them or forget them. We will commit them to memory. We will become them. We become authors. We become their books.

I am sorry. I lost something there. Like a path I was walking that dead-ended, and now I am alone and lost in the forest, and I am here and I do not know where here is any more.

You must learn a Shakespeare play: I will think of you as *Titus Andronicus*. Or *you*, whoever you are, you could learn an Agatha Christie novel: you will be *Murder on the Orient Express*. Someone else can learn the poems of John Wilmot, Earl of Rochester, and you, whoever you are reading this, can learn a Dickens book and when I want to know what happened to Barnaby Rudge I will come to you. You can tell me.

And the people who would burn the words, the people who would take the books from the shelves, the firemen and the ignorant, the ones afraid of tales and words and dreams and Hallowe'en and people who have tattooed themselves with stories and Boys! You Can Grow Mushrooms in Your Cellar! and as long as your words which are people which are days which are my life, as long as your words survive, then you lived and you mattered and you changed the world and I cannot remember your name.

I learned your books. Burned them into my mind. In case the firemen come to town.

But who you are is gone. I wait for it to return to me. Just as I waited for my dictionary or for my radio, or for my boots, and with as meagre a result.

All I have left is the space in my mind where you used to be.

And I am not so certain about even that.

I was talking to a friend. And I said, 'Are these stories familiar to you?' I told him all the words I knew, the ones about the monsters coming home to the house with the human child in it, the ones about the lightning salesman and the wicked carnival that followed him, and the Martians and their fallen glass cities and their perfect canals. I told him all the words, and he said he hadn't heard of them. That they didn't exist.

And I worry.

I worry I was keeping them alive. Like the people in the snow at the end of the story, walking backwards and forwards, remembering, repeating the words of the stories, making them real.

I think it's God's fault.

I mean, he can't be expected to remember everything, God can't. Busy chap. So perhaps he delegates things, sometimes, just goes, 'You! I want you to remember the dates of the Hundred Years' War. And you, you remember okapi. You, remember Jack Benny who was Benjamin Kubelsky from Waukegan, Illinois.' And then, when you forget the things that God has charged you with remembering, bam. No more okapi. Just an okapi-shaped hole in the world, which is halfway between an antelope and a giraffe. No more Jack Benny. No more Waukegan. Just a hole in your mind where a person or a concept used to be.

I don't know.

I don't know where to look. Have I lost an author, just as once I lost a dictionary? Or worse: did God give me this one small task, and now I have failed him, and because I have forgotten him he has gone from the shelves, gone from the reference works, and now he only exists in our dreams . . .

My dreams. I do not know your dreams. Perhaps you do not dream of a veldt that is only wallpaper but that eats two children. Perhaps you do not know that Mars is heaven, where our beloved dead go to wait for us, then consume us in the night. You do not dream of a man arrested for the crime of being a pedestrian.

I dream these things.

If he existed, then I have lost him. Lost his name. Lost his book titles, one by one by one. Lost the stories.

And I fear that I am going mad, for I cannot just be growing old.

If I have failed in this one task, oh God, then only let me do this thing, that you may give the stories back to the world.

Because, perhaps, if this works, they will remember him. All of them will remember him. His name will once more become synonymous with small American towns at Hallowe'en, when the leaves skitter across the sidewalk like frightened birds, or with Mars, or with love. And my name will be forgotten.

I am willing to pay that price, if the empty space in the book-shelf of my mind can be filled again, before I go.

Dear God, hear my prayer.

A . . . B . . . C . . . D . . . E . . . F . . . G . . .

Jerusalem

I will not cease from mental fight,
Nor shall my sword sleep in my hand
Till we have built Jerusalem
In England's green and pleasant land.
– WILLIAM BLAKE

Jerusalem, thought Morrison, was like a deep pool, where time had settled too thickly. It had engulfed him, engulfed both of them, and he could feel the pressure of time pushing him up and out. Like swimming down too deep.

He was glad to be out of it.

Tomorrow he would go back to work once more. Work was good. It would give him something to focus on. He turned on the radio and then, mid-song, turned it off.

'I was enjoying that,' said Delores. She was cleaning the fridge before filling it with fresh food.

He said, 'I'm sorry.' He couldn't think straight, with the music playing. He needed the silence.

Morrison closed his eyes and, for a moment, he was back in Jerusalem, feeling the desert heat on his face, staring at the old city and understanding, for the first time, how small it all was. That the real Jerusalem, two thousand years ago, was smaller than an English country town.

Their guide, a lean, leathery woman in her fifties, pointed.

'That's where the sermon on the mount would have been given. That's where Jesus was arrested. He was imprisoned there. Tried before Pilate there, at the far end of the Temple. Crucified on that hill.' She pointed matter-of-factly down the slopes and up again. It was a few hours' walk at most.

Delores took photos. She and their guide had hit it off immediately. Morrison had not wanted to visit Jerusalem. He had wanted to go to Greece for his holidays, but Delores had insisted. Jerusalem was *biblical,* she told him. It was part of history.

They walked through the old town, starting in the Jewish Quarter. Stone steps. Closed shops. Cheap souvenirs. A man walked past them wearing a huge black fur hat, and a thick coat. Morrison winced. 'He must be boiling.'

'It's what they used to wear in Russia,' said the guide. 'They wear it here. The fur hats are for holidays. Some of them wear hats even bigger than that.'

Delores put a cup of tea down in front of him. 'Penny for your thoughts,' she said.

'Remembering the holiday.'

'You don't want to brood on it,' she said. 'Best to let it go. Why don't you take the dog for a nice walk?'

He drank the tea. The dog looked at him expectantly when he went to put the lead on it, as if it were about to say something. 'Come on, boy,' said Morrison.

He went left, down the avenue, heading for the Heath. It was green. Jerusalem had been golden: a city of sand and rock. They walked from the Jewish Quarter to the Muslim Quarter, passing bustling shops piled high with sweet things to eat, with fruits or with bright clothes.

'Then the sheets are gone,' their guide had said to Delores. 'Jerusalem syndrome.'

'Never heard of it,' she said. Then, to Morrison, 'Have you ever heard of it?'

'I was miles away,' said Morrison. 'What does that mean? That door, with all the stencils on it?'

'It welcomes someone back from a pilgrimage to Mecca.'

'There you go,' said Delores. 'For us, it was going to Jerusalem. Someone else goes somewhere else. Even in the Holy Land, there's still pilgrims.'

'Nobody comes to London,' said Morrison. 'Not for that.'

Delores ignored him. 'So, they're gone,' she said to the guide. 'The wife comes back from a shopping trip, or the museum, and there's the sheets gone.'

'Exactly,' said the guide. 'She goes to the front desk, and tells them she does not know where the husband is.'

Delores put her hand around Morrison's arm, as if assuring herself that he was there. 'And where is he?'

'He has Jerusalem syndrome. He is on the street corner, wearing nothing but a toga. That's the sheets. He is preaching – normally about being good, obeying God. Loving each other.'

'Come to Jerusalem and go mad,' said Morrison. 'Not much of an advertising slogan.'

Their guide looked at him sternly. 'It is,' she said, with what Morrison thought might actually be pride, 'the only location-specific mental illness. And it is the only easily curable mental illness. You know what the cure is?'

'Take away their sheets?'

The guide hesitated. Then she smiled. 'Close. You take the person out of Jerusalem. They get better immediately.'

'Afternoon,' said the man at the end of his road. They'd been nodding to each other for eleven years now, and he still had no idea of the man's name. 'Bit of a tan. Been on holiday, have we?'

'Jerusalem,' said Morrison.

'Brr. Wouldn't catch me going there. Get blown up or kidnapped soon as look at you.'

'That didn't happen to us,' said Morrison.

'Still. Safer at home. Eh?'

Morrison hesitated. Then he said, in a rush, 'We went through a youth hostel, down to an underground, um . . .' He lost the word. 'Water storage place. From Herod's time. They stored the rainwater underground, so it wouldn't evaporate. A hundred years ago someone rowed a boat all the way through underground Jerusalem.'

The lost word hovered at the edge of his consciousness like a hole in a dictionary. Two syllables, begins with a C, means deep echoing underground place where they store water.

'Well, then,' said his neighbour.

'Right,' said Morrison.

The Heath was green and it rolled in gentle slopes, interrupted by oak and beech, by chestnut and poplar. He imagined a world in which London was divided, in which London was a city crusaded against, lost and won and lost again, over and over.

Perhaps, he thought, it isn't madness. Perhaps the cracks are just deeper there, or the sky is thin enough that you can hear, when God talks to His prophets. But nobody stops to listen any longer.

'Cistern,' he said, aloud.

The green of the Heath became dry and golden, and the heat burned his skin like the opening of an oven door. It was as if he had never left.

'My feet hurt,' Delores was saying. And then she said, 'I'm going back to the hotel.'

Their guide looked concerned.

'I just want to put my feet up for a bit,' said Delores. 'It's just all so much to take in.'

They were passing the Christ prison shop. It sold souvenirs and carpets. 'I'll bathe my feet. You two carry on without me. Pick me up after lunch.'

Morrison would have argued, but they had hired the guide

for the whole day. Her skin was dark and weathered. She had an extraordinarily white smile, when she smiled. She led him to a café.

'So,' said Morrison. 'Business good?'

'We do not see as many tourists,' she said. 'Not since the intifada began.'

'Delores. My wife. She's always wanted to come here. See the holy sights.'

'We have so many of them here. Whatever you believe. Christian or Muslim or Jew. It's still the Holy City. I've lived here all my life.'

'I suppose you must be looking forward to them sorting all this out,' he said. 'Er. The Palestinian situation. The politics.'

She shrugged. 'It doesn't matter to Jerusalem,' she said. 'The people come. The people believe. Then they kill each other, to prove that God loves them.'

'Well,' he said. 'How would you fix it?'

She smiled her whitest smile. 'Sometimes,' she said, 'I think it would be best if it was bombed. If it was bombed back to a radioactive desert. Then who would want it? But then I think, they would come here and collect the radioactive dust that might contain atoms of the Dome of the Rock, or of the Temple, or a wall that Christ leaned against on his way to the Cross. People would fight over who owns a poisonous desert, if that desert was Jerusalem.'

'You don't like it here?'

'You should be glad there is no Jerusalem where you come from. Nobody wants to partition London. Nobody goes on pilgrimages to the holy city of Liverpool. No prophets walked in Birmingham. Your country is too young. It is still green.'

'England's not young.'

'Here, they still struggle over decisions made two thousand years ago. They have been fighting about who owns this city for over three thousand years, when King David took it in battle from the Jebusites.'

He was drowning in the Time, could feel it crushing him, like an ancient forest being crushed into oil.

She said, 'Do you have any children?'

The question took Morrison by surprise. 'We wanted kids. It didn't work out that way.'

'Is she looking for a miracle, your wife? They do, sometimes.'

'She has . . . faith,' he said. 'I've never believed. But no, I don't think so.' He sipped his coffee. 'So. Um. Are you married?'

'I lost my husband.'

'Was it a bomb?'

'What?'

'How you lost your husband?'

'An American tourist. From Seattle.'

'Oh.'

They finished their coffee. 'Shall we see how your wife's feet are doing?'

As they walked up the narrow street, towards the hotel, Morrison said, 'I'm really lonely. I work at a job I don't enjoy and come home to a wife who loves me but doesn't much like me, and some days it feels like I can't move and that all I want is for the whole world to go away.'

She nodded. 'Yes, but you don't live in Jerusalem.'

The guide waited in the lobby of the hotel while Morrison went up to his room. He was, somehow, not surprised in the least to see that Delores was not in the bedroom, or in the tiny bathroom, and that the sheets that had been on the bed that morning were now gone.

His dog could have walked the Heath forever, but Morrison was getting tired and a fine rain was drizzling. He walked back through a green world. A green and pleasant world, he thought, knowing that wasn't quite it. His head was like a filing cabinet that had fallen downstairs, and all the information in it was jumbled and disordered.

They caught up with his wife on the Via Dolorosa. She wore a sheet, yes, but she seemed intent, not mad. She was calm, frighteningly so.

'Everything is love,' she was telling the people. 'Everything is Jerusalem. God is love. Jerusalem is love.'

A tourist took a photograph, but the locals ignored her. Morrison put his hand on her arm. 'Come on, love,' he said. 'Let's go home.'

She looked through him. He wondered what she was seeing. She said, 'We are home. In this place the walls of the world are thin. We can hear Him calling to us, through the walls. Listen. You can hear Him. Listen!'

Delores did not fight or even protest as they led her back to the hotel. Delores did not look like a prophet. She looked like a woman in her late thirties wearing nothing but a sheet. Morrison suspected that their guide was amused, but when he caught her eyes he could see only concern.

They drove from Jerusalem to Tel Aviv, and it was on the beach in front of their hotel, after sleeping for almost twenty-four hours, that Delores came back, now just slightly confused, with little memory of the previous day. He tried to talk to her about what he had seen, about what she had said, but stopped when he saw it was upsetting her. They pretended that it had not happened, did not mention it again.

Sometimes he wondered what it had felt like inside her head, that day, hearing the voice of God through the golden-coloured stones, but truly, he did not want to know. It was better not to.

It's location-specific. You take the person out of Jerusalem, he thought – wondering, as he had wondered a hundred times in the last few days, if this was truly far enough.

He was glad they were back in England, glad they were home,

where there was not enough Time to crush you, to suffocate you, to make you dust.

Morrison walked back up the avenue in the drizzle, past the trees in the pavement, past the neat front gardens and the summer flowers and the perfect green of the lawns, and he felt cold.

He knew she would be gone before he turned the corner, before he saw the open front door banging in the wind.

He would follow her. And, he thought, almost joyfully, he would find her.

This time he would listen.

Click-Clack the Rattlebag

'Before you take me up to bed, will you tell me a story?'

'Do you actually need me to take you up to bed?' I asked the boy.

He thought for a moment. Then, with intense seriousness, 'Yes, actually I think I do. It's because of, I've finished my home-work, and so it's my bedtime, and I am a bit scared. Not very scared. Just a bit. But it is a very big house, and lots of times the lights don't work and it's sort of dark.'

I reached over and tousled his hair.

'I can understand that,' I said. 'It is a very big old house.' He nodded. We were in the kitchen, where it was light and warm. I put down my magazine on the kitchen table. 'What kind of story would you like me to tell you?'

'Well,' he said, thoughtfully. 'I don't think it should be *too* scary, because then when I go up to bed, I will just be thinking about monsters the whole time. But if it isn't just a *little* bit scary then I won't be interested. And you make up scary stories, don't you? I know she says that's what you do.'

'She exaggerates. I write stories, yes. Nothing that's really been published, yet, though. And I write lots of different kinds of stories.'

'But you *do* write scary stories?'

'Yes.'

The boy looked up at me from the shadows by the door, where

he was waiting. 'Do you know any stories about Click-Clack the Rattlebag?'

'I don't think so.'

'Those are the best sorts of stories.'

'Do they tell them at your school?'

He shrugged. 'Sometimes.'

'What's a Click-Clack the Rattlebag story?'

He was a precocious child, and was unimpressed by his sister's boyfriend's ignorance. You could see it on his face. 'Everybody knows them.'

'I don't,' I said, trying not to smile.

He looked at me as if he was trying to decide whether or not I was pulling his leg. He said, 'I think maybe you should take me up to my bedroom, and then you can tell me a story before I go to sleep, but probably it should be a not-scary story because I'll be up in my bedroom then, and it's actually a bit dark up there, too.'

I said, 'Shall I leave a note for your sister, telling her where we are?'

'You can. But you'll hear when they get back. The front door is very slammy.'

We walked out of the warm and cosy kitchen into the hallway of the big house, where it was chilly and draughty and dark. I flicked the light switch, but the hall remained dark.

'The bulb's gone,' the boy said. 'That always happens.'

Our eyes adjusted to the shadows. The moon was almost full, and blue-white moonlight shone in through the high windows on the staircase, down into the hall. 'We'll be all right,' I said.

'Yes,' said the boy, soberly. 'I am very glad you're here.' He seemed less precocious now. His hand found mine, and he held on to my fingers comfortably, trustingly, as if he'd known me all his life. I felt responsible and adult. I did not know if the feeling I had for his sister, who was my girlfriend, was love, not yet, but I liked that the child treated me as one of the family. I felt like his big brother, and I stood taller, and if there was something unsettling about the empty house I would not have admitted it for worlds.

The stairs creaked beneath the threadbare stair-carpet.

'Click-Clacks,' said the boy, 'are the best monsters ever.'

'Are they from television?'

'I don't think so. I don't think any people know where they come from. Mostly they come from the dark.'

'Good place for a monster to come from.'

'Yes.'

We walked along the upper corridor in the shadows, moving from patch of moonlight to patch of moonlight. It really was a big house. I wished I had a flashlight.

'They come from the dark,' said the boy, holding on to my hand. 'I think probably they're made of dark. And they come in when you don't pay attention. That's when they come in. And then they take you back to their . . . not nests. What's a word that's like *nests,* but not?'

'*House?*'

'No. It's not a house.'

'*Lair?*'

He was silent. Then, 'I think that's the word, yes. *Lair.*' He squeezed my hand. He stopped talking.

'Right. So they take the people who don't pay attention back to their lair. And what do they do then, your monsters? Do they suck all the blood out of you, like vampires?'

He snorted. 'Vampires don't suck all the blood out of you. They only drink a little bit. Just to keep them going, and, you know, flying around. Click-Clacks are much scarier than vampires.'

'I'm not scared of vampires,' I told him.

'Me neither. I'm not scared of vampires either. Do you want to know what Click-Clacks do? They *drink* you,' said the boy.

'Like a Coke?'

'Coke is very bad for you,' said the boy. 'If you put a tooth in Coke, in the morning, it will be dissolved into nothing. That's how bad Coke is for you and why you must always clean your teeth, every night.'

I'd heard the Coke story as a boy, and had been told, as an adult, that it wasn't true, but was certain that a lie which promoted dental hygiene was a good lie, and I let it pass.

'Click-Clacks drink you,' said the boy. 'First they bite you, and then you go all *ishy* inside, and all your meat and all your brains and everything except your bones and your skin turns into a wet, milkshakey stuff and then the Click-Clack sucks it out through the holes where your eyes used to be.'

'That's disgusting,' I told him. 'Did you make it up?'

We'd reached the last flight of stairs, all the way into the big house.

'No.'

'I can't believe you kids make up stuff like that.'

'You didn't ask me about the rattlebag,' he said.

'Right. What's the rattlebag?'

'Well,' he said, sagely, soberly, a small voice from the darkness beside me, 'once you're just bones and skin, they hang you up on a hook, and you rattle in the wind.'

'So what do these Click-Clacks look like?' Even as I asked him, I wished I could take the question back, and leave it unasked. I thought: *huge spidery creatures. Like the one in the shower this morning.* I'm afraid of spiders.

I was relieved when the boy said, 'They look like what you aren't expecting. What you aren't paying attention to.'

We were climbing wooden steps now. I held on to the railing on my left, held his hand with my right, as he walked beside me. It smelled like dust and old wood, that high in the house. The boy's tread was certain, though, even though the moonlight was scarce.

'Do you know what story you're going to tell me, to put me to bed?' he asked. 'Like I said. It doesn't actually have to be scary.'

'Not really.'

'Maybe you could tell me about this evening. Tell me what you did?'

'That won't make much of a story for you. My girlfriend just moved into a new place on the edge of town. She inherited it from an aunt or someone. It's very big and very old. I'm going to spend my first night with her, tonight, so I've been waiting for an hour or so for her and her housemates to come back with the wine and an Indian takeaway.'

'See?' said the boy. There was that precocious amusement again; but all kids can be insufferable sometimes, when they think they know something you don't. It's probably good for them. 'You know all that. But you don't think. You just let your brain fill in the gaps.'

He pushed open the door to the attic room. It was perfectly dark, now, but the opening door disturbed the air, and I heard things rattle gently, like dry bones in thin bags, in the slight wind. Click. Clack. Click. Clack. Like that.

I would have pulled away then, if I could; but small, firm fingers pulled me forward, unrelentingly, into the dark.

An Invocation of Incuriosity

There are flea markets all across Florida, and this was not the worst of them. It had once been an aircraft hangar, but the local airport had closed over twenty years before. There were a hundred traders there behind their metal tables, most of them selling counterfeit merchandise: sunglasses or watches or bags or belts. There was an African family selling carved wooden animals and behind them a loud, blowsy woman named (I cannot forget the name) Charity Parrot sold coverless paperback books, and old pulp magazines, the paper browned and crumbling, and beside her, in the corner, a Mexican woman whose name I never knew sold film posters and curling film stills.

I bought books from Charity Parrot, sometimes.

Soon enough the woman with the film posters went away and was replaced by a small man in sunglasses, his grey tablecloth spread over the metal table and covered with small carvings. I stopped and examined them – a peculiar set of creatures, made of grey bone and stone and dark wood – and then I examined him. I wondered if he had been in a ghastly accident, the kind it takes plastic surgery to repair: his face was wrong, the way it sloped, the shape of it. His skin was too pale. His too-black hair looked like it had to be a wig, made, perhaps, of dog fur. His glasses were so dark as to hide his eyes completely. He did not look in any way out of place in a Florida flea market: the tables were all manned by strange people, and strange people shopped there.

I bought nothing from him.

The next time I was there Charity Parrot had, in her turn, moved on, her place taken by an Indian family who sold hookahs and smoking paraphernalia, but the little man in the dark glasses was still in his corner at the back of the flea market, with his grey cloth. On it were more carvings of creatures.

'I do not recognise any of these animals,' I told him.

'No.'

'Do you make them yourself?'

He shook his head. You cannot ask anyone in a flea market where they get their stuff from. There are few things that are taboo in a flea market, but that is: sources are inviolate.

'Do you sell a lot?'

'Enough to feed myself,' he said. 'Keep a roof over my head.' Then, 'They are worth more than I ask for them.'

I picked up something that reminded me a little of what a deer might look like if deer were carnivorous, and said, 'What is this?'

He glanced down. 'I think it is a primitive thawn. It's hard to tell.' And then, 'It was my father's.'

There was a chiming noise then, to signal that soon enough the flea market would close.

'Would you like food?' I asked.

He looked at me, warily.

'My treat,' I said. 'No obligations. There's a Denny's over the road. Or there's the bar.'

He thought for a moment. 'Denny's will be fine,' he said. 'I will meet you over there.'

I waited at Denny's. After half an hour I no longer expected him to come, but he surprised me and he arrived fifty minutes after I got there, carrying a brown leather bag tied to his wrist with a long piece of twine. I imagined it had to contain money, for it hung as if empty, and it could not have held his stock. Soon enough he was eating his way through a plate piled with pancakes, and, eventually, over coffee, he began to talk.

* * *

The sun began to go out a little after midday. A flicker, first, and then a rapid darkening that began on one side of the sun and then crept across its crimson face until the sun went black, like a coal knocked from a fire, and night returned to the world.

Balthasar the Tardy hurried down from the hill, leaving his nets in the trees, uninspected and unemptied. He uttered no words, conserving his breath, moving as fast as befitted his remarkable bulk, until he reached the bottom of the hill and the front door of his one-room cottage.

'Oaf! It is time!' he called. Then he knelt and lit a fish-oil lamp, which sputtered and stank and burned with a fitful orange flame.

The door of the cottage opened and Balthasar's son emerged. The son was a little taller than his father, and much thinner, and was beardless. The youth had been named after his grandfather, and while his grandfather had lived the boy had been known as Farfal the Younger; now he was referred to, even to his face, as Farfal the Unfortunate. If he brought home a laying fowl it would cease to give eggs; if he took an axe to a tree it would fall in a place that would cause the greatest inconvenience and the least possible good; if he found a trove of ancient treasure, half-buried in a locked box at the edge of a field, the key to the box would break off as he turned it, leaving only a faint echo of song on the air, as if of a distant choir, and the box would dissolve to sand. Young women upon whom he fastened his affections would fall in love with other men or be transformed into grues or carried off by deodands. It was the way of things.

'Sun's gone out,' said Balthasar the Tardy to his son.

Farfal said, 'So this is it, then. This is the end.'

It was chillier, now the sun had gone out.

Balthasar said only, 'It soon will be. We have only a handful of minutes left. It is well that I have made provision for this day.' He held the fish-oil lamp up high, and walked back into the cottage.

Farfal followed his father into the tiny dwelling, which consisted of one large room and, at the far end of the dwelling, a locked door. It was to this door that Balthasar walked. He put down the lamp in front of it, took a key from around his neck and unlocked the door.

Farfal's mouth fell open.

He said only, 'The colours.' Then, 'I dare not go through.'

'Idiot boy,' said his father. 'Go through, and tread carefully as you do.' And then, when Farfal made no move to walk, his father pushed him through the door, and closed it behind them.

Farfal stood there, blinking at the unaccustomed light.

'As you apprehend,' said his father, resting his hands on his capacious stomach and surveying the room they found them-selves in, 'this room does not exist temporally in the world you know. It exists, instead, over a million years before our time, in the days of the last Remoran Empire, a period marked by the excellence of its lute music, its fine cuisine, and also the beauty and compliance of its slave class.'

Farfal rubbed his eyes, and then looked at the wooden case-ment standing in the middle of the room, a casement through which they had just walked, as if it were a door. 'I begin to perceive,' he said, 'why it is that you were so often unavail-able. For it seems to me that I have seen you walk through that door into this room many times and never wondered about it, merely resigned myself to the time that would pass until you returned.'

Balthasar the Tardy began then to remove his clothes of dark sacking until he was naked, a fat man with a long white beard and cropped white hair, and then to cover himself with brightly coloured silken robes.

'The sun!' exclaimed Farfal, peering out of the room's small window. 'Look at it! It is the orange-red of a fresh-stirred fire! Feel the heat it gives!' And then he said, 'Father. Why has it never occurred to me to ask you why you spent so much time in the second room of our one-room cottage? Nor to remark upon the existence of such a room, even to myself?'

Balthasar twisted the last of the fastenings, covering his remarkable stomach with a silken covering that crawled with embroideries of elegant monsters. 'That might,' he admitted, 'have been due in part to Empusa's Invocation of Incuriosity.' He produced a small black box from around his neck, windowed and barred, like a tiny room, barely large enough to hold a beetle. 'This, when properly primed and invoked, keeps us from being remarked upon. Just as you were not able to wonder at my comings and goings, so neither do the folk in this time and place marvel at me, nor at anything I do that is in any wise contrary to the mores and customs of the Eighteenth and Last Greater Remoran Empire.'

'Astonishing,' said Farfal.

'It matters not that the sun has gone out, that in a matter of hours, or at most weeks, all life on Earth will be dead, for here and at this time I am Balthasar the Canny, merchant to the sky-ships, dealer in antiquities, magical objects, and marvels – and here you, my son, will stay. You will be, to all who wonder about your provenance, simply and purely my servant.'

'Your servant?' said Farfal the Unfortunate. 'Why can I not be your son?'

'For various reasons,' stated his father, 'too trivial and minor even to warrant discussion at this time.' He hung the black box from a nail in the corner of the room. Farfal thought he saw a leg or head, as if of some beetle-like creature, waving at him from inside the little box, but he did not pause to inspect it. 'Also because I have a number of sons in this time, that I have fathered upon my concubines, and they might not be pleased to learn of another. Although, given the disparity in the dates of your birth, it would be over a million years before you could inherit any wealth.'

'There is wealth?' asked Farfal, looking at the room he was in with fresh eyes. He had spent his life in a one-roomed cottage at the end of time, at the bottom of a small hill, surviving on the food his father could net in the air – usually only seabirds or flying lizards, although on occasion other things had been caught in the nets: creatures who claimed to be angels, or great self-important cockroach-like things with high metal crowns, or huge bronze-coloured jellies. They would be taken from the netting, and then either thrown back into the air, or eaten, or traded with the few folk that passed that way.

His father smirked and stroked his impressive white beard like a man petting an animal. 'Wealth indeed,' he said. 'There is much call in these times for pebbles and small rocks from the End of the Earth: there are spells, cantrips, and magical instruments for which they are almost irreplaceable. And I deal in such things.'

Farfal the Unfortunate nodded. 'And if I do not wish to be a servant,' he said, 'but simply request to be returned to where we came from, through that casement, why, what then?'

Balthasar the Tardy said only, 'I have little patience for such questions. The sun has gone out. In hours, perhaps minutes, the world will have ended. Perhaps the universe also has ended. Think no more on these matters. Instead, I shall procure a locking-spell creature for the casement, down at the ship market. And while I go to do that, you can order and polish all the objects you can see in this cabinet, taking care not to put your fingers directly upon the green flute (for it will give you music, but replace contentment in your soul with an insatiable longing) nor get the onyx bogadil wet.' He patted his son's hand affectionately, a glorious, resplendent creature in his many-coloured silks. 'I have spared you from death, my boy,' he said. 'I have brought you back in time to a new life. What should it matter that in this life you are not son but servant? Life is life, and it is infinitely better than the alternative, or so we presume, for nobody returns to dispute it. Such is my motto.'

So saying he fumbled beneath the casement, and produced a grey rag, which he handed to Farfal. 'Here. To work! Do a good job and I shall show you by how much the sumptuous feasts of antiquity are an improvement over smoked seabird and pickled ossaker root. Do not, under any circumstances or provocation, move the casement. Its position is precisely calibrated. Move it, and it could open to anywhere.'

He covered the casement with a piece of woven cloth, which made it appear less remarkable that a large wooden casement was standing, unsupported, in the centre of a room.

Balthasar the Tardy left that room through a door that Farfal had not previously observed. Bolts were slammed closed. Farfal picked up his rag, and began, wanly, to dust and to polish.

After several hours he observed a light coming through the casement, so brightly as to penetrate the cloth covering, but it soon faded once more.

Farfal was introduced to the household of Balthasar the Canny as a new servant. He observed Balthasar's five sons and his seven concubines (although he was not permitted to speak to them), was introduced to the House-Carl, who held the keys, and the maidmen who hurried and scurried thence and hither at the

House-Carl's command, and than whom there was nothing lower in that place, save for Farfal himself.

The maidmen resented Farfal, with his pale skin, for he was the only one apart from their master permitted in the Sanctum Sanctorum, Master Balthasar's room of wonders, a place to which Master Balthasar had hitherto only repaired alone.

And so the days went by, and the weeks, and Farfal ceased to marvel at the bright orange-red sun, so huge and remarkable, or at the colours of the daytime sky (predominantly salmon and mauve), or at the ships that would arrive in the ship-market from distant worlds bearing their cargo of wonders.

Farfal was miserable, even when surrounded by marvels, even in a forgotten age, even in a world filled with miracles. He said as much to Balthasar the next time the merchant came in the door to the sanctum. 'This is unfair.'

'Unfair?'

'That I clean and polish the wonders and precious things, while you and your other sons attend feasts and parties and banquets and meet people and otherwise and altogether enjoy living here at the dawn of time.'

Balthasar said, 'The youngest son may not always enjoy the privileges of his elder brothers, and they are all older than you.'

'The red-haired one is but fifteen, the dark-skinned one is fourteen, the twins are no more than twelve, while I am a man of seventeen years . . .'

'They are older than you by more than a million years,' said his father. 'I will hear no more of this nonsense.'

Farfal the Unfortunate bit his lower lip to keep from replying.

It was at that moment that there was a commotion in the courtyard, as if a great door had been broken open, and the cries of animals and house-birds arose. Farfal ran to the tiny window and looked out. 'There are men,' he said. 'I can see the light glinting on their weapons.'

His father seemed unsurprised. 'Of course,' he said. 'Now, I have a task for you, Farfal. Due to some erroneous optimism on my part, we are almost out of the stones upon which my wealth is founded, and I have the indignity of discovering myself to be overcommitted at present. Thus it is necessary for you and I to return to our old home and gather what we can. It will be safer if there are two of us. And time is of the essence.'

'I will help you,' said Farfal, 'if you will agree to treat me better in the future.'

From the courtyard there came a cry. 'Balthasar? Wretch! Cheat! Liar! Where are my thirty stones?' The voice was deep and penetrating.

'I shall treat you much better in the future,' said his father. 'I swear it.' He walked to the casement, pulled off the cloth. There was no light to be seen through it, nothing inside the wooden casing but a deep and formless blackness.

'Perhaps the world has entirely ended,' said Farfal, 'and now there is nothing but nothing.'

'Only a handful of seconds have passed there since we came through it,' his father told him. 'That is the nature of time. It flows faster when it is younger and the course is narrower: at the end of all things time has spread and slowed, like oil spilled on a still pond.'

Then he removed the sluggish spell-creature he had placed on the casement as a lock, and he pushed against the inner casing, which opened slowly. A chill wind came through it which made Farfal shiver. 'You send us to our deaths, Father,' he said.

'We all go to our deaths,' said his father. 'And yet, here you are, a million years before your birth, still alive. Truly we are all composed of miracles. Now, son, here is a bag, which, as you will soon discover, has been imbued with Swann's Imbuement of Remarkable Capacity, and will hold all that you place inside it, regardless of weight or mass or volume. When we get there, you must take as many stones as you can and place them in the bag. I myself will run up the hill to the nets and check them for treasures – or for things that would be regarded as treasures if I were to bring them back to the now and the here.'

'Do I go first?' asked Farfal, clutching the bag.

'Of course.'

'It's so cold.'

In reply his father prodded him in the back with a hard finger. Farfal clambered, grumbling, through the casement, and his father followed.

'This is too bad,' said Farfal. They walked out of the cottage at the end of time and Farfal bent to pick up pebbles. He placed the first in the bag, where it glinted greenly. He picked up another. The sky was dark but it seemed as if something filled the sky, something without shape.

There was a flash of something not unlike lightning, and in it he could see his father hauling in nets from the trees at the top of the hill.

A crackling. The nets flamed and were gone. Balthasar ran down the hill gracelessly and breathlessly. He pointed at the sky. 'It is Nothing!' he said. 'Nothing has swallowed the hilltop! Nothing has taken over!'

There was a powerful wind then, and Farfal watched his father crackle, and then raise into the air, and then vanish. He backed away from the Nothing, a darkness within the darkness with tiny lightnings playing at its edges, and then he turned and ran, into the house, to the door into the second room. But he did not go through into the second room. He stood there in the doorway, and then turned back to the Dying Earth. Farfal the Unfortunate watched as the Nothing took the outer walls and the distant hills and the skies, and then he watched, unblinking, as Nothing swallowed the cold sun, watched until there was nothing left but a dark formlessness that pulled at him, as if restless to be done with it all.

Only then did Farfal walk into the inner room in the cottage, into his father's inner sanctum a million years before.

A bang on the outer door.

'Balthasar?' It was the voice from the courtyard. 'I gave you the day you begged for, wretch. Now give me my thirty stones. Give me my stones or I shall be as good as my word – your sons will be taken off-world, to labour in the Bdellium Mines of Telb, and the women shall be set to work as musicians in the pleasure palace of Luthius Limn, where they will have the honour of making sweet music while I, Luthius Limn, dance and sing and make passionate and athletic love to my catamites. I shall not waste breath in describing the fate I would have in store for your servants. Your spell of hiding is futile, for see, I have found this room with relative ease. Now, give me my thirty stones before I open the door and render down your obese frame for cooking fat and throw your bones to the dogs and the deodands.'

Farfal trembled with fear. *Time,* he thought. *I need Time.* He made his voice as deep as he could, and he called out, 'One moment, Luthius Limn. I am engaged in a complex magical operation to purge your stones of their negative energies. If I am disturbed in this, the consequences will be catastrophic.'

Farfal glanced around the room. The only window was too small to permit him to climb out, while the room's only door had Luthius Limn on the other side of it. 'Unfortunate indeed,' he sighed. Then he took the bag his father had given to him and swept into it all the trinkets, oddments, and gewgaws he could reach, still taking care not to touch the green flute with his bare flesh. They vanished into the bag, which weighed no more and seemed no more full than it had ever done.

He stared at the casement in the centre of the room. The only way out, and it led to Nothing, to the end of everything.

'Enough!' came the voice from beyond the door. 'My patience is at an end, Balthasar. My cooks shall fry your internal organs tonight.' There came a loud crunching against the door, as if of something hard and heavy being slammed against it.

Then there was a scream, and then silence.

Luthius Limn's voice: 'Is he dead?'

Another voice – Farfal thought it sounded like one of his half brothers – said, 'I suspect that the door is magically protected and warded.'

'Then,' boomed Luthius Limn, decisively, 'we shall go through the wall.'

Farfal was unfortunate, but not stupid. He lifted down the black lacquer box from the nail upon which his father had hung it. He heard something scuttle and move inside it.

'My father told me not to move the casement,' he said to himself. Then he put his shoulder against it and heaved violently, pushing the heavy thing almost half an inch. The darkness that pervaded the casement began to change, and it filled with a pearl-grey light.

He hung the box about his neck. 'It is good enough,' said Farfal the Unfortunate, and, as something slammed against the wall of the room, he took a strip of cloth and tied the leather bag that contained all the remaining treasures of Balthasar the Canny about his left wrist, and he pushed himself through.

And there was light, so bright that he closed his eyes, and walked through the casement.

Farfal began to fall.

He flailed in the air, eyes tightly closed against the blinding light, felt the wind whip past him.

Something smacked and engulfed him: water, brackish, warm, and Farfal floundered, too surprised to breathe. He surfaced, his head breaking water, and he gulped air. And then he pushed himself through the water, until his hands grasped some kind of plant, and he pulled himself, on hands and feet, out of the green water, and up onto a spongy dry land, trailing and trickling water as he went.

* * *

'The light,' said the man at Denny's. 'The light was blinding. And the sun was not yet up. But I obtained these' – he tapped the frame of his sunglasses – 'and I stay out of the sunlight, so my skin does not burn too badly.'

'And now?' I asked.

'I sell the carvings,' he said. 'And I seek another casement.'

'You want to go back to your own time?'

He shook his head. 'It's dead,' he said. 'And all I knew, and everything like me. It's dead. I will not return to the darkness at the end of time.'

'What then?'

He scratched at his neck. Through the opening in his shirt I could see a small, black box, hanging about his neck, no bigger than a locket, and inside the box something moved: a beetle, I thought. But there are big beetles in Florida. They are not uncommon.

'I want to go back to the beginning,' he said. 'When it started. I want to stand there in the light of the universe waking to itself, the dawn of everything. If I am going to be blinded, let it be by that. I want to be there when the suns are a-borning. This ancient light is not bright enough for me.'

He took the napkin in his hand then, and reached into the leather bag with it. Taking care to touch it only through the cloth, he pulled out a flute-like instrument, about a foot long, made of green jade or something similar, and placed it on the table in front of me. 'For the food,' he said. 'A thank-you.'

He got up, then, and walked away, and I sat and stared at the green flute for so long a time; eventually I reached out and felt the coldness of it with my fingertips, and then gently, without daring to blow, or to try to make music from the end of time, I touched the mouthpiece to my lips.

'And Weep, Like Alexander'

The little man hurried into the Fountain and ordered a very large whisky. 'Because,' he announced to the pub in general, 'I deserve it.'

He looked exhausted, sweaty and rumpled, as if he had not slept in several days. He wore a tie, but it was so loose as to be almost undone. He had greying hair that might once have been ginger.

'I'm sure you do,' said Brian.

'I do!' said the man. He took a sip of the whisky as if to find out whether or not he liked it, then, satisfied, gulped down half the glass. He stood completely still, for a moment, like a statue. 'Listen,' he said. 'Can you hear it?'

'What?' I said.

'A sort of background whispering white noise that actually becomes whatever song you wish to hear when you sort of half-concentrate upon it?'

I listened. 'No,' I said.

'Exactly,' said the man, extraordinarily pleased with himself. 'Isn't it *wonderful*? Only yesterday, everybody in the Fountain was complaining about the Wispamuzak. Professor Mackintosh here was grumbling about having Queen's "Bohemian Rhapsody" stuck in his head and how it was now following him across London. Today, it's gone, as if it had never been. None of you can even remember that it existed. And that is all due to me.'

'I what?' said Professor Mackintosh. 'Something about the Queen?' And then, 'Do I know you?'

'We meet,' said the little man. 'But people forget me, alas. It is because of my job.' He took out his wallet, produced a card, passed it to me.

OBEDIAH POLKINGHORN

it read, and beneath that in small letters,

UNINVENTOR.

'If you don't mind my asking,' I said. 'What's an uninventor?'

'It's somebody who uninvents things,' he said. He raised his glass, which was quite empty. 'Ah. Excuse me, Sally, I need another very large whisky.'

The rest of the crowd there that evening seemed to have decided that the man was both mad and uninteresting. They had returned to their conversations. I, on the other hand, was caught. 'So,' I said, resigning myself to my conversational fate. 'Have you been an uninventor long?'

'Since I was fairly young,' he said. 'I started uninventing when I was eighteen. Have you never wondered why we do not have jet-packs?'

I had, actually.

'Saw a bit on *Tomorrow's World* about them, when I was a lad,' said Michael, the landlord. 'Man went up in one. Then he came down. Raymond Burr seemed to think we'd all have them soon enough.'

'Ah, but we don't,' said Obediah Polkinghorn, 'because I uninvented them about twenty years ago. I had to. They were driving everybody mad. I mean, they seemed so attractive, and so cheap, but you just had to have a few thousand bored teenagers strapping them on, zooming all over the place, hovering outside bedroom windows, crashing into the flying cars . . .'

'Hold on,' said Sally. 'There aren't any flying cars.'

'True,' said the little man, 'but only because I uninvented them. You wouldn't believe the traffic jams they'd cause. I'd look up and it was just the bottoms of bloody flying cars from horizon to horizon. Some days I couldn't see the skies at all. People throwing rubbish out of their car windows . . . They were easy to run – ran off gravitosolar power, obviously – but I didn't realise that they needed to go until I heard a lady talking about them on Radio Four, all "Why Oh Why Didn't We Stick with Non-Flying Cars?" She had a point. Something needed to be done. I uninvented them. I made a list of inventions the world would be better off without and, one by one, I uninvented them all.'

By now he had started to gather a small audience. I was pleased I had a good seat.

'It was a lot of work, too,' he continued. 'You see, it's almost impossible *not* to invent the flying car, as soon as you've invented the Lumenbubble. So eventually I had to uninvent them too. And I miss the individual Lumenbubble: a massless portable light source that floated half a metre above your head and went on when you wanted it to. Such a wonderful invention. Still, no use crying over unspilt milk, and you can't mend an omelette without unbreaking a few eggs.'

'You also can't expect us actually to believe any of this,' said someone, and I think it was Jocelyn.

'Right,' said Brian. 'I mean, next thing you'll be telling us that you uninvented the spaceship.'

'But I did,' said Obediah Polkinghorn. He seemed extremely pleased with himself. 'Twice. I had to. You see, the moment we whizz off into space and head out to the planets and beyond, we bump into things that spur so many other inventions. The

Polaroid Instant Transporter. That was the worst. And the Mockett Telepathic Translator. That was the worst as well. But as long as it's nothing worse than a rocket to the moon, I can keep everything under control.'

'So, how exactly do you go about uninventing things?' I asked.

'It's hard,' he admitted. 'It's all about unpicking probability threads from the fabric of creation. Which is a bit like unpicking a needle from a haystack. But they tend to be long and tangled, like spaghetti. So it's rather like having to unpick a strand of spaghetti from a haystack.'

'Sounds like thirsty work,' said Michael, and I signalled him to pour me another half pint of cider.

'Fiddly,' said the little man. 'Yes. But I pride myself on doing good. Each day I wake, and, even if I've unhappened something that might have been wonderful, I think, Obediah Polkinghorn, the world is a happier place because of something that you've uninvented.'

He looked into his remaining scotch, swirled the liquid around in his glass.

'The trouble is,' he said, 'with the Wispamuzak gone, that's it. I'm done. It's all been uninvented. There are no more horizons left to undiscover, no more mountains left to unclimb.'

'Nuclear power?' suggested 'Tweet' Peston.

'Before my time,' said Obediah. 'Can't uninvent things invented before I was born. Otherwise I might uninvent something that would have led to my birth, and then where would we be?' Nobody had any suggestions. 'Knee-high in jet-packs and flying cars, that's where,' he told us. 'Not to mention Morrison's Martian Emolument.' For a moment, he looked quite grim. 'Ooh. That stuff was nasty. And a cure for cancer. But frankly, given what it did to the oceans, I'd rather have the cancer.

'No. I have uninvented everything that was on my list. I shall go home,' said Obediah Polkinghorn, bravely, 'and weep, like

Alexander, because there are no more worlds to unconquer. What is there left to uninvent?'

There was silence in the Fountain.

In the silence, Brian's iPhone rang. His ringtone was the Rutles singing 'Cheese and Onions'. 'Yeah?' he said. Then, 'I'll call you back.'

It is unfortunate that the pulling out of one phone can have such an effect on other people around. Sometimes I think it's because we remember when we could smoke in pubs, and that we pull out our phones together as once we pulled out our cigarette packets. But probably it's because we're easily bored.

Whatever the reason, the phones came out.

Crown Baker took a photo of us all, and then Twitpicced it. Jocelyn started to read her text messages. 'Tweet' Peston tweeted that he was in the Fountain and had met his first uninventor. Professor Mackintosh checked the test match scores, told us what they were and emailed his brother in Inverness to grumble about them. The phones were out and the conversation was over.

'What's that?' asked Obediah Polkinghorn.

'It's the iPhone 5,' said Ray Arnold, holding his up. 'Crown's using the Nexus X. That's the Android system. Phones. Internet. Camera. Music. But it's the apps. I mean, do you know, there are over a thousand fart sound-effect apps on the iPhone alone? You want to hear the unofficial Simpsons Fart App?'

'No,' said Obediah. 'I most definitely do not want to. I do *not*.' He put down his drink, unfinished. Pulled his tie up. Did up his coat. 'It's not going to be easy,' he said, as if to himself. 'But, for the good of all . . .' And then he stopped. And he grinned.

'It's been marvellous talking to you all,' he announced to nobody in particular, as he left the Fountain.

Nothing O'Clock

I

The Time Lords built a prison. They built it in a time and place that are equally as unimaginable to any entity who has never left the solar system in which it was spawned, or who has only experienced the journey into the future one second at a time, and that going forward. It was built solely for the Kin. It was impregnable: a complex of small, nicely appointed rooms (for they were not monsters, the Time Lords. They could be merciful, when it suited them), out of temporal phase with the rest of the Universe.

There were, in that place, only those rooms: the gulf between microseconds was one that could not be crossed. In effect, those rooms became a Universe in themselves, one that borrowed light and heat and gravity from the rest of creation, always a fraction of a moment away.

The Kin prowled its rooms, patient and deathless, and always waiting.

It was waiting for a question. It could wait until the end of time. (But even then, when Time Ended, the Kin would never perceive it, imprisoned in the micro-moment away from time.)

The Time Lords maintained the prison with huge engines they built in the hearts of black holes, unreachable: no one would be able to get to the engines, save the Time Lords themselves.

The multiple engines were a fail-safe. Nothing could ever go wrong.

As long as the Time Lords existed, the Kin would be in their prison, and the rest of the Universe would be safe. That was how it was, and how it always would be.

And if anything went wrong, then the Time Lords would know. Even if, unthinkably, any of the engines failed, then emergency signals would sound on Gallifrey long before the prison of the Kin returned to our time and our Universe. The Time Lords had planned for everything.

They had planned for everything except the possibility that one day there would be no Time Lords, and no Gallifrey. No Time Lords in the Universe, except for one.

So when the prison shook and crashed, as if in an earthquake, throwing the Kin down, and when the Kin looked up from its prison to see the light of galaxies and suns above it, unmediated and unfiltered, and it knew that it had returned to the Universe, it knew it would only be a matter of time until the question would be asked once more.

And, because the Kin was careful, it took stock of the Universe they found themselves in. It did not think of revenge: that was not in its nature. It wanted what it had always wanted. And besides . . .

There was still a Time Lord in the Universe.

The Kin needed to do something about that.

II

On Wednesday, eleven-year-old Polly Browning put her head around her father's office door. 'Dad. There's a man at the front door in a rabbit mask who says he wants to buy the house.'

'Don't be silly, Polly.' Mr Browning was sitting in the corner of the room he liked to call his office, and which the estate agent had optimistically listed as a third bedroom, although it was scarcely big enough for a filing cabinet and a card table, upon which rested a brand-new Amstrad computer. Mr Browning was carefully entering the numbers from a pile of receipts onto the computer, and wincing. Every half an hour he would save the work he'd done so far, and the computer would make a grinding noise for a few minutes as it saved everything onto a floppy disk.

'I'm not being silly. He says he'll give you seven hundred and fifty thousand pounds for it.'

'Now you're really being silly. It's on sale for a hundred and fifty thousand.' *And we'd be lucky to get that in today's market,* he thought, but did not say. It was the summer of 1984, and Mr Browning despaired of finding a buyer for the little house at the end of Claversham Row.

Polly nodded thoughtfully. 'I think you should go and talk to him.'

Mr Browning shrugged. He needed to save the work he'd done so far anyway. As the computer made its grumbling sound, Mr Browning went downstairs. Polly, who had planned to go up to her bedroom to write in her diary, decided to sit on the stairs and find out what was going to happen next.

Standing in the front garden was a tall man in a rabbit mask. It was not a particularly convincing mask. It covered his entire face, and two long ears rose above his head. He held a large, leather, brown bag, which reminded Mr Browning of the doctors' bags of his childhood.

'Now, see here,' began Mr Browning, but the man in the rabbit mask put a gloved finger to his painted bunny lips, and Mr Browning fell silent.

'Ask me what time it is,' said a quiet voice that came from behind the unmoving muzzle of the rabbit mask.

Mr Browning said, 'I understand you're interested in the house.' The FOR SALE sign by the front gate was grimy and streaked by the rain.

'Perhaps. You can call me Mister Rabbit. Ask me what time it is.'

Mr Browning knew that he ought to call the police. Ought to do something to make the man go away. What kind of crazy person wears a rabbit mask anyway?

'Why are you wearing a rabbit mask?'

'That was not the correct question. But I am wearing the rabbit mask because I am representing an extremely famous and important person who values his or her privacy. Ask me what time it is.'

Mr Browning sighed. 'What time is it, Mister Rabbit?' he asked.

The man in the rabbit mask stood up straighter. His body language was one of joy and delight. 'Time for you to be the richest man on Claversham Row,' he said. 'I'm buying your house, for cash, and for more than ten times what it's worth, because it's just perfect for me now.' He opened the brown leather bag, and produced blocks of money, each block containing five hundred – 'count them, go on, count them' – crisp fifty-pound notes, and two plastic supermarket shopping bags, into which he placed the blocks of currency.

Mr Browning inspected the money. It appeared to be real.

'I . . .' He hesitated. What did he need to do? 'I'll need a few days. To bank it. Make sure it's real. And we'll need to draw up contracts, obviously.'

'Contract's already drawn up,' said the man in the rabbit mask. 'Sign here. If the bank says there's anything funny about the money, you can keep it and the house. I'll be back on Saturday to take vacant possession. You can get everything out by then, can't you?'

'I don't know,' said Mr Browning. Then: 'I'm sure I can. I mean, *of course.*'

'I'll be here on Saturday,' said the man in the rabbit mask.

'This is a very unusual way of doing business,' said Mr Browning. He was standing at his front door holding two shopping bags, containing £750,000.

'Yes,' agreed the man in the rabbit mask. 'It is. See you on Saturday, then.'

He walked away. Mr Browning was relieved to see him go. He had been seized by the irrational conviction that, were he to remove the rabbit mask, there would be nothing underneath.

Polly went upstairs to tell her diary everything she had seen and heard.

* * *

On Thursday, a tall young man with a tweed jacket and a bow tie knocked on the door. There was nobody at home, and nobody answered, and, after walking around the house, he went away.

* * *

On Saturday, Mr Browning stood in his empty kitchen. He had banked the money successfully, which had wiped out all his debts. The furniture that they had wanted to keep had been put into a moving van and sent to Mr Browning's uncle, who had an enormous garage he wasn't using.

'What if it's all a joke?' asked Mrs Browning.

'Not sure what's funny about giving someone seven hundred and fifty thousand pounds,' said Mr Browning. 'The bank says it's real. Not reported stolen. Just a rich and eccentric person who wants to buy our house for a lot more than it's worth.'

They had booked two rooms in a local hotel, although hotel

rooms had proved harder to find than Mr Browning had expected. Also, he had had to convince Mrs Browning, who was a nurse, that they could now afford to stay in a hotel.

'What happens if he never comes back?' asked Polly. She was sitting on the stairs, reading a book.

Mr Browning said, 'Now you're being silly.'

'Don't call your daughter silly,' said Mrs Browning. 'She's got a point. You don't have a name or a phone number or anything.'

This was unfair. The contract was made out, and the buyer's name was clearly written on it: N. M. de Plume. There was an address, too, for a firm of London solicitors, and Mr Browning had phoned them and been told that, yes, this was absolutely legitimate.

'He's eccentric,' said Mr Browning. 'An eccentric millionaire.'

'I bet it's him behind that rabbit mask,' said Polly. 'The eccentric millionaire.'

The doorbell rang. Mr Browning went to the front door, his wife and daughter beside him, each of them hoping to meet the new owner of their house.

'Hello,' said the lady in the cat mask. It was not a very realistic mask. Polly saw her eyes glinting behind it, though.

'Are you the new owner?' asked Mrs Browning.

'Either that, or I'm the owner's representative.'

'Where's . . . your friend? In the rabbit mask?'

Despite the cat mask, the young lady (was she young? Her voice sounded young, anyway) seemed efficient and almost brusque. 'You have removed all your possessions? I'm afraid anything left behind will become the property of the new owner.'

'We've got everything that matters.'

'Good.'

Polly said, 'Can I come and play in the garden? There isn't a garden at the hotel.' There was a swing on the oak tree in the back garden, and Polly loved to sit on it and read.

'Don't be silly, love,' said Mr Browning. 'We'll have a new house, and then you'll have a garden with swings. I'll put up new swings for you.'

The lady in the cat mask crouched down. 'I'm Mrs Cat. Ask me what time it is, Polly.'

Polly nodded. 'What's the time, Mrs Cat?'

'Time for you and your family to leave this place and never look back,' said Mrs Cat, but she said it kindly.

Polly waved goodbye to the lady in the cat mask when she got to the end of the garden path.

III

They were in the TARDIS control room, going home.

'I still don't understand,' Amy was saying. 'Why were the Skeleton People so angry with you in the first place? I thought they *wanted* to get free from the rule of the Toad-King.'

'They weren't angry with me about *that*,' said the young man in the tweed jacket and the bow tie. He pushed a hand through his hair. 'I think they were quite pleased to be free, actually.' He ran his hands across the TARDIS control panel, patting levers, stroking dials. 'They were just a bit upset with me because I'd walked off with their squiggly whatsit.'

'Squiggly whatsit?'

'It's on the . . .' He gestured vaguely with arms that seemed to be mostly elbows and joints. 'The tabley thing over there. I confiscated it.'

Amy looked irritated. She wasn't irritated, but she sometimes liked to give him the impression she was, just to show him who was boss. 'Why don't you ever call things by their proper names? *The tabley thing over there*? It's called "a table".'

She walked over to the table. The squiggly whatsit was glittery and elegant: it was the size and general shape of a bracelet, but it twisted in ways that made it hard for the eye to follow.

'Really? Oh good.' He seemed pleased. 'I'll remember that.'

Amy picked up the squiggly whatsit. It was cold and much heavier than it looked. 'Why did you confiscate it? And why are you saying *confiscate* anyway? That's like what teachers do, when you bring something you shouldn't to school. My friend Mels set a record at school for the number of things she'd got confiscated. One night she got me and Rory to make a disturbance while she broke into the teacher's supply cupboard, which was where her stuff was. She had to go over the roof and through the teachers' loo window . . .'

But the Doctor was not interested in Amy's old school friend's exploits. He never was. He said, 'Confiscated. For their own safety. Technology they shouldn't have had. Probably stolen. Time looper and booster. Could have made a nasty mess of things.' He pulled a lever. 'And we're here. All change.'

There was a rhythmic grinding sound, as if the engines of the Universe itself were protesting, a rush of displaced air, and a large blue police box materialised in the back garden of Amy Pond's house. It was the beginning of the second decade of the twenty-first century.

The Doctor opened the TARDIS door. Then he said, 'That's odd.'

He stood in the doorway, made no attempt to walk outside. Amy came over to him. He put out an arm to prevent her from leaving the TARDIS. It was a perfectly sunny day, almost cloudless.

'What's wrong?'

'Everything,' he said. 'Can't you feel it?' Amy looked at her garden. It was overgrown and neglected, but then it always had been, as long as she remembered.

'No,' said Amy. And then she said, 'It's quiet. No cars. No birds. Nothing.'

'No radio waves,' said the Doctor. 'Not even Radio Four.'

'You can hear radio waves?'

'Of course not. Nobody can hear radio waves,' he said, unconvincingly.

And that was when the voice said, ATTENTION VISITORS. YOU ARE NOW ENTERING KIN SPACE. THIS WORLD IS THE PROPERTY OF THE KIN. YOU ARE TRESPASSING. It was a strange voice, whispery and, mostly, Amy suspected, in her head.

'This is Earth,' called Amy. 'It doesn't belong to you.' And then she said, 'What have you done with the people?'

WE BOUGHT IT FROM THEM. THEY DIED OUT NATURALLY SHORTLY AFTERWARDS. IT WAS A PITY.

'I don't believe you,' shouted Amy.

NO GALACTIC LAWS WERE VIOLATED. THE PLANET WAS PURCHASED LEGALLY AND LEGITIMATELY. A THOROUGH INVESTIGATION BY THE SHADOW PROCLAMATION VINDICATED OUR OWNERSHIP IN FULL.

'It's not yours! Where's Rory?'

'Amy? Who are you talking to?' asked the Doctor.

'The voice. The one in my head. Can't you hear it?'

TO WHOM ARE YOU TALKING? asked the Voice.

Amy closed the TARDIS door.

'Why did you do that?' asked the Doctor.

'Weird, whispery voice in my head. Said they'd bought the planet. And the, the Shadow Proclamation said it was all okay. It told me all the people died out naturally. You couldn't hear it. It didn't know you were here. Element of surprise. Closed the door.' Amy Pond could be astonishingly efficient, when she was under stress. Right now, she was under stress, but you wouldn't have known it, if it wasn't for the squiggly whatsit, which she was holding between her hands and was bending and twisting into shapes that defied the imagination and seemed to be wandering off into peculiar dimensions.

'Did they say who they were?'

She thought for a moment. '"You are now entering Kin space. This world is the property of the Kin."'

He said, 'Could be anyone. The Kin. I mean . . . it's like calling yourselves the People. It's what pretty much every race-name means. Except for *Dalek*. That means *Metal-Cased Hatey Death Machines* in Skaronian.' And then he was running to the control panel. 'Something like this. It can't occur overnight. People don't just die off. And this is 2010. Which means . . .'

'It means they've done something to Rory.'

'It means they've done something to everyone.' He pressed several keys on an ancient typewriter keyboard, and patterns flowed across the screen that hung above the TARDIS console. 'I couldn't hear them . . . they couldn't hear me. You could hear both of us. *Aha!* Summer of 1984! That's the divergence point . . .' His hands began turning, twiddling and pushing levers, pumps, switches, and something small that went *ding*.

'Where's Rory? I want him, right now,' demanded Amy as the TARDIS lurched away into space and time. The Doctor had only briefly met her fiancé, Rory Williams, once before. She did not think the Doctor understood what she saw in Rory. Some days, *she* was not entirely sure what she saw in Rory. But she was certain of this: nobody took her fiancé away from her.

'Good question. Where's Rory? Also, where's seven billion other people?' he asked.

'I want my Rory.'

'Well, wherever the rest of them are, he's there too. And you ought to have been with them. At a guess, neither of you were ever born.'

Amy looked down at herself, checking her feet, her legs, her elbows, her hands (the squiggly whatsit glittered like an Escher

nightmare on her wrist. She dropped it onto the control panel).
She reached up and grasped a handful of auburn hair. 'If I wasn't
born, what am I doing here?'

'You're an independent temporal nexus, chronosynclastically
established as an inverse . . .' He saw her expression, and stopped.

'You're telling me it's timey-wimey, aren't you?'

'Yes,' he said, seriously. 'I suppose I am. Right. We're here.'

He adjusted his bow tie with precise fingers, tipping it to one
side rakishly.

'But, Doctor. The human race didn't die out in 1984.'

'New timeline. It's a paradox.'

'And you're the paradoctor?'

'Just the Doctor.' He adjusted his bow tie to its earlier align-
ment, stood up a little straighter. 'There's something familiar
about all this.'

'What?'

'Don't know. Hmm. Kin. Kin. *Kin.* I keep thinking of masks.
Who wears masks?'

'Bank robbers?'

'No.'

'Really ugly people?'

'No.'

'Hallowe'en? People wear masks at Hallowe'en.'

'*Yes!* They *do!*'

'So that's important?'

'Not even a little bit. But it's true. Right. Big divergence in time
stream. And it's not actually possible to take over a Level 5 planet
in a way that would satisfy the Shadow Proclamation unless . . .'

'Unless what?'

The Doctor stopped moving. He bit his lower lip. Then: 'Oh.
They wouldn't.'

'Wouldn't what?'

'They couldn't. I mean, that would be completely . . .'

Amy tossed her hair, and did her best to keep her temper. Shouting at the Doctor never worked, unless it did. 'Completely what?'

'Completely impossible. You can't take over a Level 5 planet. Unless you do it legitimately.' On the TARDIS control panel something whirled and something else went *ding*. 'We're here. It's the nexus. Come on! Let's explore 1984.'

'You're enjoying this,' said Amy. 'My whole world has been taken over by a mysterious voice. All the people are extinct. Rory's gone. And you're enjoying this.'

'No, I'm not,' said the Doctor, trying hard not to show how much he was enjoying it.

* * *

The Brownings stayed in the hotel while Mr Browning looked for a new house. The hotel was completely full. Coincidentally, the Brownings learned, in conversation with other hotel guests over breakfast, they had also sold their houses and flats. None of them seemed particularly forthcoming about who had bought their previous residences.

'It's ridiculous,' he said, after ten days. 'There's nothing for sale in town. Or anywhere around here. They've all been snapped up.'

'There must be something,' said Mrs Browning.

'Not in this part of the country,' said Mr Browning.

'What does the estate agent say?'

'Not answering the phone,' said Mr Browning.

'Well, let's go and talk to her,' said Mrs Browning. 'You coming with, Polly?'

Polly shook her head. 'I'm reading my book,' she said.

Mr and Mrs Browning walked into town, and they met the estate agent outside the door of the shop, putting up a notice saying 'Under New Management'. There were no properties for sale in the window, only a lot of houses and flats with SOLD on them.

'Shutting up shop?' asked Mr Browning.

'Someone made me an offer I couldn't refuse,' said the estate agent. She was carrying a heavy-looking plastic shopping bag. The Brownings could guess what was in it.

'Someone in a rabbit mask?' asked Mrs Browning.

When they got back to the hotel, the manager was waiting in the lobby for them, to tell them they wouldn't be living in the hotel much longer.

'It's the new owners,' she explained. 'They are closing the hotel for refurbishing.'

'New owners?'

'They just bought it. Paid a lot of money for it, I was told.'

Somehow, this did not surprise the Brownings one little bit. They were not surprised until they got up to their hotel room, and Polly was nowhere to be seen.

IV

'Nineteen eighty-four,' mused Amy Pond. 'I thought somehow it would feel more, I don't know. Historical. It doesn't feel like a long time ago. But my parents hadn't even met yet.' She hesitated, as if she were about to say something about her parents, but her attention drifted. They crossed the road.

'What were they like?' asked the Doctor. 'Your parents?'

Amy shrugged. 'The usual,' she said, without thinking. 'A mum and a dad.'

'Sounds likely,' agreed the Doctor much too readily. 'So, I need you to keep your eyes open.'

'What are we looking for?'

It was a little English town, and it looked like a little English town as far as Amy was concerned. Just like the one she'd left, only without the coffee shops, or the mobile phone shops.

'Easy. We're looking for something that shouldn't be here. Or we're looking for something that should be here but isn't.'

'What kind of thing?'

'Not sure,' said the Doctor. He rubbed his chin. 'Gazpacho, maybe.'

'What's gazpacho?'

'Cold soup. But it's meant to be cold. So if we looked all over 1984 and couldn't find any gazpacho, that would be a clue.'

'Were you always like this?'

'Like what?'

'A madman. With a time machine.'

'Oh, no. It took ages until I got the time machine.'

They walked through the centre of the little town, looking for something unusual, and finding nothing, not even gazpacho.

* * *

Polly stopped at the garden gate in Claversham Row, looking up at the house that had been her house since they had moved here, when she was seven. She walked up to the front door, rang the doorbell and waited, and was relieved when nobody answered it. She glanced down the street, then walked hurriedly around the house, past the rubbish bins, into the back garden.

The French window that opened onto the little back garden had a catch that didn't fasten properly. Polly thought it extremely unlikely that the house's new owners had fixed it. If they had, she'd come back when they were here, and she'd have to ask, and it would be awkward and embarrassing.

That was the trouble with hiding things. Sometimes, if you were in a hurry, you left them behind. Even important things. And there was nothing more important than her diary.

Polly had been keeping it since they had arrived in the town. It had been her best friend: she had confided in it, told it about the girls who had bullied her, the ones who befriended her, about the first boy she had ever liked. It was, sometimes, her best friend: she would turn to it in times of trouble, or turmoil and pain. It was the place she poured out her thoughts.

And it was hidden underneath a loose floorboard in the big cupboard in her bedroom.

Polly tapped the left French door hard with the palm of her hand, rapping it next to the casement, and the door wobbled, and then swung open.

She walked inside. She was surprised to see that they hadn't replaced any of the furniture her family had taken away. It still smelled like her house. It was silent: nobody home. Good. She hurried up the stairs, worried she might still be at home when Mr Rabbit or Mrs Cat returned.

She went up the stairs. On the landing something brushed her face – touched it gently, like a thread, or a cobweb. She looked up. That was odd. The ceiling seemed furry: hair-like threads, or thread-like hairs, came down from it. She hesitated then, thought about running – but she could see her bedroom door. The Duran Duran poster was still on it. Why hadn't they taken it down?

Trying not to look up at the hairy ceiling, she pushed open her bedroom door.

The room was different. There was no furniture, and where her bed had been were sheets of paper. She glanced down: photographs from newspapers, blown up to life-size. The eyeholes had been cut out already. She recognised Ronald Reagan, Margaret Thatcher, Pope John Paul, the Queen . . .

Perhaps they were going to have a party. The masks didn't look very convincing.

She went to the built-in cupboard at the end of the room. Her *Smash Hits* diary was sitting in the darkness, beneath the floorboard, in there. She opened the cupboard door.

'Hello, Polly,' said the man in the cupboard. He wore a mask, like the others had. An animal mask: this was some kind of big grey dog.

'Hello,' said Polly. She didn't know what else to say. 'I . . . I left my diary behind.'

'I know. I was reading it.' He raised the diary. He was not the same as the man in the rabbit mask, the woman in the cat mask, but everything Polly had felt about them, about the *wrongness*, was intensified here. 'Do you want it back?'

'Yes please,' Polly said to the dog-masked man. She felt hurt and violated: this man had been reading her diary. But she wanted it back.

'You know what you need to do, to get it?'

She shook her head.

'Ask me what the time is.'

She opened her mouth. It was dry. She licked her lips, and muttered, 'What time is it?'

'And my name,' he said. 'Say my name. I'm Mister Wolf.'

'What's the time, Mister Wolf?' asked Polly. A playground game rose unbidden to her mind.

Mister Wolf smiled (but how can a mask smile?) and he opened his mouth so wide to show row upon row of sharp, sharp teeth.

'Dinnertime,' he told her.

Polly started to scream then, as he came towards her, but she didn't get to scream for very long.

V

The TARDIS was sitting in a small grassy area, too small to be a park, too irregular to be a square, in the middle of the town, and the Doctor was sitting outside it, in a deck chair, walking through his memories.

The Doctor had a remarkable memory. The problem was, there was so much of it. He had lived eleven lives (or more: there was another life, was there not, that he tried his best never to think about) and he had a different way of remembering things in each life.

The worst part of being however old he was (and he had long since abandoned trying to keep track of it in any way that mattered to anybody but him) was that sometimes things didn't arrive in his head quite when they were meant to.

Masks. That was part of it. And Kin. That was part of it too. And Time.

It was all about Time. Yes, that was it . . .

An old story. Before his time – he was sure of that. It was something he had heard as a boy. He tried to remember the stories he had been told as a small boy on Gallifrey, before he had been taken to the Time Lord Academy and his life had changed forever.

Amy was coming back from a sortie through the town.

'Maximelos and the three Ogrons!' he shouted at her.

'What about them?'

'One was too vicious, one was too stupid, one was just right.'

'And this is relevant how?'

He tugged at his hair absently. 'Er, probably not relevant at all. Just trying to remember a story from my childhood.'

'Why?'

'No idea. Can't remember.'

'You,' said Amy Pond, 'are very frustrating.'

'Yes,' said the Doctor, happily. 'I probably am.'

He had hung a sign on the front of the TARDIS. It said:

SOMETHING MYSTERIOUSLY WRONG? JUST KNOCK!

NO PROBLEM TOO SMALL.

'If it won't come to us, I'll go to it. No, scrap that. Other way round. And I've redecorated inside, so as not to startle people. What did you find?'

'Two things,' she said. 'First one was Prince Charles. I saw him in the newsagent's.'

'Are you sure it was him?'

Amy thought. 'Well, he looked like Prince Charles. Just much younger. And the newsagent asked him if he'd picked out a name for the next Royal Baby. I suggested Rory.'

'Prince Charles in the newsagent's. Right. Next thing?'

'There aren't any houses for sale. I've walked every street in the town. No FOR SALE signs. There are people camping in tents on the edge of town. Lots of people leaving to find places to live, because there's nothing around here. It's just weird.'

'Yes.'

He almost had it, now. Amy opened the TARDIS door. She looked inside. 'Doctor . . . it's the same size on the inside.'

He beamed, and took her on an extensive tour of his new office, which consisted of standing inside the doorway and making a waving gesture with his right arm. Most of the space was taken up with a desk, with an old-fashioned telephone, and a typewriter on it. There was a back wall. Amy experimentally pushed her hands through the wall (it was hard to do with her eyes open, easy when she closed them), then she closed her eyes and pushed her head through the wall. Now she could see the TARDIS control room, all copper and glass. She took a step backwards, into the tiny office.

'Is it a hologram?'

'Sort of.'

There was a hesitant rap at the door of the TARDIS. The Doctor opened it.

'Excuse me. The sign on the door.' The man appeared harassed. His hair was thinning. He looked at the tiny room, mostly filled by a desk, and he made no move to come inside.

'Yes! Hello! Come in!' said the Doctor. 'No problem too small!'

'Um. My name's Reg Browning. It's my daughter. Polly. She was meant to be waiting for us, back in the hotel room. She's not there.'

'I'm the Doctor. This is Amy. Have you spoken to the police?'

'Aren't you police? I thought perhaps you were.'

'Why?' asked Amy.

'This is a police call box. I didn't even know they were bringing them back.'

'For some of us,' said the tall young man with the bow tie, 'they never went away. What happened when you spoke to the police?'

'They said they'd keep an eye out for her. But honestly, they seemed a bit preoccupied. The desk sergeant said the lease had run out on the police station, rather unexpectedly, and they're looking for somewhere to go. The desk sergeant said the whole lease thing came as a bit of a blow to them.'

'What's Polly like?' asked Amy. 'Could she be staying with friends?'

'I've checked with her friends. Nobody's seen her. We're living in the Rose Hotel, on Wednesbury Street, right now.'

'Are you visiting?'

Mr Browning told them about the man in the rabbit mask who had come to the door last week to buy their house for so much more than it was worth, and paid cash. He told them about the woman in the cat mask who had taken possession of the house . . .

'Oh. Right. Well, that makes sense of everything,' said the Doctor, as if it actually did.

'It does?' said Mr Browning. 'Do you know where Polly is?'

The Doctor shook his head. 'Mister Browning. Reg. Is there any chance she might have gone back to your house?'

The man shrugged. 'Might have done. Do you think—?'

But the tall young man and the red-haired Scottish girl pushed past him, slammed the door of their police box, and sprinted away across the green.

VI

Amy kept pace with the Doctor, and panted out questions as they ran.

'You think she's in the house?'

'I'm afraid she is. Yes. I've got a sort of an idea. Look, Amy, don't let anyone persuade you to ask *them* the time. And if they do, don't answer them. Safer that way.'

'You mean it?'

'I'm afraid so. And watch out for masks.'

'Right. So these are dangerous aliens we're dealing with? They wear masks and ask you what time it is?'

'It sounds like them. Yes. But my people dealt with them, so long ago. It's almost inconceivable . . .'

They stopped running as they reached Claversham Row.

'And if it is who I think it is, what I think it – they – it – are . . . there is only one sensible thing we should be doing.'

'What's that?'

'Running away,' said the Doctor, as he rang the doorbell.

A moment's silence, then the door opened and a girl looked up at them. She could not have been more than eleven, and her hair was in pigtails. 'Hello,' she said. 'My name is Polly Browning. What's your names?'

'Polly!' said Amy. 'Your parents are worried sick about you.'

'I just came to get my diary back,' said the girl. 'It was under a loose floorboard in my old bedroom.'

'Your parents have been looking for you all day!' said Amy. She wondered why the Doctor didn't say anything.

The little girl – Polly – looked at her wristwatch. 'That's weird. It says I've only been here for five minutes. I got here at ten this morning.'

Amy knew it was somewhere late in the afternoon. She said, 'What time is it now?'

Polly looked up, delighted. This time Amy thought there was something strange about the girl's face. Something flat. Something almost mask-like . . .

'Time for you to come into my house,' said the girl.

Amy blinked. It seemed to her that, without having moved, she and the Doctor were now standing in the entry hall. The girl was standing on the stairs facing them. Her face was level with theirs.

'What are you?' asked Amy.

'We are the Kin,' said the girl, who was not a girl. Her voice was deeper, darker, and more guttural. She seemed to Amy like something crouching, something huge that wore a paper mask with the face of a girl crudely scrawled on it. Amy could not understand how she could ever have been fooled into thinking it was a real face.

'I've heard of you,' said the Doctor. 'My people thought you were—'

'An abomination,' said the crouching thing with the paper mask. 'And a violation of all the laws of time. They sectioned us off from the rest of Creation. But I escaped, and thus we escaped. And we are ready to begin again. Already we have started to purchase this world . . .'

'You're recycling money through time,' said the Doctor. 'Buying up this world with it, starting with this house, the town . . .'

'Doctor? What's going on?' asked Amy. 'Can you explain any of this?'

'All of it,' said the Doctor. 'Sort of wish I couldn't. They've come here to take over the Earth. They're going to become the population of the planet.'

'Oh, no, Doctor,' said the huge crouching creature in the paper mask. 'You don't understand. That's not why we take over the planet. We will take over the world and let humanity become extinct simply in order to get you here, now.'

The Doctor grabbed Amy's hand and shouted, 'Run!' He headed for the front door –

– and found himself at the top of the stairs. He called, 'Amy!' but there was no reply. Something brushed his face: something that felt almost like fur. He swatted it away.

There was one door open, and he walked towards it.

'Hel*lo*,' said the person in the room, in a breathy, female voice. '*So* glad you could come, Doctor.'

It was Margaret Thatcher, the prime minister of Great Britain.

'You *do* know who we are, dear?' she asked. 'It would be such a *shame* if you didn't.'

'The Kin,' said the Doctor. 'A population that only consists of one creature, but able to move through time as easily and instinctively as a human can cross the road. There was only one of you. But you'd populate a place by moving backwards and forwards in time until there were hundreds of you, then thousands and millions, all interacting with yourselves at different moments in your own timeline. And this would go on until the local structure of time would collapse, like rotten wood. You need other entities, at least in the beginning, to ask you the time, and create the quantum superpositioning that allows you to anchor to a place–time location.'

'Very *good*,' said Mrs Thatcher. 'Do you *know* what the Time Lords said, when they engulfed our world? They said that as *each* of us was the Kin at a different moment in time, to kill any one of us was to commit an act of genocide against our whole species. You cannot kill *me*, because to kill me is to kill *all* of us.'

'You know I'm the last Time Lord?'

'Oh *yes*, dear.'

'Let's see. You pick up the money from the mint as it's being printed, buy things with it, return it moments later. Recycle it through time. And the masks . . . I suppose they amplify the conviction field. People are going to be much more willing to sell things when they believe that the leader of their country is asking for them, personally . . . and eventually you've sold the whole place to yourselves. Will you kill the humans?'

'*No* need, dear. We'll even make reser*v*ations for them: Greenland, Siberia, Antarctica . . . but they *will* die out, none-theless. Several billion people living in places that can barely support a few thousand. Well, dear . . . it *won't* be pretty.' Mrs Thatcher moved. The Doctor concentrated on seeing her as she was. He closed his eyes. Opened them to see a bulky figure wearing a crude black-and-white face mask, with a photograph of Margaret Thatcher on it.

The Doctor reached out his hand and pulled off the mask from the Kin.

The Doctor could see beauty where humans could not. He took joy in all creatures. But the face of the Kin was hard to appreciate.

'You . . . you revolt yourself,' said the Doctor. 'Blimey. It's why you wear masks. You don't like your face, do you?'

The Kin said nothing. Its face, if that was its face, writhed and squirmed.

'Where's Amy?' asked the Doctor.

'Surplus to requirements,' said another, similar voice, from behind him. A thin man, in a rabbit mask. 'We let her go. We only needed you, Doctor. Our Time Lord prison was a torment, because we were trapped in it and reduced to one of us. You are also only one of you. And you will stay here in this house forever.'

The Doctor walked from room to room, examining his surroundings with care. The walls of the house were soft and covered with a light layer of fur. And they moved, gently, in and out, as if they were . . . 'Breathing. It's a living room. Literally.'

He said, 'Give me Amy back. Leave this place. I'll find you somewhere you can go. You can't just keep looping and re-looping through time, over and over, though. It messes everything up.'

'And when it does, we begin again, somewhere else,' said the woman in the cat mask, on the stairs. 'You will be imprisoned until your life is done. Age here, regenerate here, die here, over and over. Our prison will not end until the last Time Lord is no more.'

'Do you really think you can hold me that easily?' the Doctor asked. It was always good to seem in control, no matter how much he was worried that he was going to be stuck here for good.

'Quickly! Doctor! Down here!' It was Amy's voice. He took the steps three at a time, heading towards the place her voice had come from: the front door.

'Doctor!'

'I'm here.' He rattled the door. It was locked. He pulled out his screwdriver, and soniced the door handle.

There was a clunk and the door flew open: the sudden daylight was blinding. The Doctor saw, with delight, his friend, and a familiar big blue police box. He was not certain which to hug first.

'Why didn't you go inside?' he asked Amy, as he opened the TARDIS door.

'Can't find the key. Must have dropped it while they were chasing me. Where are we going now?'

'Somewhere safe. Well, safer.' He closed the door. 'Got any suggestions?'

Amy stopped at the bottom of the control room stairs and looked around at the gleaming coppery world, at the glass pillar that ran through the TARDIS controls, at the doors.

'Amazing, isn't she?' said the Doctor. 'I never get tired of looking at the old girl.'

'Yes, the old girl,' said Amy. 'I think we should go to the very dawn of time, Doctor. As early as we can go. They won't be able to find us there, and we can work out what to do next.' She was looking over the Doctor's shoulder at the console, watching his hands move, as if she was determined not to forget anything he did. The TARDIS was no longer in 1984.

'The dawn of time? Very clever, Amy Pond. That's somewhere we've never gone before. Somewhere we shouldn't be able to go. It's a good thing I've got this.' He held up the squiggly whatsit, then attached it to the TARDIS console, using alligator clips and what looked like a piece of string.

'There,' he said proudly. 'Look at that.'

'Yes,' said Amy. 'We've escaped the Kin's trap.'

The TARDIS engines began to groan, and the whole room began to judder and shake.

'What's that noise?'

'We're heading for somewhere the TARDIS isn't designed to go. Somewhere I wouldn't dare go without the squiggly whatsit giving us a boost and a time bubble. The noise is the engines complaining. It's like going up a steep hill in an old car. It may take us a few more minutes to get there. Still, you'll like it when we arrive: the dawn of time. Excellent suggestion.'

'I'm sure I will like it,' said Amy, with a smile. 'It must have felt so good to escape the Kin's prison, Doctor.'

'That's the funny thing,' said the Doctor. 'You ask me about escaping the Kin's prison. That house. And I mean, I did escape, just by sonicing a doorknob, which was a bit convenient. But what if the trap wasn't the house? What if the Kin didn't want a Time Lord to torture and kill? What if they wanted something much more important. What if they wanted a TARDIS?'

'Why would the Kin want a TARDIS?' asked Amy.

The Doctor looked at Amy. He looked at her with clear eyes, unclouded by hate or by illusion. 'The Kin can't travel very far through time. Not easily. And doing what they do is slow, and it takes an effort. The Kin would have to travel back and forward in time fifteen million times just to populate London.

'What if the Kin had all of Time and Space to move through? What if it went back to the very beginning of the Universe, and began its existence there? It would be able to populate every-thing. There would be no intelligent beings in the whole of the SpaceTime Continuum that wasn't the Kin. One entity would fill the Universe, leaving no room for anything else. Can you imagine it?'

Amy licked her lips. 'Yes,' she said. 'Yes I can.'

'All you'd need would be to get into a TARDIS, and have a Time Lord at the controls, and the Universe would be your playground.'

'Oh yes,' said Amy, and she was smiling broadly, now. 'It will be.'

'We're almost there,' said the Doctor. 'The dawn of time. Please. Tell me that Amy's safe, wherever she is.'

'Why ever would I tell you that?' asked the Kin in the Amy Pond mask. 'It's not true.'

VII

Amy could hear the Doctor running down the stairs. She heard a voice that sounded strangely familiar calling to him, and then she heard a sound that filled her chest with despair: the diminishing *vworp vworp* of a TARDIS as it leaves.

The door opened, at that moment, and she walked out into the downstairs hall.

'He's run out on you,' said a deep voice. 'How does it feel to be abandoned?'

'The Doctor doesn't abandon his friends,' said Amy to the thing in the shadows.

'He does. He obviously did in this case. You can wait as long as you want to, he'll never come back,' said the thing, as it stepped out of the darkness, and into the half-light.

It was huge. Its shape was humanoid, but also somehow animal (*Lupine,* thought Amy Pond, as she took a step backwards, away from the thing). It had a mask on, an unconvincing wooden mask, that seemed like it was meant to represent an angry dog, or perhaps a wolf.

'He's taking someone he believes to be you for a ride in the TARDIS. And in a few moments, reality is going to rewrite. The Time Lords reduced the Kin to one lonely entity cut off from the rest of Creation. So it is fitting that a Time Lord restores us to our rightful place in the order of things: all other things will serve me, or will be me, or will be food for me. Ask me what time it is, Amy Pond.'

'Why?'

There were more of them, now, shadowy figures. A cat-faced woman on the stairs. A small girl in the corner. The rabbit-headed man standing behind her said, 'Because it will be a clean way to die. An easy way to go. In a few moments you will never have existed anyway.'

'Ask me,' said the wolf-masked figure in front of her. 'Say, "What's the time, Mister Wolf?"'

In reply, Amy Pond reached up and pulled the wolf mask from the face of the huge thing, and she saw the Kin.

Human eyes were not meant to look at the Kin. The crawling, squirming, wriggling mess that was the face of the Kin was a frightful thing: the masks had been as much for its own protection as for everyone else's.

Amy Pond stared at the face of the Kin. She said, 'Kill me if you're going to kill me. But I don't believe that the Doctor has abandoned me. And I'm not going to ask you what time it is.'

'Pity,' said the Kin, through a face that was a nightmare. And it moved towards her.

* * *

The TARDIS engines groaned once, loudly, and then were silent.

'We are here,' said the Kin. Its Amy Pond mask was now just a flat, scrawled drawing of a girl's face.

'We're here at the beginning of it all,' said the Doctor, 'because that's where you want to be. But I'm prepared to do this another way. I could find a solution for you. For all of you.'

'Open the door,' grunted the Kin.

The Doctor opened the door. The winds that swirled about the TARDIS pushed the Doctor backwards.

The Kin stood at the door of the TARDIS. 'It's so dark.'

'We're at the very start of it all. Before light.'

'I will walk into the void,' said the Kin. 'And you will ask me, "What time is it?" And I will tell myself, tell you, tell all Creation, *Time for the Kin to rule, to occupy, to invade. Time for the Universe to become only me and mine and whatever I keep to devour. Time for the first and final reign of the Kin, world without end, through all of time.*'

'I wouldn't do it,' said the Doctor. 'If I were you. You can still change your mind.'

The Kin dropped the Amy Pond mask onto the TARDIS floor. It pushed itself out of the TARDIS door, into the Void.

'Doctor,' it called. Its face was a writhing mass of maggots. 'Ask me what time it is.'

'I can do better than that,' said the Doctor. 'I can *tell* you exactly what time it is. It's no time. It's Nothing O'Clock. It's a microsecond before the Big Bang. We're not at the Dawn of Time. We're before the Dawn.

'The Time Lords really didn't like genocide. I'm not too keen on it myself. It's the potential you're killing off. What if one day there was a good Dalek? What if . . .' He paused. 'Space is big. Time is bigger. I would have helped you to find a place your people could have lived. But there was a girl called Polly, and she left her diary behind. And you killed her. That was a mistake.'

'You never even knew her,' called the Kin from the Void.

'She was a kid,' said the Doctor. 'Pure potential, like every kid everywhere. I know all I need.' The squiggly whatsit attached to the TARDIS console was beginning to smoke and spark. 'You're out of time, literally. Because Time doesn't start until the Big Bang. And if any part of a creature that inhabits time gets removed from time . . . well, you're removing yourself from the whole picture.'

The Kin understood. It understood that, at that moment, all of Time and Space was one tiny particle, smaller than an atom, and that until a microsecond passed, and the particle exploded, nothing would happen. Nothing could happen. And the Kin was on the wrong side of the microsecond.

Cut off from Time, all the other parts of the Kin were ceasing to be. The It that was They felt the wash of nonexistence sweeping over them.

In the beginning – before the beginning – was the word. And the word was 'Doctor!'

But the door had been closed and the TARDIS vanished, implacably. The Kin was left alone, in the void before Creation.

Alone, forever, in that moment, waiting for Time to begin.

VIII

The young man in the tweed jacket walked around the house at the end of Claversham Row. He knocked at the door, but no one answered. He went back into the blue box, and fiddled with the tiniest of controls: it was always easier to travel a thousand years than it was to travel twenty-four hours.

He tried again.

He could feel the threads of time ravelling and reravelling. Time is complex: not everything that has happened has happened, after all. Only the Time Lords understood it, and even they found it impossible to describe.

The house in Claversham Row had a grimy FOR SALE sign in the garden.

He knocked at the door.

'Hello,' he said. 'You must be Polly. I'm looking for Amy Pond.'

The girl's hair was in pigtails. She looked up at the Doctor suspiciously. 'How do you know my name?' she asked.

'I'm very clever,' said the Doctor, seriously.

Polly shrugged. She went back into the house, and the Doctor followed. There was, he was relieved to notice, no fur on the walls.

Amy was in the kitchen, drinking tea with Mrs Browning. Radio Four was playing in the background. Mrs Browning was telling Amy about her job as a nurse, and the hours she had to work, and Amy was saying that her fiancé was a nurse, and she knew all about it.

She looked up, sharply, when the Doctor came in: a look as if to say 'You've got a lot of explaining to do.'

'I thought you'd be here,' said the Doctor. 'If I just kept looking.'

* * *

They left the house on Claversham Row: the blue police box was parked at the end of the road, beneath some chestnut trees.

'One moment,' said Amy, 'I was about to be eaten by that creature. The next I was sitting in the kitchen, talking to Mrs Browning, and listening to *The Archers*. How did you do that?'

'I'm very clever,' said the Doctor. It was a good line, and he was determined to use it as much as possible.

'Let's go home,' said Amy. 'Will Rory be there this time?'

'Everybody in the world will be there,' said the Doctor. 'Even Rory.'

They went into the TARDIS. He had already removed the blackened remains of the squiggly whatsit from the console: the TARDIS would not again be able to reach the moment before time began, but then, all things considered, that had to be a good thing.

He was determined to take Amy straight home – with just a small side trip to Andalusia, during the age of chivalry, where, in a small inn on the road to Seville, he had once been served the finest gazpacho he had ever tasted.

The Doctor was almost completely sure he could find it again . . .

'We'll go straight home,' he said. 'After lunch. And over lunch, I'll tell you the story of Maximelos and the three Ogrons.'

Diamonds and Pearls: A Fairy Tale

Once upon the olden times, when the trees walked and the stars danced, there was a girl whose mother died, and a new mother came and married her father, bringing her own daughter with her. Soon enough the father followed his first wife to the grave, leaving his daughter behind him.

The new mother did not like the girl and treated her badly, always favouring her own daughter, who was indolent and rude. One day, her stepmother gave the girl, who was only eighteen, twenty dollars to buy her drugs. 'Don't stop on the way,' she said.

So the girl took the twenty-dollar bill, and put an apple into her purse, for the way was long, and she walked out of the house and down to the end of the street, where the wrong side of town began.

She saw a dog tied to a lamppost, panting and uncomfortable in the heat, and the girl said, 'Poor thing.' She gave it water.

The elevator was out of service. The elevator there was always out of service. Halfway up the stairs she saw a hooker, with a swollen face, who stared up at her with yellow eyes. 'Here,' said the girl. She gave the hooker the apple.

She went up to the dealer's floor and she knocked on the door three times. The dealer opened the door and stared at her and said nothing. She showed him the twenty-dollar bill.

Then she said, 'Look at the state of this place,' and she bustled in. 'Don't you ever clean up in here? Where are your cleaning supplies?'

The dealer shrugged. Then he pointed to a closet. The girl opened it and found a broom and a rag. She filled the bathroom sink with water and she began to clean the place.

When the rooms were cleaner, the girl said, 'Give me the stuff for my mother.'

He went into the bedroom, came back with a plastic bag. The girl pocketed the bag and walked down the stairs.

'Lady,' said the hooker. 'The apple was good. But I'm hurting real bad. You got anything?'

The girl said, 'It's for my mother.'

'Please?'

'You poor thing.'

The girl hesitated, then she gave her the packet. 'I'm sure my stepmother will understand,' she said.

She left the building. As she passed, the dog said, 'You shine like a diamond, girl.'

She got home. Her mother was waiting in the front room. 'Where is it?' she demanded.

'I'm sorry,' said the girl. Diamonds dropped from her lips, rattled across the floor.

Her stepmother hit her.

'Ow!' said the girl, a ruby red cry of pain, and a ruby fell from her mouth.

Her stepmother fell to her knees, picked up the jewels. 'Pretty,' she said. 'Did you steal them?'

The girl shook her head, scared to speak.

'Do you have any more in there?'

The girl shook her head, mouth tightly closed.

The stepmother took the girl's tender arm between her finger and her thumb and pinched as hard as she could, squeezed until the tears glistened in the girl's eyes, but she said nothing.

So her stepmother locked the girl in her windowless bedroom, so she could not get away.

The woman took the diamonds and the ruby to Al's Pawn and Gun, on the corner, where Al gave her five hundred dollars no questions asked.

Then she sent her other daughter off to buy drugs for her.

The girl was selfish. She saw the dog panting in the sun, and, once she was certain that it was chained up and could not follow, she kicked at it. She pushed past the hooker on the stair. She reached the dealer's apartment and knocked on the door. He looked at her, and she handed him the twenty without speaking. On her way back down, the hooker on the stair said, 'Please . . . ?' but the girl did not even slow.

'Bitch!' called the hooker.

'Snake,' said the dog, when she passed it on the sidewalk.

Back home, the girl took out the drugs, then opened her mouth to say, 'Here,' to her mother. A small frog, brightly coloured, slipped from her lips. It leapt from her arm to the wall, where it hung and stared at them unblinking.

'Oh my god,' said the girl. 'That's just disgusting.' Five more coloured tree frogs, and one small red, black and yellow–banded snake.

'Black against red,' said the girl. 'Is that poisonous?' (Three more tree frogs, a cane toad, a small, blind white snake, and a baby iguana.) She backed away from them.

Her mother, who was not afraid of snakes or of anything, kicked at the banded snake, which bit her leg. The woman screamed and flailed, and her daughter also began to scream, a long loud scream which fell from her lips as a healthy adult python.

The girl, the first girl, whose name was Amanda, heard the screams and then the silence but she could do nothing to find out what was happening.

She knocked on the door. No one opened it. No one said anything. The only sounds she could hear were rustlings, as if of something huge and legless slipping across the carpet.

When Amanda got hungry, too hungry for words, she began to speak.

'Thou still unravish'd bride of quietness,' she began. 'Thou foster child of Silence and slow Time . . .'

She spoke, although the words were choking her.

'Beauty is truth, truth beauty, – that is all ye know on earth, and all ye need to know . . .' A final sapphire clicked across the wooden floor of Amanda's closet room.

The silence was absolute.

The Return of the Thin White Duke

He was the monarch of all he surveyed, even when he stood out on the palace balcony at night listening to reports and he glanced up into the sky at the bitter twinkling clusters and whorls of stars. He ruled the worlds. He had tried for so long to rule wisely, and well, and to be a good monarch, but it is hard to rule, and wisdom can be painful. And it is impossible, he had found, if you rule, to do only good, for you cannot build anything without tearing something down, and even he could not care about every life, every dream, every population of every world.

Bit by bit, moment by moment, death by little death, he ceased to care.

He would not die, for only inferior people died, and he was the inferior of no one.

Time passed. One day, in the deep dungeons, a man with blood on his face looked at the Duke and told him he had become a monster. The next moment, the man was no more; a footnote in a history book.

The Duke gave this conversation much thought over the next several days, and eventually he nodded his head. 'The traitor was right,' he said. 'I have become a monster. Ah well. I wonder if any of us set out to be monsters?'

Once, long ago, there had been lovers, but that had been in

the dawn days of the Dukedom. Now, in the dusk of the world, with all pleasures available freely (but what we attain with no effort we cannot value), and with no need to deal with any issues of succession (for even the notion that another would one day succeed the Duke bordered upon blasphemy), there were no more lovers, just as there were no challenges. He felt as if he were asleep while his eyes were open and his lips spoke, but there was nothing to wake him.

The day after it had occurred to the Duke that he was now a monster was the Day of Strange Blossoms, celebrated by the wearing of flowers brought to the Ducal Palace from every world and every plane. It was a day that all in the Ducal Palace, which covered a continent, were traditionally merry, and in which they cast off their cares and darknesses, but the Duke was not happy.

'How can you be made happy?' asked the information beetle on his shoulder, there to relay his master's whims and desires to a hundred hundred worlds. 'Give the word, Your Grace, and empires will rise and fall to make you smile. Stars will flame novae for your entertainment.'

'Perhaps I need a heart,' said the Duke.

'I shall have a hundred hundred hearts immediately plucked, ripped, torn, incised, sliced and otherwise removed from the chests of ten thousand perfect specimens of humanity,' said the information beetle. 'How do you wish them prepared? Shall I alert the chefs or the taxidermists, the surgeons or the sculptors?'

'I need to care about something,' said the Duke. 'I need to value life. I need to wake.'

The beetle chittered and chirruped on his shoulder; it could access the wisdom of ten thousand worlds, but it could not advise its master when he was in this mood, so it said nothing. It relayed its concern to its predecessors, the older information beetles and scarabs, now sleeping in ornate boxes on a hundred hundred worlds, and the scarabs consulted among themselves with regret, because, in the vastness of time, even this had happened before, and they were prepared to deal with it.

A long-forgotten subroutine from the morning of the worlds was set into motion. The Duke was performing the final ritual of the Day of Strange Blossoms with no expression on his thin face, a man seeing his world as it was and valuing it not at all, when a small winged creature fluttered out from the blossom in which she had been hiding.

'Your Grace,' she whispered. 'My mistress needs you. Please. You are her only hope.'

'Your mistress?' asked the Duke.

'The creature comes from Beyond,' clicked the beetle on his shoulder. 'From one of the places that does not acknowledge the Ducal Overlordship, from the lands beyond life and death, between being and unbeing. It must have hidden itself inside an imported offworld orchid blossom. Its words are a trap, or a snare. I shall have it destroyed.'

'No,' said the Duke. 'Let it be.' He did something he had not done for many years, and stroked the beetle with a thin white finger. Its green eyes turned black and it chittered into perfect silence.

He cupped the tiny thing in his hands, and walked back to his quarters, while she told him of her wise and noble Queen, and of the giants, each more beautiful than the last, and each more huge and dangerous and more monstrous, who kept her Queen a captive.

And as she spoke, the Duke remembered the days when a lad from the stars had come to World to seek his fortune (for in those days there were fortunes everywhere, just waiting to be found); and in remembering he discovered that his youth was less distant than he had thought. His information beetle lay quiescent upon his shoulder.

'Why did she send you to me?' he asked the little creature.

But, her task accomplished, she would speak no more, and in moments she vanished, as instantly and as permanently as a star that had been extinguished upon Ducal order.

He entered his private quarters, and placed the deactivated information beetle in its case beside his bed. In his study, he had his servants bring him a long black case. He opened it himself, and, with a touch, he activated his master advisor. It shook itself, then wriggled up and about his shoulders in viper form, its serpent tail forking into the neural plug at the base of his neck.

The Duke told the serpent what he intended to do.

'This is not wise,' said the master advisor, the intelligence and advice of every Ducal advisor in memory available to it, after a moment's examination of precedent.

'I seek adventure, not wisdom,' said the Duke. A ghost of a smile began to play at the edges of his lips; the first smile that his servants had seen in longer than they could remember.

'Then, if you will not be dissuaded, take a battle-steed,' said the advisor. It was good advice. The Duke deactivated his master advisor and he sent for the key to the battle-steeds' stable. The key had not been played in a thousand years: its strings were dusty.

There had once been six battle-steeds, one for each of the Lords and Ladies of the Evening. They were brilliant, beautiful, unstoppable, and when the Duke had been forced, with regret, to terminate the career of each of the Rulers of the Evening, he had declined to destroy their battle-steeds, instead placing them where they could be of no danger to the worlds.

The Duke took the key and played an opening arpeggio. The gate opened, and an ink-black, jet-black, coal-black battle-steed strutted out with feline grace. It raised its head and stared at the world with proud eyes.

'Where do we go?' asked the battle-steed. 'What do we fight?'

'We go Beyond,' said the Duke. 'And as to whom we shall fight . . . well, that remains to be seen.'

'I can take you anywhere,' said the battle-steed. 'And I will kill those who try to hurt you.'

The Duke clambered onto the battle-steed's back, the cold metal yielding as live flesh between his thighs, and he urged it forward.

A leap and it was racing through the froth and flux of Underspace: together they were tumbling through the madness between the worlds. The Duke laughed, then, where no man could hear him, as they travelled together through Underspace, travelling forever in the Undertime (that is not reckoned against the seconds of a person's life).

'This feels like a trap, of some kind,' said the battle-steed, as the space beneath galaxies evaporated about them.

'Yes,' said the Duke. 'I am sure that it is.'

'I have heard of this Queen,' said the battle-steed, 'or of some-thing like her. She lives between life and death, and calls warriors and heroes and poets and dreamers to their doom.'

'That sounds right,' said the Duke.

'And when we return to real-space, I would expect an ambush,' said the battle-steed.

'That sounds more than probable,' said the Duke, as they reached their destination, and erupted out of Underspace back into existence.

The guardians of the palace were as beautiful as the messenger had warned him, and as ferocious, and they were waiting.

'What are you doing?' they called, as they came in for the assault. 'Do you know that strangers are forbidden here? Stay with us. Let us love you. We will devour you with our love.'

'I have come to rescue your Queen,' he told them.

'Rescue the Queen?' they laughed. 'She will have your head on a plate before she looks at you. Many people have come to save her, over the years. Their heads sit on golden plates in her palace. Yours will simply be the freshest.'

There were men who looked like fallen angels and women who looked like demons risen. There were people so beautiful that they would have been all that the Duke had ever desired, had they been human, and they pressed close to him, skin to carapace and flesh against armour, so they could feel the coldness of him, and he could feel the warmth of them.

'Stay with us. Let us love you,' they whispered, and they reached out with sharp talons and teeth.

'I do not believe your love will prove to be good for me,' said the Duke. One of the women, fair of hair, with eyes of a peculiar translucent blue, reminded him of someone long forgotten, of a lover who had passed out of his life a long time before. He found her name in his mind, and would have called it aloud, to see if she turned, to see if she knew him, but the battle-steed lashed out with sharp claws, and the pale blue eyes were closed forever.

The battle-steed moved fast, like a panther, and each of the guardians fell to the ground, and writhed and was still.

The Duke stood before the Queen's palace. He slipped from his battle-steed to the fresh earth.

'Here, I go on alone,' he said. 'Wait, and one day I shall return.'

'I do not believe you will ever return,' said the battle-steed. 'I shall wait until time itself is done, if need be. But still, I fear for you.'

The Duke touched his lips to the black steel of the steed's head, and bade it farewell. He walked on to rescue the Queen. He remembered a monster who had ruled worlds and who would never die, and he smiled, because he was no longer that man. For the first time since his first youth he had something to lose, and the discovery of that made him young again. His heart began to pound in his chest as he walked through the empty palace, and he laughed out loud.

She was waiting for him, in the place where flowers die. She was everything he had imagined that she would be. Her skirt was simple and white, her cheekbones were high and very dark, her hair was long and the infinitely dark colour of a crow's wing.

'I am here to rescue you,' he told her.

'You are here to rescue yourself,' she corrected him. Her voice was almost a whisper, like the breeze that shook the dead blossoms.

He bowed his head, although she was as tall as he was.

'Three questions,' she whispered. 'Answer them correctly, and all you desire shall be yours. Fail, and your head will rest forever on a golden dish.' Her skin was the brown of the dead rose petals. Her eyes were the dark gold of amber.

'Ask your three questions,' he said, with a confidence he did not feel.

The Queen reached out a finger and she ran the tip of it gently along his cheek. The Duke could not remember the last time that anybody had touched him without his permission.

'What is bigger than the universe?' she asked.

'Underspace and Undertime,' said the Duke. 'For they both include the universe, and also all that is not the universe. But I suspect you seek a more poetic, less accurate answer. The mind, then, for it can hold a universe, but also imagine things that have never been, and are not.'

The Queen said nothing.

'Is that right? Is that wrong?' asked the Duke. He wished, momentarily, for the snakelike whisper of his master advisor, unloading, through its neural plug, the accumulated wisdom of his advisors over the years, or even the chitter of his information beetle.

'The second question,' said the Queen. 'What is greater than a King?'

'Obviously, a Duke,' said the Duke. 'For all Kings, Popes,

Chancellors, Empresses and such serve at and only at my will. But again, I suspect that you are looking for an answer that is less accurate and more imaginative. The mind, again, is greater than a King. Or a Duke. Because, although I am the inferior of nobody, there are those who could imagine a world in which there is something superior to me, and something else again superior to that, and so on. No! Wait! I have the answer. It is from the Great Tree: *Kether*, the Crown, the concept of monarchy, is greater than any King.'

The Queen looked at the Duke with amber eyes, and she said, 'The final question for you. What can you never take back?'

'My word,' said the Duke. 'Although, now I come to think of it, once I give my word, sometimes circumstances change and sometimes the worlds themselves change in unfortunate or unexpected ways. From time to time, if it comes to that, my word needs to be modified in accordance with realities. I would say Death, but, truly, if I find myself in need of someone I have previously disposed of, I simply have them reincorporated . . .'

The Queen looked impatient.

'A kiss,' said the Duke.

She nodded.

'There is hope for you,' said the Queen. 'You believe you are my only hope, but, truthfully, I am yours. Your answers were all quite wrong. But the last was not as wrong as the rest of them.'

The Duke contemplated losing his head to this woman, and found the prospect less disturbing than he would have expected.

A wind blew through the garden of dead flowers, and the Duke was put in mind of perfumed ghosts.

'Would you like to know the answer?' she asked.

'Answers,' he said. 'Surely.'

'Only one answer, and it is this: the heart,' said the Queen. 'The heart is greater than the universe, for it can find pity in it

for everything in the universe, and the universe itself can feel
no pity. The heart is greater than a King, because a heart can
know a King for what he is, and still love him. And once you
give your heart, you cannot take it back.'

'I *said* a kiss,' said the Duke.

'It was not as wrong as the other answers,' she told him. The
wind gusted higher and wilder and for a heartbeat the air was
filled with dead petals. Then the wind was gone as suddenly as
it appeared, and the broken petals fell to the floor.

'So. I have failed, in the first task you set me. Yet I do not
believe my head would look good upon a golden dish,' said the
Duke. 'Or upon any kind of a dish. Give me a task, then, a quest,
something I can achieve to show that I am worthy. Let me rescue
you from this place.'

'I am never the one who needs rescuing,' said the Queen.
'Your advisors and scarabs and programs are done with you.
They sent you here, as they sent those who came before you,
long ago, because it is better for you to vanish of your own
volition than for them to kill you in your sleep. And less
dangerous.' She took his hand in hers. 'Come,' she said. They
walked away from the garden of dead flowers, past the fountains
of light, spraying their lights into the void, and into the citadel
of song, where perfect voices waited at each turn, sighing and
chanting and humming and echoing, although nobody was there
to sing.

Beyond the citadel was only mist.

'There,' she told him. 'We have reached the end of everything, where nothing exists but what we create, by act of will
or by desperation. Here in this place I can speak freely. It is
only us, now.' She looked into his eyes. 'You do not have to
die. You can stay with me. You will be happy to have finally
found happiness, a heart, and the value of existence. And I will
love you.'

The Duke looked at her with a flash of puzzled anger. 'I asked to care. I asked for something to care about. I asked for a heart.'

'And they have given you all you asked for. But you cannot be their monarch and have those things. So you cannot return.'

'I . . . I asked them to make this happen,' said the Duke. He no longer looked angry. The mists at the edge of that place were pale, and they hurt the Duke's eyes when he stared at them too deeply or too long.

The ground began to shake, as if beneath the footsteps of a giant.

'Is anything true here?' asked the Duke. 'Is anything permanent?'

'Everything is true,' said the Queen. 'The giant comes. And it will kill you, unless you defeat it.'

'How many times have you been through this?' asked the Duke. 'How many heads have wound up on golden dishes?'

'Nobody's head has ever wound up on a golden platter,' she said. 'I am not programmed to kill them. They battle for me and they win me and they stay with me, until they close their eyes for the last time. They are content to stay, or I make them content. But you . . . you need your discontent, don't you?'

He hesitated. Then he nodded.

She put her arms around him and kissed him, slowly and gently. The kiss, once given, could not be taken back.

'So now, I will fight the giant and save you?'

'It is what happens.'

He looked at her. He looked down at himself, at his engraved armour, at his weapons. 'I am no coward. I have never walked away from a fight. I cannot return, but I will not be content to stay here with you. So I will wait here, and I will let the giant kill me.'

She looked alarmed. 'Stay with me. Stay.'

The Duke looked behind him, into the blank whiteness. 'What lies out there?' he asked. 'What is beyond the mist?'

'You would run?' she asked. 'You would leave me?'

'I will walk,' he said. 'And I will not walk away. But I will walk towards. I wanted a heart. What is on the other side of that mist?'

She shook her head. 'Beyond the mist is *Malkuth:* the Kingdom. But it does not exist unless you make it so. It becomes as you create it. If you dare to walk into the mist, then you will build a world or you will cease to exist entirely. And you can do this thing. I do not know what will happen, except for this: if you walk away from me you can never return.'

He heard a pounding still, but was no longer certain that it was the feet of a giant. It felt more like the beat, beat, beat of his own heart.

He turned towards the mist, before he could change his mind, and he walked into the nothingness, cold and clammy against his skin. With each step he felt himself becoming less. His neural plugs died, and gave him no new information, until even his name and his status were lost to him.

He was not certain if he was seeking a place or making one. But he remembered dark skin and her amber eyes. He remembered the stars – there would be stars where he was going, he decided. There must be stars.

He pressed on. He suspected he had once been wearing armour, but he felt the damp mist on his face, and on his neck, and he shivered in his thin coat against the cold night air.

He stumbled, his foot glancing against the kerb.

Then he pulled himself upright, and peered at the blurred streetlights through the fog. A car drove close – too close – and vanished past him, the red rear lights staining the mist crimson.

My old manor, he thought, fondly, and that was followed by a moment of pure puzzlement, at the idea of Beckenham as his old anything. He'd only just moved there. It was somewhere to use as a base. Somewhere to escape from. Surely, that was the point?

But the idea, of a man running away (a lord or a duke, perhaps, he thought, and liked the way it felt in his head), hovered and hung in his mind, like the beginning of a song.

'I'd rather write a something song than rule the world,' he said aloud, tasting the words in his mouth. He rested his guitar case against a wall, put his hand in the pocket of his duffel coat, found a pencil stub and a shilling notebook, and wrote them down. He'd find a good two-syllable word for the *something* soon enough, he hoped.

Then he pushed his way into the pub. The warm, beery atmosphere embraced him as he walked inside. The low fuss and grumble of pub conversation. Somebody called his name, and he waved a pale hand at them, pointed to his wristwatch and then to the stairs. Cigarette smoke gave the air a faint blue sheen. He coughed, once, deep in his chest, and craved a cigarette of his own.

Up the stairs with the threadbare red carpeting, holding his guitar case like a weapon, whatever had been in his mind before he turned the corner into the High Street evaporating with each step. He paused in the dark corridor before opening the door to the pub's upstairs room. From the buzz of small talk and the clink of glasses, he knew there were already a handful of people waiting and working. Someone was tuning a guitar.

Monster? thought the young man. *That's got two syllables.*

He turned the word around in his mind several times before he decided that he could find something better, something bigger, something more fitting for the world he intended to conquer, and, with only a momentary regret, he let it go forever, and walked inside.

Feminine Endings

My darling,

Let us begin this letter, this prelude to an encounter, formally, as a declaration, in the old-fashioned way: I love you. You do not know me (although you have seen me, smiled at me, placed coins in the palm of my hand). I know you (although not so well as I would like. I want to be there when your eyes flutter open in the morning, and you see me, and you smile. Surely this would be paradise enough?). So I do declare myself to you now, with pen set to paper. I declare it again: I love you.

I write this in English, your language, a language I also speak. My English is good. I was some years ago in England and in Scotland. I spent a whole summer standing in Covent Garden, except for the month of Edinburgh Festival, when I am in Edinburgh. People who put money in my box in Edinburgh included Mr Kevin Spacey the actor, and Mr Jerry Springer the American television star, who was in Edinburgh for an opera about his life.

I have put off writing this for so long, although I have wanted to, although I have composed it many times in my head. Shall I write about you? About me?

First you.

I love your hair, long and red. The first time I saw you I believed you to be a dancer, and I still believe that you have a dancer's body. The legs, and the posture, head up and back. It was your smile that told me you were a foreigner, before ever I heard you speak. In my country we smile in bursts, like the sun coming out and illuminating the fields and then retreating again behind a cloud too soon. Smiles are valuable here, and rare. But you smiled all the time, as if everything you saw delighted you. You smiled the first time you saw me, even wider than before. You smiled and I was lost, like a small child in a great forest never to find its way home again.

I learned when young that the eyes give too much away. Some in my profession adopt dark spectacles, or even (and these I scorn with bitter laughter as amateurs) masks that cover the whole face. What good is a mask? My solution is that of full-sclera theatrical contact lenses, purchased from an American website for a little under five hundred euro, which cover the whole eye. They are dark grey, of course, and look like stone. They have made me more than five hundred euro, paid for themselves over and over. You may think, given my profession, that I must be poor, but you would be wrong. Indeed, I fancy that you must be surprised by how much I have collected. My needs have been small and my earnings always very good.

Except when it rains.

Sometimes even when it rains. The others as perhaps you have observed, my love, retreat when it rains, put up the umbrellas, run away. I remain where I am. Always. I simply wait, unmoving. It all adds to the conviction of the performance.

And it is a performance, as much as when I was a theatrical actor, a magician's assistant, even when I myself was a dancer. (That is how I am so familiar with the bodies of dancers.) Always, I was aware of the audience as individuals. I have found this with all actors and all dancers, except the shortsighted ones for whom the audience is a blur. My eyesight is good, even through the contact lenses.

'Did you see the man with the moustache in the third row?' we would say. 'He is staring at Minou with lustful glances.'

And Minou would reply, 'Ah yes. But the woman on the aisle, who looks like the German chancellor, she is now fighting to stay awake.' If one person falls asleep, you can lose the whole audience, so we would play the rest of the evening to a middle-aged woman who wished only to succumb to drowsiness.

The second time you stood near me you were so close I could smell your shampoo. It smelled like flowers and fruit. I imagine America as being a whole continent full of women who smell of flowers and fruit. You were talking to a young man from the university. You were complaining about the difficulties of our language for an American. 'I understand what gives a man or a woman gender,' you were saying. 'But what makes a chair mascu-line or a pigeon feminine? Why should a statue have a feminine ending?'

The young man, he laughed and pointed straight at me then. But truly, if you are walking through the square, you can tell nothing about me. The robes look like old marble, water-stained and timeworn and lichened. The skin could be granite. Until I move I am stone and old bronze, and I do not move if I do not want to. I simply stand.

Some people wait in the square for much too long, even in the rain, to see what I will do. They are uncomfortable not knowing, only happy once they have assured themselves that I am a natural, not an artificial. It is the uncertainty that traps people, like a mouse in a glue trap.

I am writing about myself perhaps too much. I know that this is a letter of introduction as much as it is a love letter. I should write about you. Your smile. Your eyes so green. (You do not know the true colour of my eyes. I will tell you. They are brown.) You like classical music, but you have also ABBA and Kid Loco on your iPod nano. You wear no perfume. Your underwear is, for the most part, faded and comfortable, although you have a single set of red-lace brassiere and panties which you wear for special occasions.

People watch me in the square, but the eye is only attracted by motion. I have perfected the tiny movement, so tiny that the passer can scarcely tell if it is something he saw or not. Yes? Too often people will not see what does not move. The eyes see it but do not see it, they discount it. I am human-shaped, but I am not human. So in order to make them see me, to make them look at me, to stop their eyes from sliding off me and paying me no attention, I am forced to make the tiniest motions, to draw their eyes to me. Then, and only then, do they see me. But they do not always know what they have seen.

I think of you as a code to be broken, or as a puzzle to be cracked. Or a jigsaw puzzle, to be put together. I walk through your life, and I stand motionless at the edge of my own. My gestures – statuesque, precise – are too often misinterpreted. I want you. I do not doubt this.

You have a younger sister. She has a MySpace account, and a Facebook account. We talk sometimes on messenger. All too often people assume that a medieval statue exists only in the fifteenth century. This is not so true: I have a room, I have a laptop. My computer is passworded. I practise safe computing. Your password is your first name. That is not safe. Anyone could read your email, look at your photographs, reconstruct your interests from your web history. Someone who was interested and who cared could spend endless hours building up a complex schematic of your life, matching the people in the photographs to the names in the emails, for example. It would not be hard reconstructing a life from a computer, or from cell phone messages. It would be like filling a crossword puzzle.

I remember when I actually admitted to myself that you had taken to watching me, and only me, on your way across the square. You paused. You admired me. You saw me move once, for a child, and you told a woman with you, loud enough to be heard, that I might be a real statue. I take it as the highest compliment. I have many different styles of movement, of course – I can move like clockwork, in a set of tiny jerks and stutters, I can move like a robot or an automaton. I can move like a statue coming to life after hundreds of years of being stone.

Within my hearing you have spoken many times of the beauty of this small city. How, for you, to be standing inside the stained-glass confection of the old church was like being imprisoned inside a kaleidoscope of jewels. It was like being in the heart of the sun. Also, you are concerned about your mother's illness.

When you were an undergraduate you worked as a cook, and your fingertips are covered with the scar-marks of a thousand tiny knife-cuts.

I love you, and it is my love for you that drives me to know all about you. The more I know the closer I am to you. You were to come to my country with a young man, but he broke your heart, and still you came here to spite him, and still you smiled. I close my eyes and I can see you smiling. I close my eyes and I see you striding across the town square in a clatter of pigeons. The women of this country do not stride. They move diffidently, unless they are dancers. And when you sleep your eyelashes flutter. The way your cheek touches the pillow. The way you dream.

I dream of dragons. When I was a small child, at the home, they told me that there was a dragon beneath the old city. I pictured the dragon wreathing like black smoke beneath the buildings, inhabiting the cracks between the cellars, insubstantial and yet always present. That is how I think of the dragon, and how I think of the past, now. A black dragon made of smoke. When I perform I have been eaten by the dragon and have become part of the past. I am, truly, seven hundred years old.

Kings come and kings go. Armies arrive and are absorbed or return home again, leaving only damaged buildings, widows and bastard children behind them, but the statues remain, and the dragon of smoke, and the past.

I say this, although the statue that I emulate is not from this town at all. It stands in front of a church in southern Italy, where it is believed to represent either the sister of John the Baptist, or a local lord who endowed the church to celebrate that he had not died of the plague, or the angel of death.

I had imagined you perfectly pure, my love, pure as I am, yet one time I found that the red lace panties were pushed to the bottom of your laundry hamper, and upon close examination I was able to assure myself that you had, unquestionably, been unchaste the previous evening. Only you know who with, for you did not talk of the incident in your letters home, or allude to it in your online journal.

A small girl looked up at me once, and turned to her mother, and said, 'Why is she so unhappy?' (I translate into English for you, obviously. The girl was referring to me as a statue and thus she used the feminine ending.)

'Why do you believe her to be unhappy?'

'Why else would people make themselves into statues?'

Her mother smiled. 'Perhaps she is unhappy in love,' she said.

I was not unhappy in love. I was prepared to wait until everything was right, something very different.

There is time. There is always time. It is the gift I took from being a statue – one of the gifts, I should say.

You have walked past me and looked at me and smiled, and you have walked past me and other times you barely noticed me as anything other than an object. Truly, it is remarkable how little regard you, or any human, gives to something that remains completely motionless. You have woken in the night, got up, walked to the little toilet, micturated, walked back to your bed, slept once more, peacefully. You would not notice something perfectly still, would you? Something in the shadows?

If I could I would have made the paper for this letter for you out of my body. I thought about mixing in with the ink my blood or spittle, but no. There is such a thing as overstatement, yet great loves demand grand gestures, yes? I am unused to grand gestures. I am more practised in the tiny gestures. I made a small boy scream once, simply by smiling at him when he had convinced himself that I was made of marble. It is the smallest of gestures that will never be forgotten.

I love you, I want you, I need you. I am yours just as you are mine. There. I have declared my love for you.

Soon, I hope, you will know this for yourself. And then we will never part. It will be time, in a moment, to turn around, put down the letter. I am with you, even now, in these old apartments with the Iranian carpets on the walls.

You have walked past me too many times.

No more.

I am here with you. I am here now.

When you put down this letter. When you turn and look across this old room, your eyes sweeping it with relief or with joy or even with terror . . .

Then I will move. Move, just a fraction. And, finally, you will see me.

Observing the Formalities

As you know, I wasn't invited to the Christening. Get
    over it, you tell me.
But it's the little formalities that keep the world turning.
My twelve sisters each had an invitation, engraved, and
    delivered
By a footman. I thought perhaps my footman had got
    lost.

Few invitations reach me here. People no longer leave
    visiting cards.
And even when they did I would tell them I was not at
    home,
Deploring the unmannerliness of these more recent
    generations.
They eat with their mouths open. They interrupt.

Manners are all, and the formalities. When we lose those
We have lost everything. Without them, we might as well
    be dead.
Dull, useless things. The young should be taught a trade,
    should hew or spin,
Should know their place and stick to it. Be seen, not
    heard. Be hushed.

My youngest sister invariably is late, and interrupts. I am
    myself a stickler for punctuality.
I told her, no good will come of being late. I told her,
Back when we were still speaking, when she was still
    listening. She laughed.
It could be argued that I should not have turned up
    uninvited

But people must be taught lessons. Without them, none
    of them will ever learn.
People are dreams and awkwardness and gawk. They
    prick their fingers
Bleed and snore and drool. Politeness is as quiet as a
    grave,
Unmoving, roses without thorns. Or white lilies. People
    have to learn.

Inevitably my sister turned up late. Punctuality is the
    politeness of princes,
That, and inviting all potential godmothers to a
    Christening.
They said they thought I was dead. Perhaps I am. I can
    no longer recall.
Still and all, it was necessary to observe the formalities.

I would have made her future so tidy and polite.
    Eighteen is old enough. More than enough.
After that life gets so messy. Loves and hearts are such
    untidy things.
Christenings are raucous times and loud, and rancorous,
As bad as weddings. Invitations go astray. We'd argue
    about precedence and gifts.

They would have invited me to the funeral.

The Sleeper and the Spindle

It was the closest kingdom to the queen's, as the crow flies, but not even the crows flew it. The high mountain range that served as the border between the two kingdoms discouraged crows as much as it discouraged people, and it was considered unpassable.

More than one enterprising merchant, on each side of the mountains, had commissioned folk to hunt for the mountain pass that would, if it were there, have made a rich man or woman of anyone who controlled it. The silks of Dorimar could have been in Kanselaire in weeks, in months, not years. But there was no such pass to be found and so, although the two kingdoms shared a common border, nobody crossed from one kingdom to the next.

Even the dwarfs, who were tough, and hardy, and composed of magic as much as of flesh and blood, could not go over the mountain range.

This was not a problem for the dwarfs. They did not go over the mountain range. They went under it.

* * *

Three dwarfs, travelling as swiftly as one through the dark paths beneath the mountains:

'Hurry! Hurry!' said the dwarf in the rear. 'We have to buy her the finest silken cloth in Dorimar. If we do not hurry, perhaps it will be sold, and we will be forced to buy her the second-finest cloth.'

'We know! We know!' said the dwarf in the front. 'And we shall buy her a case to carry the cloth back in, so it will remain perfectly clean and untouched by dust.'

The dwarf in the middle said nothing. He was holding his stone tightly, not dropping it or losing it, and was concentrating on nothing else but this. The stone was a ruby, rough-hewn from the rock and the size of a hen's egg. It would be worth a kingdom when cut and set, and would be easily exchanged for the finest silks of Dorimar.

It would not have occurred to the dwarfs to give the young queen anything they had dug themselves from beneath the earth. That would have been too easy, too routine. It's the distance that makes a gift magical, so the dwarfs believed.

* * *

The queen woke early that morning.

'A week from today,' she said aloud. 'A week from today, I shall be married.'

It seemed both unlikely and extremely final. She wondered how she would feel to be a married woman. It would be the end of her life, she decided, if life was a time of choices. In a week from now she would have no choices. She would reign over her people. She would have children. Perhaps she would die in childbirth, perhaps she would die as an old woman, or in battle. But the path to her death, heartbeat by heartbeat, would be inevitable.

She could hear the carpenters in the meadows beneath the castle, building the seats that would allow her people to watch her marry. Each hammer blow sounded like the dull pounding of a huge heart.

* * *

The three dwarfs scrambled out of a hole in the side of the riverbank, and clambered up into the meadow, one, two, three. They climbed to the top of a granite outcrop, stretched, kicked, jumped and stretched themselves once more. Then they sprinted north, towards the cluster of low buildings that made the village of Giff, and in particular to the village inn.

The innkeeper was their friend: they had brought him a bottle of Kanselaire wine – deep red, sweet and rich, and nothing like the sharp, pale wines of those parts – as they always did. He would feed them, and send them on their way, and advise them.

The innkeeper, chest as huge as his barrels, beard as bushy and as orange as a fox's brush, was in the taproom. It was early in the morning, and on the dwarfs' previous visits at that time of day the room had been empty, but now there must have been thirty people in that place, and not a one of them looked happy.

The dwarfs, who had expected to sidle into an empty taproom, found all eyes upon them.

'Goodmaster Foxen,' said the tallest dwarf to the innkeeper.

'Lads,' said the innkeeper, who thought that the dwarfs were boys, for all that they were four, perhaps five times his age, 'I know you travel the mountain passes. We need to get out of here.'

'What's happening?' said the smallest of the dwarfs.

'Sleep!' said the sot by the window.

'Plague!' said a finely dressed woman.

'Doom!' exclaimed a tinker, his saucepans rattling as he spoke. 'Doom is coming!'

'We travel to the capital,' said the tallest dwarf, who was no bigger than a child, and had no beard. 'Is there plague in the capital?'

'It is not plague,' said the sot by the window, whose beard was long and grey, and stained yellow with beer and wine. 'It is sleep, I tell you.'

'How can sleep be a plague?' asked the smallest dwarf, who was also beardless.

'A witch!' said the sot.

'A bad fairy,' corrected a fat-faced man.

'She was an enchantress, as I heard it,' interposed the pot girl.

'Whatever she was,' said the sot, 'she was not invited to a birthing celebration.'

'That's all tosh,' said the tinker. 'She would have cursed the princess whether she'd been invited to the naming-day party or not. She was one of those forest witches, driven to the margins a thousand years ago, and a bad lot. She cursed the babe at birth, such that when the girl was eighteen she would prick her finger and sleep forever.'

The fat-faced man wiped his forehead. He was sweating, although it was not warm. 'As I heard it, she was going to die, but another fairy, a good one this time, commuted her magical death sentence to one of sleep. Magical sleep,' he added.

'So,' said the sot. 'She pricked her finger on something-or-other. And she fell asleep. And the other people in the castle – the lord and the lady, the butcher, baker, milkmaid, lady-in-waiting – all of them slept, as she slept. None of them have aged a day since they closed their eyes.'

'There were roses,' said the pot girl. 'Roses that grew up around the castle. And the forest grew thicker, until it became impassible. This was, what, a hundred years ago?'

'Sixty. Perhaps eighty,' said a woman who had not spoken until now. 'I know, because my aunt Letitia remembered it happening, when she was a girl, and she was no more than seventy when she died of the bloody flux, and that was only five years ago come Summer's End.'

'. . . and brave men,' continued the pot girl. 'Aye, and brave women too, they say, have attempted to travel to the Forest of Acaire, to the castle at its heart, to wake the princess, and, in waking her, to wake all the sleepers, but each and every one of those heroes ended their lives lost in the forest, murdered by bandits, or impaled upon the thorns of the rosebushes that encircle the castle—'

'Wake her how?' asked the middle-sized dwarf, hand still clutching his rock, for he thought in essentials.

'The usual method,' said the pot girl, and she blushed. 'Or so the tales have it.'

'Right,' said the tallest dwarf. 'So, bowl of cold water poured on the face and a cry of "*Wakey! Wakey!*"?'

'A kiss,' said the sot. 'But nobody has ever got that close. They've been trying for sixty years or more. They say the witch—'

'Fairy,' said the fat man.

'Enchantress,' corrected the pot girl.

'Whatever she is,' said the sot. 'She's still there. That's what they say. If you get that close. If you make it through the roses, she'll be waiting for you. She's old as the hills, evil as a snake, all malevolence and magic and death.'

The smallest dwarf tipped his head on one side. 'So, there's a sleeping woman in a castle, and perhaps a witch or fairy there with her. Why is there also a plague?'

'Over the last year,' said the fat-faced man. 'It started in the north, beyond the capital. I heard about it first from travellers coming from Stede, which is near the Forest of Acaire.'

'People fell asleep in the towns,' said the pot girl.

'Lots of people fall asleep,' said the tallest dwarf. Dwarfs sleep rarely: twice a year at most, for several weeks at a time, but he had slept enough in his long lifetime that he did not regard sleep as anything special or unusual.

'They fall asleep whatever they are doing, and they do not wake up,' said the sot. 'Look at us. We fled the towns to come here. We have brothers and sisters, wives and children, sleeping now in their houses or cowsheds, at their workbenches. All of us.'

'It is moving faster and faster,' said the thin, red-haired woman who had not spoken previously. 'Now it covers a mile, perhaps two miles, each day.'

'It will be here tomorrow,' said the sot, and he drained his flagon, gestured to the innkeeper to fill it once more. 'There is nowhere for us to go to escape it. Tomorrow, everything here will be asleep. Some of us have resolved to escape into drunkenness before the sleep takes us.'

'What is there to be afraid of in sleep?' asked the smallest dwarf. 'It's just sleep. We all do it.'

'Go and look,' said the sot. He threw back his head, and drank as much as he could from his flagon. Then he looked back at them, with eyes unfocused, as if he were surprised to still see them there. 'Well, go on. Go and look for yourselves.' He swallowed the remaining drink, then he laid his head upon the table.

They went and looked.

***

'Asleep?' asked the queen. 'Explain yourselves. How so, asleep?'

The dwarf stood upon the table so he could look her in the eye. 'Asleep,' he repeated. 'Sometimes crumpled upon the ground. Sometimes standing. They sleep in their smithies, at their awls, on milking stools. The animals sleep in the fields. Birds, too, slept, and we saw them in trees or dead and broken in fields where they had fallen from the sky.'

The queen wore a wedding gown, whiter than the snow. Around her, attendants, maids of honour, dressmakers and milliners clustered and fussed.

'And why did you three also not fall asleep?'

The dwarf shrugged. He had a russet-brown beard that had always made the queen think of an angry hedgehog attached to the lower portion of his face. 'Dwarfs are magical things. This sleep is a magical thing also. I felt sleepy, mind.'

'And then?'

She was the queen, and she was questioning him as if they were alone. Her attendants began removing her gown, taking it away, folding and wrapping it, so the final laces and ribbons could be attached to it, so it would be perfect.

Tomorrow was the queen's wedding day. Everything needed to be perfect.

'By the time we returned to Foxen's Inn they were all asleep, every man jack-and-jill of them. It is expanding, the zone of the spell, a few miles every day.'

The mountains that separated the two lands were impossibly high, but not wide. The queen could count the miles. She pushed one pale hand through her raven-black hair, and she looked most serious.

'What do you think, then?' she asked the dwarf. 'If I went there. Would I sleep, as they did?'

He scratched his arse, unselfconsciously. 'You slept for a year,' he said. 'And then you woke again, none the worse for it. If any of the bigguns can stay awake there, it's you.'

Outside, the townsfolk were hanging bunting in the streets and decorating their doors and windows with white flowers. Silverware had been polished and protesting children had been forced into tubs of lukewarm water (the oldest child always got the first dunk and the hottest, cleanest water) and then scrubbed with rough flannels until their faces were raw and red. They were then ducked under the water, and the backs of their ears were washed as well.

'I am afraid,' said the queen, 'that there will be no wedding tomorrow.'

She called for a map of the kingdom, identified the villages closest to the mountains, sent messengers to tell the inhabitants to evacuate to the coast or risk royal displeasure.

She called for her first minister and informed him that he would be responsible for the kingdom in her absence, and that he should do his best neither to lose it nor to break it.

She called for her fiancé and told him not to take on so, and that they would still be married, even if he was but a prince and she already a queen, and she chucked him beneath his pretty chin and kissed him until he smiled.

She called for her mail shirt.

She called for her sword.

She called for provisions, and for her horse, and then she rode out of the palace, towards the east.

* * *

It was a full day's ride before she saw, ghostly and distant, like clouds against the sky, the shape of the mountains that bordered the edge of her kingdom.

The dwarfs were waiting for her, at the last inn in the foothills of the mountains, and they led her down deep into the tunnels, the way that the dwarfs travel. She had lived with them, when she was little more than a child, and she was not afraid.

The dwarfs did not speak to her as they walked the deep paths, except, on more than one occasion, to say, 'Mind your head.'

* * *

'Have you noticed,' asked the shortest of the dwarfs, 'something unusual?' They had names, the dwarfs, but human beings were not permitted to know what they were, such things being sacred.

The queen had a name, but nowadays people only ever called her Your Majesty. Names are in short supply in this telling.

'I have noticed many unusual things,' said the tallest of the dwarfs.

They were in Goodmaster Foxen's inn.

'Have you noticed, that even amongst all the sleepers, there is something that does not sleep?'

'I have not,' said the second tallest, scratching his beard. 'For each of them is just as we left him or her. Head down, drowsing, scarcely breathing enough to disturb the cobwebs that now festoon them . . .'

'The cobweb spinners do not sleep,' said the tallest dwarf.

It was the truth. Industrious spiders had threaded their webs from finger to face, from beard to table. There was a modest web in the deep cleavage of the pot girl's breasts. There was a thick cobweb that stained the sot's beard grey. The webs shook and swayed in the draught of air from the open door.

'I wonder,' said one of the dwarfs, 'whether they will starve and die, or whether there is some magical source of energy that gives them the ability to sleep for a long time.'

'I would presume the latter,' said the queen. 'If, as you say, the original spell was cast by a witch, seventy years ago, and those who were there sleep even now, like Red-beard beneath his hill, then obviously they have not starved or aged or died.'

The dwarfs nodded. 'You are very wise,' said a dwarf. 'You always were wise.'

The queen made a sound of horror and of surprise.

'That man,' she said, pointing. 'He looked at me.'

It was the fat-faced man. He had moved slowly, tearing the

webbing, moved his face so that he was facing her. He had looked at her, yes, but he had not opened his eyes.

'People move in their sleep,' said the smallest dwarf.

'Yes,' said the queen. 'They do. But not like that. That was too slow, too stretched, too *meant*.'

'Or perhaps you imagined it,' said a dwarf.

The rest of the sleeping heads in that place moved slowly, in a stretched way, as if they meant to move. Now each of the sleeping faces was facing the queen.

'You did not imagine it,' said the same dwarf. He was the one with the red-brown beard. 'But they are only looking at you with their eyes closed. That is not a bad thing.'

The lips of the sleepers moved in unison. No voice, only the whisper of breath through sleeping lips.

'Did they just say what I thought they said?' asked the shortest dwarf.

'They said, "Mama. It is my birthday",' said the queen, and she shivered.

***

They rode no horses. The horses they passed all slept, standing in fields, and could not be woken.

The queen walked fast. The dwarfs walked twice as fast as she did, in order to keep up.

The queen found herself yawning.

'Bend over, towards me,' said the tallest dwarf. She did so. The dwarf slapped her around the face. 'Best to stay awake,' he said, cheerfully.

'I only yawned,' said the queen.

'How long, do you think, to the castle?' asked the smallest dwarf.

'If I remember my tales and my maps correctly,' said the

queen, 'the Forest of Acaire is about seventy miles from here. Three days' march.' And then she said, 'I will need to sleep tonight. I cannot walk for another three days.'

'Sleep, then,' said the dwarfs. 'We will wake you at sunrise.'

She went to sleep that night in a hayrick, in a meadow, with the dwarfs around her, wondering if she would ever wake to see another morning.

*　*　*

The castle in the Forest of Acaire was a grey, blocky thing, all grown over with climbing roses. They tumbled down into the moat and grew almost as high as the tallest tower. Each year the roses grew out further: close to the stone of the castle there were only dead, brown stems and creepers, with old thorns sharp as knives. Fifteen feet away the plants were green and the blossoming roses grew thickly. The climbing roses, living and dead, were a brown skeleton, splashed with colour, that rendered the grey fastness less precise.

The trees in the Forest of Acaire were pressed thickly together, and the forest floor was dark. A century before, it had been a forest only in name: it had been hunting lands, a royal park, home to deer and wild boar and birds beyond counting. Now the forest was a dense tangle, and the old paths through the forest were overgrown and forgotten.

*　*　*

The fair-haired girl in the high tower slept.

All the people in the castle slept. Each of them was fast asleep, excepting only one.

The old woman's hair was grey, streaked with white, and was so sparse her scalp showed. She hobbled, angrily, through the castle, leaning on her stick, as if she were driven only by hatred, slamming doors, talking to herself as she walked. 'Up the blooming stairs and past the blooming cook and what are you cooking now, eh, great lard-arse, nothing in your pots and pans but dust and more dust, and all you ever ruddy do is snore.'

Into the kitchen garden, neatly tended. The old woman picked rampion and rocket, and she pulled a large turnip from the ground.

Eighty years before, the palace had held five hundred chickens; the pigeon coop had been home to hundreds of fat white doves; rabbits had run, white-tailed, across the greenery of the grass square inside the castle walls; and fish had swum in the moat and the pond: carp and trout and perch. There remained now only three chickens. All the sleeping fish had been netted and carried out of the water. There were no more rabbits, no more doves.

She had killed her first horse sixty years back, and eaten as much of it as she could before the flesh went rainbow-coloured and the carcass began to stink and crawl with blue flies and maggots. Now she only butchered the larger mammals in midwinter, when nothing rotted and she could hack and sear frozen chunks of the animal's corpse until the spring thaw.

The old woman passed a mother, asleep, with a baby dozing at her breast. She dusted them, absently, as she passed, made certain that the baby's sleepy mouth remained on the nipple.

She ate her meal of turnips and greens in silence.

* * *

It was the first great grand city they had come to. The city gates were high and impregnably thick, but they were open wide.

The three dwarfs were all for going around it, for they were not comfortable in cities, distrusted houses and streets as unnatural things, but they followed their queen.

Once in the city, the sheer numbers of people made them uncomfortable. There were sleeping riders on sleeping horses; sleeping cabmen up on still carriages that held sleeping passengers; sleeping children clutching their balls and hoops and the whips for their spinning tops; sleeping flower women at their stalls of brown, rotten, dried flowers; even sleeping fishmongers beside their marble slabs. The slabs were covered with the remains of stinking fish, and they were crawling with maggots. The rustle and movement of the maggots was the only movement and noise the queen and the dwarfs encountered.

'We should not be here,' grumbled the dwarf with the angry brown beard.

'This road is more direct than any other road we could follow,' said the queen. 'Also it leads to the bridge. The other roads would force us to ford the river.'

The queen's temper was equable. She went to sleep at night, and she woke in the morning, and the sleeping sickness had not touched her.

The maggots' rustlings, and, from time to time, the gentle snores and shifts of the sleepers, were all that they heard as they made their way through the city. And then a small child, asleep on a step, said, loudly and clearly, 'Are you spinning? Can I see?'

'Did you hear that?' asked the queen.

The tallest dwarf said only, 'Look! The sleepers are waking!'

He was wrong. They were not waking.

The sleepers were standing, however. They were pushing themselves slowly to their feet, and taking hesitant, awkward, sleeping steps. They were sleepwalkers, trailing gauze cobwebs behind them. Always, there were cobwebs being spun.

'How many people, human people I mean, live in a city?' asked the smallest dwarf.

'It varies,' said the queen. 'In our kingdom, no more than

twenty, perhaps thirty thousand people. This seems bigger than our cities. I would think fifty thousand people. Or more. Why?'

'Because,' said the dwarf, 'they appear to all be coming after us.'

Sleeping people are not fast. They stumble, they stagger, they move like children wading through rivers of treacle, like old people whose feet are weighed down by thick, wet mud.

The sleepers moved towards the dwarfs and the queen. They were easy for the dwarfs to outrun, easy for the queen to outwalk. And yet, and yet, there were so many of them. Each street they came to was filled with sleepers, cobweb-shrouded, eyes tight closed or eyes open and rolled back in their heads showing only the whites, all of them shuffling sleepily forward.

The queen turned and ran down an alleyway and the dwarfs ran with her.

'This is not honourable,' said a dwarf. 'We should stay and fight.'

'There is no honour,' gasped the queen, 'in fighting an opponent who has no idea that you are even there. No honour in fighting someone who is dreaming of fishing or of gardens or of long-dead lovers.'

'What would they do if they caught us?' asked the dwarf beside her.

'Do you wish to find out?' asked the queen.

'No,' admitted the dwarf.

They ran, and they ran, and they did not stop from running until they had left the city by the far gates, and had crossed the bridge that spanned the river.

* * *

The old woman had not climbed the tallest tower in a dozen years. It was a laborious climb, and each step took its toll on her knees and on her hips. She walked up the curving stone stairwell, each small shuffling step she took an agony. There were no railings there, nothing to make the steep steps easier. She leaned on her stick, sometimes, to catch her breath, and then she kept climbing.

She used the stick on the webs, too: thick cobwebs hung and covered the stairs, and the old woman shook her stick at them, pulling the webs apart, leaving spiders scurrying for the walls.

The climb was long, and arduous, but eventually she reached the tower room.

There was nothing in the room but a spindle and a stool, beside one slitted window, and a bed in the centre of the round room. The bed was opulent: crimson and gold cloth was visible beneath the dusty netting that covered it and protected its sleeping occupant from the world.

The spindle sat on the ground, beside the stool, where it had fallen almost eighty years before.

The old woman pushed at the netting with her stick, and dust filled the air. She stared at the sleeper on the bed.

The girl's hair was the golden-yellow of meadow flowers. Her lips were the pink of the roses that climbed the palace walls. She had not seen daylight in a long time, but her skin was creamy, neither pallid nor unhealthy.

Her chest rose and fell, almost imperceptibly, in the semidarkness.

The old woman reached down, and picked up the spindle. She said, aloud, 'If I drove this spindle through your heart, then you'd not be so pretty-pretty, would you? Eh? Would you?'

She walked towards the sleeping girl in the dusty white dress. Then she lowered her hand. 'No. I can't. I wish to all the gods I could.'

All of her senses were fading with age, but she thought she heard voices from the forest. Long ago she had seen them come, the princes and the heroes, watched them perish, impaled upon the thorns of the roses, but it had been a long time since anyone, hero or otherwise, had reached as far as the castle.

'Eh,' she said aloud, as she said so much aloud, for who was to hear her? 'Even if they come, they'll die screaming on the blinking thorns. There's nothing they can do – that anyone can do. Nothing at all.'

***

A woodcutter, asleep by the bole of a tree half-felled half a century before, and now grown into an arch, opened his mouth as the queen and the dwarfs passed and said, 'My! What an unusual naming-day present that must have been!'

Three bandits, asleep in the middle of what remained of the trail, their limbs crooked as if they had fallen asleep while hiding in a tree above and had tumbled, without waking, to the ground below, said, in unison, without waking, 'Will you bring me roses?'

One of them, a huge man, fat as a bear in autumn, seized the queen's ankle as she came close to him. The smallest dwarf did not even hesitate: he lopped the hand off with his hand-axe, and the queen pulled the man's fingers away, one by one, until the hand fell on the leaf mould.

'Bring me roses,' said the three bandits as they slept, with one voice, while the blood oozed indolently onto the ground from the stump of the fat man's arm. 'I would be so happy if only you would bring me roses.'

***

They felt the castle long before they saw it: felt it as a wave of sleep that pushed them away. If they walked towards it their heads fogged, their minds frayed, their spirits fell, their thoughts clouded. The moment they turned away they woke up into the world, felt brighter, saner, wiser.

The queen and the dwarfs pushed deeper into the mental fog.

Sometimes a dwarf would yawn and stumble. Each time the other dwarfs would take him by the arms and march him forward, struggling and muttering, until his mind returned.

The queen stayed awake, although the forest was filled with people she knew could not be there. They walked beside her on the path. Sometimes they spoke to her.

'Let us now discuss how diplomacy is affected by matters of natural philosophy,' said her father.

'My sisters ruled the world,' said her stepmother, dragging her iron shoes along the forest path. They glowed a dull orange, yet none of the dry leaves burned where the shoes touched them. 'The mortal folk rose up against us, they cast us down. And so we waited, in crevices, in places they do not see us. And now, they adore me. Even you, my stepdaughter. Even you adore me.'

'You are so beautiful,' said her mother, who had died so very long ago. 'Like a crimson rose fallen in the snow.'

Sometimes wolves ran beside them, pounding dust and leaves up from the forest floor, although the passage of the wolves did not disturb the huge cobwebs that hung like veils across the path. Also, sometimes the wolves ran through the trunks of trees and off into the darkness.

The queen liked the wolves, and was sad when one of the dwarfs began shouting, saying that the spiders were bigger than pigs, and the wolves vanished from her head and from the world. (It was not so. They were only spiders of a regular size, used to spinning their webs undisturbed by time and by travellers.)

* * *

The drawbridge across the moat was down, and they crossed it, although everything seemed to be pushing them away. They could not enter the castle, however: thick thorns filled the gateway, and fresh growth covered with roses.

The queen saw the remains of men in the thorns: skeletons in armour and skeletons unarmoured. Some of the skeletons were high on the sides of the castle, and the queen wondered if they had climbed up, seeking an entry, and died there, or if they had died on the ground, and been carried upwards as the roses grew.

She came to no conclusions. Either way was possible.

And then her world was warm and comfortable, and she became certain that closing her eyes for only a handful of moments would not be harmful. Who would mind?

'Help me,' croaked the queen.

The dwarf with the brown beard pulled a thorn from the rosebush nearest to him, and jabbed it hard into the queen's thumb, and pulled it out again. A drop of dark blood dripped onto the flagstones of the gateway.

'Ow!' said the queen. And then, 'Thank you!'

They stared at the thick barrier of thorns, the dwarfs and the queen. She reached out and picked a rose from the thorn-creeper nearest her, and bound it into her hair.

'We could tunnel our way in,' said the dwarfs. 'Go under the moat and into the foundations and up. Only take us a couple of days.'

The queen pondered. Her thumb hurt, and she was pleased her thumb hurt. She said, 'This began here eighty or so years ago. It began slowly. It only spread recently. It is spreading faster and faster. We do not know if the sleepers can ever wake. We do not know anything, save that we may not actually have another two days.'

She eyed the dense tangle of thorns, living and dead, decades of dried, dead plants, their thorns as sharp in death as ever they were when alive. She walked along the wall until she reached a skeleton, and she pulled the rotted cloth from its shoulders, and felt it as she did so. It was dry, yes. It would make good kindling.

'Who has the tinder box?' she asked.

* * *

The old thorns burned so hot and so fast. In fifteen minutes orange flames snaked upwards: they seemed, for a moment, to engulf the building, and then they were gone, leaving just blackened stone. The remaining thorns, those strong enough to have withstood the heat, were easily cut through by the queen's sword, and were hauled away and tossed into the moat.

The four travellers went into the castle.

The old woman peered out of the slitted window at the flames below her. Smoke drifted in through the window, but neither the flames nor the roses reached the highest tower. She knew that the castle was being attacked, and she would have hidden in the tower room, had there been anywhere to hide, had the sleeper not been on the bed.

She swore, and began, laboriously, to walk down the steps, one at a time. She intended to make it down as far as the castle's battlements, where she could head over to the far side of the building, to the cellars. She could hide there. She knew the building better than anybody. She was slow, but she was cunning, and she could wait. Oh, she could wait.

She heard their calls rising up the stairwell.

'This way!'

'Up here!'

'It feels worse this way. Come on! Quickly!'

She turned around, then, did her best to hurry upward, but her legs moved no faster than they had when she was climbing earlier that day. They caught her just as she reached the top of the steps, three men, no higher than her hips, closely followed by a young woman in travel-stained clothes, with the blackest hair the old woman had ever seen.

The young woman said, 'Seize her,' in a tone of casual command.

The little men took her stick. 'She's stronger than she looks,' said one of them, his head still ringing from the blow she had got in with the stick, before he had taken it. They walked her back into the round tower room.

'The fire?' said the old woman, who had not talked to anyone who could answer her for decades. 'Was anyone killed in the fire? Did you see the king or the queen?'

The young woman shrugged. 'I don't think so. The sleepers we passed were all inside, and the walls are thick. Who are you?'

Names. Names. The old woman squinted, then she shook her head. She was herself, and the name she had been born with had been eaten by time and lack of use.

'Where is the princess?'

The old woman just stared at her.

'And why are you awake?'

She said nothing. They spoke urgently to one another then, the little men and the queen. 'Is she a witch? There's a magic about her, but I do not think it's of her making.'

'Guard her,' said the queen. 'If she is a witch, that stick might be important. Keep it from her.'

'It's my stick,' said the old woman. 'I think it was my father's. But he had no more use for it.'

The queen ignored her. She walked to the bed, pulled down the silk netting. The sleeper's face stared blindly up at them.

'So this is where it began,' said one of the little men.

'On her birthday,' said another.

'Well,' said the third. 'Somebody's got to do the honours.'

'I shall,' said the queen, gently. She lowered her face to the sleeping woman's. She touched the pink lips to her own carmine lips and she kissed the sleeping girl long and hard.

* * *

'Did it work?' asked a dwarf.

'I do not know,' said the queen. 'But I feel for her, poor thing. Sleeping her life away.'

'You slept for a year in the same witch-sleep,' said the dwarf. 'You did not starve. You did not rot.'

The figure on the bed stirred, as if she were having a bad dream from which she was fighting to wake herself.

The queen ignored her. She had noticed something on the floor beside the bed. She reached down and picked it up. 'Now this,' she said. 'This smells of magic.'

'There's magic all through this,' said the smallest dwarf.

'No, *this*,' said the queen. She showed him the wooden spindle, the base half wound around with yarn. '*This* smells of magic.'

'It was here, in this room,' said the old woman, suddenly. 'And I was little more than a girl. I had never gone so far before, but I climbed all the steps, and I went up and up and round and round until I came to the topmost room. I saw that bed, the one you see, although there was nobody in it. There was only an old woman, sitting on the stool, spinning wool into yarn with her spindle. I had never seen a spindle before. She asked if I would like a go. She took the wool in her hand and gave me the spindle to hold. And then, she held my thumb and pressed it against the point of the spindle until blood flowed, and she touched the blooming blood to the thread. And then she said—'

A voice interrupted her. A young voice it was, a girl's voice, but still sleep-thickened. 'I said, now I take your sleep from you, girl, just as I take from you your ability to harm me in my sleep, for someone needs to be awake while I sleep. Your family, your friends, your world will sleep too. And then I lay down on the bed, and I slept, and they slept, and as each of them slept I stole a little of their life, a little of their dreams, and as I slept I took back my youth and my beauty and my power. I slept and I grew strong. I undid the ravages of time and I built myself a world of sleeping slaves.'

She was sitting up in the bed. She looked so beautiful, and so very young.

The queen looked at the girl, and saw what she was searching for: the same look that she had seen in her stepmother's eyes, and she knew what manner of creature this girl was.

'We had been led to believe,' said the tallest dwarf, 'that when you woke, the rest of the world would wake with you.'

'Why ever would you think that?' asked the golden-haired girl, all childlike and innocent (ah, but her eyes! Her eyes were so old.) 'I like them asleep. They are more . . . *biddable*.' She stopped for a moment. Then she smiled. 'Even now they come for you. I have called them here.'

'It's a high tower,' said the queen. 'And sleeping people do not move fast. We still have a little time to talk, Your Darkness.'

'Who are you? Why would we talk? Why do you know to address me that way?' The girl climbed off the bed and stretched deliciously, pushing each finger out before running her fingertips through her golden hair. She smiled, and it was as if the sun shone into that dim room. 'The little people will stop where they are, now. I do not like them. And you, girl. You will sleep too.'

'No,' said the queen.

She hefted the spindle. The yarn wrapped around it was black with age and with time.

The dwarfs stopped where they stood, and they swayed, and closed their eyes.

The queen said, 'It's always the same with your kind. You need youth and you need beauty. You used your own up so long ago, and now you find ever-more-complex ways of obtaining them. And you always want power.'

They were almost nose to nose, now, and the fair-haired girl seemed so much younger than the queen.

'Why don't you just go to sleep?' asked the girl, and she smiled guilelessly, just as the queen's stepmother had smiled when she wanted something. There was a noise on the stairs, far below them.

'I slept for a year in a glass coffin,' said the queen. 'And the woman who put me there was much more powerful and dangerous than you will ever be.'

'More powerful than I am?' The girl seemed amused. 'I have a million sleepers under my control. With every moment that I slept I grew in power, and the circle of dreams grows faster and faster with every passing day. I have my youth – so much youth! I have my beauty. No weapon can harm me. Nobody alive is more powerful than I am.'

She stopped and stared at the queen.

'You are not of our blood,' she said. 'But you have some of the skill.' She smiled, the smile of an innocent girl who has woken on a spring morning. 'Ruling the world will not be easy. Nor will maintaining order among those of the Sisterhood who have survived into this degenerate age. I will need someone to be my eyes and ears, to administer justice, to attend to things when I am otherwise engaged. I will stay at the centre of the web. You will not rule with me, but beneath me, but you will still rule, and rule continents, not just a tiny kingdom.' She reached out a hand and stroked the queen's pale skin, which, in the dim light of that room, seemed almost as white as snow.

The queen said nothing.

'Love me,' said the girl. 'All will love me, and you, who woke me, you must love me most of all.'

The queen felt something stirring in her heart. She remembered her stepmother then. Her stepmother had liked to be adored. Learning how to be strong, to feel her own emotions and not another's, had been hard; but once you learned the trick of it, you did not forget. And she did not wish to rule continents.

The girl smiled at her with eyes the colour of the morning sky.

The queen did not smile. She reached out her hand. 'Here,' she said. 'This is not mine.'

She passed the spindle to the old woman beside her. The old woman hefted it, thoughtfully. She began to unwrap the yarn from the spindle with arthritic fingers. 'This was my life,' she said. 'This thread was my life . . .'

'It *was* your life. You gave it to me,' said the sleeper, irritably. 'And it has gone on much too long.'

The tip of the spindle was still sharp after so many decades.

The old woman, who had once been a princess, held the yarn tightly in her hand, and she thrust the point of the spindle at the golden-haired girl's breast.

The girl looked down as a trickle of red blood ran down her breast and stained her white dress crimson.

'No weapon can harm me,' she said, and her girlish voice was petulant. 'Not any more. Look. It's only a scratch.'

'It's not a weapon,' said the queen, who understood what had happened. 'It's your own magic. And a scratch is all that was needed.'

The girl's blood soaked into the thread that had once been wrapped about the spindle, the thread that ran from the spindle to the raw wool in the old woman's hand.

The girl looked down at the blood staining her dress, and at the blood on the thread, and she said only, 'It was just a prick of the skin, nothing more.' She seemed confused.

The noise on the stairs was getting louder. A slow, irregular shuffling, as if a hundred sleepwalkers were coming up a stone spiral staircase with their eyes closed.

The room was small, and there was nowhere to hide, and the room's window was a narrow slit in the stones.

The old woman, who had not slept in so many decades, she who had once been a princess, said, 'You took my dreams. You took my sleep. Now, that's enough of all that.' She was a very old woman: her fingers were gnarled, like the roots of a hawthorn bush. Her nose was long, and her eyelids drooped, but there was a look in her eyes in that moment that was the look of someone young.

She swayed, and then she staggered, and she would have fallen to the floor if the queen had not caught her first.

The queen carried the old woman to the bed, marvelling at how little she weighed, and placed her on the crimson counterpane. The old woman's chest rose and fell.

The noise on the stairs was louder now. Then a silence, followed, suddenly, by a hubbub, as if a hundred people were talking at once, all surprised and angry and confused.

The beautiful girl said, 'But—' and now there was nothing girlish or beautiful about her. Her face fell, and became less shapely. She reached down to the smallest dwarf, pulled his hand-axe from his belt. She fumbled with the axe, held it up threateningly, with hands all wrinkled and worn.

The queen drew her sword (the blade-edge was notched and damaged from the thorns) but instead of striking, she took a step backwards.

'Listen! They are waking up,' she said. 'They are all waking up. Tell me again about the youth you stole from them. Tell me again about your beauty and your power. Tell me again how clever you were, Your Darkness.'

When the people reached the tower room, they saw an old

woman asleep on a bed, and they saw the queen, standing tall, and beside her, the dwarfs, who were shaking their heads, or scratching them.

They saw something else on the floor also: a tumble of bones, a hank of hair as fine and as white as fresh-spun cobwebs, a tracery of grey rags across it, and over all of it, an oily dust.

'Take care of her,' said the queen, pointing with the dark wooden spindle at the old woman on the bed. 'She saved your lives.'

She left, then, with the dwarfs. None of the people in that room or on the steps dared to stop them or would ever understand what had happened.

* * *

A mile or so from the castle, in a clearing in the Forest of Acaire, the queen and the dwarfs lit a fire of dry twigs, and in it they burned the thread and the fibre. The smallest dwarf chopped the spindle into fragments of black wood with his axe, and they burned them too. The wood chips gave off a noxious smoke as they burned, which made the queen cough, and the smell of old magic was heavy in the air.

Afterwards, they buried the charred wooden fragments beneath a rowan tree.

By evening they were on the outskirts of the forest, and had reached a cleared track. They could see a village across the hill, and smoke rising from the village chimneys.

'So,' said the dwarf with the beard. 'If we head due west, we can be at the mountains by the end of the week, and we'll have you back in your palace in Kanselaire within ten days.'

'Yes,' said the queen.

'And your wedding will be late, but it will happen soon after your return, and the people will celebrate, and there will be joy unbounded through the kingdom.'

'Yes,' said the queen. She said nothing, but sat on the moss beneath an oak tree and tasted the stillness, heartbeat by heartbeat.

There are choices, she thought, when she had sat long enough. *There are always choices.*

She made her choice.

The queen began to walk, and the dwarfs followed her.

'You *do* know we're heading east, don't you?' said one of the dwarfs.

'Oh yes,' said the queen.

'Well, *that's* all right then,' said the dwarf.

They walked to the east, all four of them, away from the sunset and the lands they knew, and into the night.

Witch Work

The witch was as old as the mulberry tree
She lived in the house of a hundred clocks
She sold storms and sorrows and calmed the sea
And she kept her life in a box.

The tree was the oldest that I'd ever seen
Its trunk flowed like liquid. It dripped with age.
But every September its fruit stained the green
As scarlet as harlots, as red as my rage.

The clocks whispered time which they caught in their
    gears
They crept and they chattered, they chimed and they
    chewed.
She fed them on minutes. The old ones ate years.
She feared and she loved them, her wild clocky brood.

She sold me a storm when my anger was strong
And my hate filled the world with volcanoes and
    laughter
I watched as the lightnings and wind sang their song
And my madness was swallowed by what happened
    after.

She sold me three sorrows all wrapped in a cloth.
The first one I gave to my enemy's child.
The second my woman made into a broth.
The third waits unused, for we reconciled.

She sold calm seas to the mariners' wives
Bound the winds with silk cords so the storms could be
   tied there,
The women at home lived much happier lives
Till their husbands returned, and their patience be tried
   there.

The witch hid her life in a box made of dirt,
As big as a fist and as dark as a heart
There was nothing but time there and silence and hurt
While the witch watched the waves with her pain and
   her art.

(But he never came back. He never came back . . .)

The witch was as old as the mulberry tree
She lived in the house of a hundred clocks
She sold storms and sorrows and calmed the sea
And she kept her life in a box.

In *Relig Odhráin*

When Saint Columba landed on the island of Iona
His friend Oran landed with him
Though some say Saint Oran waited
In the shadows of the island, waiting for the saint to
    land there,
I believe they came together, came from Ireland, were
    like brothers
Were the blond and brave Columba and the dark man
    they called Oran.

He was *odrán,* like the otter, was the other. There were
    others
And they landed on Iona and they said, We'll build a
    chapel.
It's what saints did when they landed. (*Oran:* priest of
    sun or fire
Or from *odhra,* meaning dark-haired.) But their chapel
    kept on crumbling.
And Columba took the answer from a dream or
    revelation,
That his building needed Oran, needed death in the
    foundations.

Others claim it was doctrinal, and Saints Oran and
    Columba

Were debating, as the Irish love debating, about Heaven,
Since the truth is long-forgotten we are left with just
their actions
(By their actions shall ye know them): Saint Columba
buried Oran
Still alive, with earth about him, buried deep, with earth
upon him.

Three days later they returned there, stocky monks with
spades and mattocks
And they dug down to Saint Oran, so Columba could
embrace him
Touch his face and say his farewells. Three days dead.
They brushed the mud off
When Saint Oran's eyes blinked open. Oran grinned at
Saint Columba.
He had died but now was risen, and he said the words
the dead know,
In a voice like wind and water.

He said, Heaven is not waiting for the good and pure and
gentle
There's no punishment eternal, there's no Hell for the
ungodly
Nor is God as you imagine—
                          Saint Columba shouted 'Quiet!'
And to save the monks from error shovelled mud onto
Saint Oran.
So they buried him forever. And they called the place
Saint Oran's.
In its churchyard kings of Scotland, kings of Norway, all
were buried
On the island of Iona.

Some folk claim it was a druid priest of sunlight that
  was buried
In the earth of good Iona just to hold the church
  foundations,
But for me that's much too simple, and it libels Saint
  Columba
(Who cried 'Earth! Throw earth on Oran, stop his mouth
  with mud this moment,
Lest he bring us to perdition!'). They imagine it a murder
As one saint entombed another underneath that holy
  chapel.

While Saint Oran's name continues,
Martyred heretic, his bones still hold the chapel stones
  together,
And we join them, kings and princes, in his graveyard,
  in his chapel,
For it's Oran's name they carry. He's embraced in his
  damnation
By the simple words he uttered. There's no Hell to spite
  the sinners.
There's no Heaven for the blessed. God is not what you
  imagine.

And perhaps he kept on preaching, for he'd died and he
  had risen,
Until silenced, crushed or muffled by the soil of Iona.
Saint Columba, he was buried on the island of Iona
Decades later. But they disinterred his body and they
  took it
To Downpatrick, where it's buried with Saint Patrick and
  Saint Brigid.
So the only saint is Oran on the island of Iona.

Don't go digging in that graveyard for the kings of old,
the mighty,
Or archbishops and their riches. They are guarded by
Saint Oran
Who will rise up from the gravedirt like the darkness,
like an otter,
For he sees the sun no longer. He will touch you,
He will taste you, he will leave his words inside you.
(God is not what you imagine. Nor is Hell and nor is
Heaven.)

Then you'll leave him and his graveyard, and forget the
shadow's terror,
As you rub your neck, remember only this: he died to
save us.
And that Saint Columba killed him on the island of Iona.

Black Dog

There were ten tongues within one head
And one went out to fetch some bread,
To feed the living and the dead.

Old Riddle

I

The Bar Guest

Outside the pub it was raining cats and dogs.
Shadow was still not entirely convinced that he was
in a pub. True, there was a tiny bar at the back of the
room, with bottles behind it and a couple of the huge taps
you pulled, and there were several high tables and people
were drinking at the tables, but it all felt like a room in somebody's house. The dogs helped reinforce that impression. It
seemed to Shadow that everybody in the pub had a dog except
for him.

'What kind of dogs are they?' Shadow asked, curious. The
dogs reminded him of greyhounds, but they were smaller and
seemed saner, more placid and less high-strung than the greyhounds he had encountered over the years.

'Lurchers,' said the pub's landlord, coming out from behind
the bar. He was carrying a pint of beer that he had poured for

himself. 'Best dogs. Poacher's dogs. Fast, smart, lethal.' He bent down, scratched a chestnut-and-white brindled dog behind the ears. The dog stretched and luxuriated in the ear-scratching. It did not look particularly lethal, and Shadow said so.

The landlord, his hair a mop of grey and orange, scratched at his beard reflectively. 'That's where you'd be wrong,' he said. 'I walked with his brother last week, down Cumpsy Lane. There's a fox, a big red reynard, pokes his head out of a hedge, no more than twenty metres down the road, then, plain as day, saunters out onto the track. Well, Needles sees it, and he's off after it like the clappers. Next thing you know, Needles has his teeth in reynard's neck, and one bite, one hard shake, and it's all over.'

Shadow inspected Needles, a grey dog sleeping by the little fireplace. He looked harmless too. 'So what sort of a breed is a lurcher? It's an English breed, yes?'

'It's not actually a breed,' said a white-haired woman without a dog who had been leaning on a nearby table. 'They're crossbred for speed, stamina. Sighthound, greyhound, collie.'

The man next to her held up a finger. 'You must understand,' he said, cheerfully, 'that there used to be laws about who could own purebred dogs. The local folk couldn't, but they could own mongrels. And lurchers are better and faster than pedigree dogs.' He pushed his spectacles up his nose with the tip of his forefinger. He had a muttonchop beard, brown flecked with white.

'Ask me, all mongrels are better than pedigree anything,' said the woman. 'It's why America is such an interesting country. Filled with mongrels.' Shadow was not certain how old she was. Her hair was white, but she seemed younger than her hair.

'Actually, darling,' said the man with the muttonchops, in his gentle voice, 'I think you'll find that the Americans are keener on pedigree dogs than the British. I met a woman from the American Kennel Club, and honestly, she scared me. I was scared.'

'I wasn't talking about dogs, Ollie,' said the woman. 'I was talking about . . . Oh, never mind.'

'What are you drinking?' asked the landlord.

There was a handwritten piece of paper taped to the wall by the bar telling customers not to order a lager 'as a punch in the face often offends'.

'What's good and local?' asked Shadow, who had learned that this was mostly the wisest thing to say.

The landlord and the woman had various suggestions as to which of the various local beers and ciders were good. The little muttonchopped man interrupted them to point out that in his opinion *good* was not the avoidance of evil, but something more positive than that: it was making the world a better place. Then he chuckled, to show that he was only joking and that he knew that the conversation was really only about what to drink.

The beer the landlord poured for Shadow was dark and very bitter. He was not certain that he liked it. 'What is it?'

'It's called Black Dog,' said the woman. 'I've heard people say it was named after the way you feel after you've had one too many.'

'Like Churchill's moods,' said the little man.

'Actually, the beer is named after a local dog,' said a younger woman. She was wearing an olive-green sweater, and standing against the wall. 'But not a real one. Semi-imaginary.'

Shadow looked down at Needles, then hesitated. 'Is it safe to scratch his head?' he asked, remembering the fate of the fox.

'Course it is,' said the white-haired woman. 'He loves it. Don't you?'

'Well. He practically had that tosser from Glossop's finger off,' said the landlord. There was admiration mixed with warning in his voice.

'I think he was something in local government,' said the

woman. 'And I've always thought that there's nothing wrong with dogs biting *them*. Or VAT inspectors.'

The woman in the green sweater moved over to Shadow. She was not holding a drink. She had dark, short hair, and a crop of freckles that spattered her nose and cheeks. She looked at Shadow. 'You aren't in local government, are you?'

Shadow shook his head. He said, 'I'm kind of a tourist.' It was not actually untrue. He was travelling, anyway.

'You're Canadian?' said the muttonchop man.

'American,' said Shadow. 'But I've been on the road for a while now.'

'Then,' said the white-haired woman, 'you aren't actually a tourist. Tourists turn up, see the sights and leave.'

Shadow shrugged, smiled, and leaned down. He scratched the landlord's lurcher on the back of its head.

'You're not a dog person, are you?' asked the dark-haired woman.

'I'm not a dog person,' said Shadow.

Had he been someone else, someone who talked about what was happening inside his head, Shadow might have told her that his wife had owned dogs when she was younger, and sometimes called Shadow *puppy* because she wanted a dog she could not have. But Shadow kept things on the inside. It was one of the things he liked about the British: even when they wanted to know what was happening on the inside, they did not ask. The world on the inside remained the world on the inside. His wife had been dead for three years now.

'If you ask me,' said the man with the muttonchops, 'people are either dog people or cat people. So would you then consider yourself a cat person?'

Shadow reflected. 'I don't know. We never had pets when I was a kid, we were always on the move. But—'

'I mention this,' the man continued, 'because our host also has a cat, which you might wish to see.'

'Used to be out here, but we moved it to the back room,' said the landlord, from behind the bar.

Shadow wondered how the man could follow the conversation so easily while also taking people's meal orders and serving their drinks. 'Did the cat upset the dogs?' he asked.

Outside, the rain redoubled. The wind moaned, and whistled, and then howled. The log fire burning in the little fireplace coughed and spat.

'Not in the way you're thinking,' said the landlord. 'We found it when we knocked through into the room next door, when we needed to extend the bar.' The man grinned. 'Come and look.'

Shadow followed the man into the room next door. The mutton-chop man and the white-haired woman came with them, walking a little behind Shadow.

Shadow glanced back into the bar. The dark-haired woman was watching him, and she smiled warmly when he caught her eye.

The room next door was better lit, larger, and it felt a little less like somebody's front room. People were sitting at tables, eating. The food looked good and smelled better. The landlord led Shadow to the back of the room, to a dusty glass case.

'There she is,' said the landlord, proudly.

The cat was brown, and it looked, at first glance, as if it had been constructed out of tendons and agony. The holes that were its eyes were filled with anger and with pain; the mouth was wide open, as if the creature had been yowling when she was turned to leather.

'The practice of placing animals in the walls of buildings is similar to the practice of walling up children alive in the foundations of a house you want to stay up,' explained the mutton-chop man, from behind him. 'Although mummified cats always make me think of the mummified cats they found around the temple of Bast in Bubastis in Egypt. So many tons of mummified cats that they sent them to England to be ground up as cheap fertiliser and dumped on the fields. The Victorians also made paint out of mummies. A sort of brown, I believe.'

'It looks miserable,' said Shadow. 'How old is it?'

The landlord scratched his cheek. 'We reckon that the wall she was in went up somewhere between 1300 and 1600. That's from parish records. There's nothing here in 1300, and there's a house in 1600. The stuff in the middle was lost.'

The dead cat in the glass case, furless and leathery, seemed to be watching them, from its empty black-hole eyes.

I got eyes wherever my folk walk, breathed a voice in the back of Shadow's mind. He thought, momentarily, about the fields fertilised with the ground mummies of cats, and what strange crops they must have grown.

'*They put him into an old house side,*' said the man called Ollie. '*And there he lived and there he died. And nobody either laughed or cried.* All sorts of things were walled up, to make sure that things were guarded and safe. Children, sometimes. Animals. They did it in churches as a matter of course.'

The rain beat an arrhythmic rattle on the windowpane. Shadow thanked the landlord for showing him the cat. They went back into the taproom. The dark-haired woman had gone, which gave Shadow a moment of regret. She had looked so friendly. Shadow bought a round of drinks for the muttonchop man, the white-haired woman, and one for the landlord.

The landlord ducked behind the bar. 'They call me Shadow,' Shadow told them. 'Shadow Moon.'

The muttonchop man pressed his hands together in delight. 'Oh! How wonderful. I had an Alsatian named Shadow, when I was a boy. Is it your real name?'

'It's what they call me,' said Shadow.

'I'm Moira Callanish,' said the white-haired woman. 'This is my partner, Oliver Bierce. He knows a lot, and he will, during the course of our acquaintance, undoubtedly tell you everything he knows.'

They shook hands. When the landlord returned with their drinks, Shadow asked if the pub had a room to rent. He had intended to walk further that night, but the rain sounded like it had no intention of giving up. He had stout walking shoes, and weather-resistant outer clothes, but he did not want to walk in the rain.

'I used to, but then my son moved back in. I'll encourage people to sleep it off in the barn, on occasion, but that's as far as I'll go these days.'

'Anywhere in the village I could get a room?'

The landlord shook his head. 'It's a foul night. But Porsett is only a few miles down the road, and they've got a proper hotel there. I can call Sandra, tell her that you're coming. What's your name?'

'Shadow,' said Shadow again. 'Shadow Moon.'

Moira looked at Oliver, and said something that sounded like 'waifs and strays?' and Oliver chewed his lip for a moment, and then he nodded enthusiastically. 'Would you fancy spending the night with us? The spare room's a bit of a box room, but it does have a bed in it. And it's warm there. And dry.'

'I'd like that very much,' said Shadow. 'I can pay.'

'Don't be silly,' said Moira. 'It will be nice to have a guest.'

II

The Gibbet

Oliver and Moira both had umbrellas. Oliver insisted that Shadow carry his umbrella, pointing out that Shadow towered over him, and thus was ideally suited to keep the rain off both of them.

The couple also carried little flashlights, which they called torches. The word put Shadow in mind of villagers in a horror movie storming the castle on the hill, and the lightning and thunder added to the vision. *Tonight, my creature,* he thought, *I will give you life!* It should have been hokey but instead it was disturbing. The dead cat had put him into a strange set of mind.

The narrow roads between fields were running with rainwater.

'On a nice night,' said Moira, raising her voice to be heard over the rain, 'we would just walk over the fields. But they'll be all soggy and boggy, so we're going down by Shuck's Lane. Now, that tree was a gibbet tree, once upon a time.' She pointed to a massive-trunked sycamore at the crossroads. It had only a few branches left, sticking up into the night like afterthoughts.

'Moira's lived here since she was in her twenties,' said Oliver. 'I came up from London, about eight years ago. From Turnham Green. I'd come up here on holiday originally when I was fourteen and I never forgot it. You don't.'

'The land gets into your blood,' said Moira. 'Sort of.'

'And the blood gets into the land,' said Oliver. 'One way or another. You take that gibbet tree, for example. They would leave people in the gibbet until there was nothing left. Hair gone to make bird's nests, flesh all eaten by ravens, bones picked clean. Or until they had another corpse to display anyway.'

Shadow was fairly sure he knew what a gibbet was, but he asked anyway. There was never any harm in asking, and Oliver was definitely the kind of person who took pleasure in knowing peculiar things and in passing his knowledge on.

'Like a huge iron birdcage. They used them to display the bodies of executed criminals, after justice had been served. The gibbets were locked, so the family and friends couldn't steal the body back and give it a good Christian burial. Keeping passersby on the straight and the narrow, although I doubt it actually deterred anyone from anything.'

'Who were they executing?'

'Anyone who got unlucky. Three hundred years ago, there were over two hundred crimes punishable by death. Including travelling with Gypsies for more than a month, stealing sheep – and, for that matter, anything over twelve pence in value – and writing a threatening letter.'

He might have been about to begin a lengthy list, but Moira broke in. 'Oliver's right about the death sentence, but they only gibbeted murderers, up these parts. And they'd leave corpses in the gibbet for twenty years, sometimes. We didn't get a lot of murders.' And then, as if trying to change the subject to something lighter, she said, 'We are now walking down Shuck's Lane. The locals say that on a clear night, which tonight certainly is not, you can find yourself being followed by Black Shuck. He's a sort of a fairy dog.'

'We've never seen him, not even on clear nights,' said Oliver.

'Which is a very good thing,' said Moira. 'Because if you see him – you die.'

'Except Sandra Wilberforce said she saw him, and she's healthy as a horse.'

Shadow smiled. 'What does Black Shuck do?'

'He doesn't do anything,' said Oliver.

'He does. He follows you home,' corrected Moira. 'And then, a bit later, you die.'

'Doesn't sound very scary,' said Shadow. 'Except for the dying bit.'

They reached the bottom of the road. Rainwater was running like a stream over Shadow's thick hiking boots.

Shadow said, 'So how did you two meet?' It was normally a safe question, when you were with couples.

Oliver said, 'In the pub. I was up here on holiday, really.'

Moira said, 'I was with someone when I met Oliver. We had a very brief, torrid affair, then we ran off together. Most unlike both of us.'

They did not seem like the kind of people who ran off together, thought Shadow. But then, all people were strange. He knew he should say something.

'I was married. My wife was killed in a car crash.'

'I'm so sorry,' said Moira.

'It happened,' said Shadow.

'When we get home,' said Moira, 'I'm making us all whisky macs. That's whisky and ginger wine and hot water. And I'm having a hot bath. Otherwise I'll catch my death.'

Shadow imagined reaching out his hand and catching death in it, like a baseball, and he shivered.

The rain redoubled, and a sudden flash of lightning burned the world into existence all around them: every grey rock in the drystone wall, every blade of grass, every puddle and every tree was perfectly illuminated, and then swallowed by a deeper darkness, leaving afterimages on Shadow's night-blinded eyes.

'Did you see that?' asked Oliver. 'Damnedest thing.' The thunder rolled and rumbled, and Shadow waited until it was done before he tried to speak.

'I didn't see anything,' said Shadow. Another flash, less bright, and Shadow thought he saw something moving away from them in a distant field. 'That?' he asked.

'It's a donkey,' said Moira. 'Only a donkey.'

Oliver stopped. He said, 'This was the wrong way to come home. We should have got a taxi. This was a mistake.'

'Ollie,' said Moira. 'It's not far now. And it's just a spot of rain. You aren't made of sugar, darling.'

Another flash of lightning, so bright as to be almost blinding. There was nothing to be seen in the fields. Darkness. Shadow turned back to Oliver, but the little man was no longer standing beside him. Oliver's flashlight was on the ground. Shadow blinked his eyes, hoping to force his night vision to return. The man had collapsed, crumpled onto the wet grass on the side of the lane.

'Ollie?' Moira crouched beside him, her umbrella by her side. She shone her flashlight onto his face. Then she looked at Shadow. 'He can't just sit here,' she said, sounding confused and concerned. 'It's pouring.'

Shadow pocketed Oliver's flashlight, handed his umbrella to Moira, then picked Oliver up. The man did not seem to weigh much, and Shadow was a big man.

'Is it far?'

'Not far,' she said. 'Not really. We're almost home.'

They walked in silence, across a churchyard on the edge of a village green, and into a village. Shadow could see lights on in the grey stone houses that edged the one street. Moira turned off, into a house set back from the road, and Shadow followed her. She held the back door open for him.

The kitchen was large and warm, and there was a sofa, half-covered with magazines, against one wall. There were low beams in the kitchen, and Shadow needed to duck his head. Shadow removed Oliver's raincoat and dropped it. It puddled on the wooden floor. Then he put the man down on the sofa.

Moira filled the kettle.

'Do we call an ambulance?'

She shook her head.

'This is just something that happens? He falls down and passes out?'

Moira busied herself getting mugs from a shelf. 'It's happened before. Just not for a long time. He's narcoleptic, and if something surprises or scares him he can just go down like that. He'll come round soon. He'll want tea. No whisky mac tonight, not for him. Sometimes he's a bit dazed and doesn't know where he is, sometimes he's been following everything that happened while he was out. And he hates it if you make a fuss. Put your backpack down by the Aga.'

The kettle boiled. Moira poured the steaming water into a teapot. 'He'll have a cup of real tea. I'll have chamomile, I think, or I won't sleep tonight. Calm my nerves. You?'

'I'll drink tea, sure,' said Shadow. He had walked more than twenty miles that day, and sleep would be easy in the finding. He wondered at Moira. She appeared perfectly self-possessed in the face of her partner's incapacity, and he wondered how much of it was not wanting to show weakness in front of a stranger. He admired her, although he found it peculiar. The English were strange. But he understood hating 'making a fuss'. Yes.

Oliver stirred on the couch. Moira was at his side with a cup of tea, helped him into a sitting position. He sipped the tea, in a slightly dazed fashion.

'It followed me home,' he said, conversationally.

'What followed you, Ollie, darling?' Her voice was steady, but there was concern in it.

'The dog,' said the man on the sofa, and he took another sip of his tea. 'The black dog.'

III

The Cuts

These were the things Shadow learned that night, sitting around the kitchen table with Moira and Oliver:

He learned that Oliver had not been happy or fulfilled in his London advertising agency job. He had moved up to the village and taken an extremely early medical retirement. Now, initially for recreation and increasingly for money, he repaired and rebuilt drystone walls. There was, he explained, an art and a skill to wall building, it was excellent exercise, and, when done correctly, a meditative practice.

'There used to be hundreds of drystone-wall people around here. Now there's barely a dozen who know what they're doing. You see walls repaired with concrete, or with breeze blocks. It's a dying art. I'd love to show you how I do it. Useful skill to have. Picking the rock, sometimes, you have to let the rock tell you where it goes. And then it's immovable. You couldn't knock it down with a tank. Remarkable.'

He learned that Oliver had been very depressed several years earlier, shortly after Moira and he got together, but that for the last few years he had been doing very well. Or, he amended, relatively well.

He learned that Moira was independently wealthy, that her family trust fund had meant that she and her sisters had not needed to work, but that, in her late twenties, she had gone for teacher training. That she no longer taught, but that she was extremely active in local affairs, and had campaigned success-fully to keep the local bus routes in service.

Shadow learned, from what Oliver didn't say, that Oliver was scared of something, very scared, and that when Oliver was asked what had frightened him so badly, and what he had meant by saying that the black dog had followed him home, his response was to stammer and to sway. He learned not to ask Oliver any more questions.

This is what Oliver and Moira had learned about Shadow sitting around that kitchen table:

Nothing much.

Shadow liked them. He was not a stupid man; he had trusted people in the past who had betrayed him but he liked this couple, and he liked the way their home smelled – like bread-making and jam and walnut wood-polish – and he went to sleep that night in his box-room bedroom worrying about the little man with the muttonchop beard. What if the thing Shadow had glimpsed in the field had *not* been a donkey? What if it *had* been an enormous dog? What then?

The rain had stopped when Shadow woke. He made himself toast in the empty kitchen. Moira came in from the garden, letting a gust of chilly air in through the kitchen door. 'Sleep well?' she asked.

'Yes. Very well.' He had dreamed of being at the zoo. He had been surrounded by animals he could not see, which snuffled and snorted in their pens. He was a child, walking with his mother, and he was safe and he was loved. He had stopped in front of a lion's cage, but what had been in the cage was a sphinx, half lion and half woman, her tail swishing. She had smiled at him, and her smile had been his mother's smile. He heard her voice, accented and warm and feline.

It said, *Know thyself.*

I know who I am, said Shadow in his dream, holding the bars of the cage. Behind the bars was the desert. He could see pyramids. He could see shadows on the sand.

Then who are you, Shadow? What are you running from? Where are you running to?

Who are you?

And he had woken, wondering why he was asking himself that question, and missing his mother, who had died twenty years before, when he was a teenager. He still felt oddly comforted, remembering the feel of his hand in his mother's hand.

'I'm afraid Ollie's a bit under the weather this morning.'

'Sorry to hear that.'

'Yes. Well, can't be helped.'

'I'm really grateful for the room. I guess I'll be on my way.'

Moira said, 'Will you look at something for me?'

Shadow nodded, then followed her outside, and round the

side of the house. She pointed to the rose bed. 'What does that look like to you?'

Shadow bent down. *'The footprint of an enormous hound,'* he said. 'To quote Dr Watson.'

'Yes,' she said. 'It really does.'

'If there's a spectral ghost-hound out there,' said Shadow, 'it shouldn't leave footprints. Should it?'

'I'm not actually an authority on these matters,' said Moira. 'I had a friend once who could have told us all about it. But she . . .' She trailed off. Then, more brightly, 'You know, Mrs Camberley two doors down has a Doberman pinscher. Ridiculous thing.' Shadow was not certain whether the ridiculous thing was Mrs Camberley or her dog.

He found the events of the previous night less troubling and odd, more explicable. What did it matter if a strange dog had followed them home? Oliver had been frightened or startled, and had collapsed, from narcolepsy, from shock.

'Well, I'll pack you some lunch before you go,' said Moira. 'Boiled eggs. That sort of thing. You'll be glad of them on the way.'

They went into the house. Moira went to put something away, and returned looking shaken.

'Oliver's locked himself in the bathroom,' she said.

Shadow was not certain what to say.

'You know what I wish?' she continued.

'I don't.'

'I wish you would talk to him. I wish he would open the door. I wish he'd talk to me. I can hear him in there. I can hear him.'

And then, 'I hope he isn't cutting himself again.'

Shadow walked back into the hall, stood by the bathroom door, called Oliver's name. 'Can you hear me? Are you okay?'

Nothing. No sound from inside.

Shadow looked at the door. It was solid wood. The house was old, and they built them strong and well back then. When Shadow had used the bathroom that morning he'd learned the lock was a hook and eye. He leaned on the handle of the door, pushing it down, then rammed his shoulder against the door. It opened with a noise of splintering wood.

He had watched a man die in prison, stabbed in a pointless argument. He remembered the way that the blood had puddled about the man's body, lying in the back corner of the exercise yard. The sight had troubled Shadow, but he had forced himself to look, and to keep looking. To look away would somehow have felt disrespectful.

Oliver was naked on the floor of the bathroom. His body was pale, and his chest and groin were covered with thick, dark hair. He held the blade from an ancient safety razor in his hands. He had sliced his arms with it, his chest above the nipples, his inner thighs and his penis. Blood was smeared on his body, on the black-and-white linoleum floor, on the white enamel of the bathtub. Oliver's eyes were round and wide, like the eyes of a bird. He was looking directly at Shadow, but Shadow was not certain that he was being seen.

'Ollie?' said Moira's voice, from the hall. Shadow realised that he was blocking the doorway and he hesitated, unsure whether to let her see what was on the floor or not.

Shadow took a pink towel from the towel rail and wrapped it around Oliver. That got the little man's attention. He blinked, as if seeing Shadow for the first time, and said, 'The dog. It's for the dog. It must be fed, you see. We're making friends.'

Moira said, 'Oh my dear sweet god.'

'I'll call the emergency services.'

'Please don't,' she said. 'He'll be fine at home with me. I don't know what I'll . . . please?'

Shadow picked up Oliver, swaddled in the towel, carried him into the bedroom as if he were a child, and then placed him on the bed. Moira followed. She picked up an iPad by the bed, touched the screen, and music began to play. 'Breathe, Ollie,' she said. 'Remember. Breathe. It's going to be fine. You're going to be fine.'

'I can't really breathe,' said Oliver, in a small voice. 'Not really. I can feel my heart, though. I can feel my heart beating.'

Moira squeezed his hand and sat down on the bed, and Shadow left them alone.

When Moira entered the kitchen, her sleeves rolled up, and her hands smelling of antiseptic cream, Shadow was sitting on the sofa, reading a guide to local walks.

'How's he doing?'

She shrugged.

'You have to get him help.'

'Yes.' She stood in the middle of the kitchen and looked about her, as if unable to decide which way to turn. 'Do you . . . I mean, do you have to leave today? Are you on a schedule?'

'Nobody's waiting for me. Anywhere.'

She looked at him with a face that had grown haggard in an hour. 'When this happened before, it took a few days, but then he was right as rain. The depression doesn't stay long. So, just wondering, would you just, well, stick around? I phoned my sister but she's in the middle of moving. And I can't cope on my own. I really can't. Not again. But I can't ask you to stay, not if anyone is waiting for you.'

'Nobody's waiting,' repeated Shadow. 'And I'll stick around. But I think Oliver needs specialist help.'

'Yes,' agreed Moira. 'He does.' Dr Scathelocke came over late that afternoon. He was a friend of Oliver and Moira's. Shadow was not entirely certain whether rural British doctors still made house calls, or whether this was a socially justified visit. The doctor went into the bedroom, and came out twenty minutes later.

He sat at the kitchen table with Moira, and he said, 'It's all very shallow. Cry-for-help stuff. Honestly, there's not a lot we can do for him in hospital that you can't do for him here, what with the cuts. We used to have a dozen nurses in that wing. Now they are trying to close it down completely. Get it all back to the community.' Dr Scathelocke had sandy hair, was as tall as Shadow but lankier. He reminded Shadow of the landlord in the pub, and he wondered idly if the two men were related. The doctor scribbled several prescriptions, and Moira handed them to Shadow, along with the keys to an old white Range Rover.

Shadow drove to the next village, found the little chemists' and waited for the prescriptions to be filled. He stood awkwardly in the overlit aisle, staring at a display of suntan lotions and creams, sadly redundant in this cold wet summer.

'You're Mr American,' said a woman's voice from behind him. He turned. She had short dark hair and was wearing the same olive-green sweater she had been wearing in the pub.

'I guess I am,' he said.

'Local gossip says that you are helping out while Ollie's under the weather.'

'That was fast.'

'Local gossip travels faster than light. I'm Cassie Burglass.'

'Shadow Moon.'

'Good name,' she said. 'Gives me chills.' She smiled. 'If you're still rambling while you're here, I suggest you check out the hill just past the village. Follow the track up until it forks, and then go left. It takes you up Wod's Hill. Spectacular views. Public right of way. Just keep going left and up, you can't miss it.'

She smiled at him. Perhaps she was just being friendly to a stranger.

'I'm not surprised you're still here though,' Cassie continued. 'It's hard to leave this place once it gets its claws into you.' She smiled again, a warm smile, and she looked directly into his eyes, as if trying to make up her mind. 'I think Mrs Patel has your prescriptions ready. Nice talking to you, Mr American.'

IV

The Kiss

Shadow helped Moira. He walked down to the village shop and
bought the items on her shopping list while she stayed in the
house, writing at the kitchen table or hovering in the hallway
outside the bedroom door. Moira barely talked. He ran errands
in the white Range Rover, and saw Oliver mostly in the hall,
shuffling to the bathroom and back. The man did not speak to
him.

Everything was quiet in the house: Shadow imagined the
black dog squatting on the roof, cutting out all sunlight, all
emotion, all feeling and truth. Something had turned down the
volume in that house, pushed all the colours into black and
white. He wished he was somewhere else, but could not run
out on them. He sat on his bed, and stared out of the window
at the rain puddling its way down the windowpane, and felt the
seconds of his life counting off, never to come back.

It had been wet and cold, but on the third day the sun came
out. The world did not warm up, but Shadow tried to pull himself
out of the grey haze, and decided to see some of the local sights.
He walked to the next village, through fields, up paths and along
the side of a long drystone wall. There was a bridge over a narrow
stream that was little more than a plank, and Shadow jumped the
water in one easy bound. Up the hill: there were trees, oak and
hawthorn, sycamore and beech at the bottom of the hill, and then
the trees became sparser. He followed the winding trail, sometimes
obvious, sometimes not, until he reached a natural resting place,
like a tiny meadow, high on the hill, and there he turned away
from the hill and saw the valleys and the peaks arranged all about
him in greens and greys like illustrations from a children's book.

He was not alone up there. A woman with short dark hair

was sitting and sketching on the hill's side, perched comfortably on a grey boulder. There was a tree behind her, which acted as a windbreak. She wore a green sweater and blue jeans, and he recognised Cassie Burglass before he saw her face.

As he got close, she turned. 'What do you think?' she asked, holding her sketchbook up for his inspection. It was an assured pencil drawing of the hillside.

'You're very good. Are you a professional artist?'

'I dabble,' she said.

Shadow had spent enough time talking to the English to know that this meant either that she dabbled, or that her work was regularly hung in the National Gallery or Tate Modern.

'You must be cold,' he said. 'You're only wearing a sweater.'

'I'm cold,' she said. 'But, up here, I'm used to it. It doesn't really bother me. How's Ollie doing?'

'He's still under the weather,' Shadow told her.

'Poor old sod,' she said, looking from her paper to the hillside and back. 'It's hard for me to feel properly sorry for him, though.'

'Why's that? Did he bore you to death with interesting facts?'

She laughed, a small huff of air at the back of her throat. 'You really ought to listen to more village gossip. When Ollie and Moira met, they were both with other people.'

'I know that. They told me that.' Shadow thought a moment. 'So he was with you first?'

'No. *She* was. We'd been together since college.' There was a pause. She shaded something, her pencil scraping the paper. 'Are you going to try and kiss me?' she asked.

'I, uh. I, um,' he said. Then, honestly, 'It hadn't occurred to me.'

'Well,' she said, turning to smile at him, 'it bloody well should. I mean, I asked you up here, and you came, up to Wod's Hill, just to see me.' She went back to the paper and the drawing of the hill. 'They say there's dark doings been done on this hill.

Dirty dark doings. And I was thinking of doing something dirty myself. To Moira's lodger.'

'Is this some kind of revenge plot?'

'It's not an anything plot. I just like you. And there's no one around here who wants me any longer. Not as a woman.'

The last woman that Shadow had kissed had been in Scotland. He thought of her, and what she had become, in the end. 'You *are* real, aren't you?' he asked. 'I mean . . . you're a real person. I mean . . .'

She put the pad of paper down on the boulder and she stood up. 'Kiss me and find out,' she said.

He hesitated. She sighed, and she kissed him.

It was cold on that hillside, and Cassie's lips were cold. Her mouth was very soft. As her tongue touched his, Shadow pulled back.

'I don't actually know you,' Shadow said.

She leaned away from him, looked up into his face. 'You know,' she said, 'all I dream of these days is somebody who will look my way and see the real me. I had given up until you came along, Mr American, with your funny name. But you looked at me, and I knew you saw me. And that's all that matters.'

Shadow's hands held her, feeling the softness of her sweater.

'How much longer are you going to be here? In the district?' she asked.

'A few more days. Until Oliver's feeling better.'

'Pity. Can't you stay forever?'

'I'm sorry?'

'You have nothing to be sorry for, sweet man. You see that opening over there?'

He glanced over to the hillside, but could not see what she was pointing at. The hillside was a tangle of weeds and low trees and half-tumbled drystone walls. She pointed to her drawing, where she had drawn a dark shape, like an archway, in the middle of a clump of gorse bushes on the side of the hill. 'There. Look.' He stared, and this time he saw it immediately.

'What is it?' Shadow asked.

'The Gateway to Hell,' she told him, impressively.

'Uh-huh.'

She grinned. 'That's what they call it round here. It was originally a Roman temple, I think, or something even older. But that's all that remains. You should check it out, if you like that sort of thing. Although it's a bit disappointing: just a little passageway going back into the hill. I keep expecting some archaeologists will come out this way, dig it up, catalogue what they find, but they never do.'

Shadow examined her drawing. 'So what do you know about big black dogs?' he asked.

'The one in Shuck's Lane?' she said. He nodded. 'They say the barghest used to wander all around here. But now it's just in Shuck's Lane. Dr Scathelocke once told me it was folk memory. The wish hounds are all that are left of the Wild Hunt, which was based around the idea of Odin's hunting wolves, Freki and Geri. I think it's even older than that. Cave memory. Druids. The thing that prowls in the darkness beyond the fire circle, waiting to tear you apart if you edge too far out alone.'

'Have you ever seen it, then?'

She shook her head. 'No. I researched it, but never saw it. My semi-imaginary local beast. Have you?'

'I don't think so. Maybe.'

'Perhaps you woke it up when you came here. You woke me up, after all.'

She reached up, pulled his head down towards her and kissed him again. She took his left hand, so much bigger than hers, and placed it beneath her sweater.

'Cassie, my hands are cold,' he warned her.

'Well, my everything is cold. There's nothing *but* cold up here. Just smile and look like you know what you're doing,' she told him. She pushed Shadow's left hand higher, until it was cupping the lace of her bra, and he could feel, beneath the lace, the hardness of her nipple and the soft swell of her breast.

He began to surrender to the moment, his hesitation a mixture of awkwardness and uncertainty. He was not sure how he felt about this woman: she had history with his benefactors, after all. Shadow never liked feeling that he was being used; it had happened too many times before. But his left hand was touching her breast and his right hand was cradling the nape of her neck, and he was leaning down and now her mouth was on his, and she was clinging to him as tightly as if, he thought, she wanted to occupy the very same space that he was in. Her mouth tasted like mint and stone and grass and the chilly afternoon breeze. He closed his eyes, and let himself enjoy the kiss and the way their bodies moved together.

Cassie froze. Somewhere close to them, a cat mewed. Shadow opened his eyes.

'Jesus,' he said.

They were surrounded by cats. White cats and tabbies, brown and ginger and black cats, long-haired and short. Well-fed cats with collars and disreputable ragged-eared cats that looked as if they had been living in barns and on the edges of the wild. They stared at Shadow and Cassie with green eyes and blue eyes and golden eyes, and they did not move. Only the occasional swish of a tail or the blinking of a pair of feline eyes told Shadow that they were alive.

'This is weird,' said Shadow.

Cassie took a step back. He was no longer touching her now. 'Are they with you?' she asked.

'I don't think they're with anyone. They're cats.'

'I think they're jealous,' said Cassie. 'Look at them. They don't like me.'

'That's . . .' Shadow was going to say 'nonsense', but no, it was sense, of a kind. There had been a woman who was a goddess, a continent away and years in his past, who had cared about him, in her own way. He remembered the needle-sharpness of her nails and the catlike roughness of her tongue.

Cassie looked at Shadow dispassionately. 'I don't know who you are, Mr American,' she told him. 'Not really. I don't know why you can look at me and see the real me, or why I can talk to you when I find it so hard to talk to other people. But I can. And you know, you seem all normal and quiet on the surface, but you are so much weirder than I am. And I'm extremely fucking weird.'

Shadow said, 'Don't go.'

'Tell Ollie and Moira you saw me,' she said. 'Tell them I'll be waiting where we last spoke, if they have anything they want to say to me.' She picked up her sketchpad and pencils, and she walked off briskly, stepping carefully through the cats, who did not even glance at her, just kept their gazes fixed on Shadow, as she moved away through the swaying grasses and the blowing twigs.

Shadow wanted to call after her, but instead he crouched down and looked back at the cats. 'What's going on?' he asked. 'Bast? Are you doing this? You're a long way from home. And why would you still care who I kiss?'

The spell was broken when he spoke. The cats began to move, to look away, to stand, to wash themselves intently.

A tortoiseshell cat pushed her head against his hand, insistently, needing attention. Shadow stroked her absently, rubbing his knuckles against her forehead.

She swiped blinding-fast with claws like tiny scimitars, and drew blood from his forearm. Then she purred, and turned, and

within moments the whole kit and caboodle of them had vanished
into the hillside, slipping behind rocks and into the undergrowth,
and were gone.

V

The Living and the Dead

Oliver was out of his room when Shadow got back to the house,
sitting in the warm kitchen, a mug of tea by his side, reading a
book on Roman architecture. He was dressed, and he had shaved
his chin and trimmed his beard. He was wearing pyjamas, with
a plaid bathrobe over them.

'I'm feeling a bit better,' he said, when he saw Shadow. Then,
'Have you ever had this? Been depressed?'

'Looking back on it, I guess I did. When my wife died,' said
Shadow. 'Everything went flat. Nothing meant anything for a
long time.'

Oliver nodded. 'It's hard. Sometimes I think the black dog is
a real thing. I lie in bed thinking about the painting of Fuseli's
nightmare on a sleeper's chest. Like Anubis. Or do I mean Set?
Big black thing. What was Set anyway? Some kind of donkey?'

'I never ran into Set,' said Shadow. 'He was before my time.'

Oliver laughed. 'Very dry. And they say you Americans don't
do irony.' He paused. 'Anyway. All done now. Back on my feet.
Ready to face the world.' He sipped his tea. 'Feeling a bit embarrassed. All that Hound of the Baskervilles nonsense behind me
now.'

'You really have nothing to be embarrassed about,' said Shadow,
reflecting that the English found embarrassment wherever they
looked for it.

'Well. All a bit silly, one way or another. And I really am feeling much perkier.'

Shadow nodded. 'If you're feeling better, I guess I should start heading south.'

'No hurry,' said Oliver. 'It's always nice to have company. Moira and I don't really get out as much as we'd like. It's mostly just a walk up to the pub. Not much excitement here, I'm afraid.'

Moira came in from the garden. 'Anyone seen the secateurs? I know I had them. Forget my own head next.'

Shadow shook his head, uncertain what secateurs were. He thought of telling the couple about the cats on the hill, and how they had behaved, but could not think of a way to describe it that would explain how odd it was. So, instead, without thinking, he said, 'I ran into Cassie Burglass on Wod's Hill. She pointed out the Gateway to Hell.'

They were staring at him. The kitchen had become awkwardly quiet. He said, 'She was drawing it.'

Oliver looked at him and said, 'I don't understand.'

'I've run into her a couple of times since I got here,' said Shadow.

'What?' Moira's face was flushed. 'What are you saying?' And then, 'Who the, who the *fuck* are you to come in here and say things like that?'

'I'm, I'm nobody,' said Shadow. 'She just started talking to me. She said that you and she used to be together.'

Moira looked as if she were going to hit him. Then she just said, 'She moved away after we broke up. It wasn't a good breakup. She was very hurt. She behaved appallingly. Then she just up and left the village in the night. Never came back.'

'I don't want to talk about that woman,' said Oliver, quietly. 'Not now. Not ever.'

'Look. She was in the pub with us,' pointed out Shadow. 'That

first night. You guys didn't seem to have a problem with her
then.'

Moira just stared at him and did not respond, as if he had
said something in a tongue she did not speak. Oliver rubbed his
forehead with his hand. 'I didn't see her,' was all he said.

'Well, she said to say hi when I saw her today,' said Shadow.
'She said she'd be waiting, if either of you had anything you
wanted to say to her.'

'We have nothing to say to her. Nothing at all.' Moira's eyes
were wet, but she was not crying. 'I can't believe that, that
fucking woman has come back into our lives, after all she put
us through.' Moira swore like someone who was not very good
at it.

Oliver put down his book. 'I'm sorry,' he said. 'I don't feel
very well.' He walked out, back to the bedroom, and closed the
door behind him.

Moira picked up Oliver's mug, almost automatically, and took
it over to the sink, emptied it out and began to wash it.

'I hope you're pleased with yourself,' she said, rubbing the
mug with a white plastic scrubbing brush as if she were trying
to scrub the picture of Beatrix Potter's cottage from the china.
'He was coming back to himself again.'

'I didn't know it would upset him like that,' said Shadow. He
felt guilty as he said it. He had known there was history between
Cassie and his hosts. He could have said nothing, after all.
Silence was always safer.

Moira dried the mug with a green and white tea towel. The
white patches of the towel were comical sheep, the green were
grass. She bit her lower lip, and the tears that had been brim-
ming in her eyes now ran down her cheeks. Then, 'Did she say
anything about me?'

'Just that you two used to be an item.'

Moira nodded, and wiped the tears from her young-old face

with the comical tea towel. 'She couldn't bear it when Ollie and I got together. After I moved out, she just hung up her paint-brushes and locked the flat and went to London.' She blew her nose vigorously. 'Still. Mustn't grumble. We make our own beds. And Ollie's a *good* man. There's just a black dog in his mind. My mother had depression. It's hard.'

Shadow said, 'I've made everything worse. I should go.'

'Don't leave until tomorrow. I'm not throwing you out, dear. It's not your fault you ran into that woman, is it?' Her shoulders were slumped. 'There they are. On top of the fridge.' She picked up something that looked like a very small pair of garden shears. 'Secateurs,' she explained. 'For the rosebushes, mostly.'

'Are you going to talk to him?'

'No,' she said. 'Conversations with Ollie about Cassie never end well. And in this state, it could plunge him even further back into a bad place. I'll just let him get over it.'

Shadow ate alone in the pub that night, while the cat in the glass case glowered at him. He saw no one he knew. He had a brief conversation with the landlord about how he was enjoying his time in the village. He walked back to Moira's house after the pub, past the old sycamore, the gibbet tree, down Shuck's Lane. He saw nothing moving in the fields in the moonlight: no dog, no donkey.

All the lights in the house were out. He went to his bedroom as quietly as he could, packed the last of his possessions into his backpack before he went to sleep. He would leave early, he knew.

He lay in bed, watching the moonlight in the box room. He remembered standing in the pub, and Cassie Burglass standing beside him. He thought about his conversation with the landlord, and the conversation that first night, and the cat in the glass box, and, as he pondered, any desire to sleep evaporated. He was perfectly wide awake in the small bed.

Shadow could move quietly when he needed to. He slipped out of bed, pulled on his clothes and then, carrying his boots, he opened the window, reached over the sill and let himself tumble silently into the soil of the flower bed beneath. He got to his feet and put on the boots, lacing them up in the half dark. The moon was several days from full, bright enough to cast shadows.

Shadow stepped into a patch of darkness beside a wall, and he waited there.

He wondered how sane his actions were. It seemed very probable that he was wrong, that his memory had played tricks on him, or other people's had. It was all so very unlikely, but then, he had experienced the unlikely before, and if he was wrong he would be out, what? A few hours' sleep?

He watched a fox hurry across the lawn, watched a proud white cat stalk and kill a small rodent, and saw several other cats pad their way along the top of the garden wall. He watched a weasel slink from shadow to shadow in the flower bed. The constellations moved in slow procession across the sky.

The front door opened, and a figure came out. Shadow had half-expected to see Moira, but it was Oliver, wearing his pyjamas and, over them, a thick tartan dressing gown. He had Wellington boots on his feet, and he looked faintly ridiculous, like an invalid from a black-and-white movie, or someone in a play. There was no colour in the moonlit world.

Oliver pulled the front door closed until it clicked, then he walked towards the street, but walking on the grass, instead of crunching down the gravel path. He did not glance back, or even look around. He set off up the lane, and Shadow waited until Oliver was almost out of sight before he began to follow. He knew where Oliver was going, had to be going.

Shadow did not question himself, not any longer. He knew

where they were both headed, with the certainty of a person in a dream. He was not even surprised when, halfway up Wod's Hill, he found Oliver sitting on a tree stump, waiting for him. The sky was lightening, just a little, in the east.

'The Gateway to Hell,' said the little man. 'As far as I can tell, they've always called it that. Goes back years and years.'

The two men walked up the winding path together. There was something gloriously comical about Oliver in his robe, in his striped pyjamas and his oversized black rubber boots. Shadow's heart pumped in his chest.

'How did you bring her up here?' asked Shadow.

'Cassie? I didn't. It was her idea to meet up here on the hill. She loved coming up here to paint. You can see so far. And it's holy, this hill, and she always loved that. Not holy to Christians, of course. Quite the obverse. The old religion.'

'Druids?' asked Shadow. He was uncertain what other old religions there were, in England.

'Could be. Definitely could be. But I think it predates the druids. Doesn't have much of a name. It's just what people in these parts practise, beneath whatever else they believe. Druids, Norse, Catholics, Protestants, doesn't matter. That's what people pay lip service to. The old religion is what gets the crops up and keeps your cock hard and makes sure that nobody builds a bloody great motorway through an area of outstanding natural beauty. The Gateway stands, and the hill stands, and the place stands. It's well, well over two thousand years old. You don't go mucking about with anything that powerful.'

Shadow said, 'Moira doesn't know, does she? She thinks Cassie moved away.' The sky was continuing to lighten in the east, but it was still night, spangled with a glitter of stars, in the purple-black sky to the west.

'That was what she *needed* to think. I mean, what else was she going to think? It might have been different if the police had been interested . . . but it wasn't like . . . Well. It protects itself. The hill. The gate.'

They were coming up to the little meadow on the side of the hill. They passed the boulder where Shadow had seen Cassie drawing. They walked towards the hill.

'The black dog in Shuck's Lane,' said Oliver. 'I don't actually think it is a dog. But it's been there so long.' He pulled out a small LED flashlight from the pocket of his bathrobe. 'You really talked to Cassie?'

'We talked, I even kissed her.'

'Strange.'

'I first saw her in the pub, the night I met you and Moira. That was what made me start to figure it out. Earlier tonight, Moira was talking as if she hadn't seen Cassie in years. She was baffled when I asked. But Cassie was standing just behind me that first night, and she spoke to us. Tonight, I asked at the pub if Cassie had been in, and nobody knew who I was talking about. You people all know each other. It was the only thing that made sense of it all. It made sense of what she said. Everything.'

Oliver was almost at the place Cassie had called the Gateway to Hell. 'I thought that it would be so simple. I would give her to the hill, and she would leave us both alone. Leave Moira alone. How could she have kissed you?'

Shadow said nothing.

'This is it,' said Oliver. It was a hollow in the side of the hill, like a short hallway that went back. Perhaps, once, long ago, there had been a structure, but the hill had weathered, and the stones had returned to the hill from which they had been taken.

'There are those who think it's devil worship,' said Oliver. 'And I think they are wrong. But then, one man's god is another's devil. Eh?'

He walked into the passageway, and Shadow followed him.

'Such bullshit,' said a woman's voice. 'But you always were a bullshitter, Ollie, you pusillanimous little cock-stain.'

Oliver did not move or react. He said, 'She's here. In the wall. That's where I left her.' He shone the flashlight at the wall, in the short passageway into the side of the hill. He inspected the drystone wall carefully, as if he were looking for a place he recognised, then he made a little grunting noise of recognition. Oliver took out a compact metal tool from his pocket, reached as high as he could and levered out one little rock with it. Then he began to pull rocks out from the wall, in a set sequence, each rock opening a space to allow another to be removed, alternating large rocks and small.

'Give me a hand. Come on.'

Shadow knew what he was going to see behind the wall, but he pulled out the rocks, placed them down on the ground, one by one.

There was a smell, which intensified as the hole grew bigger, a stink of old rot and mould. It smelled like meat sandwiches gone bad. Shadow saw her face first, and he barely knew it as a face: the cheeks were sunken, the eyes gone, the skin now dark and leathery, and if there were freckles they were impossible to make out; but the hair was Cassie Burglass's hair, short and black, and in the LED light, he could see that the dead thing wore an olive-green sweater, and the blue jeans were her blue jeans.

'It's funny. I knew she was still here,' said Oliver. 'But I still had to see her. With all your talk. I had to see it. To prove she was still here.'

'Kill him,' said the woman's voice. 'Hit him with a rock, Shadow. He killed me. Now he's going to kill you.'

'Are you going to kill me?' Shadow asked.

'Well, yes, obviously,' said the little man, in his sensible voice. 'I mean, you know about Cassie. And once you're gone, I can just finally forget about the whole thing, once and for all.'

'Forget?'

'Forgive *and* forget. But it's hard. It's not easy to forgive myself, but I'm sure I can forget. There. I think there's enough room for you to get in there now, if you squeeze.'

Shadow looked down at the little man. 'Out of interest,' he said, curious, 'how are you going to make me get in there? You don't have a gun on you. And, Ollie, I'm twice your size. You know, I could just break your neck.'

'I'm not a stupid man,' said Oliver. 'I'm not a bad man, either. I'm not a terribly well man, but that's neither here nor there, really. I mean, I did what I did because I was jealous, not because I was ill. But I wouldn't have come up here alone. You see, this is the temple of the Black Dog. These places were the first temples. Before the stone henges and the standing stones, they were waiting and they were worshipped, and sacrificed to, and feared, and placated. The black shucks and the barghests, the padfoots and the wish hounds. They were here and they remain on guard.'

'Hit him with a rock,' said Cassie's voice. 'Hit him now, Shadow, *please.*'

The passage they stood in went a little way into the hillside, a man-made cave with drystone walls. It did not look like an ancient temple. It did not look like a gateway to hell. The predawn sky framed Oliver. In his gentle, unfailingly polite voice, he said, 'He is in me. And I am in him.'

The black dog filled the doorway, blocking the way to the world outside, and, Shadow knew, whatever it was, it was no true dog. Its eyes actually glowed, with a luminescence that reminded Shadow of rotting sea-creatures. It was to a wolf, in scale and in menace, what a tiger is to a lynx: pure carnivore, a creature made of danger and threat. It stood taller than Oliver and it stared at Shadow, and it growled, a rumbling deep in its chest. Then it sprang.

Shadow raised his arm to protect his throat, and the creature sank its teeth into his flesh, just below the elbow. The pain was excruciating. He knew he should fight back, but he was falling to his knees, and he was screaming, unable to think clearly, unable to focus on anything except his fear that the creature was going to use him for food, fear it was crushing the bone of his forearm.

On some deep level he suspected that the fear was being created by the dog: that he, Shadow, was not cripplingly afraid like that. Not really. But it did not matter. When the creature released Shadow's arm, he was weeping and his whole body was shaking.

Oliver said, 'Get in there, Shadow. Through the gap in the wall. Quickly, now. Or I'll have him chew off your face.'

Shadow's arm was bleeding, but he got up and squeezed through the gap into the darkness without arguing. If he stayed out there, with the beast, he would die soon, and die in pain. He knew that with as much certainty as he knew that the sun would rise tomorrow.

'Well, yes,' said Cassie's voice in his head. 'It's going to rise. But unless you get your shit together you are never going to see it.'

There was barely space for him and Cassie's body in the cavity behind the wall. He had seen the expression of pain and fury on her face, like the face of the cat in the glass box, and then he knew she, too, had been entombed here while alive.

Oliver picked up a rock from the ground, and placed it onto the wall, in the gap. 'My own theory,' he said, hefting a second rock and putting it into position, 'is that it is the prehistoric dire wolf. But it is bigger than ever the dire wolf was. Perhaps it is the monster of our dreams, when we huddled in caves. Perhaps it was simply a wolf, but we were smaller, little hominids who could never run fast enough to get away.'

Shadow leaned against the rock face behind him. He squeezed his left arm with his right hand to try to stop the bleeding. 'This is Wod's Hill,' said Shadow. 'And that's Wod's dog. I wouldn't put it past him.'

'It doesn't matter.' More stones were placed on stones.

'Ollie,' said Shadow. 'The beast is going to kill you. It's already inside you. It's not a good thing.'

'Old Shuck's not going to hurt me. Old Shuck loves me. Cassie's in the wall,' said Oliver, and he dropped a rock on top of the others with a crash. 'Now you are in the wall with her. Nobody's waiting for you. Nobody's going to come looking for you. Nobody is going to cry for you. Nobody's going to miss you.'

There were, Shadow knew, although he could never have told a soul how he knew, three of them, not two, in that tiny space. There was Cassie Burglass, there in body (rotted and dried and still stinking of decay) and there in soul, and there was also something else, something that twined about his legs, and then butted gently at his injured hand. A voice spoke to him, from somewhere close. He knew that voice, although the accent was unfamiliar.

It was the voice that a cat would speak in, if a cat were a woman: expressive, dark, musical. The voice said, *You should not be here, Shadow. You have to stop, and you must take action. You are letting the rest of the world make your decisions for you.*

Shadow said aloud, 'That's not entirely fair, Bast.'

'You have to be quiet,' said Oliver, gently. 'I mean it.' The stones of the wall were being replaced rapidly and efficiently. Already they were up to Shadow's chest.

Mrr. No? Sweet thing, you really have no idea. No idea who you are or what you are or what that means. If he walls you up in here to die in this hill, this temple will stand forever – and whatever hodgepodge of belief these locals have will work for them and will make magic. But the sun will still go down on them, and all the skies will be grey. All things will mourn, and they will not know what they are mourning for. The world will be worse – for people, for cats, for the remembered, for the forgotten. You have died and you have returned. You matter, Shadow, and you must not meet your death here, a sad sacrifice hidden in a hillside.

'So what are you suggesting I do?' he whispered.

Fight. The Beast is a thing of mind. It's taking its power from you, Shadow. You are near, and so it's become more real. Real enough to own Oliver. Real enough to hurt you.

'Me?'

'You think ghosts can talk to everyone?' asked Cassie Burglass's voice in the darkness, urgently. 'We are moths. And you are the flame.'

'What should I do?' asked Shadow. 'It hurt my arm. It damn near ripped out my throat.'

Oh, sweet man. It's just a shadow-thing. It's a night-dog. It's just an overgrown jackal.

'It's real,' Shadow said. The last of the stones was being banged into place.

'Are you truly scared of your father's dog?' said a woman's voice. Goddess or ghost, Shadow did not know.

But he knew the answer. Yes. Yes, he was scared.

His left arm was only pain, and unusable, and his right hand was slick and sticky with his blood. He was entombed in a cavity between a wall and rock. But he was, for now, alive.

'Get your shit together,' said Cassie. 'I've done everything I can. Do it.'

He braced himself against the rocks behind the wall, and he raised his feet. Then he kicked both his booted feet out together, as hard as he could. He had walked so many miles in the last few months. He was a big man, and he was stronger than most. He put everything he had behind that kick.

The wall exploded.

The Beast was on him, the black dog of despair, but this time Shadow was prepared for it. This time he was the aggressor. He grabbed at it.

I will not be my father's dog.

With his right hand he held the beast's jaw closed. He stared into its green eyes. He did not believe the beast was a dog at all, not really.

It's daylight, said Shadow to the dog, with his mind, not with his voice. *Run away. Whatever you are, run away. Run back to your gibbet, run back to your grave, little wish hound. All you can do is depress us, fill the world with shadows and illusions. The age when you ran with the Wild Hunt, or hunted terrified humans, it's over. I don't know if you're my father's dog or not. But you know what? I don't care.*

With that, Shadow took a deep breath and let go of the dog's muzzle.

It did not attack. It made a noise, a baffled whine deep in its throat that was almost a whimper.

'Go home,' said Shadow, aloud.

The dog hesitated. Shadow thought for a moment then that he had won, that he was safe, that the dog would simply go away. But then the creature lowered its head, raised the ruff around its neck, and bared its teeth. It would not leave, Shadow knew, until he was dead.

The corridor in the hillside was filling with light: the rising sun shone directly into it. Shadow wondered if the people who had built it, so long ago, had aligned their temple to the sunrise. He took a step to the side, stumbled on something, and fell awkwardly to the ground.

Beside Shadow on the grass was Oliver, sprawled and unconscious. Shadow had tripped over his leg. The man's eyes were closed; he made a growling sound in the back of his throat, and

Shadow heard the same sound, magnified and triumphant, from the dark beast that filled the mouth of the temple.

Shadow was down, and hurt, and was, he knew, a dead man.

Something soft touched his face, gently.

Something else brushed his hand. Shadow glanced to his side, and he understood. He understood why Bast had been with him in this place, and he understood who had brought her.

They had been ground up and sprinkled on these fields more than a hundred years before, stolen from the earth around the temple of Bastet and Beni Hasan. Tons upon tons of them, mummified cats in their thousands, each cat a tiny representation of the deity, each cat an act of worship preserved for an eternity.

They were there, in that space, beside him: brown and sand-coloured and shadowy grey, cats with leopard spots and cats with tiger stripes, wild, lithe and ancient. These were not the local cats Bast had sent to watch him the previous day. These were the ancestors of those cats, of all our modern cats, from Egypt, from the Nile Delta, from thousands of years ago, brought here to make things grow.

They trilled and chirrupped, they did not meow.

The black dog growled louder but now it made no move to attack. Shadow forced himself into a sitting position. 'I thought I told you to go home, Shuck,' he said.

The dog did not move. Shadow opened his right hand, and gestured. It was a gesture of dismissal, of impatience. *Finish this.*

The cats sprang, with ease, as if choreographed. They landed on the beast, each of them a coiled spring of fangs and claws, both as sharp as they had ever been in life. Pin-sharp claws sank into the black flanks of the huge beast, tore at its eyes. It snapped at them, angrily, and pushed itself against the wall, toppling more rocks, in an attempt to shake them off, but without success. Angry teeth sank into its ears, its muzzle, its tail, its paws.

The beast yelped and growled, and then it made a noise which, Shadow thought, would, had it come from any human throat, have been a scream.

Shadow was never certain what happened then. He watched the black dog put its muzzle down to Oliver's mouth, and push, hard. He could have sworn that the creature stepped *into* Oliver, like a bear stepping into a river.

Oliver shook, violently, on the sand.

The scream faded, and the beast was gone, and sunlight filled the space on the hill.

Shadow felt himself shivering. He felt like he had just woken up from a waking sleep; emotions flooded through him, like sunlight: fear and revulsion and grief and hurt, deep hurt.

There was anger in there, too. Oliver had tried to kill him, he knew, and he was thinking clearly for the first time in days.

A man's voice shouted, 'Hold up! Everyone all right over there?'

A high bark, and a lurcher ran in, sniffed at Shadow, his back against the wall, sniffed at Oliver Bierce, unconscious on the ground, and at the remains of Cassie Burglass.

A man's silhouette filled the opening to the outside world, a grey paper cutout against the rising sun.

'Needles! Leave it!' he said. The dog returned to the man's side. The man said, 'I heard someone screaming. Leastways, I wouldn't swear to it being a someone. But I heard it. Was that you?'

And then he saw the body, and he stopped. 'Holy fucking mother of all fucking bastards,' he said.

'Her name was Cassie Burglass,' said Shadow.

'Moira's old girlfriend?' said the man. Shadow knew him as the landlord of the pub, could not remember whether he had ever known the man's name. 'Bloody Nora. I thought she went to London.'

Shadow felt sick.

The landlord was kneeling beside Oliver. 'His heart's still beating,' he said. 'What happened to him?'

'I'm not sure,' said Shadow. 'He screamed when he saw the body – you must have heard him. Then he just went down. And your dog came in.'

The man looked at Shadow, worried. 'And you? Look at you! What happened to you, man?'

'Oliver asked me to come up here with him. Said he had something awful he had to get off his chest.' Shadow looked at the wall on each side of the corridor. There were other bricked-in nooks there. Shadow had a good idea of what would be found behind them if any of them were opened. 'He asked me to help him open the wall. I did. He knocked me over as he went down. Took me by surprise.'

'Did he tell you why he had done it?'

'Jealousy,' said Shadow. 'Just jealous of Moira and Cassie, even after Moira had left Cassie for him.'

The man exhaled, shook his head. 'Bloody hell,' he said. 'Last bugger I'd expect to do anything like this. Needles! Leave it!' He pulled a mobile phone from his pocket, and called the police. Then he excused himself. 'I've got a bag of game to put aside until the police have cleared out,' he explained.

Shadow got to his feet, and inspected his arms. His sweater and coat were both ripped in the left arm, as if by huge teeth, but his skin was unbroken beneath it. There was no blood on his clothes, no blood on his hands.

He wondered what his corpse would have looked like, if the black dog had killed him.

Cassie's ghost stood beside him, and looked down at her body, half-fallen from the hole in the wall. The corpse's fingertips and the fingernails were wrecked, Shadow observed, as if she had tried, in the hours or the days before she died, to dislodge the rocks of the wall.

'Look at that,' she said, staring at herself. 'Poor thing. Like a cat in a glass box.' Then she turned to Shadow. 'I didn't actually fancy you,' she said. 'Not even a little bit. I'm not sorry. I just needed to get your attention.'

'I know,' said Shadow. 'I just wish I'd met you when you were alive. We could have been friends.'

'I bet we would have been. It was hard in there. It's good to be done with all of this. And I'm sorry, Mr American. Try not to hate me.'

Shadow's eyes were watering. He wiped his eyes on his shirt. When he looked again, he was alone in the passageway.

'I don't hate you,' he told her.

He felt a hand squeeze his hand. He walked outside, into the morning sunlight, and he breathed and shivered, and listened to the distant sirens.

Two men arrived and carried Oliver off on a stretcher, down the hill to the road where an ambulance took him away, siren screaming to alert any sheep on the lanes that they should shuffle back to the grass verge.

A female police officer turned up as the ambulance disappeared, accompanied by a younger male officer. They knew the landlord, whom Shadow was not surprised to learn was also a Scathelocke, and were both impressed by Cassie's remains, to the point that the young male officer left the passageway and vomited into the ferns.

If it occurred to either of them to inspect the other bricked-in cavities in the corridor, for evidence of centuries-old crimes, they managed to suppress the idea, and Shadow was not going to suggest it.

He gave them a brief statement, then rode with them to the local police station, where he gave a fuller statement to a large police officer with a serious beard. The officer appeared mostly concerned that Shadow was provided with a mug of instant coffee, and that Shadow, as an American tourist, would not form a mistaken impression of rural England. 'It's not like this up here normally. It's really quiet. Lovely place. I wouldn't want you to think we were all like this.'

Shadow assured him that he didn't think that at all.

VI

The Riddle

Moira was waiting for him when he came out of the police station. She was standing with a woman in her early sixties, who looked comfortable and reassuring, the sort of person you would want at your side in a crisis.

'Shadow, this is Doreen. My sister.'

Doreen shook hands, explaining she was sorry she hadn't been able to be there during the last week, but she had been moving house.

'Doreen's a county court judge,' explained Moira.

Shadow could not easily imagine this woman as a judge.

'They are waiting for Ollie to come around,' said Moira. 'Then they are going to charge him with murder.' She said it thoughtfully, but in the same way she would have asked Shadow where he thought she ought to plant some snapdragons.

'And what are you going to do?'

She scratched her nose. 'I'm in shock. I have no idea what I'm doing any more. I keep thinking about the last few years. Poor, poor Cassie. She never thought there was any malice in him.'

'I never liked him,' said Doreen, and she sniffed. 'Too full of facts for my liking, and he never knew when to stop talking.

Just kept wittering on. Like he was trying to cover something up.'

'Your backpack and your laundry are in Doreen's car,' said Moira. 'I thought we could give you a lift somewhere, if you needed one. Or if you want to get back to rambling, you can walk.'

'Thank you,' said Shadow. He knew he would never be welcome in Moira's little house, not any more.

Moira said, urgently, angrily, as if it was all she wanted to know, 'You said you saw Cassie. You *told* us, yesterday. That was what sent Ollie off the deep end. It hurt me so much. Why did you say you'd seen her, if she was dead? You *couldn't* have seen her.'

Shadow had been wondering about that, while he had been giving his police statement. 'Beats me,' he said. 'I don't believe in ghosts. Probably a local, playing some kind of game with the Yankee tourist.'

Moira looked at him with fierce hazel eyes, as if she was trying to believe him but was unable to make the final leap of faith. Her sister reached down and held her hand. 'More things in heaven and earth, Horatio. I think we should just leave it at that.'

Moira looked at Shadow, unbelieving, angered, for a long time, before she took a deep breath and said, 'Yes. Yes, I suppose we should.'

There was silence in the car. Shadow wanted to apologise to Moira, to say something that would make things better.

They drove past the gibbet tree.

'*There were ten tongues within one head,*' recited Doreen, in a voice slightly higher and more formal than the one in which she had previously spoken. '*And one went out to fetch some bread, to feed the living and the dead.* That was a riddle written about this corner, and that tree.'

'What does it mean?'

'A wren made a nest inside the skull of a gibbeted corpse, flying in and out of the jaw to feed its young. In the midst of death, as it were, life just keeps on happening.'

Shadow thought about the matter for a little while, and told her that he guessed that it probably did.

October 2014
Florida/New York/Paris

Credits